Praise for *Delphic Oracle U.S.A.*

"A curious cast of characters, a mythical town, $10,000 missing, and we're on the hoof with Steven Mayfield's captivating *Delphic Oracle, U.S.A.* With twists and turns and relationships as slippery as eels, Mayfield weaves together a story that will delight readers of all ages."

—Susan Wingate, #1 Amazon bestseller and award-winning author

"This wonderful book, spanning decades, is quirky in the best sense of the word. Hop aboard and be charmed by tornado chasers, Shakespeare-spouting gangsters on the lam, and countless others in a multi-generational romp that rolls along with the fevered pitch of a screwball comedy. Full of heart, full of fun, full of family—a splendid homage to the fine folks of *Delphic Oracle U.S.A.*"

—Alice Kaltman, Pushcart-nominated author of *Dawg Towne, Wavehouse*, and *The Tantalizing Tale of Grace Minnaugh*

"Mayfield is an astonishing storyteller—Flannery O'Connor with sunshine. I read *Treasure of the Blue Whale* and hoped he would serve up another ordered universe fluid with imperfections and missed opportunities, botched plans and deformities of all kinds. And now he has! *Delphic Oracle, U.S.A.* is a small town where unlikelies are never misfits, where idiosyncrasy is the norm, and best of all, there's a place for everyone. Closing this new Mayfield novel, you know in your deepest heart that we belong to each other."

  —Mary Rakow, award-winning author of *The Memory Room* and *This is Why I Came*

DELPHIC ORACLE, U.S.A.

Steven Mayfield

Regal House Publishing

Published by
Regal House Publishing, LLC
Raleigh, NC 27587
All rights reserved

ISBN -13 (paperback): 9781646032921
ISBN -13 (epub): 9781646032938
Library of Congress Control Number: 2021949151

Interior by Lafayette & Greene
Cover images © by C. B. Royal
Author photograph by Hunnicutt Photography

Regal House Publishing, LLC
https://regalhousepublishing.com

Printed in the United States of America

This book is dedicated to my dear mother-in-law, Netta Baker Bindel—sweet as honey-comb, tough as a leather glove, always color-coordinated.

Also by Steven Mayfield

Howling at the Moon

Treasure of the Blue Whale

Prologue

A Fair Warning

You are born with a mother and a father, always in a place. The place is part of you, as inescapable as a fingerprint. Where are you from? In your heart, you know the truth. You are from the place you were born. I am from a town in Nebraska once known as Miagrammesto Station. I have never truly lived anywhere else. I never will. You are new here. Welcome. You are about to meet a great many people, too many to keep track of at first. Don't worry. You needn't remember them all. Some will become friends, others mere acquaintances. You'll forget a few that matter, hang on to a few that don't. Our little place includes a man unable to discern the difference between destiny and storm warnings, one with religion but no faith, one with faith but no religion, a kid known as Samson the Methodist, and a quartet of confused lovers. Here's a tip: among the folks inhabiting these pages are a librarian, a con man, an enchantress, and a skeleton. Keep your eye on them. They will help answer the question of how a place called Miagrammesto Station became home to the long-lost Oracle of Delphi.

My name is Peter Goodfellow—Delphic Oracle, Nebraska city manager and inmate at the Luther Burbank Correctional Facility. I'm also the parish priest at St. Mary's—Father Peter—but don't be put off. It's a job, so these pages will not narrate a religious fable but the stories of three families: the Goodfellows, the Penrods, and the Thorntons. Some of what I'll tell you was acquired as a boy at the knee of my great-grandmother, Willa Louise Goodfellow. She was born when our town was known as Miagrammesto Station and died at one hundred years and six days old after it had become Delphic Oracle. Grammie Willa knew everything about this little settlement just south of the Platte River, including the story of Maggie Westinghouse and the notorious July Pennybaker. "In a time when Delphic Oracle was known as Miagrammesto Station, a fox named July Pennybaker came to town," Grammie Willa claimed. "The fox was sly, but he chose to pursue a clever hen. Bent on chicanery, he ended up seeking redemption."

Peter Goodfellow
July 3, 2015

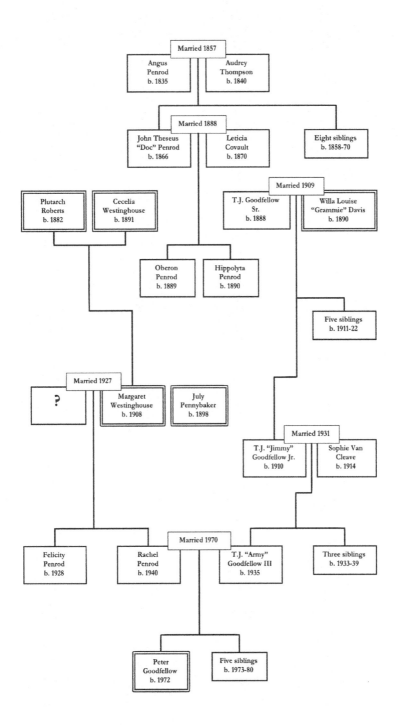

Married 1857
Angus Penrod b. 1835
Audrey Thompson b. 1840

Married 1888
John Theseus "Doc" Penrod b. 1866
Leticia Covault b. 1870
Eight siblings b. 1858-70

Married 1909
T.J. Goodfellow Sr. b. 1888
Willa Louise "Grammie" Davis b. 1890

Plutarch Roberts b. 1882
Cecelia Westinghouse b. 1891

Oberon Penrod b. 1889
Hippolyta Penrod b. 1890

Five siblings b. 1911-22

Married 1927
?
Margaret Westinghouse b. 1908
July Pennybaker b. 1898

Married 1931
T.J. "Jimmy" Goodfellow Jr. b. 1910
Sophie Van Cleave b. 1914

Married 1970
Felicity Penrod b. 1928
Rachel Penrod b. 1940
T.J. "Army" Goodfellow III b. 1935
Three siblings b. 1933-39

Peter Goodfellow b. 1972
Five siblings b. 1973-80

1

MIAGRAMMESTO STATION

"It began in 1919 after a frigid and gray winter was followed by a windy, unpredictable spring," Grammie Willa always began her story. Fortunately, the end of May welcomed a fruitful summer and long, warm autumn. It made Miagrammesto Station a hospitable place far into October, its residents quick to welcome Maggie Westinghouse and her mother after the travel-weary pair stepped off the afternoon train about a week before Halloween. The two wore thin coats and told the story of a courageous husband and father, allegedly killed in the final days of the The War To End All Wars, leaving behind his lovely wife and a daughter, then eleven years old.

All over the country the boys who had survived the Major's war had been home for months and the raging Spanish flu pandemic was on the wane. Meanwhile, the withering drought and unforgiving winds that sent many a farm swirling into the white-hot Midwestern sky were more than a decade off. Miagrammesto Station was a bustling county seat serving the dozens of farms dotting the valley—a place boasting two doctors, three car dealerships, and eight thriving religious denominations. As the new decade of the 1920s approached, most horse-drawn wagons had been replaced by Fords or Chevys, but radio had yet to take over the evenings, leaving people free to sit on their porches with glasses of lemonade, making fun of the frenetic and decadent city folk who gambled for a living at that faraway and profligate casino called Wall Street.

Like Major Westinghouse, the town's dentist, Doctor Plutarch Roberts, had also served during The War To End All Wars, although the closest he came to the trenches in Europe was a converted supply shed at Fort Benning where he spent the war rummaging through the mouths of stateside officers and the petticoats of their wives. Unblemished by combat, the unctuously handsome Doctor Roberts hired Maggie's mother as his assistant, providing a small stipend and the apartment above his office. With his encouragement, the community embraced the young widow even though visitors to their tiny flat discovered not a single photograph of brave Major Westinghouse. Even more curious, broodingly beautiful little Maggie bore a remarkable resemblance not only to silent film vamp Theda Bara but to the landlord, as well.

Maggie and her mother settled in. Maggie enrolled at the South Ward School, proving to be as clever as she was beautiful, while her mother remained ostensibly steadfast to the elusive memory of her gallant Major. A delicate woman with the singing voice of an angel, Mrs. Westinghouse slowly overcame the waggling tongues. Likewise, the perplexing history and provocative resemblance her daughter shared with Doctor Roberts was eventually overlooked, although the unveiled sniping of Violet Roberts, the dentist's thin-lipped, aspish wife, eventually forced Maggie and her mother from the unadorned pews of St. Luke's Methodist Church and into the open arms of the Episcopalians.

Five years later, in 1924, July Pennybaker appeared in Chicago with a reckless gash of a grin and a bagful of delectably outlandish claims. "He was an ace pilot in the war," some said, while others were told the story of a financial wunderkind on Wall Street who'd abandoned riches to seek wisdom and tranquility in the monasteries of Tibet. July claimed to have visited mythical Shangri-La and trekked the Khyber Pass under the protection of the Crown Prince of Afghanistan. He described traveling by camel to Damascus on the legendary Silk Road, afterward making his way to Istanbul, and then taking the Orient Express to Vienna. Eventually, he ended up in Paris, consorting in the City of Light with Picasso, Gertrude Stein, and a boisterous writer named Hemingway. July Pennybaker claimed to have been a magician and a bartender and a barber—to have ridden with Pancho Villa, discoursed with an exiled pre-revolutionary Lenin, and walked along the Great Wall with Sun Yat-sen. He was handsome with an enviable head of hair, alarmingly blue eyes, the body of a trapeze artist, and the shameless charm of a chautauqua preacher.

Bugs Moran—a member of the North Side O'Banion mob—latched on to July, moving the flamboyant adventurer into his inner circle of thugs even though the fast-talking stranger seemed more interested in Moran's accounting than his firearms. July soon had a closetful of tailored suits that draped as easily over his athletic frame as the pretty girls who hung on his arm. He affected a Chicago accent, remembered the names of everyone he met, and tipped nearly as well as rival mobster Scarface Capone. Best of all he could sing like an Irish devil and soon became a favorite at McGovern's Saloon. Bugs loved him. The rest of the O'Banion gang didn't and it wasn't long before Hymie Weiss and Schemer Drucci were in Bugs's ear, pointing out that July Pennybaker always seemed to be missing when the bullets started flying. They convinced Bugs that their dashing colleague needed to make his bones or become a pile of them.

Not long thereafter—on a January day in 1925, with glacial wind shrieking off Lake Michigan and the sky drab with overcast—July waited with Bugs, Hymie, and Schemer outside rival mob boss Papa Johnny Torrio's South Clyde Avenue apartment. Bugs, Hymie, and Schemer had their own guns. Bugs had loaned July a fully loaded .38. By the time Papa Johnny emerged, the shooters—alleged in the next day's *Chicago Tribune* to include "…a fourth unknown assailant"—had been waiting for three hours. They were cold and impatient, three of the gunmen letting loose a torrent of bullets. Afterward, the assassins headed to McGovern's to celebrate, tossing back one drink each and about to tip another, when news reached them that Torrio had survived. Bugs dispatched July to finish the job and the glib talker, without a single mob scalp to his credit, headed out. An hour passed, then two, then six. July did not return.

Soon thereafter, Bugs discovered an empty space in his office safe where ten thousand dollars had resided.

Bugs was fond of July and willing to forgive his failure to put even one bullet into Papa Johnny. However, there wasn't a man alive whose charms could compete with ten thousand dollars. Bugs raged for a while, kicking a hole in the wall of his office, throwing a paperweight through the window, and shooting out the streetlamp across the street. Afterward, he instructed Hymie and Schemer to find July, get his money back, and then offer their former associate accommodations at the bottom of Lake Michigan. The two goons were delighted and rushed over to July's apartment on North Dearborn. The flat was deserted save a dog-eared English translation of *Parallel Lives* on the bedside table and a phalanx of expensive suits in the armoire. The pockets in the suits were as empty as Bugs's safe. July Pennybaker had skipped town.

The attempted hit on Papa Johnny enraged his second-in-command, Al Capone. The violent and impulsive gangster loved Torrio—a mentor since the old days in New York—and he put a bounty on the shooters. "I'm gonna personally put their god-damned brains on a baseball bat," he vowed. Word crisscrossed the nation's criminal underbelly, but six months after the hit on Papa Johnny, the whereabouts of Bugs Moran's former favorite remained unknown.

The same year that July disappeared, Maggie Westinghouse was seventeen years old and had begun to suffer visions that visited her in a leisurely way, provoking laughter and mostly incoherent babbling. Always, they ended in a swoon and troubled sleep. She spoke while slumbering, describing exotic locales or carrying on spirited conversations with unseen beings, afterward waking with no memory of what had transpired. "Folks around town had always been a little cowed by Maggie," Grammie Willa recollected. "She was beautiful and men made fools of themselves while a lot of women tried to even things out by whittling away at her reputation." She spent a lot of time on her own, Grammie told me, taking long walks that took her to the edge of town and beyond. It was June, 1925, when Maggie walked along the tracks near the Miagrammesto Station fairgrounds and saw the door to a railroad switch-house propped open. Inside, she discovered a man asleep on a pile of gunnysacks.

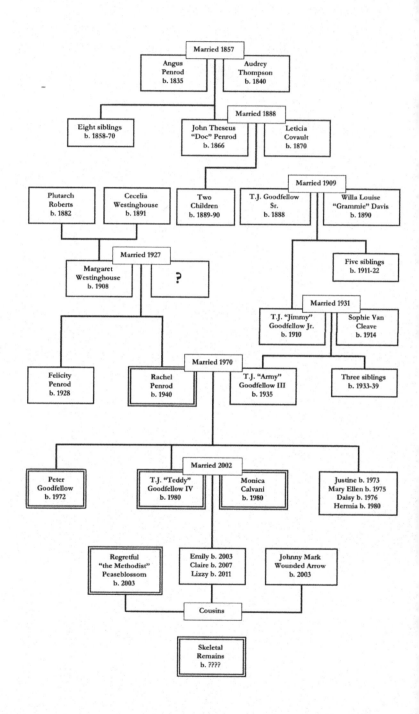

Married 1857
Angus Penrod b. 1835
Audrey Thompson b. 1840

Eight siblings b. 1858-70

Married 1888
John Theseus "Doc" Penrod b. 1866
Leticia Covault b. 1870

Married 1909
Plutarch Roberts b. 1882
Cecelia Westinghouse b. 1891
Two Children b. 1889-90
T.J. Goodfellow Sr. b. 1888
Willa Louise "Grammie" Davis b. 1890

Married 1927
Margaret Westinghouse b. 1908
?

Five siblings b. 1911-22

Married 1931
T.J. "Jimmy" Goodfellow Jr. b. 1910
Sophie Van Cleave b. 1914

Felicity Penrod b. 1928

Married 1970
Rachel Penrod b. 1940
T.J. "Army" Goodfellow III b. 1935
Three siblings b. 1933-39

Peter Goodfellow b. 1972

Married 2002
T.J. "Teddy" Goodfellow IV b. 1980
Monica Calvani b. 1980
Justine b. 1973
Mary Ellen b. 1975
Daisy b. 1976
Hermia b. 1980

Regretful "the Methodist" Peaseblossom b. 2003
Emily b. 2003
Claire b. 2007
Lizzy b. 2011
Johnny Mark Wounded Arrow b. 2003

Cousins

Skeletal Remains b. ????

2

TEDDY

Eighty-nine years after Maggie Westinghouse discovered July Pennybaker asleep in a railroad switch-house, Nick Dolny asserted to me, my little brother, Teddy, and a handful of regulars at the Cozy Lunch Bar & Grill that wives live longer than their husbands because, "they ain't married to women." A wellspring of misogyny, Nick would have gone on had the sound of thunder and a weatherman on the TV mounted on the wall behind the bar not cut him off.

"We bring this weather alert from KOLN-Channel 10," the broadcaster intoned. "The possibility of severe thunderstorms accompanied by damaging winds or tornadoes now exists in an area east of Alinin, Kansas, extending from Marysville west to Smith Center and south to Salina."

Teddy slipped off his barstool and headed for the door, abandoning a nearly full longneck Budweiser that was quickly claimed by our brother-in-law, Francis Wounded Arrow—the half-Lakota Sioux handyman carefully peeling the label from the bottle as if to preserve a treasure map on its underside.

"Hey," Nick called out, "where you goin'?"

"Alinin, Kansas," Teddy replied without slowing.

My little brother has known for years that Alinin is not a target of God's wrath—a forlorn town singled out in nearly all tornado warnings and condemned to quiver in the path of every rogue plains twister darting out of a dark summer sky. It actually isn't a town at all but a map line—not Alinin, Kansas, but *a line in Kansas*. I explained this to Teddy when he was about twelve years old. At the time, we were huddled in the basement of the rambling family home where he and I and our four siblings were raised. The same somber TV weatherman had sent us scrambling down the creaky wooden steps to a dank cellar dominated by a huge cylindrical furnace with ductwork that made the thing look like a robotic octopus. "We bring this weather alert from KOLN-Channel 10," the broadcaster had intoned. "The possibility of severe thunderstorms accompanied by damaging winds or tornadoes now exists in an area east of a line in Kansas, extending from Marysville west to Smith Center and south to Salina."

More than twenty years had elapsed since that night. Nevertheless, the latest storm warning on the TV put Teddy in the wind, sending him into one of those sweltering and ponderous Nebraska summer nights when the air is like a living thing—a night when gray-umber twilight slowly spreading across the flatlands brings Nebraskans to their knees, supplicants before the cooling rain, beacons to the jolting thunderclaps. Such weather has always made Teddy feel that destiny is upon him. On that night, he had yet to understand the difference between destiny and storm warnings.

"Just got up and left?" Teddy's wife, Monica, asked when Nick called to see if he'd made it home.

"Hopped off the stool, gave us that Myrna Lisa smile of his, and then took off," Nick reported.

"Toward the theater?" Monica asked. Teddy runs the Rialto Cinema—one of the businesses our family owns. Shuttered in 1975 when folks in town fell under the spell of a then-novel four-screen multiplex in Zenith, Teddy reopened the place in 1995, adding a beer and wine service. "If you lubricate them, they will come," he always jokes and he's right. The theater has done well with folks in Zenith now willing to drive twenty-five miles in our direction for a glass of chardonnay with their popcorn. He went into the movie business after Mom fired him from the town insurance agency—another concern we Goodfellows own, along with the Penrod Hotel and coffee shop, the *Delphic Oracle Banner-Press*, the Miagrammesto County Bank, and a parcel near the Platte River where one of my sisters keeps her horses.

For all of it, we owe thanks to the perspicacity of our progenitor, Angus Penrod, who founded our town as a trading post he christened Miagrammesto Station. I don't know how he chose that name. Aunt Felicity claims that old Angus imagined himself descended from Greek scholars even though he was mostly Scotch-Irish. As for Teddy's dismissal from the Goodfellow Insurance Agency, please understand that we love my little brother, but agreed with Mom and Dad and Uncle Grey that he was a terrible salesman and the worst claims adjustor in the history of claims adjusting. Besides, Teddy was happy to be fired. It gave him an excuse to resurrect the Rialto, something he'd always wanted to do. Teddy loves movies.

"Toward the theater?" Monica repeated when Nick didn't respond.

"No, he wasn't gonna close up. Jeez, Monica, he never closes up himself. He lets one of them high school kids do it. You *know* that."

Monica and Nick have never liked each other. Although opposites in nearly every way, Nick and Teddy have been friends since they were toddlers and Nick is a jealous sort. Monica doesn't help matters. She hauls around a bucketful of one-liners to use on Nick. He's an easy target—a scrawny chicken leg of a man with thin lips, slightly pointed ears, and a head full of conspiracy theories. She held back that night, partly because it was getting late and she was tired, but mostly because it's simply too easy to make a fool of a fellow like Nick who thinks a thesaurus is a dinosaur.

"Which way then?"

"South."

"You're sure?"

Nick made a whistling sound as he exhaled through the generous gap between his front teeth. "'Course I'm sure," he snapped. "Why would I make up something like that? I don't make up things. You *know* that."

"Right…okay then," Monica said. "By the way, it's *Mona* Lisa, not *Myrna* Lisa. You should know *that*."

She hung up and was about to phone her mother-in-law when one of her three girls called out. An hour or so later she had convinced the younger two that flies wouldn't lay eggs in their ears if they went to sleep, something their big sister had suggested. It was almost eleven o'clock by the time Monica checked in with Mom. Teddy hadn't been there either. It was June 30, 2014, and my little brother was on the clock.

✺

Around the time I left my cell at The Luther the next morning, Teddy called his wife. He was nowhere near Alinin, Kansas. During the long, moonless night he had decided to head for New York City.

"We're not home right now," Monica's recorded voice told him, "unless you're a burglar, in which case we're out separating the pit bulls."

A flutter of background giggles followed.

"...Leave a message and we'll get back to you when we can."

It ended with their three daughters growling into the phone.

"This is Teddy," he began, eyes watery with tears. "I'm sorry I didn't come home last night. I'm on the road...to the east... South Bend, Indiana. I'll call again...I love you all."

Monica, waist-deep in swimming lessons with the girls when he called, didn't listen to his message until about an hour later. Afterward, she again called her mother-in-law. My mom, Rachel Goodfellow, is from a generation reared without fear of salt or saturated fats. She believes in doughnuts and immediately came over with a fresh dozen.

"Did he run *The Searchers* last night?" she asked once seated at the kitchen table with Monica. Teddy loves *The Searchers*, a classic western from the 1950s that starred John Wayne. He has a special screening at the Rialto every few months. We Goodfellows and Penrods all come, because we're family. Not many others do.

Monica nodded. "Yeah, he wrote another poem about it too."

"I wish he would stop doing this," Mom said, nibbling on a maple donut.

In Teddy's defense, I have to point out that he was a dedicated homebody until Dad died five years ago. Shortly thereafter, he began to experience unexplained melancholy and longing that hit him like bouts of influenza. This happens to a lot of men at midlife. I don't understand such afflictions, but I've never believed life to be about what you'll miss when you're gone or what you've missed out on already. It's about enjoying good things as they happen. Things like lunch...and baseball.

"Has he called yet?" Mom asked her daughter-in-law.

Monica's youngest daughter, three-year-old Lizzy, padded into the kitchen, hair still wet, her shiny eyes rimmed in red after her morning in the swimming pool. The little girl reached out and pinched her mother's sleeve with two fingers.

"He phoned this morning," Monica said, lifting Lizzy onto her lap.

"Did he say where he was going?"

The two women studied each other for a moment and then laughed.

"New York City," they said together.

Less than an hour later Nick Dolny stopped by the Penrod Hotel, a place fragrant with cigar smoke and leather club chairs. Edmund Dogberry—town mayor and Ford dealer—was in the adjoining coffee shop, finishing off the last of the Tuesday special: chicken pot pie. "He's on the run," Nick said. Afterward, Ed went downstairs to Snug Nixon's barber shop.

"Whattaya say, Ed?" Snug yelled. Snug always yells because he's under the impression that the closer he is to a person, the louder he must speak. Our town mayor is just as loud, his own volume knob perpetually on high.

"Get the pool going," Ed yelled back.

This is how everyone in Delphic Oracle knew by one p.m. that Teddy was gone again. My aunt, Felicity Penrod, interviewed witnesses to determine when the wheels of Teddy's car had most likely cleared the city limit, then officially confirmed the starting time as June 30, 2014, at 9:30 p.m. Soon, yellow

Post-it notes—each representing a bet of ten dollars—dotted a large, homemade calendar ceremoniously propped atop the television in Snug's shop, a walk-down below the hotel with a swiveling barber chair and a row of battered seats backed up to the window well. A name, date, and time were handwritten on each note. When I dropped in for a trim Snug was explaining the logic behind his pick in the pool—July 3rd, 3:22 p.m.— three days, seventeen hours, and fifty-two minutes from Felicity's certified date and time of departure.

"I don't care what Felicity says," Snug told us "Teddy left Cozy's about nine-twenty. I was there. I looked at my watch. It was nine-twenty. The way I see it—"

"Your watch is slow," Francis Wounded Arrow—my eldest sister Justine's husband—interrupted. "The clock above the bar said nine-twenty-five...on the button. I don't care what you think you saw. That's how me and Father Peter seen it."

"...and I figure Teddy had to sneak into the garage to get his tent and stuff," Snug went on, aiming a frown at Francis, "so, I'm betting he didn't leave town until at least ten-oh-five. Now, whaddaya get if you average out the last five pools and then subtract the forty-five minutes Felicity didn't count? July third, three-twenty-two in the afternoon, that's what."

Francis sat in Snug's barber chair, idly cruising his fresh crew-cut with the palm of a meaty hand that looked as if it had been worked over by a hammer or two, which, indeed, it had. "C'mon, Snug," he rebutted. "It didn't take him no forty-five minutes to get geared up. He was already packed. He's always packed. Everybody knows that. He keeps a kit in the garage. All he has to do is toss it in the car and go." Francis raised a pair of shaggy eyebrows to underscore his point. "Besides," he added, "he was all hound-doggy. He don't get hound-doggy till he's packed. That's a historical fact."

"Who asked you, Francis?" Snug barked. "Did anybody ask you? Why do you always shove in two cents worth of bullcrap while I'm still talking?"

"I'm just sayin' Teddy was ready to go."

"Yeah, well say it on your own time…and get outta my chair. Your haircut is over. You wanna sit in the chair, it'll cost you ten bucks." Snug shot a stink-eye across the room, ominously slapping one of his straight-edged razors across a strop until Francis sullenly climbed out of the barber chair and slouched into one of the seats backed up against the window well, his two cents worth of interruption still burning a hole in his pocket.

"I already paid you for the trim, Snug," Francis grumbled. "You can't make a fella pay for just parkin' in that there chair." He looked at me for help. "I'm pretty sure that's the law, ain't it, Father?"

"I don't think it's a law, Francis," I said.

Snug suddenly pointed his straight razor at us, its edge worked over until it was nearly invisible. "Teddy likes to come back at six or so in the evening," he shouted.

"Yeah, but you picked July third," Francis threw in. "That's a Friday. Teddy likes to come back on Sundays."

Despite the ominous razor, Snug didn't seem to mind the interruption, the soon-to-be realized life of leisure promised to the winner of the town pool apparently enough to overcome his urge to cut off one of Francis's ears. He set the straight edge aside and climbed into his empty barber chair, then leaned back and linked long, bony fingers behind his head, a feathery smile on his face. "Saturday is the Fourth of July. Teddy won't miss the Fourth," he said, nodding with the sort of confidence one might expect from a three-time winner of the Greater East Central Nebraska Non-Metropolitan Barber of the Year Award. "Yup. Teddy just loves the Fourth. He'll be home by Friday afternoon…July third… Guaranteed."

Later that day I shared Snug's prediction with Mom and Monica over pie and ice cream at the Y-Knot Drive-In.

"No one ever knows exactly what time Teddy leaves town. It's just Felicity's best guess," Mom suggested. I didn't agree. There is a pattern Teddy describes before bolting: middle-of-the-night walks, bad poetry composed while sitting next to the lake on the golf course, a climb up the water tower to gaze

pensively into whatever distance is available from atop the modest structure. He typically slumps in a booth at the Cozy Lunch
for two or three evenings with an untouched beer on the table,
refusing to contribute to the usual talk about baseball or how
the government is screwing the average Joe, instead making the
same face Snug makes when someone mentions his ex-wife,
a woman who indicated her dissatisfaction with marriage, in
general, and Snug, specifically, by engaging several fellows from
nearby Zenith in a series of horizontal conversations. Eventually, it's exactly as Francis suggested. Teddy gets hound-doggy,
and within thirty minutes or so, he's on the lam.

Screening *The Searchers* at the Rialto has always been a good
predictor that Teddy is about to make a run for it. The classic
western about an odyssey to find a kidnapped girl so predictably
provokes wanderlust, Ed Dogberry claims he can calculate the
date and time of Teddy's return, based on a formula that utiliz-
es secret numbers from the movie, a flip of his lucky domino,
and a single excursion on his Ouija board. Ed and my mother
are tied for the career lead in pool wins with Ed winning the
last two. Nevertheless, he still wanted Mom disqualified, which
explains the phone call she received at the Y-Knot. She put it on
speaker so Monica and I could listen in.

"Rachel? This is Ed Dogberry."

"Hello, Ed. What's on your mind?"

"Don't play dumb with me, Rachel. I know Teddy called and
told you where he was before you made your pick. Now we
agreed…no insider information. We're supposed to call Felicity
with news as it becomes available. She's the pool adjudicator,
Rachel…not you. You don't get to decide what's in the public
domain. You got a call. I know you did. Don't deny it."

"Actually, Monica got a call, Ed."

"So you're in cahoots…whatever. You're supposed disclose.
That's the rule. You're not disclosing. That's a violation."

"Shouldn't you be reading me my rights?"

"Fine, okay. Joke about it. But I'm telling you, Rachel. This
pool will be officially protested unless you disqualify yourself."

"Hold on. Peter's here. Let's ask him about this." Mom winked at me. "Is he right, Peter?"

"I think you've been watching too many *Matlock* reruns, Ed," I said.

"Har-de-har-har," Ed barked. "You're both comedians. Har-de-frickin'-har-har. So laugh this off... You're on notice, Rachel. If I lose and you win, the pool will be forthwith, heretofore, officially protested." The mayor went on, threatening to use his influence as head of the prison board to block my upcoming October release, afterward directing a few more *forthwiths* and *heretofores* at us. We'd heard them all before, although there was general agreement that *therefore-insofar-hereafterwards* was likely a new addition to his inventory.

"He's unhappy, Rachel," Monica observed after the call ended. "Maybe you should give him a hint."

"And let that old poop win again?" Mom sniffed. "Absolutely not." She held up a spoon and peered at it as if looking through a magnifying glass.

"How are the girls taking it?" she asked Monica.

"They agree with Ed. They think you've put the fix on the town pool."

"Seriously. Are they worried about their dad?"

"I am being serious. They're on Ed's side. They want you arrested. They've been marching around the house, chanting, 'Lock her up!'"

"How about you?" I asked Monica. "Are you worried?"

She laughed. "Of course not. Teddy will be back. He always comes back." Monica looked at me. "What's your pick?" she asked.

"Saturday, 3:17," I told her.

"Gutsy," she said. "The parade starts at five. You're cutting it close."

"What about you?" Mom asked her.

"Friday, July Third, 8:12 in the evening," Monica told her.

At seven p.m. on July 1, 2014, Teddy was at the drive-up

window of a McDonald's restaurant in Mason City, Iowa. He had officially been on the road for twenty-one and a half hours and sixteen people were already out of the pool. As he waited for his order, my brother sang along with an oldie on the radio, a somewhat maudlin Harry Chapin song about a father and son. It always made him weep, and by the time a girl in a paper cap leaned out the window with his food, copious tears sloppily poured from his eyes and nose, his vocal less sung than bleated. The girl frowned. Her hair was a Medusa-like rasp of purple struggling to escape from beneath her cap, her eye makeup dark and heavy, her lips painted black. Long, also black, fingernails pinched the sack containing his food like a lobster claw gripping a clam.

"Dude," she said, "pull yourself together."

Teddy drove to a nearby park where he perched on the edge of a splintered picnic table to eat. A raggedy dog joined him—an experienced beggar satisfied with the occasional french fry until a real prize was available: the napkin Teddy used to wipe tears off his face. The mangy fellow snatched it from my brother's outstretched hand, the entire thing promptly disappearing in an impressive display of snapping and snuffling as Teddy eyed the graying sky. Overhead, barrel-shaped clouds had formed, tumbling in from the north, muffled rumblings from within them heralding an advancing storm.

"I should head south," Teddy told the dog, although he didn't, instead taking the highway that led north to Minneapolis. It had been hot most of the day, but the air was now cool and laden with the sweet musk of the coming rain. Dark, low clouds were in front of him and he peered at them through the windshield, blindly turning the radio dial until he found a resonant baritone. "Just east of a line in Kansas..." the voice said.

A few fat raindrops splattered against the windshield and Teddy eased his foot off the gas pedal, allowing his car to glide to a stop on the side of the road.

"...severe thunderstorms and possible tornadoes."

Outside, there was no wind, the rain falling straight and

unimpeded, the sound as it hit the roof much like the static on his radio. Teddy sat, listening to his scratchy radio compete with the mounting rain. A minute passed, then another. After half an hour, with the storm fully upon him and the rain now forming dense, billowing sheets, he carefully nosed his car through a U-turn and headed south, moving slowly at first, then faster and faster as the clouds chased him from behind.

I knew Ed Dogberry's pick in the pool had expired when he showed up at my office in the courthouse the next morning. It was July 2, 2014. Teddy had been away for thirty-six hours and fourteen minutes with 513 more people no longer eligible for the prize money. Perhaps, you're wondering how a prison inmate and parish priest became city manager with two offices— one at the courthouse and another at St. Mary's. It's because Ed nearly bankrupted the town after wasting most of the funds provided by the state to convert Luther Burbank College into a prison. I have a degree in accounting and Ed is afraid to bully a Catholic priest, so I was a natural fit for city manager.

"Pack your bags, Father," Ed snapped. "We're shipping you to the real pen. The free lunch is over."

"Your pick is out?" I said.

"Maybe," Ed muttered. "I'm gonna appeal it." He slumped into a chair against the wall, eyeing me sheepishly.

"Should I pack my bags?" I teased.

"No...sorry about that, Peter. I'm not mad at you. It's your mother. I should have her arrested."

So Ed was out of the pool, prompting a vigorous protest that was summarily denied by Aunt Felicity Penrod, the pool adjudicator. I was back at St. Mary's by then and missed Ed's outburst of huffing and snorting that evolved into chest pain. Felicity took him to the emergency room of our little hospital.

"Aren't you waiting with me?" he asked when she turned to go.

"Call your wife," Aunt Felicity replied, a suggestion Ed didn't welcome as he and Vivian had managed to stay married for the last forty-five years of a fifty-year marriage by agreeing to avoid each other until death parted them. Vivian—a heavy smoker and drinker—was ahead in the race, something confirmed a few minutes later when Ed's electrocardiogram was completely normal. That should have been the end of it, but Ed still had a snootful of self-righteous indignation and Vivian refused to have him back under their roof until he had calmed down.

"What do you want me to do with him?" Doc Newhouse pleaded.

"Admit him. It's a public hospital. I paid for it with my taxes," Vivian responded.

Ed remained hospitalized and spent much of his day and the night that followed leaning on his call button, asking for juice or an extra pillow, or just trying to make sure that everyone within earshot was aware that Rachel Goodfellow was a "dad-burned cheater." The poor night nurse barely made it through her shift, complaining to Doc the next morning that Ed would not see another sunrise unless he was discharged before she came back on duty. Doc prescribed a cheeseburger and sweet potato fries from the Y-Knot Drive-In, medications that reliably calmed our mayor, and then phoned my mother.

"Please disqualify yourself," he begged.

"Why should I?" Mom huffed.

"Rachel, he's driving us crazy over here. He kept my patients awake all night. If he doesn't get what he wants, he pretends to have a seizure."

"Stop complaining," Mom countered. "You're a doctor. It's the life you chose."

She refused to withdraw from the pool and Ed stayed hospitalized on a day that was hot and humid and utterly windless. The overbearing and inescapable stillness made children all over town whiny and annoying, craving the air-conditioned indoors as much as their parents craved a little peace and quiet. As the temperature flirted with 100 degrees, a wildfire rumor took off. "That Peaseblossom kid got himself kicked by a mule. He's blind," someone told Snug Nixon. Snug then told the ladies at the nail salon next door to his shop, inciting the lot of them to whip out their cell phones and Facebook the living hell out of the rumor.

What really happened was this: Regretful Peaseblossom— my sister Mary Ellen's boy and so nicknamed when people kept asking how she felt about a surprise pregnancy with a third child—was playing Samson and the Philistines with his cousin, Johnny Mark Wounded Arrow, using a bone Regretful's dog had dug up from a nearby vacant lot. Even though it was obviously a shin, Regretful proclaimed it to be the jawbone of a donkey, the perfect stage prop for a reenactment of Judges, chapters 13-16. "Samson killed a thousand Philistines with one of these," Regretful told Johnny Mark, holding up the bone. Afterward, he claimed the coveted role of the Hebrew warrior. Johnny Mark then acquitted himself as various manhandled Philistines for about thirty minutes before suggesting that they re-cast the production.

"Samson was a Methodist like me," Regretful patiently explained. "The Philistines were Catholic. You're Catholic, too, so you can't be Samson."

Johnny Mark was unconvinced. "I don't think the Philistines were Catholic," he said, his protest so lacking conviction it gave his cousin the opening he needed.

"Yes, they were," Regretful said.

Johnny Mark responded by throwing the shinbone at a pair of bored crows clinging to an overhead telephone line. The projectile went straight up and missed the birds who glanced at the heavy bone with indifference as it returned to earth and clobbered Samson the Methodist on the head.

Monica and Teddy live next door to the Peaseblossoms and my sister-in-law was the first to respond to Regretful's cries, marveling at her nephew's ability to stay in character despite a nasty cut. "'Oh God, please strengthen me just once more,'" Samson the Methodist shouted over and over, "'and let me with one blow get revenge on the Philistines for my two eyes!'" Monica held a towel against his cut until Mary Ellen could bundle the boy off to the emergency room. Meanwhile, police chief Johnson K. Johnson searched the vacant lot that had yielded the shinbone and discovered a partially unearthed human skeleton. The remains were those of a large man who had obviously been underground for years. It was an exciting and unprecedented finding, and with all the shouting and crying and Bible-quoting, a considerable crowd gathered. Reluctant to disperse after the ambulance zoomed off, a good many then transitioned to the vacant lot for some skeleton-discovering, tromping all over the evidence until Chief Johnson cordoned off the crime scene with leftover crepe paper from the Father of Our Country float that the police department had built for the upcoming Fourth of July celebration. "God-damned police business, that's why," he grumbled when folks protested.

The entire affair took up three hours, and as evening approached, Monica was behind schedule, frantically sewing cherry bomb costumes for her daughters to wear in the parade the next day. Outside, twilight had summoned early darkness and low, ominous clouds enshrouded the town. It had been a stormy summer with lightning too often preceding the rain, and when the flashes and rumbles began to coincide, Monica set aside her sewing and went to find the girls. They were in the front yard, strutting about with their cheeks sucked in like the contestants they'd seen on *America's Next Top Model.*

"Time to come in," Monica called out, a wary eye on the house across the street. Francis Wounded Arrow's grandmother, Crazy Ainitta, stood in her front yard—a small patch of land speckled with dandelions and a large flock of pink plastic flamingos. Clothed in a bathrobe and galoshes, the old woman's arms clawed at the sky like a witch beckoning the storm, her fingers dancing to the flashes of light that fitfully flickered along the bellies of the clouds. Suddenly, a jagged bolt of lightning darted earthward, followed two seconds later by a crash of thunder. Monica's daughters screamed and ran for the house. Crazy Ainitta dashed for cover, as well, slaloming between the plastic flamingos as she stumbled along in the oversized boots.

Monica watched until her neighbor was safely inside her low-slung bungalow, then returned to her sewing, pausing each time she heard the hum of an approaching a car. The vehicles all continued past the house, none turning into her driveway.

Outside, the storm had paused to the north, angrily hurling crooked, eye-popping ribbons of lightning at the ground, but it suddenly swept into Delphic Oracle, battering the roof with rain as it overtook and then rushed past 8:12 p.m. on the third of July. Monica glanced at the clock.

That's it, she thought. *I'm out of the pool.*

One minute later—at 8:13 p.m.—Teddy stopped his car on the side of the road three miles south of town. After leaving Mason City he had driven as far as Topeka before remembering that he'd forgotten to post the gas and electric bill payments before he left, the stamped envelopes still on the desk in his study. He sighed heavily, watching the storm hover over Delphic Oracle. It was going to be a terrible Fourth of July. Nick and the boys at the Cozy Lunch would make jokes at his expense, red-faced Ed Dogberry would swagger around town in the full flush of his latest victory in the town pool, and his mother would pointedly suggest that he buy a motorcycle or a flight simulator like normal middle-aged men. Worst of all Monica would be understanding and his daughters delighted to see him, the combination sure to provoke feelings of guilt more oppressive than the dark clouds gathered to the north. Teddy peered through the windshield, wondering if it would rain during the Fourth of July parade. "Probably," he muttered.

A sudden flash of lightning silhouetted the distant town water tower and its spindly supports, making it look like a giant beetle. The lightning was followed a few seconds later by a flat wave of thunder, then a second flash that illuminated the map lying on the console. Teddy glanced at it. The whole of Nebraska was there, the very top portion of Kansas as well.

Kansas.

He closed his eyes and the map suddenly appeared to him as something three-dimensional—a vast, ethereal vista populated

by familiar people and things. Monica and the girls were there
along with Mom, my siblings, and me. Nick Dolny was there,
too, with Francis Wounded Arrow and Ed Dogberry and Snug
Nixon and Aunt Felicity and our Methodist nephew, Regretful
Peaseblossom. Teddy could see the Rialto and the Cozy Lunch
and the Penrod Hotel and the Y-Knot Drive-In and the Luther
Burbank Correctional Facility and the comfortable home he
and Monica had lovingly renovated. There was more and all
of it—every field, farm, building, and person—was as deeply
engraved in his memory as the *In Perpetuum* carved into the cor-
nerstone of the venerable Penrod Hotel.

Suddenly, the fields and farms and buildings melted into a
steel-gray haze, leaving only dark, shadowed figures. The storm
seemed far away now, its flashes and rumbles dissipating as
the grimly portentous shapes slowly faded, leaving behind a
great open desert shaded in blue twilight and speckled by oddly shaped rock formations. Where the desert met the horizon
were the beginnings of stars and beyond them something inexplicably beckoning and mysterious. Something irresistible.

A clap of thunder startled him and Teddy opened his eyes,
clearing the great desert and the mysterious horizon. The entire
sky behind the water tower was now dark and the revolving
searchlight at the rarely used airport panned the low clouds,
making them seem thick and solid. More flashes and thunder
etched the night as a wall of rain began to crawl toward him.
Teddy watched it approach, his fingers drumming the roadmap
at his side. Suddenly, he reached for the radio dial. A quick twist
elicited a familiar voice from Omaha's KFAB. "…a line in Kansas," the announcer said, "extending from Marysville west to
Smith Center and south to Salina."

Teddy turned off the radio and started the car, listening to
the throaty purr of the motor. After a moment he angled a
look into the rearview mirror. "Okay," he whispered, swinging
his car through a gentle arc that put it back onto the highway.
The sky again flickered followed a few seconds later by a low
rumble and a rush of wind that sent the treetops next to the

road into an easy sway. When the rain came it brought a further darkening, and as the first drops began to hit his windshield, Teddy was again moving south…away from the town. The clock was fast approaching three days and twenty-three hours. Two thousand picks had now fallen off the board with only 257 people still in the running for the win.

Early on the Fourth of July, Monica was awakened by a phone call.

"Teddy there?"

"It's six o'clock in the morning, Nick."

Monica hung up, then rose and padded in bare feet to the living room. The couch was empty, its pillows undisturbed. She made coffee next and read the paper. Around seven-thirty I called. "Hi, Monica. Teddy come home?"

Monica ran fingers through a tangle of morning hair as if to comb out the memory of waking up with unwrinkled sheets on her husband's side of the bed.

"Not yet."

"Don't worry," I reassured her. "The parade doesn't start until five. Teddy will be home by then. I'm sure of it. He won't want to miss the girls in their costumes."

It was a holiday, which gave people around town plenty of time to be abuzz about the skeleton discovered a couple of days earlier. Chief Johnson K. Johnson wanted to keep the investigation under wraps until a forensic expert from Lincoln had weighed in, but he was off-duty, and after some prodding, the corpulent chief began to leak information.

"There was a hole between the eyes of the skull. We found a bullet from a .22 inside," he reported to a group of us gathered on the backside patio of Nick's bar and grill. "Some bone expert from the U is comin' down after the holiday. We won't know much more till then, but I can tell you a few things right now. Number one, this was no suicide; number two, he was a big fella; and number three, he's been in the ground a long time…decades, I'd say."

Around midday, Nick handed out a round of free beers to annoy Vivian Dogberry, the secretary/treasurer of the Fourth of July planning committee. Vivian had threatened to have Nick's wife, Bibsy, relegated to the clean-up committee if he served booze on the nation's birthday, a considerable irony as Vivian made friends with a couple of bottles of wine each day. Nick suggested that Vivian should go "boss around the women who put together the Ladies' Auxiliary float and let men be men," and she likely would have done just that, had Doc Newhouse not put a run in her stocking when he discharged Ed from the hospital. Vivian protested as her planning committee duties traditionally provided her with opportunities to put her nose where it didn't belong, the only thing that gave her any pleasure these days. With Ed home, she'd have to stay with him and be a caretaker or risk gossip. She reminded Doc that one foot had been smoked and drunk into the grave already, another hour with her husband likely to finish her off altogether. When that didn't work she suggested that putting up with people like Ed was the life Doc chose, but having heard the same argument from my mother a couple of days earlier, it had gone from feed to manure in the doctor's estimation, and he ignored Vivian.

Ed was less interested in going home than Vivian was in having him arrive, but Doc tricked the mayor into an ambulance by implying that he would be transported to Bergan Mercy in Omaha, a hospital filled with specialists. Ed loves specialists. They're happy to earn a paycheck ruling out the various afflictions he learns about on WebMD and he eagerly scrambled onto the gurney. However, when the ambulance turned onto Country Club Lane instead of heading south on the highway that led to Omaha, Ed knew he'd been hornswoggled and tried to climb out the rear door. The paramedic wrestled him back onto the gurney and kept him pinned down as the driver bounced their rig through a bed of chrysanthemums in front of the mayor's house. Ed had been nurturing the flowers, expecting they might elevate him from Honorable Mention to First Runner-up or even Grand Prize status at the county fair in August, and their demise caused him to mount a rather spectacular fake seizure, batting his eyes, smacking his lips, and hooting. By the time the paramedics had carried him inside and dumped him into bed, they were as happy to be rid of him as Ed's ashen-faced, chain-smoking wife was unhappy to have him home. They hadn't even made it to the bottom of the stairs before Vivian started yelling at Ed to shut up so that she could get back to dying.

A bit later my mother called to remind Ed that her pick in the town pool was still active. Vivian took the call and relayed the message, prompting our town's most prominent politician to issue a flurry of politically incorrect language.

"Thoughts and prayers, Viv," Mom blithely offered. "Give Ed my thoughts and prayers."

"If you want to pray for someone, you ought to pray for me," Vivian replied, her raspy voice as flat as a gravedigger's shovel. Mom hung up and then called Monica.

"Anything?" she asked.

"Not yet," her daughter-in-law answered. "Sorry, Rachel, but I've gotta go. I'm up to my neck in cherry bomb costumes. I'll see you at the parade."

Mom waited until the phone went dead, then hung up and leaned against the sink, looking out the window of the huge, beautifully landscaped house where she and Dad raised us. The sky was clearing, burning off the morning overcast. The clouds were moving southerly, unusual for that time of year but a good sign. There would be no storm during the parade.

A few hours earlier—around four a.m. on the Fourth of July— Teddy had arrived at the place where he figured the rest of his life would begin—a line in Kansas extending from Marysville to Smith Center and south to Salina: *Alinin, Kansas.* At that hour, dawn was merely a pink suggestion in the eastern sky and so he'd wedged himself into the cramped rear seat, sleeping until daylight was no longer a rumor. Once awake, he uncurled and stepped into the cool morning air, stale and wrung out, his joints stiff and achy. He ran in place for a few moments to get his blood moving and then took a minute or so to appreciate his surroundings.

It's peaceful here, Teddy contemplated, savoring the musical sound of the wind fluting through roadside grasses, the rich aroma of fertile earth, and the distant farmsteads dotting the countryside like orphaned stars. A small gathering of cattle grazed in a nearby pasture. One in the herd moved away from the others and stood near the barbed wire fence, staring at Teddy with the typical broad-faced expression of a cow, which was no expression at all. *I have to be here*, the big bovine seemed to be thinking. *What's your excuse?*

Overhead, a low roll of dirty gray thunderclouds—ponderous and fat with rain—threatened the sky and Teddy wondered if similar clouds hung over Delphic Oracle. In an hour or so, he mused, Nick would open up the Cozy Lunch. Later on, Ed Dogberry would deliver an address light on the birth of the nation and heavy on "dad-burned cheaters who rig town pools." Around noon, the Peaseblossom Implement & Auto Parts Giants and their star pitcher, Regretful Peaseblossom, would take on the Cozy Lunch Dodgers in a Little League game that preceded the parade.

Nothing changes there, Teddy thought.

He sighed. Even though the rest of his life was anxiously awaiting, he hated to miss it all. The girls would be cute in their cherry bomb costumes and Monica would have the best picnic dinner in town. That evening, everyone in Delphic Oracle would attend the fireworks display before heading home to sip beer or lemonade while the kids ran around in the back yard, waving sparklers.

Teddy moved to the middle of the highway and straddled the center line, the road now stretched before him like an endless golden ribbon. Holding out his arms, he faced north toward Nebraska—the old side of the line. *His* old side. It was just as he expected. Nothing had changed. Slowly he turned to the south, his eyes widening with surprise. He blinked, then

blinked again, as the ominous thunderclouds suddenly separated, allowing rays of sunlight to angle through. Even in the
unbiased glow that illuminated the flat landscape, the image was
indisputable. Standing on a line in Kansas that extended from
Marysville to Smith Center and south to Salina, Teddy knew
what lay behind him: dirt and corn and weeds and more dirt—a
barn, a few cattle, a distant power line. All of it unchanged
just as he already knew. *But to the south? On the other side of a line
in Kansas?* My little brother would later describe, over Sunday
dinner with twin sister Mia and the rest of our family, exactly
what he saw.

"Same damned thing," he would tell us.

As the clock turned on four days, nineteen hours, and thirty
minutes with only three people left in the town pool, Monica
finished dressing the girls in their cherry bomb costumes. Afterward, she walked them to the Burlington Northern parking
lot where Aunt Felicity and I, along with my sisters, Mary Ellen and Mia, were organizing the gathering of elaborate floats,
men in uniforms, women in purple hats, and kids decked out
in colorful costumes. Our other sister, Daisy, was in the parade,
resplendent in rodeo gear and riding her handsome palomino,
Prince Valiant. Monica made sure her daughters were lined up
with the Little Firecracker Brigade and then made her way to
the grassy town square where Mom had staked out places for
the family with lawn chairs recently obtained on sale from the
new Walmart over in Zenith. Monica didn't realize Teddy was
back until he appeared atop the Rialto's V-shaped marquee
across from the town square, just as a small blue-and-yellow
helicopter swooped low along the parade route, heralding the
start of the day's pageantry.

From his perch above the crowd. Teddy could easily see us
lounging in the new lawn chairs. And he could wave at his three
little cherry bombs as they waddled down the street between
the Father of Our Country float, starring police chief Johnson K. Johnson as George Washington, and Francis Wounded

Arrow's nearly cherry 1929 Chevy pickup, festooned in red, white, and blue crepe paper with my eldest sister, Justine, in the truck bed tossing hard candies to the crowd. Teddy waved and waved, and from the middle of the Little Firecracker Brigade, his girls laughed with delight and waved back. By then, Ed Dogberry had made a miraculous recovery in order to deliver his customary Fourth of July remarks and someone had managed to sabotage the public-address system so that no one would have to listen. With Aunt Felicity in charge, the parade went off without a hitch, the loudest cheers offered when the mayor's speech was delivered into a dead microphone.

That evening Teddy, Monica, their girls, and the rest of our family gathered together for a picnic and then watched the fireworks display from the soft, high grass of the lakeside. There was no rain and the sky was sprayed with stars so bright their unassuming brilliance competed with the unapologetically showy fireworks. It was one of the best displays ever, put on by a couple of Italian brothers from Omaha, and we all enjoyed it immensely.

Especially Mom…because she had won the pool.

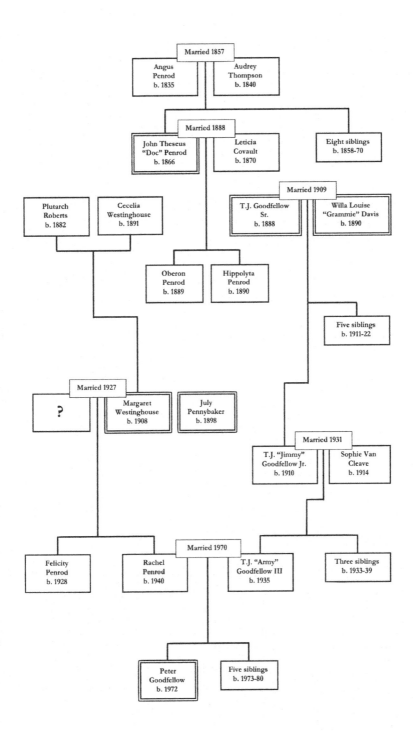

Married 1857

Angus
Penrod
b. 1835

Audrey
Thompson
b. 1840

Married 1888

John Theseus
"Doc" Penrod
b. 1866

Leticia
Covault
b. 1870

Eight siblings
b. 1858-70

Married 1909

T.J. Goodfellow
Sr.
b. 1888

Willa Louise
"Grammie" Davis
b. 1890

Plutarch
Roberts
b. 1882

Cecelia
Westinghouse
b. 1891

Oberon
Penrod
b. 1889

Hippolyta
Penrod
b. 1890

Five siblings
b. 1911-22

Married 1927

?

Margaret
Westinghouse
b. 1908

July
Pennybaker
b. 1898

Married 1931

T.J. "Jimmy"
Goodfellow Jr.
b. 1910

Sophie Van
Cleave
b. 1914

Felicity
Penrod
b. 1928

Rachel
Penrod
b. 1940

Married 1970

T.J. "Army"
Goodfellow III
b. 1935

Three siblings
b. 1933-39

Peter
Goodfellow
b. 1972

Five siblings
b. 1973-80

3

THE LONG LOST ORACLE OF DELPHI

It was not a time for young girls to approach a drifter," Grammie Willa remembered when describing Maggie Westinghouse and the stranger asleep on a pile of gunny-sacks. "...as if there's ever a good time for such nonsense." As for July, he opened his eyes and sat up straight when he first saw Maggie framed by the doorway of the switch-house. Her hair was black, her lips full, and though her stunning figure was silhouetted by the sun through a thin cotton dress, all he saw were her eyes, dark and fearless.

"'Did my heart love till now? Forswear it, sight! For I ne'er saw true beauty till this night,'" he instinctively exclaimed.

Maggie sniffed. "You're not supposed to be here," she said.

"July was six feet two inches of good-looking rascal, the sort accustomed to weakening female knees," Grammie recalled. "He was used to women tumbling pretty quickly when they heard Shakespeare spill from those handsome lips and knew right away that Maggie was no typical woman. She was formidable."

"You're not supposed to talk to strangers, I'll warrant," July replied.

"True," Maggie confessed. She leaned against the doorjamb and looked him over. "You're a mess," she said.

It was true. The breast pocket of July's coat was torn, the cuffs of his trousers seriously frayed. He looked broke and was, the money lifted from Bugs's safe—ten thousand dollars—still hidden under a floorboard in his old Chicago apartment. July needed a shower and smelled like it, but shot the beautiful girl in the switch-house doorway a smile. Then, he stood, smoothed back his hair, and carefully buttoned his coat as if about to sweep into McGovern's Saloon back in Chicago.

"I am July Pennybaker," he announced, offering a jazzy two-fingered salute. "You've no doubt heard of me."

"You look like a rail-hopper," Maggie replied, "and a pecker-wood. Why should anyone know of you?"

July moved closer, his eyes narrow as if searching for meaning in a piece of abstract art. Maggie stood her ground. "You're a brave one," he said, "and wise to see that I present no threat. I shall call you Athena."

Maggie stiffened. "You *shall* not do any such thing," she mocked. "My name is Margaret Westinghouse." She shook back her hair and instinctively struck a pose—chin up, face pointed at the disheveled stranger. "And you'll call me *Miss* Westinghouse or nothing at all."

"Ah," July replied, "that I will."

"Maggie tended to put most men in her rearview mirror pretty quickly," Grammie recalled. "There'd been too many devils like Plutarch Roberts in her life. But there had also been a real shortage of charming, square-jawed devils like July Pennybaker and she was intrigued. Besides, she'd had one of her visions that very morning and her defenses were always down afterward."

"I have spells," she told July, uncharacteristically volunteering unsolicited information about herself, a surprise to both of them. "I like to walk when I wake up…clear my head." She went on to describe a dream in which a man had appeared, riding a bicycle and wearing the robes of a Bedouin prince. The man was short and swarthy with a dark, tangled beard and terrible body odor. He produced a small dog from beneath his robes and gave it to her, promising that the animal would protect her from devils. The dog stank.

"You stink too," Maggie told July.

"And like your Arab sheik I've come to protect you from devils," July responded, "but the aroma you disdain is freedom, Miss Westinghouse, a most delectable fragrance that I heartily recommend if you're not too faint-hearted."

July Pennybaker spoke as if to an audience and the words he

used, grandiose coming from most, tripped from his tongue as easily as birds to flight. Maggie knew better, but took him home anyway, where he spent a long time in the shower washing off several weeks of tramping. As the water rushed over him, July sang and his rich baritone drew her to the bathroom door to listen. She had just cracked it for a look when he stepped out of the shower and sent her running for the kitchen. "Maggie decided to fry some sausage and an egg," Grammie Willa would recount, chuckling. "Not much of a cook, that one, but a naked man in the house can be downright inspirational." A few minutes later, July appeared in the kitchen doorway, wearing a suit taken from the closet in Mrs. Westinghouse's bedroom.

"Better?" he asked, producing a gold collar pin as if from thin air and then securing it behind the knot of his tie.

Maggie looked him over. "What else did you steal?" she asked. "Never mind. You can have those clothes. I don't care."

"I figured," July answered. "Your ex-husband's? Didn't see a ring on that lovely finger."

"Don't be stupid," Maggie sniffed. "I'm seventeen years old. They belong to my mother's lover. He's not her husband, either. He's not anything."

July sat and Maggie slid a plate onto the table with the only hot food he'd encountered in weeks. He leaned forward and inhaled deeply, then wrinkled his nose.

"What is that smell?" he asked.

"It's egg and sausage," Maggie snapped, bristling. "You don't have to eat it."

"No, not that…the other… The indecorous aroma."

"Indecorous?" Maggie retorted. "Really? That's not the right word. Aromas can't be rude. We have dictionaries here, too, buster. I know what indecorous means. I'm not stupid."

July took a bite from his sandwich and chewed thoughtfully. "No, you are not stupid. That I can see," he said.

"He made Maggie mad," Grammie Willa contended, "though mostly at herself because July had tipped her over and she knew it. It wasn't her fault. She was no flibbertigibbet like a lot of girls her age, but July had a way about him that tended to flibbertigibbetize a woman."

"Not stupid at all," July added. "'You are beautiful and therefore to be wooed. You are woman and therefore to be won.'"

This simply made Maggie angrier. She had been wooed plenty in her life, but never won, fully expecting that when true love arrived she'd manage it with a firm hand. Now that it had sashayed through the front door without knocking, true love had put her in an uncharacteristic dither, explaining the regrettable deluge of words she suddenly let pour.

"So you sing silly Irish songs and quote Shakespeare. What are you? An actor? Just so you know, I hate actors. They pretend to be people they could never be in real life, then behave as if it's an actual accomplishment...as if they were as important as the people they portray. Rudolph Valentino isn't really an Arabian sheik and Lon Chaney isn't a hunchback. They're just really good fakes. I hate fakes. You may talk like a college professor, but you're just a rail-hopper. You can't hold a job and so you ride around the country in a cattle car until somebody is dumb enough to buy into your big words and your singing and your... your...blue-eyed nonsense. You sit there with your curly hair and silly grin and think I'll jump into bed with you, but that's not going to happen, Mister...Mister—"

"July Pennybaker."

"Right...Mister July Pennybaker. So if that's why you've come here, then be on your way. Just head out the door and keep walking, okay?"

Maggie was accustomed to men bloviating, then turning marble-mouthed and red-faced as they tried not to stare at her breasts. *This must be what it feels like,* she thought, suddenly wanting July to leave nearly as much as she wanted him to stay. It was an unfamiliar predicament and she took a few moments to gather herself, nervously fingering the hem of her dress while offering the numbers on the wall calendar and the round clock above the stove a great deal more attention than either of the things warranted. She desperately wanted him to say something brazen or put a hand on her knee—anything that might justify a slap across his stupidly good-looking face. He did neither, forcing Maggie's eyes to the floor.

"You must think I'm a silly fool," she said.

"No," July replied, "I don't."

Maggie looked up and July fashioned an expression that made her want to believe him. And so she did.

"Let's start over," July said. "What is that smell?" A pungent odor, redolent of petroleum and rubbing alcohol, permeated the apartment. "It's some sort of medicine, isn't it?"

Maggie sniffed tentatively. "Oh…that," she said. "It's from below. Our landlord is a dentist. He started using a new kind of painkiller a while back…a gas you breathe in. Sometimes, we can smell it up here. He's promised to make it right, but he won't. He makes a lot of promises. I'm not holding my breath."

"Pun intended?"

"What?"

"Never mind," July replied. He finished eating and wiped his mouth with a napkin. His hands were beautiful, Maggie thought, strong with long, elegant fingers—so unlike the lumpy-knuckled farmers' sons in Miagrammesto Station. He stood and took her hand in his, pressing it to his lips.

"I thank you for providing this wayfarer with shelter and sustenance, fair lady." He straightened and winked. "And I take leave knowing full well that we shall meet again…*Miss* Westinghouse." And then July Pennybaker was gone, departing so quickly Maggie had no time to consider that the bracelet once gracing her wrist was missing.

Grammie Willa's husband and my great-grandfather—T.J. Goodfellow, Sr.—was the sheriff. "He caught up with July about a mile south of town," Grammie remembered. "July denied everything at first, but then he socked T.J. in the nose and tried to run. Big mistake. July was not a small fellow, but your great-grandpa was a bear of a man." There was a scuffle with July getting the worst of it and he was soon on his way back to Miagrammesto Station, jammed into the cramped rear seat of a patrol car with handcuffs adorning his wrists. He'd been stunned by a left hook the sheriff had landed, necessitating a side trip to Doc Penrod's where the long-time town physician was in the middle of an effort to restore Maggie Westinghouse after she'd suffered another swoon. When July was escorted into the doctor's small treatment room, she abruptly awoke, sitting bolt upright.

"We must *attack*!" she cried out from one of two exam tables, her eyes foggy. She pointed at July. "*He* is the one," she proclaimed. "*You* are the one," she said, climbing off the table and then stumbling into his arms.

"T.J. and Doc were momentarily transfixed," Grammie Willa always claimed, "and who could blame them? Miagrammesto Station had a movie house and an annual melodrama put on by the Thespians Society, but high drama was an uncommon occurrence in our neck of the woods."

"We must *attack*," Maggie repeated with quiet certainty, attempting a wink that went badly even for a girl as beautiful as she, one side of her face turning lopsided and drunken. "*He* is the one," she told the doctor, sloppily tapping on July's chest with a finger. "*He* will show you the way."

July lifted Maggie and carried her back to the exam table, then turned to face Doc Penrod and the sheriff, noting the doctor's heavy ring. It bore the symbol of the Masons. "July's instinct was to put some distance between himself and Miagrammesto Station," Grammie contended. "However, he was a businessman, too, and knew that a superstitious town stalwart like Doc Penrod and a girl with honest-to-God visions were ingredients in a recipe that might bake up a batch of profit."

"I am July Pennybaker," he said, directing his opening salvo at the open-faced physician. "You've no doubt heard of me." Doc Penrod shook his head. "The Heinrich Walterscheid Institute? Berlin? You know it, of course."

"Doc hadn't," Grammie told me, "but he'd spent about three decades in our little town having all the answers and felt a lot of pressure to maintain his image."

"It sounds familiar," Doc lied.

"I knew you'd heard of us," July said, shifting his attention to Sheriff Goodfellow. "As the good doctor well knows, Sheriff, the Walterscheid Institute employs Jungian philosophies to unearth the collective unconscious…that place in the primordial broth from which ancestral beings call out to us." He looked to Doc Penrod for affirmation, and with one foot already in the pond, the doctor waded into the lie.

"Yes…uh…it's called a collective unconscious," he said. "I've heard of it." He glanced at the sheriff and was met by a frank expression of disbelief that made him feel guilty. "But we don't have call for such things around here," he added, frowning at July.

"Ah, understandable…understandable," July replied. "That would explain why I was summoned."

"Summoned?" the sheriff echoed, eyeing his prisoner suspiciously. "You were summoned?"

July studied the collection of diplomas and certificates on Doc Penrod's wall, squinting as if to discern coded messages within the embossed seals. Finally, he sighed. "I suppose it had to come out," he said, his voice heavy. He moved to Maggie's side and lightly stroked her cheek. She had fallen asleep on the exam table, her long lashes grazing her cheek, her mouth forming a tiny bow. "Gentlemen, I have not been honest with you," he continued. "I am, in point of fact, not connected with the Walterscheid Institute. Yes, I am familiar with their work…paltry and unenlightened as it is…but, indeed, I have not studied there nor would I recommend it."

He hesitated, then went on as if relieved to unload the burden of a long-kept secret. "Have you heard of the Oracles of Delphi?" he asked.

Doc Penrod and the sheriff shook their heads and a delighted July then described Delphi, a place in Greece once thought to be the center of world, telling the men about the Temple of Apollo overlooking the Pleistos valley. Sheriff Goodfellow and the doctor remained quiet as July told them of mysterious labyrinthine caves where young girls, providentially selected by the priests of Delphi, were visited by oracular visions—glimpses of the future for a populace eager to get a leg up on fate.

"Gentlemen," July related, "little more than five years ago there were three remaining Oracles of Delphi: the beautiful maidens Clotho, Lechesis, and Atropos."

July's claim caused Doc Penrod to tip his head suspiciously and then fashion the same expression he offered teenaged girls who cited immaculate conception when facing a diagnosis of acute pregnancy. "That's from Greek mythology, isn't it?" Doc interrupted. "I remember it from college. They were called, uh...the Fates, right? That's it...the Fates. I remember now. They were old hags. They scared the hell out of the other gods." He eyed July warily. "What was the name of that place in Berlin?"

"You are obviously a classically educated man, Doctor Penrod," July improvised. "However, I refer not to such evanescent beings as the mythical Fates but to mortals terrestrially imbued with their gifts of divination."

The onslaught of grandly unfamiliar language reset the hook in the doctor's mouth, but Sheriff Goodfellow was clearly unconvinced, one hand on the butt of his service revolver as he sniffed the bait. "Good sirs," July implored. "I cannot easily explain how the winds of myth and matter became one. However, make no mistake, the Oracles of whom I speak were real."

He paused, swiveling his gaze from one man to the other.

"Not so many years ago on a day very much like today, Lechesis and Atropos each fell into a trance from which neither recovered. At the same time, Clotho...perhaps the most beautiful of all the Oracles...began to age as if each passing day spanned a hundred years. I was still recovering from wounds incurred in the Great War when I was called to Delphi by the High Priest. I am, of course, a Knight of Zeus and an Interpreter."

"In Delphi," he went on, "I found frail Clotho near death, her skin as brittle as parchment, her voice a mere echo, her eyes hazy with the coming unknown. 'And you shall find her in the

New World,' Clotho intoned before infinity claimed her, 'and she will be as a pearl among stones and they shall know her as *Margarita.*'"

"Gentlemen," July continued, "since the day of poor Clotho's transcendence there has been for the first time in more than two thousand years no Oracle of Delphi. Throughout the Mediterranean crops now wither and die, babies are born bearing the marks of devils, and pestilence moves among the people of the ancient civilizations—fearsome blights, that even now as we speak, are slowly making their way to the new empires…to England and America."

July glanced at Maggie, momentarily so beguiled by her flawless skin and cupid's bow mouth he almost lost his way. When he went on, his voice was softer, devoid of evangelical hills and valleys, but no less mesmerizing.

"Good friends, my search is at an end. I had thought myself mistaken, but you, Sheriff, were sent to retrieve me…to lift the cowl of suspicion from my eyes. The legend foretold a descendent of the three Oracles of whom I speak, a lamp whom Heaven would light, a vessel the gods would fill for us to draw upon, a chosen one who would guide us from darkness."

He knelt reverently before the slumbering girl.

"Good fellows," July intoned as Maggie issued a long, rattling snore, "the trees of destiny planted by the gods are about to bear fruit. Look upon the teller of things to come, the hope of the mortal world, the bridge between what has been and what shall be." He rose from his knees, the pitch of his voice rising, his eyes filled with tears. "MY FRIENDS, LOOK UPON THE ORACLE…THE LONG-LOST DELPHIC ORACLE!"

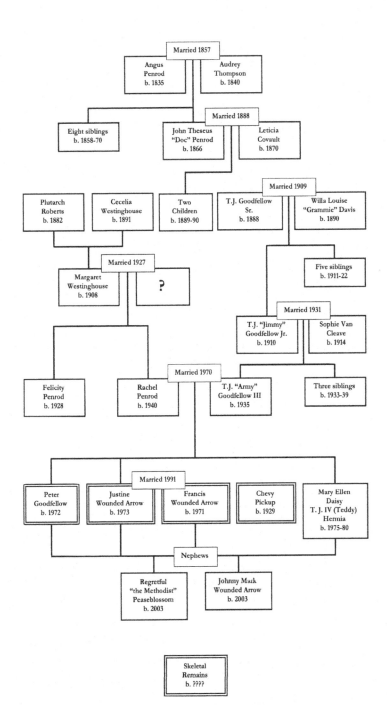

4

FRANCIS AND JUSTINE

I am the oldest of six children. Teddy and his twin sister, Hermia "Mia" Goodfellow, are the youngest with Justine, Mary Ellen, and Daisy in the middle. Justine is married to Francis Wounded Arrow, who got his arm stuck in his pickup last year on the day before the Fourth of July. At the time, Teddy was still on the run, Ed Dogberry was out of the pool, Samson the Methodist was on the mend, and we still didn't know the identity of the full human skeleton discovered in a vacant lot.

I had stopped by Peaseblossom Implement & Auto Parts around 2:30 p.m. and found Francis out front under the hood of his nearly cherry 1929 Chevy pickup, one arm jammed into a jumble of grimy metal and rubber belts and hoses. He was praying. Francis has always been a religious man. He just lacks faith, torn between the Catholic rigors of his Czech-American mother and the ecclesiastical flexibility of a full-blooded Sioux father who was descended from shamans.

"I'm a damned fool," he told me after he'd pleaded with the Great Father and then followed it up with a few tugs on his arm. "I trusted the fork-tongued long-knives from that new Walmart over in Zenith."

The day before, Francis told me, he'd used a coupon to get a car battery charger from the discount outlet and then gone fishing at the reservoir that evening. His buddy, Beagle Gibbs, was with him and they'd spent the night drinking and philosophizing about the newly discovered skeleton. "It's a sign from the Great Father," Francis had suggested to Beagle.

"It's nothing but a pile of dry bones," Beagle countered, afterward spending much of the night trying to knock Francis off

his opinion. This made Francis want to knock Beagle entirely
out of the boat, an urge he resisted with prayers to the Blessed
Uncle of Blasted Fools, a few beers, and some Jägermeister.

"I had to let Beagle drive home," Francis told me, and although pretty drunk himself, Beagle had managed to squeeze
Francis's nearly cherry 1929 Chevy pickup into his friend's
garage. He then stumbled off, sober enough to turn off the
engine—a good thing since Francis was asleep in the truck-
bed—but not distilled enough to turn off the headlights. At
first, the beams nicely illuminated the cluttered workbench at
the front of the garage and the picture of the Virgin Mary that
Francis's Catholic grandmother, Crazy Ainitta, had given him
before she was crazy. However, the rays of light slowly faded
over the next few hours, and by noon, the truck's battery was as
dead as Crazy Ainitta's amputated, diabetic toe.

"Wake up!" my sister Justine, shouted when she discovered
Francis asleep atop a half dozen decomposing catfish. It was
stiflingly hot, the still air in the garage redolent of spilled oil
and deceased fish.

"The Blessed Uncle of Hungry Catfish was on me and
Beagle's side last night," Francis told her. "He sat back in that
heavenly old La-Z-Boy recliner of his and watched us haul in
fish as quick as we could get bait on our hooks."

"I don't care, Francis," Justine scolded. "Get up!"

She went inside for a broom—her weapon of choice when
a need to rouse him presented itself—and as soon as she was
gone Francis scrambled into the truck cab where a turn of the
ignition key produced an engine noise very much like the cluck-
ing tongues that have shadowed him all his life. The truck's
battery was dead.

"Justine came back with a honey-do list but no broom,"
Francis told me. "She thought I stunk." He winked, chuckling.
"I did too," he confessed.

"You still do," I told him.

Francis then explained how his wife had scheduled a nail appointment and needed a lift since he'd been unable to find time

to figure out why her car was stuck in reverse gear. "I probably shoulda told her about the dead battery," he confessed, even though my sister had long ago made clear that knowing nothing about motor vehicles was exactly the correct amount of information.

"My appointment's at three o'clock," she shouted on her way back into the house. "We need to leave here at two-fifty sharp."

"I'll try," Francis replied, even though everyone in town knew that he'd squeezed out of his mother two weeks late and had subsequently managed over the next forty-three years to never be on time for anything.

"So I looked over that there honey-do list and had to laugh," Francis told me. "She wanted me to buy a new broom."

He grinned.

"I sawed the old one in half last week after she caught me full on the butt with it. Tossed that sucker into the vacant lot across the street."

Francis then scanned the other items on Justine's list, determining that none were of sufficient urgency to put off retrieving the bottle of Pabst Blue Ribbon he'd stashed under the seat of the pickup. He popped the top and took a swallow, frowning at the garage door. It was partially stuck open, offering a sliced view of the vacant lot across the street. The previous day, a skeleton had been found there and treasure hunters had crushed or bent many of the hip-high weeds and sunflowers, the rest blurred by translucent heat lines that rippled upward from his asphalt driveway. The undulations reminded him of old movies where the screen was distorted into waves to indicate a flashback, which reminded him of Justine's magic, which recalled for him that she could make herself disappear at will, which elicited a memory of the last of the Cocoa Puffs that he hoped hadn't disappeared after he hid them in the pantry, which, last of all, made him acutely aware that all he'd had for breakfast was trail mix and Jägermeister.

"I was starvin' to death," he told me. "Me and Beagle was gonna cook one of the catfish the night before, but he fell in the damned water tryin' to get outta the boat and soaked our only book of matches. So I figured to sneak into the house and get somethin' to eat." He never made it. Justine headed him off, abruptly materializing in the doorway, her posture and jaw-set making clear that Francis was not to traipse about their house enveloped in a cloud of dead catfish smell.

"Hose off…and burn those clothes," she niggled, pinching her nose shut. "And don't forget. We need to leave at two-fifty." Then, she popped off as magically as she had popped up.

"Your sister can make herself invisible, you know," Francis told me. It was a claim he often forwarded, accusing our family of keeping it a secret until the couple had safely exchanged vows. "I was just a kid, Father. Me and Justine were right out of high school. You shoulda told me."

"She can't make herself invisible, Francis," I replied.

"Hell if she can't. After we was hitched she started poppin' up willy-nilly every time I drank milk direct from the carton or farted out loud or took a leak with the toilet seat down. I love her, mind you, but you shoulda told me," Francis bemoaned. "You're a priest. You're supposed to advise folks about things. If I'd known, I woulda got me a pre-nup that put a limit on how many times she could go all invisible on me."

He paused to give his arm another pull. It was no use. He remained stuck.

"Anyway, I was still starvin', so after she went back inside, I looked around for somethin' to eat," Francis went on, revealing that his initial search yielded merely an orange Life Saver stuck to the truck's registration certificate and a suspiciously green Hostess cupcake. He found a single M&M under the seat, but the real prize came after he stuffed his hand into the crack between the pickup's seat cushions, happily excavating a semi-fossilized salted nut roll. Carefully nibbling on the candy to avoid a crown that had been wiggling for months, Francis then shuffled across the garage, slipped under the door without breaking stride, and lurched into the blinding sunlight. Squinting, he made his way to the lopsided shed behind the house where he retrieved his new battery charger, taking a couple of minutes to read the instructions.

"Instructions never make sense," he suggested, nevertheless, soldiering through the first paragraph of the insert before crumbling it in one fist and tossing it into an open bag of fertilizer. He then grabbed the charger and went back to the garage, issuing an appreciative whistle as he ducked under the door. With his door opener broken, one splintered row of panels hung below the sagging header with not more than an inch separating them from the roof of his pickup.

"Beagle must have had some powerful magic to get the truck into the garage," he told me. "Ship in a bottle magic, I'll wager." It was good magic he hoped to sustain, although the odds were against it if his successful brother, Russell Wounded Arrow, were to be believed. Russell captained the Dakota Casino, a gambling ship that cruised the Missouri River. "You have bad odds, Francis," he often said. "Don't bet on yourself." Russell wasn't religious, which Francis found puzzling since the Great Father seemed to have answered most of his brother's prayers. "He ain't nothin' special," Francis often opined, "yet he gets to wear a tie to work, live in a big house on the river, and hobnob at country clubs with them rich South Omaha meatpackers. Sounds like a heap o' answered prayers to me."

"So you got the charger to work?" I said, shifting Francis's gears, as talk of his brother sometimes sends him off on irretrievable rants. "I mean you got the truck from your garage to here… The engine started after you charged the battery, right?"

"Sort of," Francis replied.

His battery charger, he told me, was about the size of a shoebox. Black and glossy, it had a serious-looking dial and a pair of ebony cables snaking out the back panel. "It was pretty easy to figure out," he told me. "Didn't need no instructions. Positive to positive, negative to negative." He'd attached the lobster claw contacts at the ends of the cables to the battery posts of his Chevy, plugged in the device, and then waited as the box began to hum. Fifteen minutes later the needle on the

dial still vibrated on zero. That's when he peered more close-
ly at the charger and noticed a tiny switch. Black like the box
itself, the switch blended into the face of the device, making
Francis wonder if Justine had made it partially invisible to trick
him. He flipped it and the needle on the dial-face immediately
jumped into the red zone at the top end of the instrument's
range, accompanied by an accusatory buzz that made Francis's
heart flutter dangerously.

"It was some kind of devil switch," Francis soberly suggested, temporarily embracing the Catholic side of his family. "Put
Satan himself in that damned thing, Father. I wasn't havin' no
part of it."

He'd jerked the plug from the wall socket, afterward neatly
repacking the device in its original container and then pitching
the demonic thing into the vacant lot across the street. With
the devil cast out, Francis then climbed into the pickup cab,
breathed a prayer to the Blessed Uncle That Gives Life, and
turned the ignition key. "It started kaplunka-kaboomin' like
all get-out," he happily reported, its bad carburetor giving it a
sloppily drunken voice as he drove downtown to Peaseblossom
Implements & Auto Parts.

Our brother-in-law, Big Bob Peaseblossom—married to my
sister, Mary Ellen—was well acquainted with Francis's credit
history as he was still owed for the Chevy's dying battery as
well as a fuel filter, four quarts of oil, the deodorizer shaped
like a pine tree that hung from the truck's rearview mirror,
and a bag of chips from the vending machine in the employee
lounge. "No more credit, Francis," Big Bob had insisted, but
Francis was undaunted. A savvy trader, he eventually talked our
brother-in-law out of a new battery by offering to swap it for
a slightly used charger he promised to deliver after retrieving it
from the vacant lot across the street from his house. Big Bob
put the agreement on paper, then brought a battery out from
the back. By then, the Chevy's engine had backfired a couple of
times and then died.

"It was already one-thirty," Francis reported. "I was gonna

have just enough time to install the new battery and still get Justine picked up on time…if the Great Father hadn't decided to screw me, that is."

Before jumping into the work, Francis had offered a prayer to the Blessed Uncle of Daylight Savings Time, asking him to spring the clock forward or make it fall back—whichever of those things would give him an extra hour. Afterward, he rummaged through the cluttered truck bed, looking for a wrench. That's when he remembered that the Blessed Uncle of Things Made by Dumb-asses had failed to answer his prayer the previous week when he was trying to fix the garage door opener, making Francis so mad he'd chucked his toolbox into the vacant lot across the street from his house.

"I didn't have nothin' to trade Big Bob for a wrench so I borrowed one when he wasn't lookin'," Francis told me.

"You stole it," I countered.

"I was gonna put it back, Father. That makes it borrowed." He frowned. "Besides, you're the one bunkin' in jail every night, not me. Priest or not, you ain't one to talk."

Put in my place, I kept quiet as Francis next described snugging his borrowed wrench over the nut that secured the engine cable to the negative post of his moribund truck battery. He gave it a careful turn. It yielded easily. Delighted, Francis loosened the nut until he could turn it without the wrench, then reached in and gave the cable a tug. It didn't give. Using the wrench, Francis scraped off most of the whitish crust that covered the battery post and then loosened the nut until it nearly came off in his fingers. He gave the cable another pull. It gave only a little. He pulled again and it gave a little more. Squaring his shoulders, Francis leaned into the engine compartment and braced one hand on the positively charged post of the battery while getting a good grip on the negatively charged cable with the other. That's when he discovered that the ignition key was turned on and his allegedly dead battery had not quite made it to the Afterlife.

From inside the store Big Bob heard a pop, then saw a few

sparks fly out of the Chevy accompanied by a puff of smoke and a thumping sound as Francis hit the plate glass window of Peaseblossom Implement & Auto Parts butt-first and hard. Momentarily suspended against the window, he then sank slowly to the sidewalk and lay there like an unstuffed scarecrow.

Now, Big Bob was forty years old at the time and far too young to be a full-fledged curmudgeon, but he was one and still is. Moreover, like any self-respecting curmudgeon, he does not ordinarily leap into a breach created by another's misfortune, preferring to remain at a distance that will facilitate I-told-you-so-ing. However, Francis was family, and besides, the previous month's premium payment for the store's liability insurance had been a couple of days late. "Even if the policy was still active, I wasn't sure it covered an electrocution in my parking lot," he later told me. So he went out to determine if Francis was as dead as the battery of his nearly cherry 1929 Chevy pickup. He jostled him with the toe of his boot.

"You all right?"

Francis's heart was in the flopping portion of a significant flip-flop and he couldn't feel the fingers of one hand or make a fist with the other, but as the town handyman, he had already been nearly electrocuted a couple of times in his life. He knew from experience that he'd be fine.

"Francis, are you okay?" Big Bob repeated.

"Never better," Francis replied in a hoarse whisper, managing a crooked grin. Big Bob went back inside, and a minute or so later, Francis felt well enough to regain his feet and wobble back to the Chevy. He peered into the engine compartment, searching for the wrench, which had clattered through the jungle of belts and hoses into some secret pocket within the great belly of the thing. When his search came up empty, he cursed, then jammed his arm into the maze of rubber hoses, fan belts, and rough metal edges filling the engine compartment. Within seconds he realized that his arm was too short to reach the wrench and too thick-wristed to pull free. "It's like I told you, Padre," he told me. "The Great Father screwed me. I was stuck."

Not long thereafter I dropped by the store to lodge a protest with Big Bob, a town councilman, about Methodist Mayor Dogberry's proposal to reduce property taxes by putting up parking meters on all the streets around my St. Mary's Catholic church. I never made it inside, instead listening to Francis describe the sequence of events I've just shared.

"Maybe we should call Justine," I suggested.

Francis paled, then ground his eyes shut and concentrated, afterward explaining that he had just beseeched the Great Father and his minion, the Blessed Uncle of Things Not Seen, to make his hammy hand with its walnut knuckles thinner, or better yet, invisible. "An invisible hand is a ghost, Father," he told me. If his hand were invisible, Francis figured he could easily whip it free of the Chevy, his ghost-arm whistling through the radiator and chrome grill like winter wind through leafless trees. "Afterward," Francis promised, "I'll find Justine and tickle her silly while my hand is still invisible. Then I'll find that lazy beer barrel of a cat of hers and give his tail a pull or two... Watch that old fatso scratch and paw at nothin' but air."

He stopped talking for a few moments, his head bowed in prayer, then gave his arm another jerk. It didn't come loose, the effort making his entire hand tingle.

"Yipes!" he shouted.

Three o'clock came and went with Francis still trapped, none of his Blessed Uncles willing to make his arm invisible. "All my life I been prayin' to those sons o' bitches, Father, and I ain't got nothin' to show for it but disappointment," he grumbled.

"Maybe you're praying to the wrong God," I offered.

Francis studied me. He faithfully attended Mass with Justine every week, even though he generally deferred to his Native American roots in spiritual matters, unwilling to put all his eggs in a Catholic basket. "What the heck," he decided, bowing his head. "Holy Mary, Mother of God," he intoned, "please try to talk some sense into the Great Father who has refused to make my arm invisible."

Around three-thirty, Regretful Peaseblossom and Johnny

Mark Wounded Arrow wandered over from the Y-Knot Drive-In down the street, chocolate from a pair of dip cones smeared across their faces like war paint. Regretful—Samson the Methodist—had a bandage on his forehead from his scuffle with the human shinbone his dog had dug up. The boys peered at Francis as if he were a zoo animal.

"Whacha doin', Uncle Francis?" Johnny Mark asked him.

"Changin' my car battery," Francis answered.

Regretful licked at his ice cream cone, then lifted his chin.

"Why are you bent over the truck like that?"

"This is how you change a battery," Francis said. "You have to get the old one out first."

Regretful stepped closer, then cocked his head like a terrier.

"But it's right here." He pointed at the old battery with its crusty posts. "You're nowhere near it."

"Have you ever changed a car battery?"

"No, but—"

"Right...'No but' about covers it. You ain't never done this, so you don't know what you're talkin' about, and I don't have time to explain it to you. Now beat it."

Regretful appraised his uncle for a few seconds before looking at me. "He's stuck, isn't he, Uncle Peter?" he said. "Stuck inside that engine?"

"I don't know," I said. "Maybe."

Regretful looked at Johnny Mark. "He's definitely stuck," he said.

After the boys left I suggested that it might be time to call the fire department, but Francis declined. Delphic Oracle is a small town. It never takes long for an embarrassing situation to circulate and he knew it. "No frickin' way, Father," he protested. "Knowin' them boys, they'd probably chop my arm clean off. You know I don't deserve Justine as it is. A one-armed man's got no chance with her at all."

"That's not true, Francis," I said. "Justine loves you."

I then went inside the store for a little air-conditioning and some talk with Big Bob, while Francis pulled and tugged and twisted his arm, adding a few prayers between snippets of profanity that might well have blackened the rest of Crazy Ainitta's toes had she heard them. It was no use. Nothing worked and so he gave up, figuring he might as well sleep off his hangover. This plan, too, was thwarted when Ed Dogberry showed up.

"Hey, Francis, how's things? How's the boy?" Ed chirped. He was fresh off a luncheon with the Ladies' Auxiliary. My mom is president of the organization and had invited him to speak, figuring a cockwomble like Ed was good for a few laughs. Unfortunately, the mayor had interpreted all the snickering and eye-rolling as voter approval and was on the hunt for more, a constituent trapped in a pickup like a chicken in a fox's den.

"Nice truck you have here, Francis," Ed offered as his opening salvo. "Very...uh, cherry. It's a very cherry truck."

"Thanks," Francis answered, "but it's really just *nearly* cherry. I still have—"

"So, Mister Francis Wounded Arrow," Ed interrupted, "can I count on your vote in the next election?"

Francis grinned. "You betcha, Ed," he said, even though he never votes.

The mayor beamed. "That's my boy," he boomed. He grabbed Francis's free hand and heartily pumped it, then approached the entry to the auto parts store, pausing with a hand on the door handle. "By the way," he asked, "what're you doing there?"

"Stuck," Francis answered.

Ed nodded, forehead wrinkled. "Stuck?"

"Yeah...stuck."

"How in the heck—?"

Big Bob and I emerged from the store before Ed could finish. Big Bob had a Coke from the employee lounge for Francis, the can dripping with condensation. It was an unusual gesture from a man typically more inclined to donate a kidney than unlock his precious Coke machine and give away a free soft drink, but Bob was curious. Curiosity will do that. "Thought you might be thirsty," he said, handing Francis the Coke.

"Thanks," Francis answered.

"So...what're you doing there?" Big Bob asked.

"He's stuck," Ed tattled.

Francis closed his eyes, something Crazy Grandmother Ainitta claimed could make a person invisible. After a few seconds he re-opened them, then sighed when it was apparent that we could still see him.

"I'm stuck," he said, his voice nearly a whisper.

"Stuck?" Big Bob echoed.

"Yeah...stuck."

Big Bob pulled a small penlight from his shirt pocket and directed its beam into the engine compartment. After a moment he straightened, his face clouded with anger.

"Did you drop that wrench you stole?"

"I was gonna return it when I was done."

"Damn straight you were. I saw you take it. I woulda called Chief Johnson if I thought you were gonna keep it. That was a twenty dollar Husky, Francis. I woulda rented it to you for five, but now you're gonna pay me the full twenty or find yourself in court."

Big Bob often threatened to take someone to court, but never had. He didn't this time, either, instead blowing off a bit more steam before heading back inside to call the fire department and Police Chief Johnson K. Johnson. A few minutes later Johnson rolled up in a powder-blue squad car and laboriously eased out his 300-pound frame from behind the wheel. He waddled to the front of the Chevy and peered at Francis, then retrieved a notepad and pencil from his pocket, opened it to a blank page, and was about to conduct a proper interrogation when interrupted by the wavering hee-haw of Delphic Oracle's only fire engine. Seconds later the big truck lurched into the parking lot followed by a dangerously swaying mobile rescue unit. In a flash, volunteer firefighters dressed in civvies, save their helmets and boots, poured off the truck. Snug Nixon and Beagle Gibbs began to unroll the huge fire hose while Nick Dolny grabbed a sturdy ax. He ran for the store's entrance and unleashed a mighty swing that shattered the plate glass. This elicited a great roar of outrage from Big Bob who charged at the volunteer fire chief and might have crushed him had Beagle not intervened, tackling the implement dealer and wrestling him to the sidewalk.

"Don't look, Bob!" Beagle pleaded. "It's better if you don't look. Just let us do our jobs!"

By then, Snug Nixon had dragged the fat firehose to the front door. He planted his feet and gripped the hose with the nozzle pointed toward the interior of the store.

"Okay, boys," he shouted. "Let 'er rip!"

Chief Johnson is an officer of the law, but a bit of an anarchist at heart. He'd watched all this transpire with a perverse smile on his face, but when he caught my eye, his better angels visited. "Better hold off there, Snug," he advised.

A considerable crowd had gathered, not as sizeable as the audience for the previous day's production of Samson the Methodist and the Shinbone, but a decent showing. Samson, himself, and Johnny Mark had returned by then and the chief motioned to them. "Run down to the Y-Knot and get me a Dilly Bar," he said, handing Johnny Mark a fiver. "Keep the change." The two boys dashed off and Johnson eased his huge frame onto the curb fronting the store. A small blue-and-yellow helicopter now hovered overhead and he waved it off, then lowered his eyes until they rested on Francis.

"Whacha doin' in there?"

"Stuck," Francis told him.

"Stuck?"

"Yup."

The chief then pulled out his cell phone and checked on baseball scores until Regretful and Johnny Mark returned from the Y-Knot with his Dilly Bar. Nick Dolny had emerged from the store and he and Big Bob were chin-to-chin, arguing.

"We received a 911 call," Nick explained.

"You received no such thing, you blasted idiot!" my brother-in-law shouted. "*I* made the call and I *didn't call* 911!" They went back and forth for a while, most of the onlookers enormously entertained, although those rooting for a fistfight were disappointed when Nick noticed Francis. He formed a T with his hands.

"Time out, Big Bob," he said. He approached the Chevy. "Whacha doin' in there?"

"Stuck," Francis answered.

Nick's eyes lit up. Delphic Oracle's volunteer fire department had only recently spent the accumulated proceeds of over ten years of bake sales on a knockoff rescue device: the Teeth of Life. Nick had worried a little about the allocation of funds, given that the department's slow-pitch softball uniforms—faded T-shirts and wrinkled caps—were undeniably shabby when compared to rival Zenith's blue shirts, pants with satin piping, and snazzy belts. However, his concern about their investment had been quickly erased after the Teeth of Life arrived. A serious-looking contraption resembling the skull of a small dinosaur, it looked exactly like the legitimate Jaws of Life Nick had seen in Lincoln at the state fair. He and the boys had uncrated their new toy and carefully battened it down inside the cavernous storage bin of the fire truck. Six months later it was still there, unused.

"Teeth o' Life, boys," Nick shouted. "Get out the Teeth o' Life."

Snug Nixon and Beagle retrieved the device and hauled it to the curb where it remained until the entire Delphic Oracle Fire Department figured out that nobody knew how to operate it.

"We thought you knew how to run it," Snug said to Nick.

"What about you, Father?" Nick asked me. "You're smart. Can't you can figure it out?"

"Do you have the owner's manual?" I asked. This was greeted by a tidal wave of silence and averted eyes. I sighed. "I'll retrieve it," I said. I set off, returning twenty minutes later to find the parking lot nearly deserted. Francis was still stuck in the engine compartment of his pickup, while Big Bob slumped disconsolately on the curb, looking exactly like a fellow with a shattered nine hundred dollar glass door and an insurance policy with a one thousand dollar deductible.

"Where is everybody?" I asked Francis.

He nodded toward the crowd milling about at the Y-Knot Drive-In down the street, most of them licking ice cream cones or drinking milkshakes while pumping Chief Johnson for more information about the skeleton discovered the previous day. I was as anxious as anyone to hear what the chief had to say and set the owner's manual for the Teeth of Life on the fender of Francis's pickup.

"Read this," I said. "I'll be back."

"I don't read instructions," Francis replied, but I was already headed for the Y-Knot. A minute or so later, Big Bob joined me, leaving Francis alone in the parking lot, his arm still stuck inside his nearly cherry 1929 Chevy pickup.

It was summer and hot, the brief storm that would visit us that evening yet to declare itself. The sun had slipped behind a stand of stately cottonwoods to the west of the store, a humid breeze causing the branches to undulate gracefully. Francis squinted at the sky. It was pushing four o'clock. Justine hadn't shown up yet and he offered a prayer to the Blessed Uncle of Temporary Amnesia, asking for his wife's mind to be wiped clean of the entire afternoon. Then he went to sleep while still bent over the front end of his nearly cherry 1929 Chevy pickup, his hand and arm still stuck, his rumbling snores reverberating against the underside of the open hood until it seemed that the engine had come alive on its own.

Francis slept and dreamed. He dreamt that the reservoir was filled with fat, succulent catfish impatiently jumping into his boat to get at his bucket of earthworms. He dreamt that he could fly, soaring into an azure sky to watch the Blessed Uncles play poker and tie one on. He dreamt Justine's cat could talk and that Crazy Grandmother Ainitta's diabetic amputated toe had magically reappeared on her foot. He dreamt that the moon caught fire and the sun turned to ice, that he was once again a high school senior—young and thin—with sophomore

Justine Goodfellow shyly eyeing him from across a makeshift dance floor in the high school gym. He dreamt that his face was unlined and callow, his back straight and strong, his eyes clear and hopeful. He dreamt of winning the lottery and losing his gut. He dreamt that the Great Father decided to answer all his prayers. He dreamt he was invisible.

When Francis woke up, Justine stood next to the Chevy. Her nails were perfectly manicured and painted rose.

"Francis, move a little," she said, her voice gentle.

Francis looked into her dark eyes and felt her warmth, her magic.

"Trust me," she said.

Justine leaned against him to reach deep into the great heart of the pickup, her small hand massaging his arm and wrist. He felt her magic stream down his forearm and across his hand. It was thick and wet. Francis closed his eyes. He knew what his wife was doing.

She's making my arm invisible.

"There," she said at last, stepping away from the Chevy. "You can do it, now."

Francis wiggled his fingers. They felt invisible. He twisted his wrist to and fro. It also felt invisible.

"Go ahead," Justine said. "You can do it."

And he did. Francis Wounded Arrow straightened and pulled his arm free of the Chevy. It came out easily—as if nothing were there to impede it, as if it were invisible. It came free like winter wind through leafless trees and he suddenly stood tall and unfettered in the parking lot of Peaseblossom Implement & Auto Parts, breathing a prayer of thanks to the Great Father for giving the wife of Francis Wounded Arrow such powerful magic. He looked at his arm and hand, both green and foamy, but no longer invisible. His face fell.

"Short-acting magic," he grumbled.

Justine glanced at the bottle of liquid magic she'd retrieved from underneath the kitchen sink after word of her husband's plight reached her. "New and improved," she said. She handed him the bottle and then thrust her arm deep into the engine compartment. When she straightened, the wrench was in her hand. Francis took it and grinned. Justine grinned back, then went to the truck cab and climbed in.

Francis installed the new battery, afterward firing up the Chevy until it purred like Justine's cat. He wrestled the truck into gear and they headed out, cautiously zigzagging between the fire truck, rescue unit, and patrol car. At home, he cleaned the biggest of the catfish caught the night before and divided it. Afterward, he took a shower and then coated the fillets with pancake batter before slapping them onto the grill. Justine put plates on the picnic table behind the house, made a salad with garden lettuce and tomatoes, and brewed a pitcher of strong, dark iced tea. They ate slowly, afterward falling asleep on the couch during a rerun of *NCIS*. Francis slept through the storm that rolled in around eight o'clock. Justine waited until the rain had passed, then opened a couple of windows, turned off the TV, and re-joined her husband on the couch.

Sunset was late in coming that summer night and the twi-light's glow didn't fade until just after nine-thirty. Francis and Justine slept in each other's arms, hardly moving. It was a qui-et night early in the lunar cycle and blackness settled over the town, something that would have pleased Francis had he been awake. Fishing was better in the dark, and while his revered Uncles had excellent night vision, Francis believed it much harder for Crazy Grandmother Ainitta's retributive archangels to find him after sundown. A far-off sound caused him to stir for a few moments just after midnight *Today was an interesting day*, he mused in the darkness as Justine slept with her head on his shoulder, her soft hair smelling sweet—a mystical and im-portant day, with the Great Father allowing him to glimpse the power of Justine's magic. He stroked his wife's hair and kissed the top of her head, offering a prayer of thanks that she had chosen him over all others. Moments later his breathing again deepened and settled. Francis didn't stir again until past first light, sleeping through the lazy ascent of the days-old moon in the night sky—a razor-sharp, cool blue scimitar that offered no more help to the pale, incandescent halos of Delphic Oracle's wide-spaced streetlamps than did the slowly fading beams coming from his nearly cherry 1929 Chevy pickup…sitting out in the garage with its headlights on.

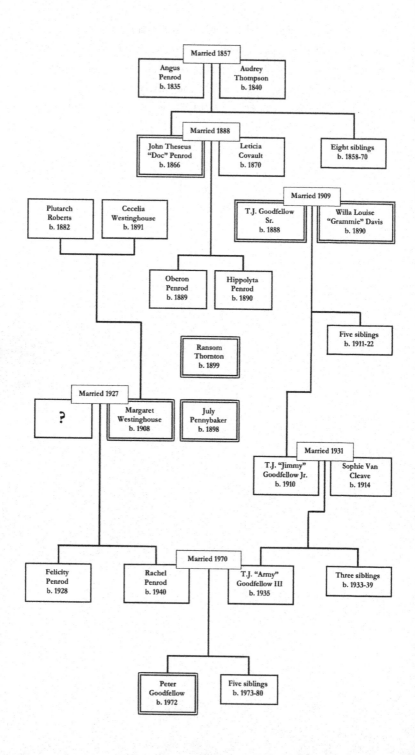

Married 1857

Angus Penrod b. 1835

Audrey Thompson b. 1840

Married 1888

John Theseus "Doc" Penrod b. 1866

Leticia Covault b. 1870

Eight siblings b. 1858-70

Married 1909

Plutarch Roberts b. 1882

Cecelia Westinghouse b. 1891

T.J. Goodfellow Sr. b. 1888

Willa Louise "Grammie" Davis b. 1890

Oberon Penrod b. 1889

Hippolyta Penrod b. 1890

Five siblings b. 1911-22

Ransom Thornton b. 1899

Married 1927

?

Margaret Westinghouse b. 1908

July Pennybaker b. 1898

Married 1931

T.J. "Jimmy" Goodfellow Jr. b. 1910

Sophie Van Cleave b. 1914

Married 1970

Felicity Penrod b. 1928

Rachel Penrod b. 1940

T.J. "Army" Goodfellow III b. 1935

Three siblings b. 1933-39

Peter Goodfellow b. 1972

Five siblings b. 1973-80

5

Betta Dar Es Laam En Thur

The long-lost Oracle of Delphi had been a spur of the moment thing for July," Grammie Willa recollected. "It seeded the clouds but then he had to make sure it rained." Fortunately, Sheriff Goodfellow gave July time to work on the next chapter of his story by accommodating him in the county jail. "T.J. wanted to keep things quiet," Grammie recalled of her lawman husband, "but he mentioned to our oldest, Jimmy, that an honest-to-God rascal was in custody, rather than one of the usual drunk-and-disorderlies. Jimmy was fifteen years old at the time and had a crush on Sophie Van Cleave. He told her and she then told her father. That pretty much told the whole town since Myron Van Cleave never met a secret he wasn't willing to part ways with before the steam was off."

Within a couple of hours, Grammie revealed, several versions of July's claim made their way around town. Van Cleave—bank president and mayor—offered up a shamelessly apocryphal rendering for Sophie and her older brother Johann, one of Maggie's former suitors. The Van Cleaves were having dinner. "This fellow, July Pennybaker, is obviously in the grip of booze or cigarettes or who knows what?" the mayor announced. "Thinks he's God or Jesus Christ or some-such nonsense. I heard he's an out-of-work actor or a hobo, although I don't know how you tell the difference. He attacked that Maggie Westinghouse you're so sweet on, Johann...knocked her unconscious is what I heard."

That evening Doc Penrod, who coached the Miagrammesto Station Bugeaters baseball team, provoked a brawl against the hated Rivercats from nearby Zenith after the Rivercats' ace, Cyclone Charlie Dickenson, threw a pitch that sent the Bugeaters' lead-off man diving to the ground. "Doc may have played the skeptic in his office when July anointed Maggie as an oracle, but he was a Mason and secretly superstitious," Grammie Willa divulged. "Our Bugeaters hadn't beaten the Rivercats in over ten years and he was sure that occult forces were in play."

"WE MUST ATTACK!" Doc cried out, as he lurched from the dugout and made straight for the Rivercat hurler, echoing the inexplicable invocation Maggie had offered up in his clinic. Both benches promptly cleared in a hell of a fight that ended when Cyclone Charlie loosened a molar in catcher Ulysses Wounded Arrow's jaw, breaking a knuckle in the process. With the Zenith star's hand in a bucket of ice, Miagrammesto Station lit up the scoreboard, beating the Rivercats twenty to fourteen. It prompted a town-wide celebration. Homemade booze flowed freely, and by midnight, people were happy to believe that Cecelia Westinghouse's beautiful daughter was a legitimate soothsayer.

A few minutes past eight o'clock the next morning, Dr. Plutarch Roberts was sizing up the recently dislodged molar he was about to jerk from Ulysses Wounded Arrow's jaw when Maggie's mother burst into his treatment room.

"Plutie!" she yelled. "Come quick!"

Dr. Roberts shut off the ether that had put Ulysses into a blissful stupor and dashed up the narrow steps to the apartment above his office. He found Maggie on the floor babbling in a tongue he didn't recognize. "Betta dar es laam en thur," she repeated over and over. When Doc Penrod was summoned, he took the young woman's pulse and blood pressure, then made an unexpected recommendation.

"Let's see what that Pennybaker fellow has to say," he suggested.

July had downed his breakfast and was leafing through the *Miagrammesto Station Banner-Press* when the doctor and Sheriff Goodfellow appeared outside his cell.

"Good fellows, prithee what tidings of our fair Oracle?" he greeted them. "'She sleeps; therefore she dreams,' I'll wager."

Doc was anxious to share the story of Maggie's latest swoon and went right to it after the sheriff unlocked the cell door. July listened, his fingers stroking the nubby surface of the thin wool blanket stretched across his bunk. "Now think carefully," he cautioned when Doc was finished. "You're sure…'betta dar es laam en thur'?' That's exactly what she said?"

"I'm sure," Doc answered. "'Betta dar es laam en thur.'"

July crossed to the only window in his cell. It was high on the cinderblock wall, allowing a view of green cornfields in the distance, the rows of stalks moving in gentle waves. He studied their rhythm and motion as if searching for secret messages, then began to chant in a singsong voice, rocking side-to-side with his hands above his head.

"Chanting and such was exactly the sort of behavior Doc expected from any self-respecting mystic," Grammie Willa told me, "but T.J. was a good Catholic and believed matters of fate best left in the hands of the Father, Son, and Holy Ghost."

"All right, that's about enough of that," the sheriff demanded.

July whirled and stumbled into him, neatly pickpocketing the key to his cell. "Dar es Salaam," he cried out. "Can you see it? It's right in front of us! Dar es Salaam…Dar es Salaam." He pulled away and pointed at the newspaper on his bunk. It was open to the post assignments for Van Berg Field, a quarter horse racetrack on the outskirts of Zenith. Doc picked up the paper and looked it over, afterward handing it to Sheriff Goodfellow. The lawman then balanced a pair of reading glasses on his nose and peered at the postings. After a few seconds, he frowned.

"I told you this was a waste of time, Doc," he said.

"Sheriff!" July cried out. He retrieved the newspaper from the lawman and waved it like a banner. "It's right here…third race, four-to-one odds. Don't you see? It's a prediction. She's predicting the future. 'Betta dar es laam en thur'… Bet Dar es Salaam in the third."

Goodfellow snatched the paper from July's hand and gave it

another look. "There isn't a Doorslam racing in the third," he said, tossing the newspaper onto the bunk. He nodded at Doc Penrod and the two men exited, the clang of the door echoing throughout the cellblock.

"It's not Doorslam," July called out. "It's Dar es Salaam... and you're right. There is no horse by that name. However, there is a province of Dar es Salaam in the African nation of Tanzania." July flicked his fingers and produced a playing card as if from thin air—a three of diamonds. "And in the third race, there's a horse named Tanzanian Dream."

July again reached into empty space and magically retrieved two more cards: a four of clubs and an ace of hearts.

"Gentleman," he added solemnly, "I believe the odds on that horse are four-to-one, are they not?" He grabbed the newspaper, then handed it to Doc Penrod through the bars. The credulous physician searched for the posting, his mouth forming a perfect O when he found it.

"I'll be darned," he said. At the same time, July unlocked his cell door and stepped out, afterward handing Sheriff Goodfellow the key he'd boosted.

"I'll be damned," the big lawman muttered.

An hour or so after Sheriff Goodfellow thoroughly patted down July Pennybaker and locked him in his cell, an employee of the Miagrammesto Station Bank left work and drove to nearby Zenith where he placed one thousand dollars to win on Tanzanian Dream. It was June 15, 1925, and Ransom Thornton had been in town nearly a year. "Long enough to soften up Myron Van Cleave with a daily helping of Irish blarney," Grammie Willa recalled. The corpulent bank president and town mayor had taken an immediate shine to Thornton upon his arrival in town, and after the young fellow was on the job only a few weeks, had impulsively named him Head of Accounting. It was a position that did not previously exist, because teller Hippolyta Penrod had done the books for years without a title. "Hippolyta figured Ransom got the promotion instead of her because he laughed at Myron's jokes," Grammie told me. According to my great-grandmother, Hippolyta then suggested that Myron Van Cleave was about as entertaining as a heart attack. "Myron didn't take it well," Grammie recalled.

"It was a sorry day, Hippolyta, when women were given the vote, I'll tell you that, by golly," the banker shouted before escaping to the Penrod Hotel where a slab of pecan pie and a chocolate soda blew the froth off his indignation. He returned to the bank and grudgingly demoted Ransom to Acting Head of Accounting, a position the good listener with a hearty laugh used to embezzle a hard grand over the next several months.

The town later learned that Ransom was a former Chicago Bears halfback who had fallen on a bad knee and then hard times, forcing him to become a bag man for crime boss Al Capone. After a year traipsing around the Windy City with another man's cash, Ransom had skimmed a little for himself and then gone on the lam, leaving behind a pregnant police captain's daughter. "Ransom loved her," Grammie Willa told me, "and figured he could use the bank's money to fix a horse race in Zenith, then refill the empty spot in the vault and return to Chicago to pay back Scarface before starting a new life with his girl."

The plan began well. Tanzanian Dream was a reasonable pick at four-to-one—odds that wouldn't arouse too much suspicion over a one thousand dollar bet. The horse won by a length with the colluding jockeys nearly choking their losing mounts to death. Ransom collected his winnings, paid off his co-conspirators, and made it back to Miagrammesto Station where he sewed the remaining loot into the lining of his suit, save the unauthorized loan he planned to surreptitiously repay the next day. Going straight—even partially so—was a new addition to young Thornton's repertoire and one he regretted when Van Cleave, Sheriff Goodfellow, and a regional bank examiner appeared in the doorway to his office the following morning. An obviously flustered and image-conscious Van Cleave, worried that the public's faith in his bank's security might drive them to

Zenith Savings and Loan, wanted to let Ransom off the hook. However, the bank examiner was an unrelenting little weasel, which is why Ransom was instead bundled off to the county jail.

Myron's former Acting Head of Accounting merely lifted an eyebrow when he was shown into the cell opposite July Pennybaker, but as soon as Sheriff Goodfellow was gone, the prisoners began to hurl whispers back and forth. Meanwhile, Tanzanian Dream's improbable victory, on the heels of the Bugeaters' win over the Rivercats, seemed not only to confirm the oracular bona fides of Maggie Westinghouse for the citizens of Miagrammesto Station, but also the credentials of July Pennybaker as a Knight of Zeus and Interpreter for the Delphic Oracle. He was released and offered a free room at the Penrod Hotel while Miagrammesto Station's elders pondered how the town might take advantage of the situation. Two days later Ransom Thornton mysteriously escaped in the middle of the night. He made his way back to Chicago and married the girl whose limited options had encouraged faithfulness. At their wedding, both the bride and the infant she held were dressed in brazen white. Ransom wore a suit coat lined with almost two thousand seven hundred dollars in cash.

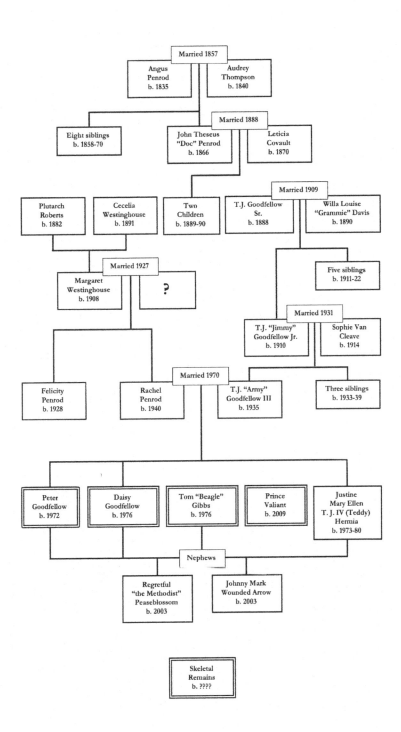

6

BEAGLE AND DAISY

On the same Fourth of July that brought Teddy home from Alinin, Kansas, the day broke sunny and by mid-morning the air was already fragrant with the aroma of barbeque and spent firecrackers. A carnival was in town with a baseball game, hot rod races, and a greased pig scramble scheduled for the afternoon, followed by an evening parade and fireworks.

"The P.A. system's down for the count," Tom "Beagle" Gibbs happily notified a few fellows who had gathered at the Cozy Lunch around ten a.m for early beers. The malfunction promised to effectively silence Mayor Ed Dogberry, a religious fundamentalist and concrete thinker who frustrated an existentialist like Beagle.

Now, if my brother-in-law, Francis Wounded Arrow, is a man of religion without faith, then his fishing buddy, Beagle, could be seen as a man who stumbled upon faith but found himself short of religion. He harbored a casual belief in a higher intelligence, but figured the Almighty was too busy to pay much attention to a fellow who simply wanted to mind his own business. "I'm flying under God's radar," he'd once told me, and this had worked well for a number of years. As he saw it, God didn't nag him about his lackluster work ethic or lack of ambition. He looked the other way when Beagle drank too much or slipped a free pack of smokes into his pocket over at the Hinky Dinky. God had given Beagle a mother with enough money to support them both and got him fired from the jobs he really hated. And on that particular Independence Day, as Beagle watched the parade begin from a spot on the grass near Mom, my sister-in-law, Monica, and me, God had laid out another perfect Fourth of July.

The spectacle began with a blue-and-yellow helicopter flying low over Scout Street, towing a streamer that proclaimed: GOD BLESS AMERICA AND DOGBERRY MOTORS. The fire truck came next, issuing short, shrill bursts from its siren, the department's still unused Teeth of Life contraption proudly mounted atop the cab. It was followed by the Purple Hat Ladies, the high school band, and an army of sweaty cheerleaders. The best—slow-moving floats with papier maché scenery, balloons, and brightly colored streamers—was yet to come, all of it leading to a big finale the planning committee had entrusted to the Zenith Shriners' clown car.

"Did you hear about the skeleton they found across the street from Francis's house?" Beagle asked us. The Father of Our Country float was lumbering past with Chief Johnson K. Johnson striking what he figured was a George Washington-like pose, one leg atop a bale of hay, his cotton-ball wig slightly askew.

"Of course," I replied. Mom and Monica ignored the question.

"Heck of a parade," Beagle said, eyeing my mother even though he knew no magnifying glass in the world was powerful enough to find her interest in his opinion. "One heck of a parade," he repeated as the moody and brilliant palomino, Prince Valiant, high-stepped down the street with my sister, Daisy, in the saddle. The horse stopped in front of us and Daisy gave the reins a tug that sent Prince Valiant rearing, his front hooves pawing at the air, his golden mane shimmering in the sunshine. Daisy—an attractive woman short by a couple of years from her fortieth birthday—pulled off her substantial cowboy hat and waved it high above her head. Beagle cheered and waved back.

"Did you ever notice," he inexplicably volunteered, "how when a horse catches your eye, it poops?"

A moment later Prince Valiant lifted his tail and noisily validated Beagle's observation onto the street, marking the start of the Beagle Gibbs Religious Period. The idea that his offhand remark was perceived by the Almighty as prayer was a consideration he would be unable to brush off, making Prince Valiant's contribution to the Fourth of July parade a propitious event. However, like many things that begin with promise only to butt up against fate, Beagle's Religious Period was destined to end a few weeks later when he accidentally nailed his balls to the roof of his mother's house.

෯

On the Monday after the parade Beagle appeared in the doorway of my office at the courthouse.

"I've received a sign from God," he announced.

"Have you been drinking?" I responded. "It's not even noon yet."

"Why do you always ask me that?" Beagle said. "You're in prison. I don't make fun of you for it. Could you, for once, be a pal like when we were kids?"

"Sorry," I said.

Beagle then reminded me of Prince Valiant's portentous contribution to the Fourth of July parade. "I think God was trying to tell me something," he said.

I didn't think so, but had to prepare for a town council meeting and didn't have time to argue. "What do you want from me, Beagle?" I asked.

"I need to find a church," he replied, "and not just any church. I'm on a quest. I'm looking for *the* church. No offense, Peter. I know you've got a dog in the hunt, but this is a once-in-a-lifetime decision. I'll probably throw in my hat with you Catholics, but I really need to check out your competition before committing."

"And this involves me because—?"

"There are a lot of churches, Peter...er, I mean, *Father*...but I think there's an expiration date on my message from God. I need help getting started. I'll figure out the rest as I go along."

I quickly scribbled down a list of religious denominations, providing a brief summary of each one. Beagle took the list and headed out, his good intentions tank filled to the brim. About a block from the courthouse he ran into Francis. Our town handyman was taking a day off to recover from his previous day off and convinced Beagle that the Blessed Uncle of Hungry Catfish had orders issued directly from the Great Father for the pair of them to go fishing. They did, and by the time the two men returned from the reservoir that evening, Beagle had lost the list. He was afraid to hit me up for another and there was a baseball game on TV that wasn't about to watch itself; hence, his quest was postponed until the following Sunday when he showed up at St. Luke's Methodist church, joining my sister, Mary Ellen Peaseblossom, and her family. Mary Ellen wasn't happy about it. Even though she converted after marrying Big Bob, my sister always fingers her rosary during Methodist services as a proper hedge against eternal damnation. A pagan in her pew put her prayer beads to the test more than she liked, an intuition that bore fruit when the pastor made too much eye contact with Beagle while straying from his planned sermon, "I'd Like To Change The World, But I Just Don't Have The Time," instead improvising a fiery diatribe drawn from the gospel according to Edgar Allen Poe.

After the service, Beagle stopped by the rectory, figuring an hour's worth of Methodist absolution was enough to tell me that he'd lost the list I'd prepared for him.

"Don't know what the heck I did with it, Padre," he told me. "Sorry about that."

"What did you think of the Methodists?" I asked as I scribbled down a new one.

"Borefest," Beagle replied, "except for that stuff about the fires of hell. That was exciting. Who was he talking about?"

Over the next few weeks, using the new list I gave him, Beagle auditioned the Lutherans, Congregationalists, Episcopalians, and Presbyterians, appraising the lot of them as uncomfortably prosecutorial. The Quakers in Zenith, a small city twenty-five miles to the north, were next and he later described them as promising—no long-nosed pastor, no daunting rituals, no endless sermons. "They mostly sit around," Beagle reported. "Every so often someone stands up and badmouths nuclear weapons or air pollution. Then, they leave. There's no homework."

After the Quaker service he'd invited the pastor to join him for a beer. "I don't imbibe, Friend," the soft-spoken Quaker quietly informed him. About Beagle's age, the man wore a clean open-collar shirt, corduroy jacket, and Hush Puppies. The part in his hair was as perfect as the carefully ironed crease in his trousers.

"At all?" Beagle gulped.

The tall man shook his head, offering the knowing smile of a fellow who has decided to get an early start on atonement, thus putting him in the express lane when it came time to meet his maker.

"What about smoking?" Beagle asked.

Another head shake.

"I gotta go," Beagle said.

"Will you join us again next week?"

Beagle shook his head. "I get what you guys are tryin' to do here," he responded, "but I got a pal back home who's a priest and I'm afraid he'll be pissed off if I don't sign with the Catholics."

For the next several mornings Beagle struggled with Catholic catechism under the tutelage of Sister Josepha, who had lost a coin flip with me. Beagle didn't listen to much of what she said, but enjoyed his time at St. Mary's. My church is quiet and comforting, its statuary and ornate carvings seductive, Sister Josepha's description of the liturgy marvelously mysterious. When he asked about the ring on the old nun's wrinkled finger she tried to explain her relationship with God.

"You're married to God?" Beagle marveled.

"Not exactly."

Sister Josepha didn't elaborate, instead sighing in a decidedly non-ecclesiastical way. "I'm not sure we have what you want, Beagle," she told him. "Do you know Fan Wang Ling, who runs the Shanghai House in Zenith? I think he taught Buddhism in China. You should check him out."

The following morning, as Sister Josepha sat in my office and admitted that she'd unashamedly borne false witness, Beagle's planned visit to the Shanghai House was delayed when his mother demanded that he mow the lawn before surrendering her car keys. He cut the grass in the front yard and then provided an IOU for the rest of the job, afterward driving to Zenith where he discovered the Shanghai House to be a tiny room located in a walk-down at the edge of the business district. Gaudily decorated in red and gold, the entire place was filled with delectable aromas, the shrill sounds of an argument spilling into the dining room each time the door to the kitchen swung open. Beagle took a table and asked for Mr. Ling, the owner.

"I want to be a Buddhist," he told him. "Can you help me out?"

"I'm a Lutheran from Council Bluffs," Mr. Ling revealed.

When Beagle's face fell, Mr. Ling offered him a conciliatory ten percent off coupon that the disappointed postulant applied toward a plate of General Tso's chicken atop a heap of fried rice. Beagle polished off the entire order in record time, then cracked open a fortune cookie and extracted a tiny scroll with the following message: GOOD THINGS COME TO THOSE WHO ARE OPTIMISTIC. On the back of the paper was a set of one and two-digit numbers.

"What are these?" Beagle asked Mr. Ling.

"They are lucky numbers."

"Like for the lottery?"

"Perhaps."

"Is that a Buddhist thing?"

"How would I know?"

∽

Beagle had never held a permanent job, driving the tractor mower at the golf course in the summer and manning a snow plow in the winter. Mostly, he went fishing with Francis or hung out at Nick Dolny's Cozy Lunch. That's where I found him when I stopped in for a beer after giving the Saturday evening Mass. He was five weeks into his Religious Period. My brother, Teddy, Snug Nixon, and Francis Wounded Arrow were there with Francis providing an update on the skeleton discovered across the street from his house. Beagle listened, thoughtfully stroking the back of his neck as if searching for the mullet Snug had finally convinced him to lose earlier that day.

"The forensic man from the U completed his report," Francis told us. "He didn't add much. The hole in the skull was made by a slug from a .22." He further reported that the scientist had also unearthed a label from a suit coat. It identified the garment as having been purchased from the Kuppenheimer Company of Chicago, circa 1920s. The investigation had otherwise hit a dead end and the victim's identity remained a mystery despite rampant speculation that included former Teamsters boss Jimmy Hoffa, mysterious skyjacker D.B. Cooper, and July Pennybaker, the former Knight of Zeus and Interpreter for the Oracle of Delphi.

A beer or two later, the conversation shifted to criticism of various politicians, the unexpected success of that summer's incarnation of the Chicago Cubs, and an unnecessarily pedantic comparison of the television programs *Law and Order* and *Law and Order: SVU*. Eventually, Beagle gained the floor and got some laughs when he described how Prince Valiant had launched him on his voyage of discovery.

"Daisy's a great gal," Snug said when he was finished. The rest of the us agreed.

Beagle nodded. "I dated her once," he recalled, looking at me. "You may not remember, Padre. You were in college. Anyway, we had one date…senior prom. She wanted to try drinking. She'd never had a drink and I'm an idiot, so I says, 'Sure,' and next thing I know, she downs half a bottle of cherry vodka and barfs in my mom's car."

"I heard about it," I said. "Daisy was embarrassed."

Beagle sighed. "I know. I never called her after that. I shoulda."

Sometimes, I think Beagle was fishing for encouragement that night, hoping I'd act as a matchmaker. I didn't. Beagle is a nice-looking fellow and there was no doubt that he and Daisy would make pretty babies. However, Daisy is my sister and I couldn't help wishing that she might opt for someone with a savings account and at least one shirt that didn't promote a heavy metal band. Now, I think of that evening and feel small, given that I'm not supposed to be in the judgment trade, but at the time all I could manage was to change the subject.

"How's your quest coming along?" I asked.

Beagle's mood further darkened. "I've had a bit of a setback," he said. He explained that the Buddhists had fallen out of the running after his mother washed his trousers with the paper containing his fortune cookie numbers still in the pocket.

"There was nothing left of it," he complained. "You'd think something that important could take a little soap and water without crumbling into pieces. It really shook my faith."

"Who's still in the running?" I asked.

"Catholics, of course," Beagle reassured me. "Don't worry, Padre. I've already got you penciled into the finals. But I still have to scout the Baptists. I'm checking them out tomorrow morning."

He seemed about to add something when his eyes suddenly shifted to the bar's entry. I followed his gaze. My sister, Daisy, was framed in the doorway, her long hair tied back with a ribbon. She wore a pink tank top and white shorts that favored her legs. The boys greeted her with a chorus of "Evening Daisy's," and she approached, her thick-soled flip-flops softly slapping against the soles of her feet.

"ATM's out of cash, Peter," she reported. "Can I borrow some money? I'll pay you back on Monday."

"Sure, sis," I replied. "How much do you need?"

"Ten dollars," she said. Daisy glanced at Beagle, adding, "For the movies."

I extracted a couple of bills and handed them over. Daisy tucked the money into her pocket, then hesitated.

"Hi, Beagle," she said.

After she was gone, there was some hooting. "Hi, Beagle," Francis warbled in a cracked falsetto until his fishing buddy was ready to take a swing at him. Nick ended it by kicking everyone out and closing up early. Beagle and I were the last to leave.

"See you boys in church," Nick called out as I left. It's something he always says to me, even though he never goes to church.

"See you in church, Nick," I called back.

"Yeah," Beagle added, "see you in church."

That night Beagle dreamt about the Fourth of July parade. He was aboard Prince Valiant with Daisy behind him, her arms wrapped around his waist. Each time the stallion reared, Daisy held on so tight it took his breath away. The next morning he awoke early. He showered and shaved, afterward slipping into a hand-me-down suit from his dead father. His beaming mother—pleased to see her son freshly shaved, wearing a suit and tie, and sporting a haircut fit for a grown man—prepared a sumptuous breakfast. Afterward, Beagle walked to the First Baptist Church where he was nearly crushed in a bear hug by a huge Black man with mountainous shoulders and a grin as wide as the grill of Ed Dogberry's vintage '56 Ford Thunderbird. Other than me, the Reverend Oscar Redwine was the only clergyman in Beagle's spiritual odyssey who hadn't run for cover.

"Brother Beagle," the reverend exclaimed, his deep, melodious voice resonating throughout the crowded church. "Within lies what ye seek. Within, Jesus has made a place among the faithful. Be not discouraged for your wandering is at an end."

Beagle looked over the congregation. Mostly women, their faces were filled with a mixture of longing and adoration as they watched their pastor welcome a new lamb into the fold. Minutes later, the place was alive with music and celebration, the choir singing and dancing as Reverend Oscar cavorted about, a Bible in one hand, his voice thundering, his huge arms reaching out as if he might suddenly pull the entire congregation into his embrace. The rafters shook and the stained-glass windows threatened to vibrate from their frames, but Reverend Oscar boogied on, pulling out one red satin handkerchief after another, using each to wipe his brow before tossing it into the forest of frenzied, outstretched arms.

Beagle shook his head with wonder as a large, energetic woman hiked up her skirt and galloped sideways down the center aisle, her voice as rich and syrupy as molasses. Reverend Oscar met the huge woman near the pulpit and they faced the congregation together, improvising lyrics that turned the rest of the choir into mere chorus, the two giant people singing louder and louder, faster and faster, while an ancient Black man on an upright piano relentlessly kept pace, his long, gnarled fingers flying over the keys. Beagle stood with the rest as the air seemed to thicken and grow sweeter. He could smell the sweat of his fellow worshippers and feel his own perspiration dripping down his back as he swiveled his hips and clapped. "They had me right then and there," he later told me. "They were fun! And Reverend Oscar? He's frickin' James Brown!"

The worshippers went through several verses of the hymn, a few singers adding nearly endless runs as if reluctant for the song to end. Eventually they gave way to the large woman, who belted out a final measure or two, as Reverend Oscar took his place behind the pulpit. When the last of the congregation was finally seated Reverend Oscar's honeyed baritone drew them back onto their toes, their arms swirling about in the sanctified air, swimming in absolution.

"Praise God! Praise Jesus!" the faithful cried out. "His Glory! His Wonder!"

"Praise Guh-aw-DUH," the reverend proclaimed. "Praise JEE-zus!"

It was a pep rally with everyone rooting for devotion and acceptance and the desire to be good—the hot, stuffy chapel filled with noisy, jubilant folks, the men with sweat stains on their shirts and undone neckties, the women shaking their hips while belting out songs with boisterous, unapologetic delight.

"Best church service ever, Padre," Beagle later told me. "Better than any bender I've ever been on." And he'd wanted desperately to be part of it, for them to know that he *got* it. He was one of them. He was applying to be part of the team, because Reverend Oscar had guaranteed his followers that Jesus was still hiring.

"Praise God!"

"Praise Jesus!"

"His Glory!"

"His Wonder!"

At last, Beagle had found his spiritual home. The unbridled joy of the Baptists was intoxicating. They were more playful than the austere Presbyterians, more accessible than the cerebral Episcopalians, more dedicated than the pop-culture Unitarians, and far less ascetic than the teetotaling Quakers. Only my ritualistic Catholics with our statues and medallions and baroque cathedral could compete. Beagle screwed his eyes shut, recalling his few days of Catholic catechism, searching for a devotion to add to the cries about him. *It's all symbolic*, Sister Josepha had told him, and with the joyous exclamations of faith flying through the air on all sides, he suddenly understood what she'd meant. "Sister Josepha isn't actually married to God," Beagle later suggested to me, further submitting that she wasn't even interested in Him that way because her relationship with the Almighty had matured over time, moving past the initial girlish flush to a more comfortable place. According to Beagle, God now went to work each day and Sister Josepha stayed home to garden and cook and do laundry and smack the children around until they behaved.

The congregation suddenly launched into another gospel tune—something they all seemed to know—and Beagle tried to join them, tossing in an incoherent jumble of "by, for, and of-the-Lords." When the song ended, he was ready, jumping to his feet and then testifying the living daylights out of the place.

"FUCKIN' A JESUS," he shouted.

❧

After Reverend Oscar took him aside to gently suggest that my Catholics deserved another shot, Beagle took a break from his quest to shingle his mother's roof. He convinced Francis to help and they agreed on a time that Francis ignored, showing up about two hours late. He'd brought tools but only one set of kneepads.

"We could trade off," Beagle suggested.

"We could also ask the Great Father to turn them into chewing tobacco, but neither thing is happening," Francis sniped. "I ain't about to skin my knees raw on your account."

Without pads, Beagle's knees soon began to scream in protest and he decided to sit on his backside, holding the shingle he was nailing with his heels. From across the street, Regretful Peaseblossom and Johnny Mark Wounded Arrow were witnesses to what happened, later reporting that they heard a shriek and then watched Beagle sled down the roof of his mother's house on a loose shingle, a nail-gun wedged between his legs. A second later the slack on the air hose attached to the gun went taut with a loud snap and Beagle came to a jerky stop just above the gutter, at the same time firing off an 8-penny galvanized nail that attached his loose scrotum to the sub-roof.

As a result of his injury Beagle missed his next catechism class at St. Mary's. He was disappointed as Sister Josepha, when informed that Beagle wanted to give the Catholics a call-back audition, had managed to dump the job on me. "She's moved me up the chain," Beagle told me. "Says I'm an *advanced* student." Subsequently, I made an end run around Sister Josepha by visiting Beagle in the hospital where I left enough reading material to successfully put the doleful aspirant off Catholicism altogether. A few days later, Beagle was queued up to the checkout stand of the Hinky Dinky, waiting to buy a lottery ticket, when I emerged from one of the aisles with a full grocery cart. My first instinct was to back up, but with both Beagle and God making eye contact, I rolled my cart in behind him. Beagle had the look of a fellow anxious to confess.

"I've given up on regular religion, Padre," he told me. He

explained how he had switched to Francis Wounded Arrow's spiritual Uncles who seemed to be part of a more diverse and user-friendly menu of deities. "No offense, but it makes more sense to have individual gods of thunder and lightning and Powerball and NASCAR and so forth," Beagle opined. "Don't get me wrong. I see the big picture. I still think there's a grand poobah up there directing traffic, but there's a lot going on down here. It's too much for one person even if that person is God. Let's face it…a good leader delegates…right, Padre?"

"Sure thing," I said.

When it was Beagle's turn to buy a lottery ticket he bowed his head, thrusting a folded ten-spot at the clerk. Bibsy Dolny—Nick's wife and a good Catholic—took his money, then held the lottery ticket just outside his reach.

"Gods of thunder and lightning!" she sniffed. "What's wrong with you, Beagle? Father Peter is a man of the cloth. You can't talk to a man of the cloth like that. Especially you. You'll need someone like Father Peter when it's time to meet your maker. You may not believe in God, Beagle, but God is real. I have proof." This was a segue-way to the exploding brains story she'd been circulating around town for a week or so. Bibsy had been on her way home with a sack of groceries in the back seat when a can of crescent rolls exploded, plastering the back of her head with dough. She'd never touched brains, but the sticky, uncooked rolls clinging to her skull seemed to her exactly how brains might feel had one's head unexpectedly detonated.

"It was just like that poor fellow they found buried across the street from Francis and Justine's house," she claimed. "My brains were oozing out of my skull…right out of my skull. Doc Newhouse said he'd never seen anything like it. 'Bibsy,' he said, 'I've seen a lot of things in my day, but you take the cake.' His words…gospel truth. I took his cake. Anyway, I somehow made it to the hospital…God only knows how because I had to steer with my knees so I could hold my brains in…and when I got to the emergency room, God had healed my wound. It was a miracle, Beagle. Miracles do happen. Isn't that right, Father?"

I'll be honest. I don't think God punishes his children with hurricanes and starvation, cares a whit about which team wins a football game, or agrees with politicians who invoke the Ten Commandments over the Sermon on the Mount. Frankly, I think God has more than enough to do without flitting about, making miracles pop up willy-nilly like dandelions. However, I knew better than to argue with Bibsy when she was all lathered up with Godliness. It colored my response.

"Miracles?" I echoed. "Absolutely…happen all the time." I glanced at Beagle, his guileless acceptance triggering my Catholic guilt. "Listen, Beagle," I expanded, hefting a leafy head of cabbage in one hand, "miracles aside, maybe you've been searching for the wrong thing."

I put the cabbage on the conveyor belt and then went on.

"Your interest in religion started because Daisy's horse did his business in front of you…but maybe you got the wrong message. Maybe it wasn't about religion at all."

Beagle nodded solemnly. "Something to think about, Padre," he said.

After the lottery drawing that evening, Beagle learned that his ticket was a dud—not a single matching number. When he complained to Francis the next day, his fishing buddy suggested that the Blessed Uncle of Powerball was a sadistic deity whose alter ego must be the Blessed Uncle of Irony as the only people who ever won big had one foot in the grave and the other in a randomized, prospective trial for the hottest new drug used to treat a terminal illness.

"*Now* you tell me," Beagle said.

"Now you *ask* me," Francis replied.

That afternoon Beagle retrieved a letter from his mailbox, listing him among the five finalists in the Publishers' Clearinghouse Sweepstakes. He immediately filled out his entry and then ran down to the Cozy Lunch.

"Drinks for the house," he called out upon entering, the house comprised entirely of Francis Wounded Arrow. "All I had to do is buy one magazine subscription," Beagle told him—a paltry investment, he figured, for such a high rate of return. Francis agreed, knocking back his free beer and then another while he and Beagle made plans for a luxury fishing expedition to Mexico that was later kiboshed when a ninety-year-old woman on her deathbed in Fort Wayne, Indiana, won the sweepstakes' top prize. One day after that, Beagle and I were sharing a booth at the Cozy Lunch around noon when Daisy came in. In addition to running her ranch, my sister is a nurse at the hospital. It was her turn to pick up burgers and fries for the staff lunch.

"I'm running behind," Nick Dolny told her, offering a free soft drink. "Give me a few minutes." He hurried into the small galley.

Daisy claimed a seat on one of the high barstools, swiveling to face us. "What's new?" she asked. It was a rhetorical question, since no news in Delphic Oracle remained new for long, forcing one to put a different spin on the old stuff.

"Same old, same old," I said, and with the tantalizing smell of sizzling hamburgers and grilled onions filling the air, we re-hashed the latest dope: Teddy's promise to never again run away; Bibsy Dolny's exploding brains; the decision by Vivian Dogberry on the day after the Fourth of July to follow through on an oft-made promise to die; the upcoming championship contest between the one-loss Cozy Lunch Dodgers and the undefeated Peaseblossom Implement & Auto Parts Giants; and the recent incarceration of former Cornhusker football star Tag Thornton at The Luther, a minimum security correctional facility in our town. Beagle didn't join our conversation, instead disconsolately swatting at a fly with a rolled-up copy of his just-arrived first issue of *Horse & Rider*.

"What are you reading, Beagle?" Daisy asked.

Beagle unfurled his magazine to display its cover, his eyes still following the erratic flight-plan of the fly. Daisy's face brightened.

"I didn't know you were a horse person," she said.

The fly moved on and Beagle looked at Daisy for the first

time since she'd entered the bar. "I've known your sister all my life," he later told me; yet he had never fully appreciated the faint spray of freckles across her nose, the shine of her hair, or the brown eyes that suddenly seemed as vividly brilliant as those of her moody palomino, Prince Valiant.

"Daisy..." he murmured, turning a bit saucer-eyed and lightning-struck as Nick emerged from the galley, carrying two paper sacks speckled with dark grease spots.

"Is Beagle botherin' you, Daisy?" the bartender growled. "'Cuz I'll kick his ass outta here if he starts botherin' you."

Daisy laughed. "Thanks, but I don't think that will be necessary, Nick."

She dug through her purse and extracted a few bills and some coins.

"I like them," Beagle suddenly blurted.

"What?" Daisy queried, head tipped quizzically.

"Horses...I like them. They're...good."

Daisy laughed, revealing dimples that made her seem new and irresistible. "Okie doke," she said. She hopped off the barstool and headed for the exit. Beagle scrambled from our booth and beat her there.

"I've got it," he said, pulling open the door.

"Thanks," Daisy said, her voice low and sultry. She studied him for a moment. "Did I tell you that I like your haircut? I do. It's much better."

Beagle grinned. "It's not just a haircut. Snug *styled* it."

"He did, huh?"

"It's shorter."

"I can see that."

Beagle then ran out of words, unable to escape the memory of how pretty Daisy had looked in her prom dress before throwing up in his mother's car.

"Well, I guess I'd better be go—" my sister began.

"Daisy," Beagle interrupted, "you heard about my message from God?"

She nodded.

"Right…everybody heard about it. So I've been checking out churches. I thought God wanted me to be more religious. But here's the thing…maybe it's like your brother told me. Maybe it wasn't about religion at all."

"I don't understand what you're talking about, Beagle," Daisy replied, checking her wristwatch. "I really have to get going."

Beagle considered the religious odyssey that had ended on his mother's roof with an incident that still had people laughing when they passed him on the street. Daisy had been one of his nurses at the hospital. She hadn't laughed. She'd brought him extra cups of tapioca pudding. Beagle loved tapioca.

"Uh…thanks, Daisy," he stammered.

My sister cocked her head prettily. "Thanks? For what? Thanks for *going*?" she teased, winking at me. "You *want* me to leave?"

"No, what I meant was thanks for…"

"For liking your haircut?"

Beagle grinned with relief. "That's it. Thanks for liking my haircut."

Daisy smiled. My sister is a lovely and very smart woman who would have been married already had she not chosen to spend fifteen years as a barrel rider on the rodeo circuit. She'd always had a thing for Beagle and well knew that he was teetering and about to tumble. Still, after their inauspicious prom date so many years before, she couldn't resist making him squirm a bit before reeling him in.

"I gotta go," she said. She waved at me. "Bye, Peter."

Beagle held the door open wider and Daisy squeezed through, so close he caught the scent of her hair and felt the warmth of her body. Outside, Prince Valiant waited, his reins draped over a bicycle rack near the curb. She slipped the lunches into his saddlebags, and by the time she'd climbed onto the palomino's broad back, Beagle and I were outside the tavern, watching in the shade of an awning. Daisy gathered up Prince Valiant's reins and then offered Beagle the sort of frankly expectant expression most women bestow upon men with better jobs than mowing the lawn at the golf course. He waved, and when she waved back, it recalled for him the Fourth of July—Prince Valiant prancing down the street, his mane rippling. And Daisy on his back, her shining hair flowing out from beneath the huge cowboy hat.

"Bye," Beagle called out.

Daisy clicked her tongue and Prince Valiant moved into the street.

"Bye, Daisy," Beagle repeated, stepping out from under the awning, a hand shading his eyes. "So long."

Daisy tugged on Prince Valiant's reins and then twisted in the saddle, shaking back her hair in a way that made Beagle feel as if he had won the Publishers' Clearinghouse Sweepstakes after all.

"So long, Beagle," she responded. "See you in church."

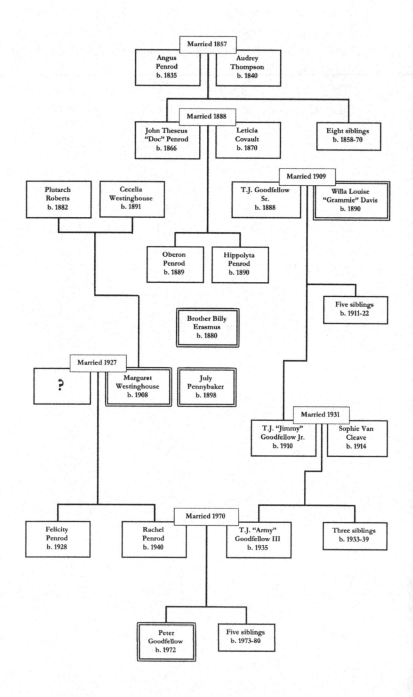

7

BROTHER BILLY AND A KNIGHT OF ZEUS

Grammie Willa believed that people who walk through life's murky puddles while remaining uncannily free of the splatter are mostly scoundrels. A rare few are so charming they make a lifted wallet seem more a donation than a theft. July was one of those. "A life in politics had once been predicted for him," Grammie Willa claimed, "but he learned early on to disdain politicians as amateurs…tinhorns who knew how to tap a mark but not when to shut off the flow and run." There was a warped integrity to the properly accomplished con, July often mused, because the mark eventually knew the truth, a sort of absolution for the grifter already hightailing it out of town.

The life July Pennybaker had chosen required luck and he was lucky—not fortunate or blessed but flat-out lucky. As a soldier in The War To End All Wars, July had risen from private to captain by bravely leading men into the desolate and shell-hole-pocked No Man's Land of Europe. Fifty-caliber machine gun fire shredded the waves of doughboys caught between the trenches, but July incurred nary a scratch. His comrades called him "Houdini," and like the legendary magician, July was confident he could escape any water tank, wriggling free of the heaviest chain long before the air in his lungs was exhausted. He'd had no idea that Ransom Thornton fixed the race won by Tanzanian Dream. He simply knew that the horse would win. He knew it instinctively and his instincts had so often proven true he no longer muddled them with doubt.

After the war, July briefly returned to the States, then hopped a steamer to Europe where he tramped around for a year. He spent a summer in Delphi, a Greek town on the southwestern spur of Mount Parnassus. There, he learned about the Oracles

of Delphi—teenaged girls who fell into swoons upon visiting
a sacred cave, afterward issuing predictions and counsel that
seemed nonsensical to all save the priests appointed to inter-
pret the visions. July visited the cave, where the last of the
Oracles' pronouncements had been offered in AD 380. There,
a friendly tour guide explained how a geologist in the 1800s
had discovered a rift in the cave floor that allowed ethylene gas
to escape from deep inside the earth. The ethylene combined
with surface oxygen and hydrogen to form ether, the famed
Oracles of Delphi thus revealed to be mere adolescents in the
throes of drug-induced euphoria. "He'd been in his share of
field hospitals during the war," Grammie remembered, "and
immediately recognized the sickly sweet aroma of ether wafting
through the floorboards from the dental office below Maggie
Westinghouse's apartment. It was all he needed."

Several weeks after July facilitated Ransom Thornton's escape, he was still at the Penrod Hotel, a guest in exchange for
his services as an interpreter for the Oracle of Delphi. With the
self-proclaimed Knight of Zeus translating her ether-induced
mutterings, Maggie correctly predicted the winners of a few
horse races in Zenith, directed Ulysses Wounded Arrow to a
shallow end of the lake where he found a Mason jar filled with
nickels, and located several lost pets. She exposed an affair between the principal of the high school and the president of the
PTA and advised Mayor Myron Van Cleave and the town council to use money from the town's general fund to invest in the
previously disdained stock market, a proposition still soaring in
1925. Stock prices rose and a starry-eyed town council provided Maggie and her mother with part of their profits, another
fraction paid to the only one in town who could decipher the
Oracle's babbling: July Pennybaker.

"Maggie tried to set the record straight," Grammie recalled,
"but she had no say in the matter." Her visions came without
warning, rendering her unconscious and then amnestic upon
waking. When Mrs. Westinghouse apprised Maggie of the prediction or advice July claimed she'd offered, the young woman

was distraught. She was already sensitive to whispers and pinch-nosed disapproval, given her unmistakable resemblance to Dr. Roberts. "She kept her guard up," Grammie told me, "which some folks took as snooty." The idea that *crazy* might gain a toehold distressed her and Maggie vociferously renounced all responsibility for miracles and prognostications. Such protests were to no avail. Most folks equated Maggie's denials with the sort of humility Nebraskans expected from one another, an admirable quality they believed further authenticated her extra-sensory powers.

Maggie's mother was happy to go along, her respect for God and Ouija boards roughly equivalent. "None of what you say makes any sense, dear," Mrs. Westinghouse cheerfully admitted to her daughter not long after the nickels-in-a-Mason-jar affair made the front page of the *Miagrammesto Station Banner-Press*. "It all seems like gobbledygook to me, but it's crystal clear to Mr. Pennybaker. He seems quite proficient in this Oracle language of yours."

"So he's fluent in gibberish?" Maggie scoffed. "That's what you're saying?"

"Margaret Westinghouse! Mind your tongue!" her mother scolded, glancing warily toward heaven.

"I won't mind my tongue. This Oracle business is a lot of horse-feathers, Mother, and I'm going to put a stop to it."

But Maggie didn't. She was in love with July and feared a dry well would put an end to his morning visits, their afternoon walks, and the evening stargazing on nights when he was not Knight of Zeusing.

Meanwhile, July had expected a short run, figuring he'd orchestrate enough successful visions to bankroll a leisurely sabbatical to Spanish Majorca or a solo voyage up and down the Mexican Baja. But as summer meandered toward August he remained in town, dawn arriving with thoughts of Maggie, his evenings ending the same way. "July had never been one to tether himself to anyone, particularly a woman," Grammie Willa contended. "It unnerved him." To make matters worse, the handsome grifter was running out of miracles. He could only fix so many horse races before one of the colluding jockeys talked, and cats lost and then found had quickly become routine for the townsfolk. "However, July knew that the size of a miracle is not nearly as important as its credentials," Grammie remembered. Not long thereafter, some credentials rolled into Miagrammesto Station in the form of con man Brother Billy Erasmus—former Inmate No. 45973 at the Rahway State penitentiary in New Jersey, where he'd shared a cell with a young fellow from New York City doing one-to-three for violation of the Mann Act.

Brother Billy had been working the Ozarks circuit as a faith healer when July reached him and was happy to stop speaking in tongues long enough to fabricate further evidence of Maggie's oracular authenticity, his caravan of five brightly painted trucks rumbling into Miagrammesto Station in early August. His crew set up camp at the fairgrounds, pitched the chautauqua tent, and dispatched shills to drum up business for the premiere revival service the following evening. Maggie had already experienced two visions that day, the first predicting rain for the following morning, the second positing the notion of a clear sky at dawn.

"I've found it best to get more than one rumor in the wind," July told Brother Billy that evening. "One always settles to the ground with convincing logic and I can chalk up the other to oracular whimsy."

Brother Billy issued a low whistle. He was a great bear of a man with a voice as smooth as caramel and a face that could soften the most unyielding judgment. Fully four inches over six feet tall and about sixty years old, Brother Billy was a former Roughrider who had learned from Colonel Teddy Roosevelt that unmitigated gall was redeemable currency in both the White House and the backwoods water-stops of small town America. With a face men trusted and a line of bull women couldn't resist, Brother Billy Erasmus could lift the front end of a car and then make love to a woman with gentleness she'd never forget. His hair was full and wavy, his eyes green as jade, his hands covered with snakebites. "Dangerous thing it is to dance on the razor's edge, young July," he advised. "It's a good way to get tarred and feathered."

July chuckled. "These folks are believers, Billy. Most want to believe so badly they'll eat the rind and throw away the fruit if they think it will get them closer to heaven." They sat near the pulpit inside Billy's huge tent, sharing a jug of fiery Arkansas jack. Dusk had already settled in and the traveling cathedral was empty save a very drunk Chinese woman who sprawled on the ground near an overturned chair. As the men talked, the woman softly snored.

"What about the girl?" Brother Billy asked. "Is she in on this?"

"Maggie's an innocent," July answered.

Billy laughed. "Careful, young July. In our line of work, there are no innocents." He took a drink from the jug, then called out to the sleeping woman. "Shu Chen! Get your drunk ass to bed."

The woman named Shu Chen lifted her face from the flattened grass and belched.

"For crissakes, Shu Chen," Billy pleaded. "Go to bed!" He eyed July, sighing. "She drinks too much, but I love her. She's the best damned cripple I ever had. Bloody contortionist is what she is. She can twist her knees until her feet are backward and dislocate both shoulders at the same time. I think she could make her head spin completely around if she wanted. She's got some sort of condition that gave her rubber joints." Billy went to the sleeping woman and covered her with his coat, a hand lingering on her cheek. "Best not to see them as innocents, young July," he said.

With the arrival of Brother Billy, the reputation of the Delphic Oracle began to spread. Billy provided a pulpit from which July decoded Maggie's dreams and cherry-picked faithful from the crowd to commune with deceased loved ones. "A few chautauqua parlor tricks strengthened Maggie's bona fides," Grammie Willa confided. With help from the stock players in Brother

Billy's troupe of actors, the Oracle of Delphi predicted sight for a blind woman and eloquence for a tongue-tied teen. She untwisted Shu Chen's pitifully deformed feet and facilitated a handspring performed by an arthritic septuagenarian. Donations flowed in, and before long, Miagrammesto Station's clergy began to sniff around, hoping to get their snouts in the trough. Brother Billy obliged, encouraging his followers to tithe not only his traveling road show but also their local churches. "Brothers and Sisters, I rely on the Almighty for sustenance," the Brother proclaimed. "I thirst and He brings the rain. I am hungry and He feeds me. I need less your coin than your hearts. Give both to the churches that nourish you." Of course, this merely encouraged the generous and devout townsfolk to give more to the chautauqua preacher, dipping into their cookie jars or searching beneath the sofa cushions for loose coins they could drop into his collection plates.

Two weeks after the revival troupe's arrival, an *Omaha World-Herald* reporter was on his way home after covering a story in Zenith about a giant barbed-wire statue of William Jennings Bryan. The journalist had arrived to find that a prankster had given the Great Commoner a Coke bottle erection and had to wait until the icon was de-tumesced before snapping a picture and heading home. Miagrammesto Station was on the way and he stopped for a sandwich and a root beer at the Cozy Lunch.

"You here about the Oracle?" one of the boys in the bar asked.

"Oracle?" the reporter replied.

The local gave him the low-down, pointing out the beautiful young prophet when she coincidentally emerged from the Penrod Hotel across the street.

"There she is," the local said. "That's Maggie Westinghouse, her own self."

Inclined to dismiss the story, at first, the lascivious correspondent took one look at the Oracle of Delphi and immediately hatched a plan to investigate both the story and Maggie's undercarriage. He was partly successful. After a night at the Penrod and a morning of journalism, he returned to Omaha with a story and a mark on his face where Maggie had slapped him. He then filed an entertaining article that had little to do with the facts. The piece ran on page one:

A LADY OF LOURDES IN MIAGRAMMESTO STATION, NEBRASKA?
Mysterious beauty predicts future, heals sick

A considerable stir ensued, and within days, Brother Billy's cavernous chautauqua tent included not just folks from nearby Zenith and Wahoo but more distant ports like Grand Island to the west and Council Bluffs, Iowa, to the east. They came in search of an exhilarating tingle of health, a peek into the forbidding future, or a fleeting reunion with a loved one firmly ensconced in the hereafter. "Where're you headed?" their friends asked when they loaded up a picnic basket with fried chicken, deviled eggs, and the fervent hope that a cure for their troubles and ailments might reside with a strange young woman in Miagrammesto Station, Nebraska. "We're goin' to see that there Delphic Oracle," the pilgrims answered.

In Miagrammesto Station, cottage industries to service the new tourists mushroomed. Kids sold sandwiches and lemonade from their front lawns while their mothers took in laundry and their dads carved small totems used to summon the dead. The town was overrun with Bible salesmen and reporters, all hard-drinking fellows who kept the local bathtubs swirling with bootleg gin. Shop owners couldn't keep their shelves stocked and many homes became boarding houses. It was a bonanza unlike anything the hard-rooted and unassuming townsfolk had ever experienced. With money spilling over their coffers like tassels on August cornstalks, mail-order clothes with looser collars and higher hemlines appeared at the Legion Club dances, houses long-neglected were painted shamelessly bright colors, brick storefronts were sanded and varnished, and more autos replaced horse-drawn wagons on the city streets.

It didn't take long for a taste of affluence to evolve into genuine hunger. The same ascetic Nebraskans, who had disdained the faraway New York Stock Exchange, eagerly embraced rabid capitalism when it fell into their laps. Astutely recognizing the value of a brand name, the city council unanimously supported Mayor Van Cleave's suggestion that Miagrammesto Station be reincorporated as "Delphic Oracle." After all, Myron reasoned, the town had only existed since 1867, the year Nebraska became a state. "That's less than sixty years," he opined. "Hell, in England they've got public outhouses older than that." A few protests were forwarded, but the stodgy traditionalists were assuaged by assigning a new name to the county. Henceforth, the collection of small farming settlements just south of the Platte River would be known as Miagrammesto County, the 25th largest of all the counties in Nebraska, its newly christened county seat of Delphic Oracle home to the wondrous and increasingly famous Oracle of Delphi. It was nearing Labor Day of 1925. July Pennybaker had been in town for almost two months.

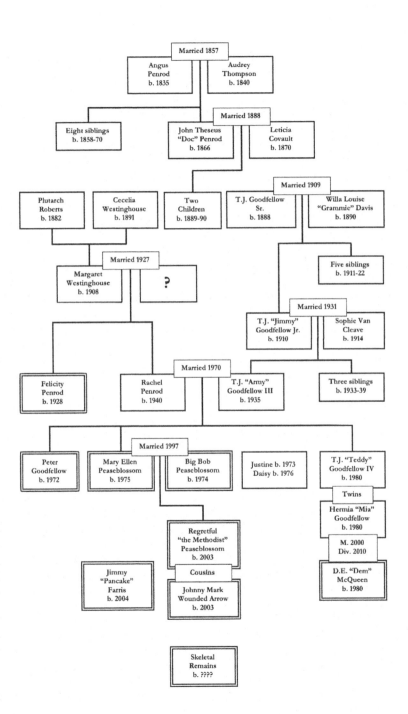

8

REGRETFUL PEASEBLOSSOM

Walt Whitman was right. Baseball is the American game—at once sobering and optimistic, exhilarating and disappointing, unforgiving and redemptive. Occasionally the prescribed innings extend into extra ones but in the end, there is an end. As with death, there are no draws, no do-overs. A baseball game on the Fourth of July is a tradition in Delphic Oracle. On the Independence Day that Teddy found Alinin, Kansas, Beagle Gibbs's message from God was delivered, and Francis Wounded Arrow drove his nearly cherry 1929 Chevy pickup in the parade, the Peaseblossom Implement & Auto Parts Giants took the field against the Cozy Lunch Dodgers in a Little League game. The contest progressed as expected until the final inning, when the Giants' pitcher—with his team clinging to a 2-1 lead—struck out the first two batters and then walked the next three on purpose, filling the bases. He'd done this before and had no doubt about the outcome as the next hitter dug in at the plate and took a few practice swings. Both pitcher and catcher were my nephews.

Regretful took his wind-up, loose and easy, ignoring the base runners. His fingers were firm on the ball, the reassuring texture of the stitches holding fast to the unyielding cowhide. The factory-imprinted *Tim Lincecum* signature was against the meat of his knuckles—a personal touch from the major league pitcher that filled him with confidence and certainty. A hush settled over the crowd save the rough Camels-and-Jack Daniels voice of Coach Dean Emmet "Dem" McQueen.

"Hey battuh, hey battuh, hey battuh, hey suh-WING battuh!"

The afternoon had grown long and a sudden line of shadow partially eclipsed the narrow lane between pitcher's mound and batter's box, casting the hitter into gray. He stood with the bat resting heavily on his shoulder, his breathing erratic, face filled with grim foreboding.

"Hey battuh, hey battuh, hey battuh, hey suh-WING battuh!"

Regretful's arm came forward, a blur in the sun, its sweep as true and precise as the chimes at St. Mary's. The crowd was silenced, his teammates stilled, gloves dangling limply at their sides, while the Dodgers slumped in their dugout, save the three to whom Regretful had bequeathed first, second, and third, a disconsolate trio staring at the ground as inevitability washed over them.

"Hey battuh, hey battuh, hey battuh, hey suh-WING battuh!"

The ball came out of Regretful's hand, up and dead center with a wicked spin. It screamed toward the plate as the batter— Jimmy "Pancake" Farris—instinctively leaned away, fighting the urge to step into the proverbial bucket just behind his right foot. In a monumental display of courage Pancake stood his ground, squeezing his eyes shut and swinging with all his strength as the ball darted in and down, hitting catcher Johnny Mark Wounded Arrow's mitt with a pop that reverberated to the far edges of the baseball diamond.

"STEE-RIKE THREEEEEEE!" umpire Johnson K. Johnson bellowed, gyrating behind home plate to signify the strikeout, an impressively graceful performance from a man weighing better than 300 pounds. "AND THAT'S THE GAME!" he added, flinging his arms outward as he declared another victory for the undefeated Peaseblossom Giants.

The three Dodgers my nephew had intentionally walked just for kicks began the long, slow shuffle back to the dugout where their coach, Nick Dolny, fumed and paced. Pancake Farris remained in the batter's box, staring at the bat that lay in the dust at his feet as the catcher, Johnny Mark, watched. Regretful left the mound and approached, bending to pick up the bat upon reaching them.

"Here you go, Pancake," he said. Regretful and Johnny Mark then trotted to the Giants' dugout and plopped onto the bench. Coach Dem McQueen—my little sister Mia's ex-husband— had already launched into his postgame speech, an incendiary Pattonesque exercise more suitable for samurai warriors than Delphic Oracle Little Leaguers. Reeking of last night's beer and that morning's cigarettes, McQueen paced up and down the line of players scattered along the bench, filling the air with a cloud of mangled platitudes and spittle, occasionally thrusting his stubbly face close to one of the boys. Regretful only half-listened, his eyes on Pancake Farris. The boy's mother had joined her son, a hand on his shoulder. Thin and pale, Pancake seemed far too small for his uniform, his oversized batting helmet looking like a saucepan atop a cabbage, his blue shirt hanging from his shoulders like drapery. The little Dodger wasn't much of a player, earning his nickname after sitting on his glove for so many games it looked like a leather hubcap as he stumbled out to right field each week for the single inning of play mandated by Little League rules.

Johnny Mark leaned toward Regretful. "Pancake's sick," he whispered as the boys watched the forlorn little outfielder trudge off the ballfield with his mother. "He's got some disease. Grandma Ainitta told me."

Regretful sniffed. He took a narrow view of Crazy Ainitta, a woman who believed Cheetos could cure diarrhea. "What disease exactly?" he asked.

"I'm not sure," Johnny Mark answered, eyeing Coach McQueen. "Maybe rabies?"

Across the diamond Pancake and his mother reached their car and Mrs. Farris opened the trunk. Pancake tossed his bat and glove inside. He looked tired.

"It's not rabies," Regretful said.

"How do you know? It could be rabies. It might be."

"It's not rabies, Johnny Mark," Regretful insisted. The boys watched Pancake climb into the car, then gathered up their own gear and headed home, pedaling along the tree-lined streets of their north-end neighborhood. Regretful broke the uneasy silence.

"We'll ask Aunt Felicity and Uncle Peter about it," he said. "They'll know."

"Read this," Aunt Felicity told Regretful a few days later. We were in the library, a full week into July with things around town back to normal. Teddy was home, Francis Wounded Arrow was a free man, Beagle Gibbs was still a few weeks away from correctly deciphering his message from God, and we still didn't know the identity of the man whose skeleton had been found in a vacant lot. I was at the periodicals table, the *Omaha World-Herald* spread out before me. I stop by the library around mid-morning on weekdays to chat with Aunt Felicity and read the paper. "Start here," she told Regretful, tapping her finger on a section midway through the imposing volume she'd pulled from one of the library's high shelves. He took the book and sat next to me, his finger moving beneath the words as we both read.

Leukemia. A type of cancer involving white blood cells.

Regretful read the description twice, then looked up.

"Is Pancake gonna die?" he asked Aunt Felicity.

"I don't know," she said. "Maybe."

Regretful re-read the page several times, afterward bombarding us both with questions: *What causes it? Why did Pancake get it? Can they cure him? Can someone catch it?* Later that day, he and Johnny Mark sat on a pew outside the confessional at St. Mary's, waiting for me to finish up with another sinner. Regretful told his cousin what he'd read.

"Pancake might be dying," he added.

Johnny Mark shook his head. "Kids don't die," he said.

Regretful is my sister Mary Ellen's boy and has been raised a Methodist at the insistence of his father, Big Bob Peaseblossom.

Big Bob—just "Bob" about seventy pounds ago—is suspicious of nonfat foods and Catholics. He persuaded Mary Ellen to raise their kids as Protestants, but Regretful is imaginative and we Catholics, with our rosary beads and holy water and oils and Latin, are right up his alley. He often sneaks into the booth at St. Mary's with Johnny Mark, providing him with sins to confess. I never kick him out. Frankly, without something to break them up, confessions are a monotonous litany of coveting, false witnessing, and Lord's-name-in-vaining. I appreciate a guest Protestant who can concoct enough entertaining sins to make things more interesting. I figure God does too.

The boys had to wait while I attended to Ed Dogberry. Ed is a Methodist, as well, but he confesses every now and then. "I'm covering my bases," he explains if anyone asks. On that morning he was anxious to unburden. The day after the Fourth of July his wife, Vivian, had acted upon an oft-repeated threat to drop dead, slipping into the beyond around the same time Ed was conjuring up impure thoughts about piano teacher and former Broadway showgirl Jewel Tomek. Vivian undoubtedly drank and smoked herself into an early grave, but the timing still unsettled Ed, and after apologizing to the Almighty while facing the altar at St. Luke's Methodist church, he wanted a pass from me too. "God oughta get the lowdown from all the horses' mouths now that Viv's in Heaven," he told me. "She could never get a story straight and I don't want to have a lot of explaining to do on Judgment Day."

Ed is very loud, and from a nearby pew, Bibsy Dolny heard every word while offering her daily prayer of thanks to God for giving her new brains after her head exploded. Regretful and Johnny Mark listened in, as well, and I heard them snicker as Ed admitted that he often contemplated what septuagenarian Jewel Tomek looked like in her underwear. Eventually, he finished and Johnny Mark slipped behind the curtain. Regretful followed and sat on the floor.

"Bless me Father for I have sinned," Johnny Mark began.

"Ask him about Pancake," Regretful whispered.

"I need a sin first."

"Ask him."

"He needs a sin, Regretful," I interrupted. "We can talk about Jimmy Farris afterward."

Regretful thought for a moment.

"Johnny Mark tried on his sister's bra," he said.

After I explained that a boy test-driving a bra wasn't a sin, we sat in the huge nave, a cavernous place where light filtered through stained glass windows, painting the alabaster statuary in carnival colors. We talked about leukemia.

"We can't always understand the ways of God," I told the boys.

"But why Pancake?" Regretful asked. "Why not me...or Johnny Mark?"

I gave him an answer that has become increasingly perplexing to me over the years. "Only God knows," I replied.

Some weeks later, with the Little League championship game approaching, Beagle Gibbs nailed his balls to the roof of his mother's house. My nephews witnessed the whole thing. They'd been on their way to the vacant lot across from Francis and Justine Wounded Arrow's home to hunt for more skeletons, when they pedaled their bikes past the Farris house and saw Pancake alone in the driveway, arms spread like wings, his face pointed upward. The boys cruised to a stop and watched. Pancake's eyes were closed, his face ghostly pale, wisps of downy hair feathering out from beneath a blue baseball cap. He was smiling. After a few seconds he let his arms fall and opened his eyes.

"Hey, guys," he said. "Whacha doin'?"

"We're gonna check out the lot where they found the skeleton," Regretful told him. "Wanna go?"

"Sure," Pancake replied. "I have to tell my mom first."

After Pancake went inside, Johnny Mark protested. "What if we catch it...that disease?"

"You can't catch it."

"You don't know that."

"I *do* know that. Aunt Felicity said so. Some people just get it. Nobody knows why."

Johnny Mark typically didn't argue with his cousin as Regretful could debate a chick back into its eggshell, but their talk with me had reminded him that there might, indeed, be a higher authority than the redoubtable Aunt Felicity Penrod. It stiffened his spine.

"Father Peter says that God knows," Johnny Mark muttered.

The morning was suddenly interrupted by a hair-raising scream and the boys whirled around just in time to see Beagle Gibbs sled down the slanted roof of the house across the street. A moment later, he jerked to a stop and a gunshot rang out, followed by another shriek. Pancake and his mother were quickly out the door, Mrs. Farris sighing with relief when she saw Regretful and Johnny Mark on the ground, rolling with laughter. She put in a 911 call, and before long, Chief Johnson K. Johnson and Sheriff Faron Troutfedder were on the scene, offering equally impressive demonstrations of police restraint when they managed to interview the young eyewitnesses without laughing. Meanwhile, Mrs. Farris went inside, returning with three PB&J sandwiches and a pitcher of lemonade. By then, an ambulance had arrived and a small blue-and-yellow helicopter was on the street with the pilot leaning against the cab of the aircraft, watching Snug Nixon and Nick Dolny argue.

"You're the fire chief," Snug whined. "You oughta pull it out."

"You got that right. I am the chief, and as the chief, I'm orderin' *you* to pull it out," Nick countered.

While the men played rock-paper-scissors to assign the duty, Beagle's mother propped a ladder against the house, then climbed up and used a pair of pliers to extract the nail her son had accidentally fired through his scrotum. Afterward, she helped Beagle to the ground and then into the back of the ambulance where he waited for the two volunteer firemen to stop bickering. By the time the rescue unit sped off with lights and siren at full tilt, it was nearly one o'clock.

"We gotta go to baseball practice," Regretful told Pancake. "Maybe we can go look for more skeletons tomorrow."

"It's okay. This was better," Pancake replied.

"Way better," Johnny Mark agreed.

Regretful and Johnny Mark raced off on their bikes, short-cutting through several rutted dirt alleys and then bouncing along the cinder-lined railbed as they made their way to a baseball diamond next to the alfalfa plant. Coach McQueen was already there, hitting grounders to the infielders while the outfielders played catch. Johnny Mark hopped off his bike and sat on the ground, panting as he tightened the laces on his sneakers.

"Pancake's an okay guy," he said to Regretful. "And I don't think he's dying. I don't think he's even sick. I think Aunt Felicity is wrong."

Regretful slipped a hand into his glove. "Aunt Felicity is never wrong," he said.

Johnny Mark strapped on his shin-guards and chest protector, then flipped his cap around and looped the catcher's mask over his head. When he was ready the two boys walked to the mound together, flipping a ball back and forth. They reached the pitching rubber and Johnny Mark dropped the ball into his friend's glove. "I think she's wrong," he reiterated. "Pancake's not dying. It's like I already told you. Kids don't die."

Johnny Mark trotted toward the plate, while Regretful turned to face the outfield. In the distance, a crop-duster lazily circled one of the cornfields west of town. Suddenly, it swooped downward—a misty waterfall of insecticide streaming from nozzles beneath its wings. It disappeared behind the long line of fence that described the outfield, then seconds later, reappeared, veering into the sky before curling about and again plunging earthward. Regretful watched the plane, recalling a crop-duster that once landed on the dirt road near his aunt Daisy's farm and horse ranch. The pilot had offered to take them up. Daisy declined, but Regretful jumped at the chance, and although thrilled at first, the wild, roller-coaster turns and pitches quickly emptied his stomach. Afterward, the good-natured pilot blamed it on the bug spray. "It kills good, but makes a feller sicker'n blue blazes sometimes," he offered, hoping to make his young green-faced passenger feel better.

The borers were bad that summer, but within days of the crop-duster's visit, the cornstalks perked up, their leaves still mottled but no longer drooping or spotted in brown. Following the harvest in October, Daisy told Regretful that it was the best yield she'd ever had, nearly 166 bushels per acre. "I'd probably have hit one-seventy if you hadn't puked on part of my crop," she teased.

"At least I went up," Regretful countered, winking at his aunt. "I didn't chicken out like you... I wasn't scared. That counts for something."

The stands were already full when the Cozy Lunch Dodgers took the field for the Little League championship game against the Peaseblossom Giants. Aunt Felicity and I were there. We have nieces and nephews on both teams and rotate the side we sit on, even though we secretly root for the Giants. Regretful is our favorite nephew.

"Dink Nixon's pitching?" Aunt Felicity observed after Dink—Snug's boy and the Dodgers' usual shortstop—fired a pitch from the mound that darted into the catcher's mitt with ferocious speed. He followed up with several more pitches, each nastier than the last.

"Whaddaya think o' them apples, Dem?" Dodger skipper Nick Dolny shouted from across the diamond.

Dem McQueen watched Dink throw a few more pitches, smacking one meaty palm with a bat until his hand was nearly as red as his face. Finally, he turned to face his team.

"Awright, listen up, Giants," he growled, his hacksaw voice easily audible to those of us in the bleachers behind the Giants' dugout. "Last game. They got one loss. We got none. We win and we're the champs. We lose and they tie us. I don't like no ties. Ties are for losers. Winners don't tie. They kick butt. So what's it gonna be today? Whattaya wanna be? Winners…or frickin' losers?"

"Winners," the team droned.

Dem McQueen is the reason I'm in prison. At Delphic Oracle High he was the school's greatest athlete, something he parlayed into a job on the police force and marriage to my beautiful little sister. Neither his job nor the marriage lasted. He knocked Mia around one too many times and she divorced him for it. I shot him for the same reason, hence my incarceration. After Mia left him, Big Bob kept Dem as the Giants' coach. I'm not sure why, although Big Bob dated Dem's older sister in high school. Regardless, it was a fortunate turn of events for Dem, especially after his love affair with whiskey and fistfights forced Chief Johnson to fire him. It gave the former high school star something to break up his days other than pro wrestling on TV, collecting unemployment, and waiting for his next high school class reunion.

Dem grabbed the Giants' first batter, Reynaldo "Runt" Diaz and shoved him toward the plate. A tiny hitter, prone to pop-ups and dribbling grounders, McQueen had taught Runt to crouch in the batter's box, forcing an enemy hurler to hit a spot the size of a postage stamp to get a called strike. "When you lead off, a walk is as good as a hit," his coach assured him.

Runt settled in at the plate, curling into a fetal position, his eyes nearly disappearing under the brim of his batting helmet. Dink Nixon, unperturbed by the prospect of a strike zone as narrow as a mail slot, promptly fired a screamer at Runt's head—the little hitter diving into the dirt of the batter's box to avoid being hit, then staying there until certain the shelling had stopped.

"Is that legal?" he asked, looking up at Ump Johnson. The big umpire nodded and Runt regained his feet, then nervously resumed his crouch, eyes large as quarters, knees quivering. Three more times Dink eyed Runt's helmet as if it displayed a target, then fired called strikes that looped toward the batter's head before darting inward to swoop over the plate. Runt

frantically recoiled each time and struck out. Beagle's nephew—
Kenny Gibbs—was the next batter and he fanned on three
straight fastballs, a final swing sending his helmet tumbling to
the ground where it spun in the dirt around home plate. In the
Giants' dugout Johnny Mark looked at Regretful and shook his
head.

"Wow," he said.

The third Giant batter was lanky first baseman Eli Gibbs,
Kenny's older brother. A patient hitter, Eli managed to get his
bat on the ball several times, fouling it down the lines and once
lifting it nearly to the right field fence before the clothesline
drive curved foul. In the end he struck out, too, afterward
trudging back to the dugout where he flung his bat into the
rack. "Don't fool around," he told Regretful. "We're in for a
game. No walking guys on purpose, okay?"

A cool front had swept in overnight, providing relief from
the sweltering days of August. Most in town had taken the
afternoon off to see the championship game and the stands
were full, with small children playing in the grass behind the
backstop while a few older boys slouched against the fence,
their long fingers entwined in the chicken wire. After the Dodgers trotted back to their dugout, the Giants took the field with
Regretful on the mound and Johnny Mark behind the plate,
their teammates filling the air with the odd music of baseball.

"Hey battuh, hey battuh, hey battuh, hey suh-WING battuh!"

Regretful showed the Dodger lead-off man a pair of
screeching fastballs, followed by a changeup so excruciatingly
slow, the thoroughly bamboozled hitter swung at it twice.

"Stee-rike threeeeee!" Ump Johnson K. Johnson sang, getting a big laugh from the crowd with, "Stee-rike fooooooour!"
The next two hitters each sauntered to the plate from the on-
deck circle and faced Regretful with steady, taunting eyes, their
bats waggling ominously. Six swings later, they had both struck
out.

"No hits, no runs," I heard Johnny Mark tell Regretful as
they reached their dugout.

"No one left on base," Regretful replied.

Johnny Mark, the Giants' best hitter, led off the top of the second inning and worked Dink to a full count before taking first base on a ball four that put Coach Nick Dolny in Ump Johnson's face, the tip of his finger dangerously close to the big man's nose. It was an entertaining dispute and the Dodger fielders were riveted as Johnny Mark casually trotted all the way to third base. Nick lost the argument and was halfway to the Dodgers' dugout before he realized that a runner awarded first base on a walk was unexpectedly in scoring position on third.

"Wait a minute! He can't do that!" he shouted. He dashed back to home plate to confront Ump Johnson. "You gotta send him back to first base," Nick fumed. "I called time out."

"You didn't call time—"

"Did so!"

"…and if your boys don't tag him out, that young fella can circle the bases."

"Listen you big, fat tub o'—"

The chief reached into a pocket, retrieved his badge, and pinned it to his chest protector. "Get off the field or I'll run you in, Nick," he growled.

The next two batters swaggered to the plate, spitting and crotch-grabbing like the major leaguers on TV. It didn't help. They both struck out. Now, there were two outs with Johnny Mark still in scoring position on third base as the next batter approached the box and settled into his stance. Dink quickly fired a sizzler that caught the inside corner. The batter, Regretful Peaseblossom, didn't move. Strike one. The next pitch was a ball, low and outside—the third another called strike, this one belt high with a hop.

"Swing battuh, swing!" Coach Dolny taunted from the Dodger bench. "Swing battuh, suh-WING!"

With the count at one ball and two strikes, Dink delivered a pitch that came in high before veering outside.

"BALL TWO!" Ump Johnson bellowed.

"Hey battuh, hey battuh, hey battuh, hey suh-WING

battuh!" the Dodgers shouted as Dink tried a changeup. It was dead center but low.

"BALL THREE!" Ump Johnson proclaimed.

Regretful ground his feet into the dirt as Dink went into his windup for the next pitch, arm dangling low to the ground, his leg-kick high in the air. Suddenly the young pitcher unwound and the ball shot from his hand, an artillery shell heading straight for the catcher's mitt. Regretful squared his body over the plate, bat held horizontal, hands widespread.

"Bunt!" Nick shouted from the Dodger bench. "It's a bunt!"

The ball clunked against the barrel of Regretful's bat and then squiggled down the foul line as my nephew dropped his bat and flew down the basepath.

"YOURS! YOURS!" Dink shouted at Emily Goodfellow as she dashed for the ball and he ran to cover her position at first base. "YOURS! YOURS!"

Emily was fast, her arm strong. But the drag bunt had been perfect. Everyone in the stands knew that she wouldn't reach the ball in time. Even if Dink beat Regretful to first base, her throw would be too late. Regretful would make it and Johnny Mark would score. The Giants would own the lead.

What happened next was both dreadful and hilarious. As Regretful zipped up the first base line, his knees began to wobble and it suddenly seemed as if he were wading chest-deep in the Platte River instead of running down the faint chalk line that marked the basepath. He stumbled, nearly fell, then stumbled again. Aunt Felicity reached over and squeezed my wrist.

"Oh dear," she murmured, and as if he'd heard her, Regretful fell down, landing with a thud a full six feet short of the bag. The next sound was the pop of the ball hitting Dink's glove as he took Emily Goodfellow's throw to end the inning with the teams still in a scoreless tie.

"OUT!" Johnson shouted.

Silence followed, then laughter—at first sporadic, like the first kernels of popcorn to burst, then growing into a rumble. Out on the field, Regretful remained in the dirt of the basepath, motionless. Emily approached and touched his shoulder. He didn't move and she put her lips close to his ear, her words inaudible. He rolled over and she helped him to his feet, then walked with her cousin to the mound where Johnny Mark waited with his best friend's glove. From a few rows behind me, Francis Wounded Arrow turned to his wife, Justine. "Gonna take a while to live that one down," he said. "You should probably make him invisible for a while."

The next three and a half innings elapsed without a single batter making contact with the ball, turning the contest into a game of catch between the opposing pitchers and their catchers. Meanwhile, the large turnout for the game had prompted considerable theatrics from Chief Johnson and the opposing coaches. The huge umpire added dance moves to his "Yer out!" calls, galloping about at home plate and occasionally performing a full pirouette, while Nick Dolny and Dem McQueen heckled so mercilessly, Johnson threatened to arrest them both. Leading off the top of the sixth and final prescribed inning for a Little League game, left-handed Eli Gibbs hit a screamer down the right field line. The Dodger outfielder nearly fainted when Eli turned on the pitch, but gamely sprinted for the ball, the fly taking him all the way to the outfield fence where he slammed hard into the chicken wire and then bounced off, blood trickling from a cut on his forehead. Inside the webbing of his glove was the ball.

"YER OUT!" Johnson shouted, performing a Motown-worthy grapevine down the third base line. The crowd cheered, the injured player was escorted to the dugout for a Band-Aid and an orange slice, and Pancake Farris replaced him, trotting out to right field as his mother watched from the stands, her hands clasped as if in prayer. Dink Nixon quickly struck out the next two hitters to end the top half of the inning with Regretful retiring the side on ten pitches in the bottom half. After six frames, both boys had pitched no-hitters, the second inning base-on-balls granted to Johnny Mark Wounded Arrow marring what were otherwise a pair of perfect games: no runs, no hits, no walks, no errors.

"Extra innings," Ump Johnson announced to the crowd. "We're goin' to extra innings."

There's an old superstition in baseball—*Don't talk about a no-hitter in progress*—a venerable adage unknown to Beagle Gibbs's mother, an affably plump woman partial to polyester ponchos with bright floral patterns.

"Has anyone gotten a hit yet?" she asked as the Dodgers took the field for the top of the seventh. "If someone did, I don't remember it."

"Mom!" Beagle cautioned.

"I'm sorry, but if someone got a hit I simply missed it or something. Has anyone on either team—"

"Mom!" Beagle repeated. "You're not supposed to talk about it."

"Talk about what? I just wanted to know if anyone—"

"Mom! No talking about it. Stop talking."

Mrs. Gibbs and Beagle have a history of public tiffs nearly as entertaining as the roller derby she loves, but her son and my sister, Daisy, had become an item and she didn't want to run off the woman who had convinced Beagle to clean himself up and take summer classes at Zenith State. She frowned, then demurely folded her hands in her lap as Dink Nixon took the mound.

"Yay, Kenny. Yay, Eli," she unenthusiastically called out to her two grandsons.

Dink struck out the first two hitters to open the seventh. Cleanup hitter Johnny Mark Wounded Arrow was next. He waited for Ump Johnson to finish sweeping dirt off home plate, then swung and missed a pair of rockets. Strike one, strike two. A reverential quiet had settled over the crowd, making it easy to hear Pancake Farris's tinny voice from right field.

"Hey battuh, hey battuh, hey battuh, hey suh-WING battuh!" he shouted, his uniform hanging on his slender frame, his thin arms and legs poking out like sticks. "Hey battuh, hey battuh, hey battuh, hey suh-WING—"

Pancake's cry was cut off by the unmistakable crack of a well-hit ball as Johnny Mark Wounded Arrow sent a shot that split the gap in right-centerfield. Pancake and the Dodgers' centerfielder both raced for it as Coach Dolny leapt to the top step of the Dodgers' dugout.

"GET OUTTA THE WAY, PANCAKE!" he shrieked.

Both players kept going, Pancake stumbling as he approached the right-centerfield fence, his flat, round glove held upward.

"GET OUTTA THE WAY, PANCAKE! GET OUTTA THE WAY!"

Pancake's mother rose, glaring at her son's coach.

"Get it, Jimmy!" she cheered. "Get it!"

"GET OUTTA THE WAY!"

"Get it, Jimmy!"

"GET OUTTA THE WAY, PANCAKE!"

The two players simultaneously reached the fly ball and crashed into one another. Pancake's teammate hit the ground, but the little rightfielder somehow kept his feet, glove still held upward.

"Get it, Jimmy!"

"GET IT, PANCAKE!"

The ball hit Pancake's glove.

"HANG ON TO IT!" Nick yelled. "HANG ON!"

Pancake tried. The ball bounced off his glove and he grabbed at it with his bare hand, juggling it once, twice, a third time. Then, it was suddenly beyond his reach and dropped, hitting the grass and dribbling to a stop at the base of the fence.

"OH MY GOD," Nick shouted, "GET IT! THROW IT! THROW THE BALL, PANCAKE!"

The young Dodger ran for the ball, picked it up, and had the stitches beneath his fingers just as Johnny Mark Wounded Arrow rounded third base and dashed for home.

"THROW IT…THROW THE BALL!" Coach Dolny exhorted.

The benches had cleared, the players crowding their baselines as Pancake made a running start.

"Throw it, Jimmy, throw it!" Mrs. Farris called out.

"THROW IT, PANCAKE, GODDAMIT!" Dolny bellowed.

Pancake's arm came forward. He released the throw, then fell as the ball sailed sideways, hit the ground, hopped twice, and rolled to a stop in the outfield grass.

"OH NO!" Nick bawled.

"Oh no," Pancake's mother whispered.

"Oh no," Aunt Felicity sighed, squeezing my wrist as Johnny Mark Wounded Arrow crossed home plate to score the first run of the game.

The distant peal of the church bell at St. Mary's echoed across the diamond as the Giants took the field for the bottom of the seventh with a 1-0 lead. Merely three outs separated Regretful and his teammates from the league championship. The bell sounded five times and then once more. It was six o'clock—time to wrap things up. The previous inning had ended after Dink Nixon struck out the final batter. A short delay then followed when Nick Dolny filed a series of protests and then threw a temper tantrum that got him handcuffed to the snack cart behind the bleachers. My brother Teddy came out of the stands to replace him. "Just make contact," he told his first batter, Dink Nixon. "You don't have to kill it. Just get on base." Dink then swaggered to the batter's box and swung so hard at Regretful's first two pitches he nearly corkscrewed into the dust.

"Just make contact," Teddy called out from the dugout, clapping his hands. "Just make contact."

Dink impassively watched the next two pitches—a pair of balls low and outside—then dug in as Regretful kicked high and threw a dangling changeup that fluttered off his fingers and meandered toward the plate. Twice fanned by tantalizing off-speed pitches, Dink leapt on the ball and drove it to centerfield where it was hauled in with the outfielder's back touching the deepest part of the diamond. One out.

With the next batter at the plate, Coach McQueen visited the mound, squeezing the elbow on Regretful's pitching arm until the boy grimaced. He had just reached the Giants' dugout on his return when two distinct cracks sounded—the batter tagging one of Regretful's fastballs followed by a smacking sound when the screaming liner hit the first baseman's glove. Two outs.

As the next batter left the on-deck circle, Dem McQueen yelled at Regretful from the bench.

"PEASEBLOSSOM!"

Regretful looked to his coach.

"PEASEBLOSSOM!" the coach repeated, his finger pointed at first base. Behind home plate Ump Johnson straightened and tucked his hands inside his chest protector. Johnny Mark stood, too, slipping off his mask as a hush drifted across the ballpark.

"PEASEBLOSSOM!" McQueen bellowed again, finger still pointed. "PEASEBLOSSOM!"

Both Dink Nixon and my nephew had pitched no-hitters, Dink's marred only by a second inning walk and Pancake Farris's seventh inning dropped ball error in right field. But Regretful had pitched more than a no-hitter. He had pitched a perfect game—no hits, no walks, no runs, no errors. Not a single batter had reached base, and if the next Dodger hitter were retired, my nephew's accomplishment would be historic, unprecedented in Delphic Oracle. Over more than 130 years of organized baseball in our little town, not a single pitcher had ever thrown a *perfect* game—not in the Little League, the Pony League, with the Junior Legion team, our minor league Delphic Oracle Haybalers, or the legendary Bugeaters, a team that had beaten the Zenith Rivercats in a 1925 game-of-the-century folks still recalled with reverence. Regretful was one out away from achieving the once-thought unachievable, but his coach wanted him to sacrifice it by intentionally walking the next batter.

Regretful lowered his eyes to the pitcher's rubber. It was red, covered with crescent-shaped cuts made by the spikes of the high schoolers on the Junior Legion team.

"PEASEBLOSSOM!"

Johnny Mark called time out and trotted out to the mound. He took the ball from Regretful's hand and studied it carefully, afterward tossing it to Chief Johnson. The umpire immediately dispatched a fresh, unblemished baseball.

"PEASEBLOSSOM!" McQueen barked from the dugout, arm still extended, finger pointed at first base. Johnny Mark dropped the ball into Regretful's glove, then reached out and tapped his cousin on the chest with his fat catcher's mitt. Afterward, he jogged back to the plate and stood, the arm with his huge glove held outward. A moment later Regretful unexpectedly fired a fastball that would have struck Johnny Mark in the chest had the batter not hit it foul. The ball carried all the way to the left field fence where it wedged in the chicken wire. It was an impressive shot but still a foul ball. Strike one.

Coach McQueen called a time-out and went to the mound. Johnny Mark joined him. The crowd was eerily silent, and with Dem's foghorn voice, we heard every word.

"Walk the damned batter, Peaseblossom," McQueen growled.

"But, Coach," Johnny Mark argued, "he's pitched a perfect game."

"You wanna be champions?" McQueen barked.

The boys nodded glumly.

"Are you winners or losers?"

"Winners."

"Then do what I say," Dem snapped. He took the ball from Regretful's hand and rubbed it between his palms, grinding at the stitches as if trying to erase them. "Walk 'im," he ordered. He returned to the dugout and Johnny Mark went back to home plate where he caught the next four pitches while standing— each a toothless thing intentionally thrown far outside the strike zone. The hitter's bat never left his shoulder, and after the walk was issued, he trotted to first base as if ashamed. Emily was the next batter. She stepped into the box and took two level practice swings. Regretful looked at his coach, and after McQueen once again pointed at first base, she was intentionally walked as was the next batter. The bases were now loaded with two outs.

Only a few minutes had passed since the resonant bells of the church proclaimed the hour. The temperature had not changed nor had the clouds floating about the sun nor the gentle flutter of the wind. The stands remained packed, the whisk-and-grind of the alfalfa mill churned in the distance, and mockingbirds hidden within the bordering cottonwoods still competed with the strident hecklers from both teams. Suddenly, we heard the faraway melancholy whistle of the evening Burlington Northern. It was on time and would soon pass through the outskirts of Delphic Oracle.

At the edge of the Dodgers' dugout, Teddy handed a bat to his next hitter and then moved aside. Pancake Farris—the batter Dem McQueen had heartlessly set up to be the final out—then began the long trip to the batter's box.

"OH MY GOD!" Nick Dolny wailed, peering between the open planks of the bleachers as he tugged on the handcuffs that anchored him to the snack cart. "FOR GOD'S SAKE, NO!"

Stunned silence followed as Ump Johnson left home plate and approached the Dodger dugout. He shared a few words of warning with Teddy, who relayed them to Nick. The chief then returned to the plate, accompanied by the mournful howl of the Burlington Northern as it clattered through Delphic Oracle on tracks sitting between the baseball diamond and a dot of sun hovering above the western horizon.

"Play ball," the umpire called out.

Gradually, the noise again picked up, the patter of the players filling the air as the actors in our final scene settled into their roles: Pancake in the batter's box, knees locked, back arched, the oversized helmet nearly hiding his eyes; Johnny Mark crouched behind home plate, his glove positioned to take the pitch; Ump Johnson behind him, ready to make the call; and Regretful forty-six feet away, squinting under the brim of his cap as he bent to take the sign. Johnny Mark lowered a single finger.

Fastball.

Regretful toed the rubber and threw. Pancake swung mightily, hitting nothing but air.

Strike one.

Regretful followed up with another fastball that the little batter badly missed.

Strike two.

The train had passed and the first sounds of evening now floated across the diamond: the nesting trill and rustle of birds, the early chirp of an impatient cricket, the distant growl of a lawn mower. The sun would soon slip behind the trees, and once the game was over, it would remain light for a time, but inevitably night would come and the season would be over—possibly a final season for some. Next summer, Regretful and Dink would move up to a higher division, one where fastballs that screamed over the plate in Little League might be nothing more than lazy batting practice pitches for the older boys. And Aunt Felicity was approaching ninety years old. She was fit and stubborn, but there comes an age when the promise of a next year is no longer made. As for Pancake Farris… Well, as I told my nephews, maybe only God knew?

On the mound Regretful rotated the ball on his fingertips, studying its seams, the delay prompting Pancake to step out of the box. He slapped at the air with the bat, spat and grabbed his crotch, scooped up a handful of dirt and carefully rubbed it between his palms.

"Come on, Jimmy! Come on!" his mother called out from the stands.

"One more strike!" Dem McQueen bawled.

"You can do it, buddy," Teddy shouted.

"For crying out loud…play ball!" Ump Johnson pleaded.

Pancake wiggled back into his crouch, a wad of gum forming a lump in one cheek, the heavy bat wobbling. His face was pale, but his eyes were steady. He was not afraid. Regretful studied the frail young player, his own lips slightly parted, and when Johnny Mark gave a sign for the next pitch, the star hurler shook his head. Johnny Mark gave another sign, prompting another head shake. The Giants' catcher then shoved his mask atop his head and trotted out to the mound where he listened as Regretful spoke, the quiet words prompting him to glance at Coach McQueen and then lower his eyes to the dirt of the pitcher's mound. After a few moments, Johnny Mark looked up. The boys nodded at each other and the young catcher returned to home plate. He squatted, and gave a sign. This time, his pitcher nodded.

Regretful took his wind-up, loose and easy, ignoring the base runners. His fingers were firm on the ball, the reassuring texture of the stitches holding fast to the unyielding cowhide. The factory-imprinted *Tim Lincecum* signature was against the meat of his knuckles, a personal touch from the young major league pitcher that filled him with confidence and certainty. A hush settled over the crowd save the gravelly Camels-and-Jack Daniels voice of Coach Dem McQueen.

"Hey battuh, hey battuh, hey battuh, hey suh-WING battuh!"

The afternoon had grown long and a sudden line of shadow partially eclipsed the narrow lane between pitcher's mound and batter's box, casting Pancake Farris into gray. He stood with the bat held high, his breathing steady, face filled with a mixture of wonder and anticipation.

"Hey battuh, hey battuh, hey battuh, hey suh-WING battuh!"

Regretful's arm came forward, a blur in the sun, its sweep as true and precise as the chimes at St. Mary's. The crowd was silenced, his teammates stilled, gloves dangling limply at their sides, while the Dodgers slumped in their dugout, save the three to whom Regretful had bequeathed first, second, and third, a disconsolate trio staring at the ground as inevitability washed over them.

"Hey battuh, hey battuh, hey battuh, hey suh-WING battuh!"

The ball came out of Regretful's hand up and dead center, delightfully slow and devoid of spin as it sailed toward Johnny

Mark's glove. It ran true to the batter without a hint of tail as
Jimmy "Pancake" Farris's bat moved forward, the sudden and
surprising strength in his thin arms lending such swiftness, a
collective gasp was issued by the fans filling the bleachers on
both sides. Jimmy's mother stood, her eyes filled with tears, as
the ball stayed up and true, piercing the shadow between pitcher's mound and home plate. There was no deflection, no curve.
It was a pitch lacking cunning or guile—a gift—a ball as fat and
round as Jimmy Farris's eyes as his bat came steadily and surely
forward with astounding speed, a grin on his tiny face, the roar
of the crowd already ringing in his ears.

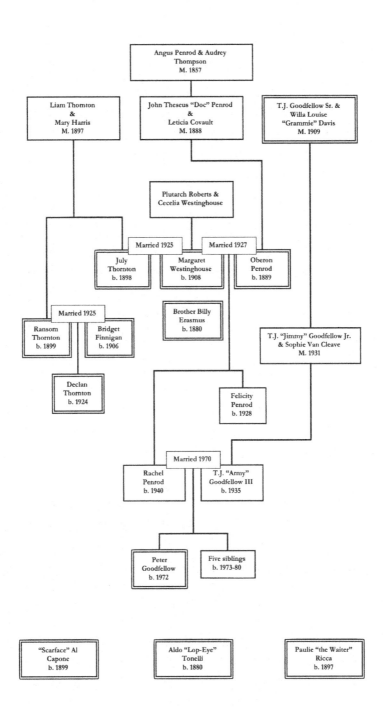

9

The Hounds Catch the Fox

Maggie Westinghouse watched July from the window of her small bedroom above the dental office. She loved his long stride and unwavering blue eyes, the way he greeted each person as an old friend. "She thought him a bounder for certain," Grammie Willa used to say, "but Maggie knew there was good in him too." She suddenly heard a thump, then a metallic crash as the floor shook from a wrestling match going on below. Dr. Plutarch Roberts had never quite mastered the administration of ether and it wasn't uncommon for a patient to wake up in the middle of a tooth extraction. Myron Van Cleave had shown up that morning, squinting in agony from a bad molar and Maggie imagined the ether-sozzled mayor tossing roundhouse punches at the man everyone knew to be her father. She hoped one landed.

Maggie crossed to her small dressing table and sat in front of the mirror. Her hair was lustrous and dark like her father's, her lips full, her skin flawless. She picked up a pair of scissors and put the point on her cheek. Sometimes she wanted to cut out the liquid brown eyes and high, elegant cheekbones. *Maybe that would put an end to the whispers*, she thought. Her mother had tried to protect her, concocting the myth of a husband and father who had died bravely in The War to End All Wars, but Maggie knew the truth. There was no Major Westinghouse. There never had been. Her mother, the former Cecelia Butterfield, had met young Plutie Roberts during his last year at the Baltimore College of Dental Surgery, allowing him to slip into her bed with promises of marriage that she held tight even as she boarded the train for Buffalo where she would "vacation" with her aunt and uncle. Once the encumbered young woman

was gone, the prominent Roberts family expeditiously reminded their son that his allowance would not see another sunrise
unless he married the bird-faced, poison-tongued daughter of
a Maryland senator. Young Plutie—a practical fellow when his
inheritance was in the mix—agreed, marrying Violet Monroe
Mandrake around the time his daughter's heels were clearing
her mother's womb.

"Cecelia was provided a small endowment by the Roberts
family to offset the inconvenience of an illegitimate grand-
child," Grammie Willa told me, but a few years later, the money
ran out and Cecelia began an exchange of letters with Dr. Roberts that led to the train platform in Miagrammesto Station,
Nebraska. Her new name, Westinghouse, had been taken from
the logo on her uncle's parlor radio.

Maggie pressed harder, the point of the scissors threatening
to pierce the skin of her cheek. She could still recall meeting her
father for the first time. Only eleven years old, she'd instinctively known that he would eventually try to slip from her mother's bed and into her own. "He waited until she was thirteen,"
Grammie Willa divulged, "showing up in Maggie's bedroom
with an excess of pomaded hair and a deficiency of pants." The
young girl laughed at him, a weapon as lethal as a knife when
brandished in the face of a coward. Dr. Roberts never again
bothered her.

Maggie set the scissors back on the dressing table, scowling.
The face in the mirror was beautiful—a gift and a curse. Men
thought her a siren, women a succubus, making her feel less a
person than a rumor. It is difficult to be friends with a rumor
and Maggie had few of them, none close. She was a curiosity.
Everyone wanted to know her, but no one truly knew her—at
least until she discovered a man sleeping in the switch-house
near the tracks.

She had surprised July when they became lovers, instinctively
skillful and shockingly aggressive. "You're a modern girl," July
said after they made love the first time. Maggie hadn't blushed,
even though she was as surprised as July at the passion that

overcame her. She was not a virgin. Mayor Van Cleave's vapid son, Johann, had taken care of that although it was Maggie who spurred him on, simply wanting to get on with it, to see what all the uproar was about. Afterward, she unabashedly apprised her mother of her deflowering and Cecelia Westinghouse began to make plans. "Maggie's mother was good at putting jam on burnt toast," Grammie Willa always claimed. "She figured a night in the back seat of Johann's roadster was tantamount to an engagement ring, but the Van Cleaves weren't about to agree to that match. They wanted Johann to hold out for a Penrod girl that would merge their families." After Maggie and Johann broke up, Mrs. Westinghouse quickly set aside her disappointment. Maggie was beautiful and her mother was confident another big fish could be reeled in. July Pennybaker was an angle not foreseen, and when it became apparent that the glib rainmaker was a broom about to sweep away the web she was spinning, Cecelia determined to end the affair. "It was a short battle," Grammie Willa recalled. "Maggie would not be swayed and Cecelia gave up, knitting another sweater for Plutie Roberts that would infuriate his wife."

Maggie returned to the window. At night she often stood there, imagining the moonlight blanketing the countryside to be an ocean, her little apartment a lighthouse that might someday attract a gliding Yankee Clipper. In her dream the ship was skippered by a swashbuckling captain who had heard her name carried on the wind. She sighed. July had arrived on the wind, but he was no mariner. A man no more real than the ethereal Major Westinghouse, his profession was more in shadows than sunlight. She had yet to tell him of the child she carried, the baby due in 1926. Maggie well knew from sad experience that the feminine species loves beautiful women considerably less than it hates beautiful women and prayed that July would carry her off long before she had to waddle around town with a massively pregnant belly—another cautionary tale for Violet Roberts and her toxic band of gossips to snicker and snipe over.

A wooden staircase allowed access to Maggie's bedroom

from outside and she heard the sound of someone taking the steps two at a time. Moments later July opened the door and Maggie rushed into his arms, fumbling with the buttons on his shirt, her lips seeking his as if years had separated them—indeed, as if only minutes remained before the walls of her tiny room fell inward and crushed them. After they made love, she draped a leg across his thigh.

"When will you make an honest woman of me, Mister July Pennybaker?" she asked.

July brushed the soft skin of her leg with his fingers. "'Hasty marriage seldom proveth well,'" he said, his hand moving downward. Maggie slapped it away, unexpected tears of anger forming in her eyes.

"You have to leave now," she said.

He laughed.

"I'm not joking, July." She sat up and wrapped her arms around her knees, suddenly bathed in perspiration. The pregnancy had proven annoying thus far with morning nausea, unpredictable hot flashes, and peaks of insatiable passion followed by valleys of irritability and melancholy. She glared at July, angry with him for the child she carried and with herself for loving him.

"July... Where did *that* come from? Who would give a person such a name?"

"It's short for Julius...Julius Caesar Pennybaker," July said. "What's wrong with you anyway? Why are you mad at me?"

"Julius Caesar? Your parents named you Julius Caesar? That's your story? If so, it's a stupid story."

July leaned toward her, separating his hair to reveal a purplish birthmark in the shape of a crown. It was flat, its edges confluent with the surrounding skin. "Ma called this my mark of royalty," he said.

Maggie touched the curious nevus, and as she traced its margin with her finger, the hot flash subsided and her mood inexplicably softened. "Julius Caesar Pennybaker," she said. "That sounds like a lie." Neither spoke for a very long time. Then

Maggie reached up and stroked his cheek and they made love again. Afterward, there were no more questions. She felt quite certain that Pennybaker was not July's real name, but it didn't matter. There had never been a Major Westinghouse, either.

As evening approached Maggie left the bed and slipped into her skirt, then crossed to the small bathroom naked from the waist up. July watched her through the open door as she used a washcloth to rinse her underarms, her breasts falling away from her torso as she leaned forward. Always full, they seemed slightly larger, the nipples more pronounced.

"What are you looking at, Mister Julius Caesar Pennybaker?" Maggie demanded.

July winked at her. "Just the most beautiful girl in the world," he said.

"Well, stop it!" Maggie snapped, wanting desperately to tell him the truth. She couldn't yet, fearing he would say all the right things, his words as light as butterfly kisses. He would be overjoyed at the prospect of fatherhood. They would plan a life together. And then July Pennybaker would beg her pardon to take a brief leave—*for only a few minutes*, he would tell her—just long enough to gather his things from the Penrod Hotel. He would kiss her hard and offer up a jazzy, two-fingered salute. And then she would never see him again.

Maggie crossed to the window and looked out. August and the first part of September had been dry. Dust filled the sky in the distance, obscuring the horizon and making the world seem small and dirty. "I have to tell you something," she said, but before Miss Margaret Westinghouse—the Oracle of Delphi—could go on, July was behind her, pulling her against him, whispering promise after promise until her head swam with both joy and despair.

⤫

"Your great-grandfather, T.J., was the town sheriff," Grammie Willa always insisted on reminding me. I knew. Everyone in town knows about the legendary peace officer whose name is still emblazoned over the entry to THEODORE JAMES GOODFELLOW

SR. CITY-COUNTY HALL. "He was a good lawman," Grammie Willa bragged. "He had a nose for trouble and a way about him that headed it off before things got out of hand. That's why July and Brother Billy so worried him. They were filled with enough liquid charm to grease the wheels of everyone else in town, but T.J. was never fooled. Given his way, the pair would long ago have been escorted to the city limit and sent packing." Instead, the sheriff had turned a blind eye in deference to Mayor Van Cleave and a city council that equated the out-of-towners flooding Delphic Oracle with an improved golf course, less potholes in the streets, and a pair of ceiling fans in the stuffy courtroom.

A few weeks after Brother Billy showed up, Sheriff Goodfellow was at his desk, going through WANTED flyers. My great-grandfather was a large man, broad in the chest with thick wrists and an enviable jawline. Father to six sons, including my grandpa Jimmy, he was a man who tolerated nonsense when he rough-housed with his boys, but was deadly serious in his role as the chief law officer of newly christened Miagrammesto County. The heavy door to the jailhouse opened and a teenaged boy entered with his little brother in tow. Fifteen-year-old T.J. "Jimmy" Goodfellow, Jr. was a smaller version of his dad, his body solid and muscular, his brown eyes penetrating. His fingers were long, his feet a pair of riverboats that predicted he would one day be eye to eye with his six-foot-three-inch father. Three-year-old Greyson "Grey" Goodfellow, clung to his brother's hand, his toddler's face already lengthening in a way that made him seem manly and handsome.

"Mom says come home," Grey commanded, the words perfectly articulated. His father chuckled.

"That so?" he teased. "Who's boss here...me or Mom?"

The boys grinned. "Mom!" they chimed.

"Seriously, Dad," Jimmy said as his little brother crawled onto their father's lap, "it's late. Mom's holding dinner and we're starving."

The sheriff leaned back in his swivel chair and yawned,

appraising the piles of documents on his desk. After sending
out requests weeks earlier, the WANTED circulars had come in
from all over the country, a trickle in the beginning but now a
daily deluge. He'd avoided them for a long time, certain he'd
come across the faces of July Pennybaker or Billy Erasmus. The
two men were obviously as crooked as a pair of birch-willow
branches and he should have run them out of town a long time
ago. But the mayor was right, he told himself. Newly named
Delphic Oracle was doing well. Packages from *Sears & Roebuck*
were now commonplace, more cars than wagons were cruising
about town, and the bellies of the local clergy were fuller as collection plates overflowed with greenbacks rather than coins. It
was all a sham, T.J. knew, but thus far no one had been hurt and
the dedicated lawman was reluctant to point out that the gold
fever gripping the community he loved was fueled by feldspar.
Besides, he had come to enjoy Brother Billy's company.

The sheriff attended each revival service, at first watching
for a slip-up that would justify an arrest. But one night, after the
last of Brother Billy's flock had cleared out, the hearty preacher
approached him with a pair of cigars in one hand and a jug in
the other. They sat, assessing the cut of each other's jibs, and
by midnight the two men were friends, smoking cigars, sharing
stories, playing chess. "T.J. needed a buddy... Not a best friend,
like me, but a real buddy," Grammie Willa always asserted.
"Most people couldn't relax around him. They all acted as if
they were guilty of something. Brother Billy was undoubtedly
guilty of a great many things, but he didn't pretend otherwise.
T.J. appreciated that sort of honesty."

"One more, boys," the sheriff said to his sons, plucking another flyer from the stack of unread notices.

STATE OF NEW YORK
WANTED: WILLIAM CHARLES O'HARE
FOR MAIL FRAUD, SECURITIES FRAUD, RELIGIOUS FRAUD,
FORGERY, EMBEZZLEMENT, COUNTERFEITING, CHAR-
LATANISM, GRAND THEFT, PETTY THEFT, UNLAWFUL

FLIGHT, PERJURY, BRIBERY, IMPERSONATING A POLICE
OFFICER, ADULTERY, VIOLATION OF THE MANN ACT,
BIGAMY

AGE: APPROXIMATELY 60 YEARS OLD
HT: 6'4"
WT: APPROXIMATELY 250 POUNDS
HAIR COLOR: VARIABLE
DISTINGUISHING FEATURES: MULTIPLE BITE SCARS ON
HANDS, SCAR FROM GUNSHOT WOUND LEFT UPPER ARM,
TATTOO OF DOLPHIN ON RIGHT UPPER ARM, SCAR ABOVE
RIGHT EYEBROW

Sheriff Goodfellow scanned the flyer, his eyes lingering on
the photo. It was old, its subject nonplussed by his predicament, the amiable face lit up by an unabashed grin. The sheriff
frowned and stared harder at the picture as if doing so might
lengthen the man's chin or flatten his nose—anything to make
the image less recognizable.

"Jimmy, take your brother and go home," T.J. suddenly ordered his eldest son. The sheriff eased Grey off his lap. "Tell
your mother I'll be along soon."

"But, Dad—"

"Go," he repeated. "Start dinner without me."

After his sons were gone, the sheriff finished reading the
flyer:

ALIASES: WILLIAM CHARLES, CHARLES WILLIAMS, BIL-
LY CICERO, CHARLIE CICERO, ERASMUS CICERO, ERAS-
MUS CHARLES

DESCRIPTION: WILLIAM CHARLES O'HARE IS A CONFI-
DENCE MAN WHO TRAVELS THROUGHOUT THE UNITED
STATES AND CANADA, OFTEN IN THE COMPANY OF CIR-
CUS PEOPLE. HE MAY BE ACCOMPANIED BY AN ORIENTAL
WOMAN THAT HE REPRESENTS AS HIS WIFE. HE SPEAKS

WITH AN ACCENT INDIGENOUS TO THE SOUTHERN UNIT-
ED STATES, BUT HAS ALSO AFFECTED ACCENTS FROM NEW
ENGLAND, NEW YORK, AND SEVERAL FOREIGN COUN-
TRIES INCLUDING ENGLAND, GERMANY, ITALY, FRANCE,
AND EGYPT. HE IS NOT THOUGHT TO BE ARMED, BUT
SHOULD STILL BE APPROACHED WITH CAUTION.

Sheriff Goodfellow set the circular on his desk. The window was open and a sudden puff of wind lifted it into the air.
It hovered briefly like a small magic carpet and then floated
to the floor in broad, gentle sweeps, landing with the printed
side up—the face of Brother Billy Erasmus taunting the Miagrammesto County law officer.

T.J. rose and went to the window. On the street outside, a
pair of boys three or four years older than little Grey laughed
and shouted as General Bill Dogberry, the Ford dealer, drove by
in a new Model T touring car. He had the top down and wore
his driving hat and gloves along with a rakish scarf. The boys
ran alongside the car, touching its shiny fenders as General Bill
furiously honked the horn and bellowed at them. T.J. watched
the boys chase after the general until the car had disappeared
from view, then returned to his desk and sat, letting his head
fall back until he was staring at the elaborately embossed ceiling
tiles.

"Crap," he muttered.

୬

I promised to tell the story of three families, but other than
Ransom—who fixed the horse race in Zenith—there's been a
dearth of Thorntons. It's time to change that.

"I always suspected they were brothers," Grammie Willa
claimed when recalling Ransom and July Thornton. "Same
ears. Ears are almost as good as fingerprints." Ransom was
the second born to Liam and Mary Thornton, his brother,
July, one year older to the day. Raised in the rough and-tumble
Five Points section of New York City, their shanty Irish father
worked the docks, bringing home a meager paycheck that paid

half their bills, the other half set aside in favor of a pint or two after work. Mary covered the rest of their obligations, working eighty hours per week at Lennox Garments where she sewed clothes destined for children with full bellies and clean fingernails.

"Money and the Irish kept separate houses in those days," Grammie Willa revealed, and it wasn't long before July and his younger brother had to sing for pennies on Wall Street, their sad Irish ballads making businessmen and their wives feel appropriately blessed. "But for the grace of God, there go we," the fashionable gentry told their immaculate children as they slipped a coin into each Irish hat, smiling at the grimy faces while wrinkling their noses against the unfamiliar scent that clung to the boys' clothing.

July was a gifted student, and by the time he turned sixteen, had caught the attention of Father Brennan who convinced Wall Street titan Carlton Fitzwalter "C.F." Pennybaker to sponsor the poor Irish lad. Mary pirated a substantial wool remnant from work to make July a new suit and Liam put down his bucket of beer long enough to sourly shake the boy's hand. Then the Thorntons bade their eldest goodbye and he was off to Yale University in New Haven, Connecticut, where he met his first college roommate: C.F.'s son, Carlton Fitzwalter Pennybaker Jr.

With the Pennybaker imprimatur, July pledged the prestigious Zeta Psi fraternity, where he quickly appreciated that ascendancy in Greek society was facilitated by the distance he could put between himself and Five Points. "He learned to lie as blithely as Mephistopheles," Grammie Willa claimed. Three years later, July was scheduled to begin law school in the fall when Junior brought an overnight date to the farewell-to-seniors bash in Atlantic City. "When it turned out that the girl was only fifteen years old," Grammie Willa told me, "the only defense Junior could muster was a finger pointed at his roommate." Five hundred dollars from C.F. Senior scripted the girl's testimony in court and July was given one to three years for violation of the Mann Act. Off to Rahway Prison, where he met Brother Billy, July was released in 1917 to join the American Expeditionary Force. He was fighting in Europe when his father was crushed on the dock by a huge crate of tractor parts.

"Ransom was running with the notorious Hudson Dusters when their father died," Grammie Willa contended, the athletic younger Thornton picking up a few dollars on fall weekends as a ringer for eastern seaboard college football teams. A few months later, their mother joined her husband in the hereafter, an early victim of the Spanish flu pandemic that would rage across the planet for nearly two years, and with July still overseas, Ransom left New York for Chicago. It was there that his path crossed with July, the brothers members of rival mobs. After the ill-fated assassination attempt on Papa Johnny Torrio, July blew town and the brothers did not see each other again until the summer of 1925 when the younger Thornton was thrown into the cell opposite July's in Miagrammesto Station, Nebraska. Both were on the run from Al Capone, July for his part in the attempted hit on Papa Johnny and Ransom for skimming money from the scar-faced mob boss.

"After July helped him escape, Ransom went back to Chicago for the police captain's daughter he'd gotten pregnant," Grammie Willa told me. "He figured his Tanzanian Dream winnings would be enough to square things with Capone and then pay for a new start with a wife and child," she alleged, "but it wasn't."

"Ya fuckin' mick," Al Capone snarled from a straight-backed chair at the center of Ransom's spare apartment, his jaw thrust forward, the scar along his cheek purple and angry. Paulie "The Waiter" Ricca stood nearby with swarthy Frank Nitti and Greasy Guzik, a fellow so bald and browless he resembled a turtle in a three-piece suit. Ransom was in the grip of mountainous Aldo Tonelli, struggling to regain his breath after the ex-boxer had landed a few punches to his gut. Bridget sat on the bed, her face bloodless, with little Declan in his crib a few feet away.

"Mister Capone, I don't know anything," Ransom cried. "I swear…I don't know where he is."

Capone nodded at Tonelli and the thug they called Lop-Eye grabbed Ransom and then threw him into the wall, the former bagman crumpling to the floor like a rag doll. A toy baseball bat with a Cubs logo was on the floor. Capone picked it up and began to pace about the small apartment as if caged, smacking it against his leg. When a framed photo on the mantel caught his eye, he stopped. The picture displayed a smiling Ransom with Bridget at his side and Declan in his arms. They were on the Navy Pier, the whitecaps of Lake Michigan highlighted in the water behind them. The day was sunny. Capone peered at the picture, head cocked as if one of the figures in the photo had whispered to him, telling him the whereabouts of the man he now knew was Ransom's brother.

"Nice lookin' family," he hissed.

Suddenly he flipped the framed photo into the air and then clubbed it with the bat as if hitting a fungo to the White Sox outfielders at Comiskey Park. The picture crashed into the wall, its glass shattering.

"Oh God! Oh God!" Bridget screamed.

Capone glared at her. "Shuddup!" he roared.

"Oh God, Ransom! Oh God!"

"I said 'shuddup!'"

"Oh God! Oh God!"

The mobster raised the bat to hit her but Ricca stopped him, putting a hand on his boss's shoulder, his soft Italian accent evident. "Al," he said, "not'a here."

Capone stared at Ricca, his eyes wild with rage.

"Not'a here," Ricca repeated. The little underboss eyed Bridget. "You gonna be a doll and shut up now, ain't ya, honey?" Bridget nodded, her face ashen and Ricca gently took the bat from Capone's hand. "See, Al?" he said. "She's okay, now. She ain't gonna make'a no more noise."

Capone went into the apartment's small bathroom and urinated without closing the door, afterward studying his image in the mirror above the sink, his lips moving as if carrying on a private conversation. When it was done, he smiled at his reflection, tapped the underside of his chin with his fingers, and stepped back into the main room of the flat. His face was once again pink, his breathing even.

"Okay, ya fuckin' mick," he directed at Ransom. "I'm a civilized man. And civilized fucks conduct their business wit'… whaddaya call it, Greasy?"

"Quid pro quo, Al," Greasy Guzik answered.

"Yeah. Dat's it. Quid pro quo. Dat means I give youse sumpin', you gimme sumpin' back. Dat's your quid pro quo, asshole. Got it?" Ransom nodded. "So you're gonna give up your brother and maybe I won't kill youse and yer entire fuckin' family until later, okay?"

"That's not exactly how quid pro quo works, Al," Greasy interjected.

Capone's gaze slowly shifted to Guzik, his eyes cold and detached. He pulled out a pistol and pointed it at him. "Shut da fuck up, Greasy," he snarled, the scar on his cheek as white as the finger he pressed against the trigger. Ricca saved the little accountant.

"Al," he said quietly, "a lotta people see us come in'a dis building."

Capone stared at his underboss for a few moments, then nodded, afterward tucking the pistol back into his belt. "Okay," he said, facing Ransom, "let's try it again. Where's yer brother?"

"I don't know."

Capone nodded at Tonelli and the big ex-boxer grabbed the lapel of Ransom's coat and pulled him to his feet. "Where is he?" Capone repeated. "You tell me, or swear to God, I let Lop-Eye punch yer fuckin' face out yer goddamned ear hole."

The threat elicited a smile from Tonelli—a crooked thing that made him look deranged.

"Where is he, goddamit?" Capone raged on. "I ain't askin' again!"

From his crib against the wall Declan suddenly began to

wail. The sound seemed to confuse Capone and he squinted at the little boy as Bridget rushed to pick up her son.

"What's wrong wit' yer kid?" he asked her. "He hungry or sumpin'?"

"He's scared."

"Scared? Who of…me?"

Bridget nodded.

Capone fingered the handle of his pistol for a moment, his forehead wrinkled. "I don't get it," he said. "Kids love me." He made a funny face, snorting like a pig and jumping about. Declan didn't laugh.

"What da hell's wrong wit' 'im?" the mob boss demanded, glowering at Bridget. "He some kind o' cretin?" For a moment, it seemed he might shoot both Bridget and Declan. Then, his eyes widened. "Wait a minute," he said, peering at her, "…I know youse. You're Tommy Finnigan's kid, right? I know yer old man. I done business wit' 'im."

Capone stroked his cheek thoughtfully. "She's a cop's kid," he said to Ricca. "We probably shouldn't kill 'em."

He nodded at Lop-Eye and the big thug let Ransom drop to the floor.

"Gimme my hat, Greasy," the mobster ordered. Guzik handed over a dress fedora with a wide white band. Capone donned it and then returned to the bathroom. "Tell ya what, you mick sonuvabitch," he said as he assessed his reflection in the mirror. He stepped back into the main room. "You and me's gonna have a contract. Dat means both sides gotta get sumpin'. Ask one o' my Jew lawyers, ya don't believe me."

He retrieved a pair of plush leather gloves from his coat pocket.

"And it ain't no fuckin' quid pro quo," he added, slanting a pair of lizard eyes at Guzik. "Dat okay wit' youse, Greasy? Ya wanna argue 'bout dis, too?"

Guzik cringed. It was apparent that his boss wanted to kill someone—anyone—but was confounded by a lack of expendable people.

"A-okay with me, Al," he squeaked.

Capone stretched his neck from side to side, making the bones pop. The sounds settled him and he turned back to Ransom. "Okay," he said, "Here's da deal. I want da sonuvabitches dat hit Papa Johnny and I ain't gonna stop till every goddamned one of 'em is dead…You hear me? Dead. So I give youse one week to find and deliver Mister *Jew-lie* T'ornton or Pennybaker or whatever da fuck he calls hisself."

Capone reached down and tapped Ransom on the forehead, thick lips pulled back to reveal a snarl of yellowed teeth.

"One week is all…Got it? One week. You gimme dat fucker or…cop's kid or not…I kill every goddamned one of youse."

Grammie Willa knew Maggie Westinghouse was pregnant even before Maggie did. "Even as a little girl, she preferred carrots and celery to pie and cake," Grammie Willa told me, "so when I saw her go through an ice cream sundae at the Penrod coffee shop with hardly a breath between bites, I figured she was eating for two." My great-grandmother also knew about carnies like Shu Chen who sometimes turned pregnant girls back into virgins. "Some folks convinced themselves that it was magic," Grammie Willa believed, "but there was nothing magical about it."

"You not too far 'long. I can do," Shu Chen said when Maggie sought her help. The Oracle of Delphi was seated on a trunk inside the travel trailer the Chinese woman shared with Brother Billy. The tiny contortionist studied Maggie's face for a moment, then abruptly pinched the girl's chin and tipped her head up. "I t'ink you wan' dis baby," she said, frowning. Shu Chen picked up a jar from a small table and angrily spat a stream of red betel juice into it. "Damn, Maggie Oracle," she scolded, "you t'ink dat July he say, 'Oh, pretty girl, you so knock up I not be crook no more and be farmer or banker man. I get house with pickey fence and give up all pretty girls just for Maggie nookie.'"

Shu Chen waggled a cautionary finger, issuing a laugh that

sounded more like a dry cough. "Dat July he not marry nobody, 'specially no dumb farmer girl nookie."

Maggie bristled. "I'm not a farm girl," she said. "And I don't need anyone to marry me. I can take care of myself."

Shu Chen scowled. "I t'ink dat too," she said, "long time 'go. T'ink I come 'Merica…marry banker man…live in proper house…get proper maid and cook." Shu Chen let her gaze drift to an outdated calendar tacked to the wall. It displayed a picture of a long, colorful paper dragon that formed a huge *S* on a wide street lined with people. Her scowl deepened, the late afternoon shadows deepening the lines on her face. "T'ings not be way we want, Maggie Oracle," she said. "T'ings not dat easy."

Shu Chen picked up the jar and again spat into it, her eyes lingering as if reading tea leaves. Abruptly, she slammed the jar down on the table and glared at Maggie, her finger swiveling back and forth like a metronome. "T'ings fucked! I no marry banker man. I be whore for banker man. Banker men, dey beat Shu Chen, den more men fuck me, but dey no banker men. No farmer men. Dey worse men." She sank to the floor and then wrapped her arms around her knees, rocking gently. Perhaps thirty-five years old, premature wrinkles had hardened her face, and yet Maggie could see that the wizened Chinese woman had once been beautiful. Suddenly, Shu Chen rose with the ease and grace of a ballerina, her expression softened.

"Not all men dirty fuckers," she said, adding a sly smile. "Billy save me." She chuckled, displaying a row of red-stained teeth. "Maybe I save Brother Billy, too, I t'ink." She went to Maggie and gently touched the girl's tummy, cocking her head as if talking to both mother and baby. "Who know? Maybe dat July he marry you…be good papa."

Maggie fought back tears. She'd never envisioned motherhood, dreaming, instead, of romance and travel and adventure—perhaps riches, although people like Plutarch Roberts, his serpentine wife, and the emotionally flatulent Van Cleaves had shown her how money could make a person small.

"What it gonna be, Maggie Oracle?" Shu Chen persisted.

Maggie sighed with exhaustion. The whistle of a freight train had roused her from sleep at three o'clock in the morning. She had remained awake, staring into the dark, thinking about a book July had given her to read. Anna Karenina had chosen to end her life in the face of unhappy prospects and Maggie suddenly wondered how long the pain would last if she threw herself in front of the 10:10 to Omaha.

Shu Chen suddenly snorted impatiently, waving Maggie off the trunk. She opened its lid and retrieved an undecorated clay pot from inside. "Sit," she commanded. Maggie didn't move, staring at the jar as if it were filled with poisonous snakes. "Sit," Shu Chen repeated, and once Maggie was again perched on the edge of the trunk, the little Chinese contortionist opened the canister, reached inside, and pulled out a brown root. It resembled a mummified baby squid, its tuberous body attached to long, thick tendrils. She put the root to her nose and sniffed.

"Dong quai," she said. "Baby killer."

She held it up and Maggie recoiled as if offered a dead rat.

"What it gonna be?" Shu Chen asked, twisting the root in her hands as if trying to awaken it. A knock at the door sounded before Maggie could answer.

"Shu Chen," Brother Billy yelled, "unlock the door!"

"Go 'way, Billy."

"Dammit, Shu Chen!"

Shu Chen went to the door, issuing an angry string of words in Chinese.

"C'mon, Shu Chen," Brother Billy pleaded. "Please open the door."

"You go 'way, Brother Billy," Shu Chen answered in English. "Go 'way or no more Shu Chen nookie for you. Go 'way!"

The big preacher remained silent for a few moments, and when he responded, his anger had been replaced by concern. "Are you all right in there?" he asked. "What's going on?"

"No worries," the Chinese woman answered, her voice softened. "You go 'way, now Billy. Shu Chen fine. No worries...no worries."

"Who's in there with you?"

"Maggie Oracle."

Shu Chen remained at the door for a few moments, one ear against it, then turned to face Maggie, the dreadful dong quai root still in her hand.

"Shu Chen ain't got all day. What it gonna be?"

Maggie stared at the ugly root. "I have to tell July," she said.

"Okay, you go tell. Come back later."

"Not now...tonight. I'll tell him tonight and we'll decide together."

"Okay. Tonight you tell Mister July."

"...or maybe tomorrow morning."

"Okay, you tell. Den come back tomorrow you still wan' baby gone."

"Definitely tomorrow."

"Okay."

"I'll tell him tomorrow."

"Okay."

∽

Hours later, July stood beneath a starry sky outside Brother Billy's huge chautauqua tent. The air was crisp with evening, the field adjacent to the encampment fragrant with dark, moist earth and freshly cut hay. It was the last cutting of the season, a harbinger for the approach of the autumnal equinox in a few days. Less than three weeks later a huge harvest moon would glow on the second day of October. Another full moon—a blue moon—was predicted for Halloween night.

The revival tent was dark inside, the door flaps pulled aside. Brother Billy's trucks were parked about fifteen yards away, forming a *U* around a small campfire. Billy, Shu Chen, and the rest of the Brother's troupe of hucksters were scattered around the fire, allowing July to hear snatches of conversation occasionally punctuated by a roar of laughter. July joined them, listening as they told oft-repeated stories of their travels, the group thinning out as midnight approached. Eventually, only Billy and July were left, trading swigs from a jug. Billy was in a dark mood. His friend, T.J. Goodfellow, had turned up for their chess game earlier that day with coyote eyes. Something had changed and Billy knew the big sheriff was about to go on the hunt again.

"We've milked this cow near dry, young July," Brother Billy said. "Attendance is waning, suspicion is up. It's time to move on." July didn't answer, his eyes on Shu Chen. She slept at Brother Billy's feet, covered by his coat. Billy followed his gaze, then sighed. "You're in love with Miss Maggie," he said. The ex-Roughrider took a pull from the jug, shivering slightly at the burn of the corn whiskey. "She's gonna get you killed, boy," he added.

They sat in silence for a few minutes. Then, Brother Billy brightened. "July, you should ham it up with me for a while. It would be like old times... Better than old times."

July shook his head. "I don't think so, Billy," he said.

"Bring Maggie," Brother Billy offered. "I mean it, July. Bring her along. Tell her to pack a bag and come with us. She hates this one-horse town and you can't tell me she doesn't know the score here. She knows exactly what we're doing...hell, what she's doing. I think she enjoys it as much as we do. The girl's a natural." He took another swig, again shivering slightly. "We could make this Oracle of Delphi con work someplace else," he went on. Suddenly, he grinned. "Wait a minute...I've a better idea. We'll go to Bethlehem, Pennsylvania...scrap the whole Oracle bit and trot her out as the second coming of the Virgin Mary. Think about it! The Virgin Mary suddenly reappears in Bethlehem frigging Pennsylvania! I'll guarantee you one thing, young July. That girl can pull it off. She's a natural...just a frigging natural. She needs a little encouragement, that's all. Just a little push."

July picked at the fire with an ancient walking cane. Its tip blackened, the cane had seen hundreds of campfires and once more did its job, an ember bursting to life. Just as quickly, the flame died, and with it, July suddenly felt as if he were the victim of a timeless con, as if *he* were the mark. "July loved Maggie and knew she loved him," Grammie Willa contended, "but they had been living in denial on the thinnest part of an eggshell and it was about to crack."

"Maggie might think someone worthy of fleecing," July told Billy, "but she's not cut out for grifting."

"Have you considered telling her the truth?" Billy posed. "Mind you, it's not an approach that's borne fruit for me, but it's not one I've often employed either."

July searched the darkness as if something out of place had emerged from the usual sounds of the night. Once satisfied they were alone, save the sleeping Shu Chen, he faced Billy, his eyes shadowed. "I can't tell her the truth," he said. He then told Brother Billy about Bugs Moran, Al Capone, the attempted hit on Papa Johnny Torrio, and his reunion with Ransom in the Miagrammesto Station jail. "Ransom has a girl in Chicago," July revealed to his friend. "Eventually he'll go back for her. But he skimmed Capone on some numbers money and he'll need leverage to stay alive. Something big. Something Capone wants."

July eyed Billy, his face made angular in the moonlight. "I know what you're thinking...Ransom is my brother. He won't give me up. But he will. He won't have a choice. Capone doesn't give people choices. He gets what he wants, and right now, he wants the people who went after Papa Johnny. That includes me. Ransom will go back for his girl, thinking he can charm his way out of the fix he's in. But he can't. He never could. When we were kids, it was always me doing the talking. He'll have to give me up."

Brother Billy listened in silence, and when July was finished, the big preacher picked up Shu Chen and carried her to the travel trailer. He took her inside and put her to bed, then returned and knocked July off his chair with a backhanded slap.

"You've got the mob on your ass?" he growled. "Crissakes, young July, you had no right to drag me into this. Bugs Moran! Al Capone! For crying out loud...Al fucking Capone! Do you have any idea how long his arms are? Crissakes, young July, he probably already knows you're here."

July gingerly swiveled his jaw from side to side, then reached out. Billy took his hand and helped him up. "He doesn't know," July said, retaking his seat next to the fire. He picked up the cane and once again began to poke at the embers. A few glowed orange, but none came to life.

"How the hell do you know?"

"He doesn't know."

"Fuck he doesn't. Crissakes...for crissakes, July."

Brother Billy loved the young fellow who had shown quick fists in the yard at Rahway along with a hunger to learn from an aging master who wanted to bequeath his rascal's legacy to a deserving protégé. He was willing to do almost anything to help him *Almost anything,* Billy anguished as the two friends gave up the night to the arrhythmic chirp of a cricket, snoring from one of the Brother's actors, and the rustling of insects and other small creatures skittering about at the edge of the campsite. After a while the big man's expression softened and he bent to retrieve the jug.

"What about the baby?" he asked.

July dropped the cane he'd used to stoke the fire, staring at his friend. "What...what baby?" he stammered.

"Great Scott, young July! You didn't know?" Billy exclaimed. "Maggie hasn't told you?"

July had successfully navigated the academic rigors of Yale, bloodied the noses of Rahway's most vicious inmates, faced murderous gunfire on the killing fields of Europe, and successfully bamboozled Bugs Moran despite the threat posed by a pair of cement galoshes and a swim in Lake Michigan. But until that moment, with the moon bright enough to reveal his astonishment, he had never felt utterly helpless.

"You...you're sure? She...Maggie...she told you?"

"Shu Chen told me," Brother Billy answered.

"Maggie told Shu Chen?"

"I don't know that Maggie's told anyone. Shu Chen just understands such things. She's got some sort of Chinese intuition or something. You know...inscrutable."

July stared at the ground, remembering Maggie's slightly rounded belly, her fuller breasts and more prominent nipples. Earlier that evening she'd clung to him when he tried to go, holding on like a sailor secured against the mast during a squall.

"I should have guessed," he confessed.

"Fuck sake," Billy replied.

The night was interrupted by the distant sound of a whistle as the Union Pacific freight train approached from the east. It would slow as it passed through town, with as many as a hundred cars rumbling across the tracks behind a pair of powerful locomotives. Once the caboose had rolled through the last crossing, the lead engineer would pull the cord on his whistle, offering a farewell as they picked up speed and headed west, moving faster and faster. By the next day, the train would be on the outskirts of Laramie, Wyoming, a bustling cowboy town well clear of Delphic Oracle and far outside the reach of Bugs Moran and Al Capone. The whistle sounded again and July stood, looking up into the cloudless sky. It was fat with stars and he quickly located Vulpecula, the Fox, and Andromeda, the Princess, both faint in the northern sky. He looked to the south. Bright in the firmament was the belt of Orion, the Hunter.

"Tomorrow night," he said, lowering his gaze to Brother Billy. "We leave… Do one more show and then go."

"And Maggie?" his friend asked.

July shook his head. "She stays," he said.

Around twenty-four hours later, July closed his new leather valise and engaged the polished brass buckles. Ordered from the *Montgomery Ward* catalog, the grip had arrived that morning, its frame sturdy, the leather soft and fragrant, the initials JTP embossed in gold just below the handle. July set the valise on the floor and put an ear to the door. It was past midnight and the Penrod Hotel was quiet. He went into the bathroom and retrieved the last of his money from inside the toilet's water tank. Five hundred thirteen dollars remained from his work as a Knight of Zeus and Interpreter for the Oracle of Delphi. The rest he had invested with a boy genius from Idaho who claimed he could invent a machine that would transmit moving pictures over the airwaves. "That one sounds like a scam," Brother Billy had cautioned him, but July was undeterred. "One man's crazy is another man's bold, Billy," he'd told his old friend. "Besides, I'd rather go broke betting on a rocket ship than a plug mule." He tucked the cash into a money belt, then opened a window and clambered down the fire escape to the alley.

Delphic Oracle's wide-spaced streetlamps cast haloes of light onto the ground, as he made his way to the railroad tracks on the west edge of town, thinking about Maggie. She had come to his room earlier, again asking, "When will you make an honest woman of me?" His answer was the same as always. "'Hasty marriage seldom proveth well.'" He trudged along the railbed, counting the crossties, the distance between houses lengthening as he neared the fairgrounds. Eventually, only one was left: a small home on a corner lot with light-colored siding and shutters as black as a horse's blinders. A grassy ditch with a wooden walkover separated the property from the street and a pair of leafy maple trees canopied the front yard. He stopped. He knew the family—had once shared Sunday dinner with them. The mother was hearty and red-cheeked, her husband the manager of the lumber yard. There were two daughters, pretty and demure, and two sons, scrubbed and mischievous. The family went to church every Sunday and said grace before meals. Thanksgiving was thick with noisy relatives, Christmas brought presents for all, and eggs were colored at Easter. It was a life according to *Currier & Ives*—as foreign to July Thornton of Five Points as one on the moon. He had never considered that his life could be different.

But perhaps with Maggie…

He was twenty-seven years old and had been to Yale and prison, had killed men in war, adventured on four continents, sold fool's gold stocks to wizened Wall Street investors, foisted fake prophecies on wide-eyed, backwater hayseeds, swum with sharks like Bugs Moran and Al Capone, and shared the camp-fire fellowship of Brother Billy and his band of good-hearted crooks. He had known many women and bedded his share, but was absolutely certain, that until he saw Miss Margaret Westinghouse silhouetted in the doorway of a railroad switch-house, he had loved none.

July reached the fence that bordered the fairgrounds and slipped between the rails, afterward making his way through a thick grove of aspens, and then onto the parade ground where Brother Billy's troupe had been fully encamped the night before. The big chautauqua tent was already stowed, the campfire extinguished, the truck engines rumbling.

"Ready?" Billy asked after July climbed into the cab of his truck. July nodded and Brother Billy ground the vehicle into gear, then headed for the exit gate of the fairgrounds, the rest of his crew following in four trucks. When they reached the gate July jumped out to open it and the caravan rumbled through, afterward heading south on the narrow gravel road that led to Highway 30. Halfway there, they passed a single farmstead with an impressive barn. Beside it, a high, terraced haystack loomed in the darkness like an Egyptian pyramid, a dog baying as they drove past. They reached Highway 30 and headed east toward Omaha, the road newly paved, the wheels of the truck humming. July closed his eyes and tried to sleep. Billy drove, occasionally glancing at his friend. When they entered the approach to the Missouri River Valley, the flat countryside began to turn hilly and more wooded. They were less than two miles from the small town of Wahoo, when Billy broke the silence.

"You sure about this?" he asked.

"Yes," July replied.

"You're jumping from the frying pan into the fire, boy."

"I know."

"Don't be a fool, young July," Billy pleaded. "You don't have to go back to Chicago. It's not worth the risk. We can make ten G's easy. We'll go west to San Francisco, run a stock scheme, make a bundle, and then head for New Zealand. I've always wanted to go to New Zealand. It's like America, only more gull-ible. We'll get filthy rich. C'mon now, boy. You know old Billy is right. Hell, let's turn around right now. Let's head for San Francisco."

Billy tapped on the truck's squeaky brakes and eased the ve-hicle toward the roadside.

"Keep going, Billy," July said.

"C'mon, July."

"Billy, take me to the station in Omaha or let me out here. Either way, I'm going back for my money."

Billy eased the truck to a stop on the soft shoulder of the highway and then put a hand on July's knee. "Everybody's milk spoils eventually, young July," he told him. "No need to make yours turn sour any sooner than it will on its own."

July knew his friend was right. The money he'd hidden be-neath a floorboard in his old Chicago apartment might well be gone, his effort to retrieve it merely earning a bullet. But if it were there, the ten thousand dollars stolen from Bugs Moran could secure a *Currier & Ives* future with Maggie.

"I'm going to Chicago," he said.

Billy studied July's face. He loved the boy. They had always been so alike, smarter than most and unafraid because the risks they took were calculated, the odds in their favor, the house al-ways winning. But the girl, Maggie, had changed him, spun him around until he was too dizzy to avoid betting the one thing Brother Billy Erasmus had advised him never to wager—his life. *I should just clobber him,* Billy thought. *Put him in the travel trailer with Shu Chen.* Once there, she could keep him happy on opium until they reached San Francisco.

"You're a goddamned fool, young July," he said, wrestling the truck into gear before gunning the engine and then veering back onto the highway.

July wadded his coat into a pillow and wedged it against the doorframe of the truck. Closing his eyes, he rested his head against it.

"Wake me when we reach Omaha," he said.

❧

Maggie struggled to carry her heavy bag across the town square. The night before, at his hotel room, July had been different and she'd gone home and told her mother about the baby. "Cecelia wasn't much help," Grammie Willa told me. "She was a lovely woman...porcelain features, a wonderful singing voice...but too much the victim if you ask me. Maggie was the backbone in that house."

"Will July marry you?" Mrs. Westinghouse asked her daughter.

"I don't know. He loves me. That much I know."

"That much isn't enough," her mother sighed. Nevertheless, she'd helped her daughter pack and sent her off with a prayer that July Pennybaker would turn out to be a better man than Plutarch Roberts.

It was mid-morning in early autumn. Cooler September evenings had taken August's yellow burn off the grass, but it was still warm enough to leave a thin film of perspiration on Maggie's skin as she pulled open the heavy door to the Penrod Hotel. Inside, the lobby was empty of guests, save ninety-year-old Angus Penrod, a permanent resident of the establishment he'd founded. The old man dozed in his favorite chair near the entry, while his grandson and the current proprietor, Oberon "Obie" Penrod, stood behind the front desk, his face making clear that he would have floated across the lobby to meet Maggie had unassisted flight been possible.

"Good morning, Maggie...er, Miss Westinghouse," Obie stammered. Tall and homely, the bookish fellow was a reluctant hotelier after a summa cum laude education at Princeton that was heavily weighted in the classics. "Four years of Latin and Greek... Worth about as much as spit in our little town," Grammie Willa suggested when recalling Obie Penrod's pedigree.

"You're looking for Mister Pennybaker?" Obie asked Maggie.

She let her suitcase drop to the marble floor, the sound echoing across the lobby. "Watch this for me, would you, Obie?" she said.

"Miss Westinghouse—"

"Don't call ahead. I want to surprise him."

"Miss Westinghouse, if you could give me a moment—"

Maggie headed for the wide staircase, an elegant structure that swirled upward in a graceful curve to the mezzanine. Near the foot of the stairs, the blood rushed from her face and she felt the beginnings of a swoon. Seated in a narrow settee, his huge frame nearly spilling over its upholstered arms, was Sheriff T.J. Goodfellow.

"Maggie knew right away that he'd brought bad news," Grammie Willa recalled. "T.J. occasionally had to inform someone of a death in their family, but had no experience as a purveyor of heartbreak. Such things broke his heart, too, and he didn't hide it well." Maggie's legs buckled and the sheriff leapt from his chair to break her fall, afterward helping her to the settee.

"Obie, bring us some water," he called out.

Obie Penrod had long waited for an opportunity to save Maggie from something or another and he quickly made for the coffee shop to retrieve water, then froze when his grandfather called out.

"Obie...I think I crapped my drawers!" Angus Penrod shouted.

Obie was instantly paralyzed, his panicked eyes swiveling back and forth between Maggie and Angus.

"Obie! Didja hear me?"

"Decision-making was not Obie's strong point," Grammie Willa remembered. "T.J. later told me that he thought Obie might crap his own drawers before he figured out which way to jump, so he bailed him out."

"She's okay for now, Obie," the sheriff reported as he checked Maggie's pulse. "Just a little woozy. Go ahead and take care of Angus."

Obie promptly went to his grandfather and sniffed the air, cautiously touching the crotch of the old man's trousers. "I think you're okay, Grandpa," he said. "No accident."

"Get your hands off my privates," Angus shouted. "Where's my grandson? It's freezin' in here."

Maggie watched Obie help his grandfather to a sofa and cover him with a light throw. The old man fell instantly to sleep, his face relaxed, the troubles of the world so far off it seemed he might well consider the next moment a perfect time to die. She envied him.

"July's gone, isn't he?" she said to the sheriff.

T.J. nodded. Around one o'clock in the morning he had watched from a small grove of trees outside the fairgrounds as Billy's caravan of trucks rumbled through the gate.

"He was a crook, wasn't he?" Maggie said. "Just a con man."

The sheriff didn't answer right away. He'd not shaved that morning and rubbed his cheek as if to erase the stubble, at the same time looking through the glass of a large window near the entry. It framed a giant elm in the town square across the street. A pair of squirrels cavorted in the branches of the tree, one of them suddenly leaping to the roof of the courthouse. His companion remained behind, clinging to the swaying limb.

"Yes, they were grifters," T.J. said, shifting his attention back to Maggie. "I found an old WANTED circular on Brother Billy a few days ago. I should have told you about it, but I just didn't have the heart. I'm sorry, Maggie. It was only a matter of time before something turned up on July too."

"You should have told me."

"I know. I'm sorry."

"You should have arrested both of them. Why didn't you arrest them?"

"They didn't actually break any laws," Goodfellow said. "A fella can sell snake oil in our town if he likes." He hesitated, then went on. "But if I'm being honest, I turned a blind eye mostly because people liked having them here. Hell, I liked having Brother Billy around."

The sheriff softly chuckled.

"You know, Maggie, being from Miagrammesto Station never meant much, did it? But being from a place called Delphic

Oracle was different. It was special and everyone in town felt special. It was like we were all part of a fairy tale. Like you were the princess and we were your happy subjects."

"But it was all fake," Maggie said. "It was a fraud."

The sheriff smiled. "Not all of it. When people believe in something that much there's got to be a little truth in there somewhere." He took Maggie's hand. "I liked July and I liked Billy. There's a lot of good in those two fellows. I know July broke your heart, and I'm sorry. I truly am. But, overall, I think the town's better off because of them."

Maggie scowled. "Better off? You think we're better off?"

"Think about it, Maggie," T.J. explained. "Those two boys really never took any money they weren't entitled to. Granted, it was money exchanged for a lot of hooey, but most of it belonged to folks from out of town and those people pretty much got what they wanted. They left town happy. I'm not sure how long it lasted, but I'll tell you, Maggie, the better part of being happy is letting happy in the door. July and Billy were good at that…letting happy get inside people. In my book I guess that makes the pair of them sort of legitimate."

Maggie sighed and the sheriff squeezed her hand.

"I know they cared about our little town. That was part of their charm. Men like Billy and July make people like them by liking them first. And I know July cared about you. Doggonit, he still cares about you, Maggie. I know he does. It was plain as day every time he was around you. But he and Billy knew that I would eventually find a reason to lock them up. They were a pair of foxes. I was the hound. They had to run while they had the chance."

He paused, his eyes resting on a painting across the lobby. Angus had been partial to seascapes when he opened the hotel and this one depicted a Yankee clipper, the sails on its three masts full and billowing. The ship seemed to have been cast adrift with neither a pilot manning the helm nor deckhands clinging to the rails. The sheriff put an arm around Maggie.

"It's no life…on the run," he said. "July knew that."

Obie had quietly joined them. He offered Maggie a glass of water and a clean handkerchief. She took a sip of the water and then dabbed at her eyes with the handkerchief as the gangly hotelier stood over her, shifting from one foot to the other like a fellow with a full bladder. He was a tall dandelion of a man, his head too big for his body, hair carefully combed to cover a growing bald spot, trousers hanging on his thin frame as if held in place by clothes-pins. Maggie studied him for a few moments and then suddenly straightened, angrily swiping at the tears on her cheeks. "I'm pregnant," she announced. "What do you think of that, Obie? Would you marry a girl who carries another man's child? Would anybody?"

"At the time, Obie was thirty-six years old," Grammie Willa recalled. "In those days, a fellow that age without a wife or sweetheart provoked a lot of nasty gossip and poor Obie too often felt like an apple in an archery tournament." He'd learned to ignore the rumormongers by living a good deal of his life inside his head. However, Maggie spoke of marriage—an unexpected wind that blew him so far back on his heels it seemed he might well fall over.

"Well?" Maggie demanded. "Would you?"

"I don't know," Obie stammered. "I'd want to, but…"

Maggie stood, her eyes dry. "Will you take my bag to the train station?" she said to Sheriff Goodfellow. "It's very heavy." She didn't wait for the answer, sweeping across the lobby and out the front door. The sheriff waited until she was gone, then stood.

"Yes," Obie suddenly blurted. "Yes, I'll marry her. Tell her that, Sheriff. Tell her that I don't care what anybody thinks. I'll marry her."

"Obie—" T.J. began.

"Just tell her."

The sheriff appraised the eldest heir to the Penrod fortune, wishing the town gossips could see how over the moon the poor lovesick fool was for Maggie Westinghouse.

"Tell her," Obie repeated.

The sheriff nodded. "I will," he said.

"I'm serious," Obie added.

"I know," T.J. replied.

The big sheriff retrieved Maggie's suitcase and then stepped into the bright sunlight outside the Penrod Hotel. She'd already made it as far as the Five-and-Dime on the far side of the town square, passing a pair of good-sized fellows who'd arrived on the seven a.m. train from Lincoln. They'd been sitting on a bench in the square for a couple of hours, and except for their size, the sheriff wasn't worried about them. Out-of-towners weren't unusual. The place had been filled with them since the anointing of the Oracle of Delphi, although he figured it would soon wind down now that July and Billy were gone. He welcomed it. Strangers too often evolved into trouble, and as if they'd read his mind, the two men stood and followed Maggie, one of them hauling a portmanteau heavy enough to make his gait lopsided.

T.J. hurried to catch up, and upon reaching the train station, went around the side of the building to the platform. It was deserted and he went inside where he found stationmaster Ulysses Wounded Arrow behind the ticket counter, ogling a postcard photo. In it, a naked woman luridly posed on a bearskin rug, her lips syrupy, her breasts globular. The appearance of the sheriff surprised Ulysses and he quickly flipped the postcard over, pasting on an expression that was one part innocent and nine parts mug shot.

"Have you seen Maggie?" the sheriff asked.

Ulysses, relieved that someone else was in the sheriff's crosshairs, exhaled in a rush. "Yeah," he reported. "She bought a ticket for Omaha on the 10:10. She was waiting over there last time I looked." He pointed across the lobby where three heavily lacquered wooden benches were affixed to the floor. A nearby hallway led to the restrooms. A newspaper stand was shoved against the wall beneath a picture of Calvin Coolidge, the famously taciturn president's lips pursed with puritanical disapproval. The benches were empty.

"Anyone else come in?"

"Couple o' big fellas…from Kansas City."

"Watch this," T.J. ordered, setting Maggie's suitcase on the floor.

The sheriff hurried across the lobby, unholstering his revolver. He went directly into the hallway that led to the restrooms, first searching the ladies' room. It was deserted and he cautiously approached the door of the men's room next, pressing his ear against it. He heard whispers on the other side and then the click of a heel on the tiled floor. Using the barrel of his gun he knocked on the door.

"This is the sheriff," he yelled. "Come out of there." He stepped back, gun raised. "Come on out now," he reiterated. "Come out with your hands up."

The door opened a crack.

"Come on now," Goodfellow repeated.

The opening widened and the sheriff sighed with relief.

"Maggie," he said, lowering his weapon. "What the heck is going on?"

Maggie stepped back, motioning for him to come in, and he did. Inside, a chipped urinal was mounted on the wall, its chlorine cleansing cake doing a bad job of hiding the odor of past users. The single toilet stall was missing its door. In the center of the space, the two men from the town square sat on their large portmanteau, bound with their own neckties and gagged with handkerchiefs. Their eyes were panicky and sweat poured down their faces. Beneath a high, frosted window July Pennybaker leveled a gun at the men, his eyes steady, his expression so grim the sheriff instantly understood that the erstwhile Knight of Zeus had killed men before and would not hesitate to do so again.

"My God, July, what have you done?" T.J. said. "Who are these two? Are they cops?"

July shook his head.

"Then, what are you—?"

"They aren't cops," July cut him off. "They're killers,

Sheriff...killers. I spotted them at the train station in Omaha."

"Killers? I don't understa—"

"They talked about Doctor Roberts," July elaborated. "They knew where his office was. They planned to kidnap Maggie... trade her life for mine."

"How do you—?"

"Just listen, T.J. You have to arrest them. You can have me too. I'll confess to whatever you want."

"July, I still don't understand—"

"You will. I'll explain it all. But you have to protect Maggie. Promise me, Sheriff. You have to promise me." He handed over his pistol. It was a long-barreled .22 six-shooter with a detachable chamber, the type used by Wild West show sharp-shooters—more a carnival gun than the sort favored by gang-sters.

"It was the Roaring Twenties and T.J. knew that a pair of gangsters alongside a photogenic fugitive like July Pennybaker would get unwanted attention in the newspapers," Grammie always reminded me. "He worried that we'd be portrayed as a bunch of backwater hicks stupid enough to rename our town after a side-show act." Of course, my great-grandfather wasn't the only one worried, and for a little while, a lot of pondering went on in that lavatory, most of it about magic. July and Mag-gie pondered the absence of magic if a set of prison bars were to separate them; the two bound and gagged strangers pon-dered the decidedly magical drama playing out in front of them, watching Maggie and July and the sheriff as if the trio were actors emoting on the screen of the Rialto down the street; and T.J. Goodfellow pondered unwelcome notoriety for the town versus the magic of genuine true love. It forced a decision, and after just a few moments, he made it.

"I brought your bag. It's in the lobby," Sheriff Goodfellow said to Maggie, breaking the silence just as a whistle announced the arrival of the 9:52 from Grand Island. It would stop long enough to detrain passengers and board new ones before de-parting for Omaha at 10:10. He returned the six-shooter to

July and then pointed his service revolver at the large men still perched on the portmanteau. "You two better get going," he said to July and Maggie. "You'll miss your train."

Grammie Willa told different versions of the next part: long speeches from July or the sheriff, a scuffle with the two strangers, an exchange of tearful embraces. In my favorite account, and the one most likely to be true, July stared at the six-shooter as if the Holy Grail had suddenly materialized in his hand while Maggie gave T.J. Goodfellow the sort of look a daughter gives a father on her wedding day.

"Get going," Goodfellow growled. He faced the two men on the trunk, giving July and Maggie his back. There were no goodbyes. The sheriff heard the whoosh of the restroom door as it was opened and a soft thud when it closed. A few minutes later the muffled voice of Ulysses Wounded Arrow issued a final boarding call.

As the train left the station with a hiss and the clank of its wheels engaging the tracks, Sheriff Goodfellow eyed the two bound and gagged strangers. Clearly relieved that a smelly urinal and an open toilet stall would not be the last things they witnessed before exiting the mortal coil, they seemed more curious than dangerous. "Not at all the types accustomed to shooting people or being shot at," T.J. would later tell Grammie Willa; indeed, the sheriff had never met a gangster, but close up, this pair seemed more like cattle-buyers than criminals.

"Who are you boys anyway?" he asked as he removed their gags, the distant final whistle of the 10:10 to Omaha announcing that the train had crossed the town limit. "They weren't gangsters," Grammie always chuckled. "They were dental supply salesmen in town to show Doctor Roberts the latest tools of his trade. There was no plan to kidnap Maggie. Traveling salesmen away from their wives have a predilection for propositioning beautiful women. That's all it was." Fortunately, the pair were veterans of their own scrapes with the law, and after the sheriff untied them, they were happy to be alive with a story to tell. "They accepted an apology along with a case of Ulysses

Wounded Arrow's bathtub gin as sufficient restitution for their ordeal," Grammie reported.

That night, while the two salesmen tied one on in their room at the Penrod Hotel, T.J. Goodfellow recounted what had happened in the train station rest room. He and Grammie Willa were in bed, the silver ha'penny moon outside their window providing enough light to reassure the sheriff that his little town was safe and secure.

"Would July and Maggie have gone if they'd known the truth about those men?" Grammie Willa asked her husband.

T.J. pulled his wife closer.

"I suspect so," he said. "Somebody's after July. Sooner or later the hounds would have turned up here."

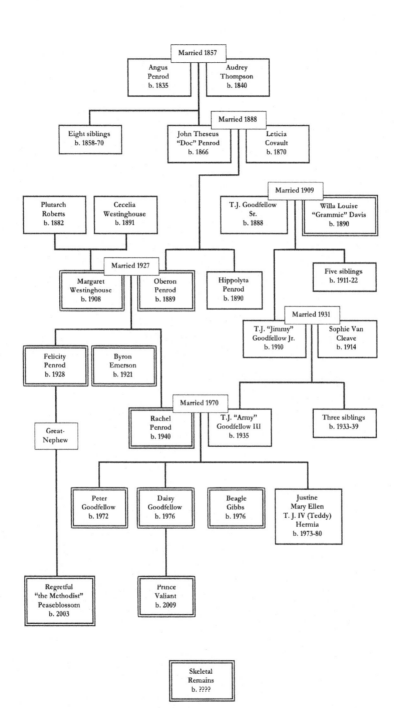

10

AUNT FELICITY

Not long after Pancake Farris hit a grand slam home run to win the final game of the season for the Cozy Lunch Dodgers, I dropped by the library to see my aunt, Felicity Penrod. She has the sort of voice that sweeps away nonsense the same way a Nebraska twister turns a barn into a pile of splintered lumber. She tries to soften things, prefacing her opinions with, "Don't get me wrong," but like the horizontal rain that precedes a tornado, there's no way a person can get wrong what follows.

"Don't get me wrong, but it was just a matter of time," I heard her tell Regretful as I climbed a short flight of steps to the main floor of the library. Regretful sat in an ancient swivel chair behind Felicity's giant desk, half-listening as the old librarian re-shelved periodicals, hurling the magazines into wall-mounted bins as if adding exclamation points to her observations. The previous night Snug Nixon's goat had gotten loose and chewed bare patches into the new putting green at the Delphic Oracle golf course.

"I told Snug how many times?" Felicity fumed. "'Fix your gate,' I said, 'or your goat will get out and cause some damage,' I said. And did he listen? Does anyone ever listen?"

Regretful's nose was in *The Kid from Tomkinsville*, a baseball fable by John Tunis. "No, Aunt Felicity," he said.

"I tried to tell him, but no one listens to a woman."

"He probably came crying to you afterward," Regretful offered, a safe response when his aunt was on a toot.

"Don't get me wrong. I'm not saying…"

෨

"Felicity Penrod was an odd duck from the beginning," my

great-grandmother always contended. She would know. A midwife, Grammie Willa delivered the baby, drying her off and then handing her over to a mother who was just a girl herself. It was 1928. "She even cried with an opinion," Grammie Willa chuckled the first time she shared Aunt Felicity's story with me. "From the very beginning that little girl wanted to make sure that nobody got her wrong."

Aunt Felicity's father, Oberon "Obie" Penrod—my grandfather on the Penrod side—knew that his daughter put people back on their heels and did his best to tone her down. "It is very important to tell the truth, but remember that people can only handle so much truth at one sitting," he advised her. At the time, Felicity was smaller than a May cornstalk with a face as perpetually serious as a Midwestern January. "If you feel the urge to be blunt, start with 'Don't get me wrong,'" Obie added. "It removes a little of the bite that follows." Little Felicity tried, but even though she resembled her father—a tall, modest fellow with long fingers, thin shoulders, an ungainly carriage, and a potato of a face—her disposition was her mother's. The former Maggie Westinghouse cared little about the attitudes of others and was unafraid to put teeth into her words. Only seventeen years old when she ran off with a grifter, July Pennybaker, Maggie had returned a year later with a scandalous history and the resolve to never again count on a man. A dark-eyed beauty with shadowy parentage and a figure that made men silly, she quickly spurned all suitors and settled on Obie. He was nineteen years older than the beguiling Miss Westinghouse and asked her to marry him on their first date.

According to Grammie Willa, Obie's parents—the austere Doc Penrod and his wife—mightily disapproved of Maggie, but harbored not so secret doubts about their son's virility and figured a wife would put the rumors to rest. "Besides," Grammie Willa recalled, "Doc was superstitious and Maggie's visions were unsettling. He was reluctant to cross her, in case she was a witch." So Obie and Maggie were married, briefly honeymooning in Kansas City before settling into the guest house at the rear of the Penrod estate. Maggie was already pregnant, and nine months to the day after the wedding, she gave birth to a girl christened Felicity Philostrata Penrod.

Felicity was only seventeen when she graduated from Delphic Oracle High in 1945. Tall, plain, and brilliant like her father, she spurned local Luther Burbank College and nearby Zenith State in favor of the University of Nebraska's large library and Lincoln's paved streets. There, she studied art, literature, and history and worked part-time in the cavernous campus library. Much of her free time was spent at the Temple building where theater and art majors discussed dangerously socialist ideas. One of them, a flop-haired young Communist from Des Moines with wire-rimmed glasses and crooked teeth, took her to the movies a few times. He held her hand when she cried during *The Best Years of Our Lives*, shared her amusement at Joan Crawford's histrionics in the maudlin *Mildred Pierce*, and, on one chilly February evening, stole a kiss outside Felicity's dormitory. While the first tingle of a boy's lips on hers was exciting, the young Bolshevik's awkward groping and grandiose babbling doomed any possibility of romance. Aunt Felicity considered him to be a trifle, a self-important and overly earnest fellow long on dogma and short on conviction. "He'll be a Republican by 1955," she predicted to her friends.

In the fall of 1946, she audited a class on nineteenth-century American poetry taught by a fragile wisp of a fellow with pale blue eyes, slender hands, and the faint, sweet scent of pipe tobacco. Byron Emerson was a first-year assistant professor whose PhD from Harvard was overshadowed by painful shyness and a pronounced stutter. Both had limited his job options after graduation, and when the University of Nebraska made clear that they were in a lather for a genuine Harvard man, he gratefully accepted a faculty position. "I have to warn you," the department chairman apologized after Byron's contract was signed. "Most of the students here consider the fragrance of manure considerably more practical than literature." Byron took the chairman's advice to heart, then gave up that same heart on the first day of the semester after Felicity Penrod spoke up from the back of his classroom, her voice forthright and unafraid. "Don't get me wrong…" she began, followed by an observation as brilliant as any he'd heard in his Harvard years. Byron was instantly smitten.

"I duh-don't see you on muh-my…muh-my," he began, his stutter confounding further attempts to form words.

"I'm Felicity Penrod," my aunt interceded. "I'm auditing the class. You won't find me on your roster."

"Wuh-well, thu-that's a guh-good start, iz-isn't it?" Byron replied.

The next week, he asked her to remain after class and they went for coffee, afterward lingering at the Student Union until dark. From then on she waited after class without being asked. A month passed. Both admitted they hated coffee and switched to tea. My aunt began to swallow her harsher opinions. Byron's nervousness eased. She baked cookies for him. He ate every one even though they were burned. She researched speech impediments. He began to stutter less. She wrote a poem about him. He wrote a short story about her. One night they supped at the Union and then walked across campus to a set of huge, freestanding Romanesque pillars near the football stadium. Known as the Columns, the site was a traditional destination for first kisses.

"I-I-I shu-shu-shouldn't have duh-done that," Byron said after their lips touched.

"You aren't grading me. It's okay," Felicity reassured him. She let the young professor pull her closer, but when he began to stroke the small of her back, she stiffened.

"Don't," she said.

Byron recoiled as if slapped, nearly falling when his heel caught on a crack in the sidewalk.

"I'm so suh-sorry—"

Felicity took his hands. "Don't get me wrong, Byron. It's okay. I want you to hold me. I just don't like people to touch my back. I'm like a wild horse. You know…skittish."

"Ski-skittish?" Byron echoed.

She smiled. "Wild horses don't like to be saddled… They're skittish."

Byron put his arms around her.

"Is thi-this okay?" he whispered.

"Perfect," she replied.

"Wuh-well that's a guh-good stuh-start," he said. "Iz-isn't it?

With an official first kiss, Felicity and Byron were now a couple. Between classes they met with friends at the Union or lunched at the Quad. On weekends they took long walks, read Shakespeare aloud to one another, cheered the football Cornhuskers on crisp Saturday afternoons, and stole demure kisses under moonlight. They joined a literary society, unraveled the allure of bourbon and soda, preferred Henry Wallace to Harry Truman, and decried Strom Thurmond. Byron began a novel. Felicity pursued a degree in library science. In the spring of 1947 he proposed. "I want to marry you, Byron, but we should wait until you have tenure," she told him. He reluctantly agreed.

Felicity received her degree with honors in May of 1949 and the young couple spent the summer tramping around Europe, returning in the fall to find the campus flooded with students, a product of the recently enacted GI Bill and a benevolent admissions policy that matriculated anyone with a warm body and a high school diploma. Byron's courses were packed, and with Felicity now in graduate school, the leisurely walks and long lunches were replaced by hurried exchanges between classes and long nights in adjoining study carrels. "It was a hectic time," Grammie Willa recalled, "one that might have caused an ordinary couple to come undone. And yet they were happy. They were in love." Indeed, Felicity Penrod and Byron Emerson were building a life together and Lincoln was now home, Delphic Oracle a memory. On a crisp and sunny October afternoon in 1949, with the campus blanketed by thousands of huge golden-yellow elm leaves, it all ended.

❧

Aunt Felicity's mother, Margaret Westinghouse Penrod, was

dead. Just forty years old, her car was struck by the southbound Burlington Northern midway between Delphic Oracle and Zenith. She and a companion were instantly killed. "The car burst into flames after it was hit," Grammie Willa told me. "There wasn't much left other than the blackened fragment of a leather valise with the initials JTP on it." According to Grammie Willa, the couple had been spotted in Zenith before the accident, sitting at a picnic table in the city park. The witness claimed that Maggie was crying. The man with her was white-haired and sported a dashing goatee. Curiously, their car was headed east when it collided with the train—back toward Delphic Oracle. "I think they decided to turn around after they reached Zenith," Grammie always surmised.

Only sixty years old but already elderly and frail, a heartbroken Obie Penrod was a wreck. "I'm not sure what comes next," he told Felicity over the phone. "Should I have a funeral?" He then handed the telephone to Felicity's nine-year-old little sister, Rachel—a surprise addition to the family in 1940.

"Are you coming home?" Rachel asked.

"Of course I am," Felicity answered.

"Will you stay?"

"I'll catch the morning Greyhound."

"But will you stay?"

"I'll see you tomorrow. If you need anything before then, go to Willa Goodfellow. She'll take care of you."

Felicity told Byron that night, the news resurrecting his stutter. "It won't be forever, darling," she whispered. They were at the Columns, their cheeks ruddy in the chill of the early evening. To the west, the university's majestic football stadium was silhouetted against a sky soft with twilight, reminding her of their tickets for the home game on Saturday: the Cornhuskers versus the Kansas Jayhawks. Neither of them fully understood the appeal football held for their raucous fellow fans in Section 129. Nevertheless, they loved the games. *Who will go with him?* she wondered.

"Muh-marry me," he pleaded.

Felicity took his face in both hands.

"I can't," she said. "You know I can't."

"Wuh-wuh-why not, Felicity? Whu-whu-why cuh-cuh-can't you? Wuh-wuh-we cuh-cuh-could live in Duh-duh-Del—"

"We've talked about this, Byron," Felicity interrupted. "You can't come with me. Lincoln was hard enough on you. You'd shrivel up and die in Delphic Oracle." She put a finger to his lips. "I'll go home... Figure out a plan for Father and Rachel and then come back. It will be weekends and holidays for a while, but eventually we'll get on with our life. It will be like I never left. I promise."

A pair of undergrads approached, the click of their footsteps echoing between the Columns and then northward to the open fields beyond. When they passed, the girl shyly smiled. The boy, a strapping young fellow wearing a school letter jacket, nodded at Byron.

"Prof," he said.

The students went to the far end of the Columns where the girl leaned against one of the huge stone pillars.

"Thu-that's Duh-Declan Thornton," Byron said, unable to disguise his bookwormish awe of the university's All-American halfback. Young Thornton and his girl began to kiss and Felicity leaned into Byron. He pulled her close, his fingers brushing her back.

"Don't," she protested softly.

"I love you," he said.

"I love you too."

Byron remained silent for a moment, his eyes moist, his face sagging. Then a soft smile replaced his doleful expression.

"Wuh-wuh-well that's a guh-good start," he said, "iz-isn't it?"

Three years later, with a hapless and prematurely senile Obie Penrod in otherwise excellent health and my aunt firmly entrenched as the only librarian at the Delphic Oracle Library, Byron Emerson was killed while serving with the newly-formed 502nd Military Intelligence Battalion in Korea. "The silly boy enlisted," Grammie Willa revealed. "He wanted be a hero like the GIs in his classroom, then got himself killed by stepping in front of a bus in Taegu. He never saw any action."

The years passed. Obie died and Rachel grew up, but Felicity Penrod remained in Delphic Oracle. She almost went to Hollywood with Rachel after a talent scout spotted her sister—by then a Husker coed and cheerleader—in a telecast of the 1962 Gotham Bowl. She also booked passage to England on the *Queen Mary* in 1965, and in 1970, purchased a one-way ticket on a Pan American flight from Omaha to Rome. She didn't go either time, instead dragging her suitcase back into the house eventually shared with Mom, Dad, me, and my siblings. More years passed. The face in the mirror grew older. And then one day Byron Emerson was a fading memory, and what had once been possible was neither future nor past.

A few days after Snug Nixon's goat tore up the putting green at the golf course, heavy rain began with the quarterly meeting of the Platte Valley Society of Librarians scheduled to convene that afternoon in nearby Zenith. It was August—far too deep into the summer for a deluge—and more than a few folks blamed Francis Wounded Arrow. Set to exchange his part-time handyman job for a full-time appointment to the county road crew, he went fishing with Beagle on the evening before his first day. It predictably turned into an entire night, and around five in the morning, permanent employment lost its allure.

"Those boys don't work in the rain," Beagle assured his fishing buddy after a rumble of thunder sounded. This encouraged Francis to perform an impromptu rain dance that magically spawned swollen clouds. However, the shower that followed was incongruously timid, and despite Beagle's promise, the road crew was on the job at seven o'clock sharp. Francis showed up about a half hour later, but only made it to nine a.m. before resigning. Rather than head home to face Justine, he ducked into the library and started an argument with Felicity Penrod.

"He was shot in the head," she growled, after Francis claimed that the skeleton discovered in the vacant lot across the street from his house belonged to a defiant Lakota Sioux medicine man the Great Father had struck with lightning. Francis thought her argument excessively cluttered with inconvenient facts and countered by asserting that his special relationship with the Great Father trumped forensic science. That was it for my aunt, who casts a doubtful eye on spiritual explanations, preferring the practicality of *The Farmer's Almanac* in the morning and the mortal comfort of a stiff bourbon and bitters in the evening.

"Don't get me wrong, Francis," she ended the dispute, "but you're an idiot."

Not long thereafter, whether meteorological or metaphysical, a significantly more ominous wave of menacing thunderheads swept in from the west and settled over the town, bellowing and hissing for an hour, before cracking open just as Felicity gathered her things for the drive to Zenith.

"Storm's a bad one, Felicity," Francis said as she shooed him out of the library and then locked the door. "River's likely to flood. Better stay off the road."

"I can't," Aunt Felicity told him. She was president of the PVSL and well knew that Cornelia Flowers from Zenith—the late Vivian Dogberry's notoriously ambitious cousin—would stage a coup should she be even a minute late.

"I'll say a prayer for you," Francis offered.

"Suit yourself," Felicity replied.

She drove to the town limit and then headed north, her little car flying along the narrow, lumpy highway. For a few miles it seemed she might outrun the bad weather, but near my sister Daisy's ranch, the storm caught her, its heavy clouds opening to release a dense curtain of rain. Soon, water swirled across the windshield of Felicity's car as she gripped the steering wheel, anxiously peering through a narrow crescent of unsteamed glass just above her dashboard. Suddenly, four horses from Daisy's ranch galloped onto the highway, their manes flaring as if ablaze.

"Look out! Look out!" Felicity shouted, stomping on the brake pedal as the ponies leapt over the hood of her car. A skim of oily water coated the asphalt and her vehicle—out of control—skated across it, describing two full circles as it crossed into the opposite lane and then shuddered to a stop on the shoulder of the highway. Daisy's horses—three fillies and a rambunctious gelding—didn't slow, racing for the nearby Platte River save a petulant roan who stopped on the far side of the road, pawing at loose stones as she eyed my aunt.

Aunt Felicity slowly eased her foot off the brake pedal. The engine had stalled, and with the storm suddenly reduced to uneven gusts of wind and the sound of scattered raindrops dimpling the roof of the car, she could almost hear her heart hammering inside her chest. *I could have been killed*, she thought, a notion that was surprisingly unnerving. My aunt has always prided herself as someone whom Death cannot frighten, and yet, she *was* frightened. She peered through the windshield. In the distance, a sign marked a railroad crossing. More than sixty-five years earlier, her mother and a companion had been killed there. The woman she remembered would not have been frightened; indeed, she would have defiantly raced at the train once a collision was inevitable, challenging the great beast to kill her if it dared.

"For crying out loud," Felicity muttered angrily. "Get ahold of yourself."

Across the road, the impertinent roan had not moved, and my aunt was about to get out of the car and retrieve her, when the horse threw back her head and whinnied, afterward trotting down a shallow embankment next to the road. Felicity glanced at her watch. Her PVSL meeting was to convene in fifteen minutes and she knew that Cornelia Flowers was already eyeing the empty chairperson's seat like a shark circling a seal. "I've got to get going," she said aloud, turning the ignition key. The car's engine purred back to life.

As she crossed the Platte River south of Zenith, my sister's horses were visible in the river shallows far below. "Daisy,"

Felicity whispered to herself. "How many times have I told you to fix that corral gate?" She let the car glide to a stop in the middle of the bridge, then climbed out and went to the balustrade, leaning over for a better look. Far below, the Platte meandered along. It wasn't much of a river, years of upstream irrigation drain-offs transforming the once great waterway into a series of channels that streamed around giant sandbars. The ponies had ventured nearly to the center, cavorting like puppies in the muddy, knee-high water.

"Don't get me wrong," Felicity grumbled as the young horses pranced across the sandbars and weaved between tangles of bleached driftwood, "but I don't have time to fetch you."

Suddenly, the clouds rose slightly and flattened. At the same time three of the horses in the riverbed stopped frolicking, watched the roan filly wade toward the far shore, and then followed her. When the last one had safely splashed onto the riverbank, Felicity went on to Zenith, arriving at the Holiday Inn Convention Center with Cornelia Flowers poised to strike the gavel in the Gardenia Meeting Room and the rain once again falling in earnest.

"I'm here," Felicity announced and the meeting proceeded nicely, although Cornelia's pouty point-of-order objections prolonged the session, making it nearly six o'clock before they adjourned.

෨

Sunset was almost three hours off, but the sky was eventide dark as Felicity neared the Platte River Bridge on the way back to Delphic Oracle. A parked police cruiser was on the approach and a solemn, square-jawed state patrolman stood at the steel balustrade, his yellow slicker and broad-brimmed hat beaded with droplets of rain. Felicity stopped and joined him, gasping when she looked over the railing. Below, the typically dribbling Platte was a raging torrent nearly a quarter-mile wide. Most of the sandbars that typically dominated the riverbed were underwater, allowing driftwood to careen downstream in the powerful current like gigantic crawfish. A small blue-and-yellow helicopter hovered about thirty feet above a narrow strip of land in the middle of the river. Huddled together on the tiny sandbar were Daisy's four young horses with a regiment of Delphic Oracle firemen across the water on the south shore, eyeing them from the gravelly riverbank.

The door of the chopper opened and my brother Teddy—wearing fire department coveralls and a football helmet—climbed out. He balanced precariously on one of the narrow skids as a second fireman—Francis Wounded Arrow—followed. Suddenly, a gust of wind buffeted the helicopter and Francis fell, arms and legs wind-milling as he tumbled through the air and smashed into the water. Teddy jumped in after him, the pair of them struggling with each other as much as the current before reaching the sandbar.

"Somebody's gonna get killed if they ain't careful," the state trooper casually observed, but Felicity never heard him, already running back to her car. Moments later she had joined the group gathered on the riverbank. I was there, along with Regretful, Daisy, and her magnificent stallion, Prince Valiant, the big horse nervously pacing about at the edge of the churning water as we watched my brother work to position a canvas sling on the underside of a chestnut filly. The sling was attached to a sturdy hawser that had been lowered from the chopper. Francis sat nearby on the sandbar, a hand gingerly supporting his rib cage.

"Don't get me wrong, but you need to stop them," my aunt said, gripping Sheriff Faron Troutfedder's arm. "That's a Robinson Raven Two helicopter. It can't lift that horse."

Troutfedder, a wiry and capable fellow with a pencil-thin moustache and long sideburns, reached for his walkie-talkie, but was too late. Teddy gave the pilot a thumbs-up and the chopper rose, its engine whining, the horse's hooves nearly grazing the sandbar as the helicopter headed toward shore. Halfway there, the aircraft began to shudder and then descend. The filly's hooves hit the water first, and when the barrel of her torso was submerged, the machine began to shake violently, forcing the pilot to release the hawser. The chopper immediately careered

skyward while the horse was swept downstream, frantically trying to keep her head above water as the sling dragged her under.

Beagle Gibbs saved the terrified filly. Dashing along the riverbank he deftly twirled a lasso above his head and cast it out,
the loop swirling through the air before neatly settling around
the horse's neck, the heels of his boots digging deep grooves in
the mud as he skidded along the riverbank. More firemen ran to
help, and together, they pulled the horse to safety.

"Don't get me wrong," Felicity observed to Sheriff Troutfedder as they watched Daisy put a leader on the rescued horse,
"but that was a stupid idea."

"Wasn't time to try much else, Felicity, gosh-darn it," Troutfedder groused, rubbing one of his long sideburns. "Water rose
too fast. We was hopin' the chopper could haul 'em off."

"We'll have to *lead* them off," Felicity said, scanning the river. "Find a place where we can ford to the center. There have
to be shoals out there." She lifted her chin to indicate a small
bluff twenty or thirty yards downstream, its summit about ten
feet above the water. The Platte dog-legged around it. "Beyond
that bend," she suggested. "It's wider there...better chance of
shallow water."

"What about a human chain?" Fire Chief Nick Dolny suggested. This was greeted by a derisive snort from Ed Dogberry
and an argument followed with the pro-human chain disciples
lining up behind Nick and the anti-chain apostates position-
ing themselves with Ed. While they carried on, Felicity joined
Prince Valiant at the edge of the water. Regretful and I went
with her, all of us studying the current.

"We'll have to lead them off," my aunt reiterated after a few
moments. She looked at us. "I'm going. Who's with me?" She
began to hike downriver without waiting for an answer, Regretful and Prince Valiant promptly following. I didn't.

"Shouldn't we let the sheriff decide?" I suggested, eyeing
the raging current while recalling Matthew 4:7, where Jesus in-
structs us to not "tempt the Lord, thy God."

Felicity turned to face me, then glanced at the rescue crew. A

horse trailer had been backed down the shallow embankment
leading to the highway. Its rear gate was open and Daisy was
inside with the filly Beagle had rescued, one hand stroking the
pony's neck to calm her. Beagle stood outside the trailer, watching them. Nick and Ed were still debating the human-chain
proposal with Sheriff Troutfedder refereeing.

"By the time they're done mansplaining why my way won't
work, Daisy's horses will have drowned," my aunt sniffed. "I'm
going. Are you coming or not?" She aimed a look at me that
evoked the only part of Deuteronomy 31:6 that matters to an
agnostic like her: "Be strong and courageous."

"Well?"

I took a deep breath and then released it.

"Peter?"

"I'm coming," I said.

The four of us—Aunt Felicity, Regretful, Prince Valiant,
and I—headed downriver toward the overhanging bluff
that marked the knee of the dogleg, the sand sucking at our
feet, the wet wind cutting through our clothes, a steepening
embankment narrowing the riverbank to a rim as we went
along. We cleared the muddy bluff and headed southeast, the
embankment slanting away to reveal eerily exposed tree roots,
the gnarled appendages reaching out like the fleshless arms of
ghouls. At the same time we ran out of shore altogether and
had to wade in ankle-to-knee deep water, warily eyeing clumps
of sticks lest one of them be a nest of deadly water moccasins.
Suddenly, Felicity stopped and held up a hand, peering at the
churning river as if reading tea leaves.

"What do you see?" I asked.

"Out there," she replied. She moved to mount Prince Valiant, but Regretful was quicker, grabbing a handful of mane and
then pulling himself onto the big stallion's back. Boy and horse
then plunged into the main body of the river, wading in chest-
deep water. About ten yards offshore they scrambled onto a
sandy shoal. From there, Regretful sat up higher on the horse,
looking upstream toward Daisy's trapped ponies.

"There's a shadow," he shouted, pointing. "Right there. It's right there."

"How wide?" Felicity yelled.

Regretful dug a knee into Prince Valiant's side, urging the golden stallion back into the water. When they reached us, he leaned down and offered her a hand.

"Wide enough," he said. "Let's go."

"Get down," Aunt Felicity replied. It was an order, not a request.

"Aw, c'mon, Auntie—"

"Down."

Regretful's face wrinkled into a pout. "I want to go," he protested.

"Down."

"But—"

"No buts. Get down."

Regretful dismounted and then linked his fingers together to make a stirrup that our aunt used to mount Prince Valiant.

"You're treating me like a child," he muttered.

"You *are* a child," Felicity responded.

"Am not! I'm almost—"

"Stop whining," Felicity snapped, ending the debate as she studied the current from atop the big horse. The rushing water was dotted with debris: cans and plastic bottles, uprooted shrubs, clumps of wild grass, branches still filled with leaves. A rolled-up sleeping bag floated past, pushed along by a small log that spun and bobbed in the water.

"Both of you head upriver," she instructed us. "Meet me back here with halters and lead ropes."

"Are you sure about this?" I asked. Before the seminary, I earned a degree in accounting and have a healthy respect for actuarial tables and risk odds. My aunt understands such data as well as I do, but she didn't answer and her silence shamed me.

"You don't have to go, Auntie," I offered, unable to hide the reluctance in my voice. "If you insist that we do it, let me go."

Felicity glanced upward. The rain had diminished to

wide-spaced droplets but the storm was ready to break open again, the wind picking up, the chill deepening as dark clouds descended.

"Don't get me wrong, Peter," my aunt said, "but I'm a better rider than you."

She tapped her heels on Prince Valiant's flanks. He waded into the river, but after negotiating no more than ten feet the stallion dipped violently, his head nearly underwater as Felicity clutched at his long mane, fighting to stay with him. For a moment or two, her legs churned freely, but then his broad back was once again beneath her, lifting her up as he reached a shoal and clambered onto it, panting noisily from the effort, the water glistening on his coat. Sitting up higher on the horse, Felicity began to scout the river from the shoal, while I grabbed a tree root and pulled myself partway up the embankment next to us, surveying the current along with her. From there, I could see the underwater shadow Regretful had spotted. It followed the bend of the river before heading upstream to the shrinking sandbar that sheltered Daisy's horses. Beyond them, the bridge was silhouetted against the gray horizon, the revolving light of the state patrolman's cruiser reflecting against its steel towers. The ponies were once again alone, the blue-and-yellow helicopter cruising shoreward with Teddy and Francis balanced on its skids.

"Get going, dammit!" Aunt Felicity shouted at me. I looked to her voice. She had stopped scouting the river and was glaring at Regretful and me. "Get going!" she repeated, angrily pointing upstream. She then grabbed a handful of mane, lightly tapped Prince Valiant's flanks with her heels, and they cautiously began to wade upriver through knee-deep water with Regretful and I matching their progress from the riverbank. They quickly cleared about half the distance to the trapped ponies, then ran out of shoal and had to swim. At the same time, the wind abruptly hastened, whipping the river into a frenzy of choppy whitecaps as Prince Valiant struggled to make progress against the powerful current, his hindquarters dipping, his head flung back and forth as he tried to keep his huge nostrils above water.

"Let's go!" I heard my aunt shout. She began to paddle with her hand, and for one giddy moment, it seemed as if her feeble contribution might be enough. Then, they began to slowly drift downstream, away from the trapped ponies, a cushion of water inexorably forming between horse and rider. Suddenly, Prince Valiant's head dipped, and with Aunt Felicity's fingers entwined in his mane, they both went under. For a few moments they were completely submerged, lost in the murky underwater darkness. Then they once again broke through the waves, both of them gasping for air, the rhythm of the big horse's body uneven, his snorting panicky and irregular. *He can't do it*, I thought. The magnificent palomino was brave and stalwart, but the river was too strong.

I have been close to the deaths of others—prayer vigils for sick parishioners, offering Last Rites, saying a funeral Mass—indeed, I was a bit close to my own demise after I shot hulking Dem McQueen through the earlobe, the crime that landed me in the Luther Burbank Correctional Facility. I feared for my life that day, running like hell until McQueen's love affair with cigarettes put him out of breath and off the chase. But with my aunt, as it had been with Grammie Willa when she died on New Year's Eve, 1990, it was different. There was no running away. The river had Aunt Felicity. She and Prince Valiant were too far away to reach, the current too powerful to fight. I glanced up. The last sky she would ever see was leaden, the last sound she would ever know was the deafening roar of the river. *This is not the death she imagined,* I anguished. *It won't be the obituary she would have written for herself.*

FROM THE BANNER PRESS:

LAST THURSDAY, AUGUST 14, 2014, FELICITY PENROD OF DELPHIC ORACLE, NEBRASKA DROWNED IN THE PLATTE RIVER. HER LAST BATTLE WITH UNKIND FATE WAS DISAPPOINTINGLY UNPOETIC—NO MYSTERIOUS COMPANION AT HER SIDE, NO CRYPTIC INITIALS

ON A CHARRED LEATHER FRAGMENT, NO CLEANSING
FIRE. HER MOTHER'S ASHES WERE SWIRLED AWAY ON
THE TAIL OF THE WIND, BUT MS. PENROD'S BLOATED
REMAINS WERE DISCOVERED DOWNSTREAM BY A DEPU-
TIZED STRANGER AND A BOY WITH A FISHING POLE.

Prince Valiant continued to struggle as if oblivious to Fate
and Aunt Felicity pulled herself forward until her lips were near
his ear. She said something, the horse tipping his head as if to
better listen. Then, she loosened her grip, and almost instantly,
the river took them both down. A moment later, my aunt unexpectedly re-emerged, face-up, coughing and sputtering. I heard
her shout, her cry not a prayer but a command.

"Get on with it!" she yelled at the sky as if furious. "Get on
with it, goddammit!"

The current now seemed to rush around her, as if she were
anchored in place. Overhead, the chopper had returned and
hovered above, the pilot's face in the rain-splattered side window, her mouth moving silently. A second hawser had been
attached to the winch and its free end wildly snapped about in
the air like a live snake held by the tail.

"What do you want?" Felicity shouted.

The chopper rolled slightly and then righted itself.

"I can't," my aunt cried out, "I can't!"

Suddenly, Regretful gripped my elbow. "Look," he cried out.
"Look, Uncle Peter!"

Across the raging water, Prince Valiant had re-emerged with
Felicity's fingers still caught in his mane. With my aunt in tow,
he began to cut steadily across the current toward an island of
sand that ran along the center of the river.

"Look, Uncle Peter," Regretful repeated, sobbing. "Look!"

And we did, both laughing and crying as the big horse managed to reach the sandbar and then scramble out of the water
with Aunt Felicity once again atop his broad back. For a few
moments, he panted with exhaustion, tremors radiating along
his great muscles, his chest heaving. Then, the wind gusted and

he reared proudly as if performing at the Fourth of July parade, droplets of water flying off his mane. It was a triumphant moment, something the people of Delphic Oracle would forever claim as legend and my modest, no-nonsense aunt would merely recall as Thursday.

The thin sandbar Prince Valiant had claimed went upriver toward the trapped ponies for nearly a third the length of a football field, then became yet another shoal, its underwater shadow curving like a bow into the dissipating sandbar that sheltered Daisy's marooned horses. Downriver, behind my aunt and Prince Valiant, a second shadow in the water marked a shoal that formed an underwater bridge to the near bank. Felicity looked up to the chopper and waved. It veered skyward and headed back toward the main rescue party. Meanwhile, Regretful and I had not moved beyond the muddy bluff and Felicity suddenly spotted us.

"For crying out loud, get going!" she shouted, motioning upstream. Then, she dug her heels into Prince Valiant's flanks and they once again ventured upriver, this time making short work of the distance to the trapped horses. Once there, the three castaways greeted them with nervous whinnies. Prince Valiant quickly steadied them, nudging each with his nose, before plunging back into the cold water. He was followed by the rambunctious roan, then the filly and the gelding—the caravan moving steadily downriver through knee-deep water.

By the time Regretful and I reached the rescue party's staging area, Felicity and Prince Valiant had cleared the dogleg and were no longer visible. We retrieved halters and lead ropes and headed back with Daisy and Beagle, re-negotiating the muddy bluff just as Felicity and the horses splashed onto the mud-sand riverbank about thirty yards downriver. We reached them a minute later and bridled the horses. Then, we headed back upstream along the riverbank with Aunt Felicity in the lead aboard Prince Valiant. The temperature had dropped even further, and near the approach to the muddy bluff, she arched her back and put a hand on her chest.

"You okay, Auntie?" I called out.

"I'm fine," she said. "Pay attention to that pony you're leading. I can take care of myself."

Minutes later, we reached the main group where Teddy helped Aunt Felicity dismount and wrapped a blanket around her shoulders. "You should sit down," he said, putting his fingers on her wrist to take her pulse. She shrugged him off, watching as Daisy pressed her forehead against Prince Valiant's handsome face, softly whispering. Aunt Felicity frowned.

"Don't get me wrong, Daisy," she scolded from a few feet away, "but you should stop gushing over that stallion and get the rest of your ponies squared away before they run off again."

My sister looked at Felicity, her face wet with tears. "Oh, Auntie," she sobbed, rushing to embrace the old librarian. Felicity put up with it for a few moments and then pulled free.

"Enough," she reproached Daisy, making clear that she didn't view saving the day as gush-worthy. "I mean it. Get those ponies in the trailer unless you want to fetch them yourself. Don't get me wrong, but I'm not going back out there if you let them wander off again."

Daisy swiped at her tears. "Okay," she said. "You're right, Auntie."

While Daisy and Beagle helped load the ponies into the horse trailer and the rest of the crew began to disperse, Felicity, Regretful, and I retreated to the riverbank, the blanket still around my aunt's shoulders. Ragged waves had eaten away most of the sandbar where the horses had been stranded, and as we watched, it became a shard, a ribbon, a sliver, and then was gone, the river at last sated. I looked at Aunt Felicity. Her eyes were closed, her face slightly upturned. When a single raindrop struck her cheek, she shuddered almost imperceptibly and I put my hand on her back.

"Don't, Byron," she whispered.

Regretful looked at me, then his aunt, brow wrinkled. "Who's Byron?" he asked.

Felicity studied his face for a moment, her eyes foggy with

memory, then shifted her gaze back to the river. "I was remembering something," she said, "from a long time ago… A storm like this one." She laughed quietly. "We must have looked ridiculous…Byron and I…frantically pedaling our bicycles back into town… Sheets of rain, the wind shrieking, soaked to the bone." She looked at Regretful.

"Byron was my fiancé," she explained. "We'd bicycled to Pioneer Park for a picnic and got caught in a storm. The park was five miles outside of Lincoln and we were freezing by the time we got back to my apartment. We made soup and then listened to *Red Skelton* on the radio… Took off all our clothes to let them dry. Byron made a joke. 'This is a good start, isn't it?' he said."

She smiled with the memory.

"That was Byron's little joke. 'Isn't it this, isn't it that.' He was always saying it."

The sky rumbled again and I glanced upward. "We'd better get going, Auntie," I said.

"I wore a woolen nightgown," Felicity went on as if she'd not heard me. "Byron wore my bathrobe. It fit him perfectly. He was a reed of a fellow. He usually went home, but stayed that night. The next day I got the phone call… Mother was dead. Killed by the train."

More thunder interrupted her story and my aunt glanced skyward where gray clouds roiled and swirled.

"We really should get going," I repeated gently. "River's still rising."

The small beachhead filled with people just minutes before was now nearly empty, the grass of the riverside trampled flat, the mud-gravel shore covered in footprints. Big Bob Peaseblossom was aboard a tractor hooked to the horse trailer and he fired up the diesel engine, then dragged the trailer up the embankment with Beagle perched on the running board. Afterward, they headed down the highway and we moved to follow.

"You know, it was just a matter of time before something like this happened," Aunt Felicity scolded my sister as we scrambled up the shallow slope that led to the highway. "You can't let those horses run wild. You have to corral them. If you don't, we'll be out here next week doing this all over again."

"I know, Auntie. I'm sorry."

"This same thing happened when Snug's goat tore up the golf course. Of course, the town will end up paying for that little debacle."

"I know. You're right. I'll be more careful from now on."

"Don't get me wrong. I just think that this sort of thing doesn't need to happen."

"That's true."

"How many times did I try to tell Snug Nixon to keep that goat penned up? And not just him. I tried to tell a lot of people, but nobody wanted to listen. Now we have to repair the putting green that billy half ate and it's going to cost a lot of money… taxpayers' money…and a *lot* of it."

We reached the road and Daisy climbed aboard Prince Valiant. A few hundred yards away the horse trailer had already pulled into her ranch. Its rear door was open and Beagle was leading one of the fillies down the ramp. Aunt Felicity pointed her chin at him.

"That Beagle Gibbs is sweet on you," she said.

Daisy glanced shyly at Regretful and me. "I know," she replied.

"He's only worth about half a damn," Aunt Felicity sniffed.

The trace of a smile played with my sister's lips. "Maybe," she said. "So far, anyway. But he got a haircut. I think he's got potential." She blushed. "To be honest," she said, her voice nearly a whisper, "I kind of like him too."

The clouds above growled another warning and Felicity glanced upward. The sky was ominous, but then the wind shifted, shoving the hazy curtain of approaching rain to the opposite side of the river, the dark clouds and sheets of rain moving rapidly as the storm veered to the northeast.

"You kind of like him too," my aunt echoed, studying my sister with soft eyes as lighter clouds chased the northbound rain, allowing muted rays of low sunlight to accent the bridge and the river and the modest hills and surrounding fields, casting them into bas-relief. "Well," she went on as the first pinks and purples of sunset began to glow in the western sky, "I guess that's a good start...isn't it?"

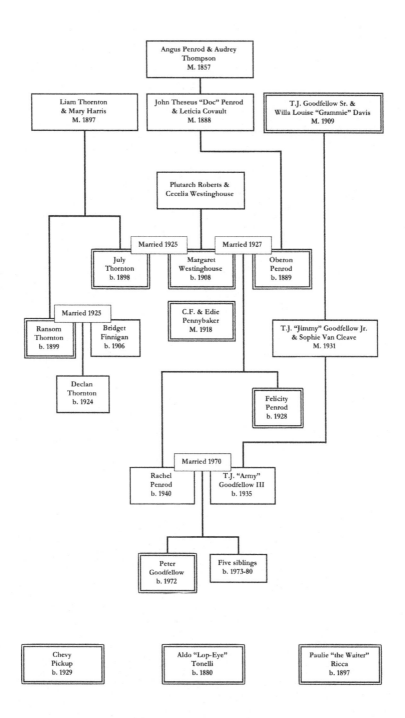

Angus Penrod & Audrey
Thompson
M. 1857

Liam Thornton
& Mary Harris
M. 1897

John Theseus "Doc" Penrod
& Leticia Covault
M. 1888

T.J. Goodfellow Sr. &
Willa Louise "Grammie" Davis
M. 1909

Plutarch Roberts &
Cecelia Westinghouse

Married 1925

Married 1927

July
Thornton
b. 1898

Margaret
Westinghouse
b. 1908

Oberon
Penrod
b. 1889

Married 1925

Ransom
Thornton
b. 1899

Bridget
Finnigan
b. 1906

C.F. & Edie
Pennybaker
M. 1918

T.J. "Jimmy" Goodfellow Jr.
& Sophie Van Cleave
M. 1931

Declan
Thornton
b. 1924

Felicity
Penrod
b. 1928

Married 1970

Rachel
Penrod
b. 1940

T.J. "Army"
Goodfellow III
b. 1935

Peter
Goodfellow
b. 1972

Five siblings
b. 1973-80

Chevy
Pickup
b. 1929

Aldo "Lop-Eye"
Tonelli
b. 1880

Paulie "the Waiter"
Ricca
b. 1897

11

Twenty-Four Step Charlie

"After T.J. turned them loose, Maggie and July got on the 10:10 and then detrained in Omaha just long enough to marry," Grammie Willa remembered. It was a hurried affair performed by a wizened and cranky justice of the peace with hair as scattered as his command of the legal prescription for matrimony. Blaming his lost spectacles as much as the impertinence of an interrupted lunch, the Douglas County official quickly dispensed with the prerequisites and jumped straight to the "Do you takes." After a ceremony lasting less than a minute he pronounced them man and wife with a hand extended: two dollars for the marriage certificate and a buck for gold rings sure to turn green with time. His wife—a gnomish woman with facial warts, lumpy legs, and a ratty black hairnet—was the sole witness. "A bargain at four bits," the magistrate assured them. The place had smelled of cats.

They left Omaha after the wedding and rumbled over the rails through a series of small Iowa towns—Red Oak, Creston, Osceola, Ottumwa. An unscheduled layover in Mount Pleasant put them six hours behind schedule. "Loose tracks up near Burlington," the conductor reassured them. Still, July was suspicious. Well aware of Capone's reach, he remained awake as Maggie dozed on a bench inside the depot. Several times he went outside to circle the station, searching the darkness beyond the reach of streetlights. It was well after midnight before their journey resumed.

During the layover July had slipped the conductor a few bills for an upper in one of the sleeper cars and the newlyweds gratefully climbed into it, made love, then fell asleep. When Maggie woke up it was still dark, the car swaying gently as it raced over the tracks. July was next to her. She could smell him—his hair and his breath and the fading scent of their lovemaking. The window curtain in their sleeping berth was drawn, but Maggie could easily imagine the countryside—dark and flat—interrupted by occasional clusters of light as the train rolled through towns too small to merit a station. She drew back the curtain. The moon outside was streaked with clouds at half-month, its ghostly light lending a gleam to the gold band around her finger.

Several hours passed. July dreamt unsettled dreams, and when the train sounded its whistle, he bolted upright.

"Over the top, boys!" he called out.

Maggie cupped his face and kissed him. Then, they made love again and when it was done she wrapped her arms and legs around him, keeping him inside until a distant voice announced the upcoming stop.

"Carthage… Next station, Carthage, Illinois," the conductor called out as he walked through their car. The long night was over, the next day upon them.

After breakfast July and Maggie sat in the club car and watched the countryside scroll past, briefly disembarking to stretch their legs at a series of whistle-stops. Twenty-seven hours after leaving Delphic Oracle, they reached their destination, the train wheezing to stop at Union Station in Chicago.

"What now?" Maggie asked.

"The future," July answered.

They prepared to disembark, but at the door of their coach, July hesitated, furtively scanning the crowded platform. Porters rushed about pushing luggage carts, one of them narrowly missing a large, noisy family surrounding a slender young man with black, wavy hair and eyes dark as cinder. Nearby, a man in uniform and a tearful woman embraced. Behind them, a pair of knickered youngsters hawked newspapers while ogling a hair-bobbed flapper showily smoking a cigarette. A number of solemn-faced men were there, neckties tightly knotted, their noses in the *Tribune*. July sighed with relief. Although a few lumbering hulks wandered the platform, their rumpled trousers and checkered wool jackets identified them as meatpackers or dockworkers, men with the massive shoulders and knotty fingers of mobsters, but none with the tell-tale bulge of a concealed weapon.

They exited the train, July firmly gripping Maggie's hand as they weaved through the crowd, his hat pulled low. Outside the station he hustled them into a cab and gave the driver an address just off Michigan Avenue. "No rush," he told the cabbie who promptly ignored him, racing through the city with one hand on the wheel and the other on his horn. Maggie clutched July's hand as the taxi darted about in the speeding traffic—narrowly missing fenders, side-swiping curbs. She was relieved when the car finally screeched to a stop in front of a forlorn boutique hotel with bricks in need of paint and a sign that hung unevenly over the door: CLARK HOTEL.

Inside, they were greeted by a tiny, hairless fellow with a sloping forehead and constantly twitching nostrils. His round eyes made him look so nearly like a rat Maggie fully expected long whiskers might suddenly sprout alongside his wriggling nose. A freestanding nameplate next to the hotel register identified him as Mr. Quill. July checked them in as the Fitzwalters from Minneapolis, requesting a room with a good view of the street. Mr. Quill then took them upstairs in an elevator that creaked and banged as it traversed each floor, eventually shuddering to a stop with the deck of the car two inches above the threadbare carpet of the third floor.

"Don't worry. This is temporary," July whispered to Maggie as Mr. Quill led them down a dimly lit corridor to a room that offered a double bed with a faded chenille cover, a chipped dresser with a crack in its mirror, and a writing desk, its chair wobbling dangerously when Maggie sat on it. July went to the window and peeked through a part in the drapes as Mr. Quill outlined the house rules. There weren't many.

"Bathroom's up the hall. It has its own lock," he finished up, placing two keys on the dresser.

"Mr. Quill was a fellow who knew suspicious behavior when

he saw it," Grammie Willa always forwarded. "He made it clear that his discretion was for sale and July bought some."

"You haven't seen us," July said, slipping a few bills into the clerk's open palm.

"Gotcha," Mr. Quill answered.

After the clerk was gone July sat on the end of the bed. Maggie remained on the wobbly chair, watching her husband. His lips were slightly parted, eyes downcast. Of July Penny-baker's many faces this was one Maggie had never seen and she suddenly longed for the raffish, fast-talking fellow who had breezed into her life just a few months earlier, full of ginger and bereft of commitment.

"July, are you sorry—?"

Before she could finish he rushed across the room and took her in his arms. "No, darling," he whispered, "that's not it."

Maggie rested her head against his chest. She wondered what her real name was. July had penned "Fitzwalter" on the ink-smudged hotel register, but she suspected it was an incarnation no more real than "Pennybaker."

"I want you to remember something," July told her, his face grim. "You must memorize it. Don't write it down...ever. Can you do that?" He gave her a name and address in New York City, then made her repeat them. "You must never write them down," he reiterated.

"I understand," Maggie answered. He released her and went to the window, once again surveilling the street below. "Now what?" Maggie asked. "What's next?"

July turned. "We sleep," he said.

When Maggie woke up, light from a streetlamp sliced through an opening in the curtains. It was evening. Her slumber had been dreamless, seemingly an instant long even though she'd obviously slept away the afternoon. Across the room July sat on the wobbly chair, his face creased with worry, the .22 revolver on the desk. He was already dressed.

"It's almost seven, Maggie," he said. "You need to get up."

She cautiously swung her legs over the edge of the bed, letting her feet dangle above the shabby carpet as if it were coated in ice.

"Get dressed," July urged. "We have to go."

Maggie frowned. "July Pennybaker, a woman needs some time to put herself together."

"Maggie—"

"Don't 'Maggie' me unless you want this to be the shortest marriage on record."

July chuckled softly, the worry lines on his forehead disappearing. "'Come, come, you wasp,'" he said, "'i' faith, you are too angry.'"

"I just woke up. Could you not throw Shakespeare at me until I've had something to eat?" Maggie pulled on a bathrobe, then gathered her toiletries and was about to pad down the hall in bare feet when July pulled her into his arms.

"Still love me?" he whispered.

Maggie did and she kissed him. "Just barely," she said, smiling.

While his new wife was in the bathroom, July retrieved coffee and day-old croissants from a deli up the street, and by eight p.m. they were off, avoiding the noisy elevator in favor of a back stairwell. July had called for a taxi, instructing the driver to meet them in the alley. He gave the cabbie an address and they lurched off, the car's tires screeching in protest as they skidded onto Michigan Avenue. An old-timer, the cabbie knew every shortcut in Chicago and soon had them on a block lined with four- and five-floor walk-ups. Tucked in among the buildings were a Greek restaurant, a tavern, a tiny market, and a tobacco shop. They stopped in front of one of the apartment buildings, a painted sign on its face identifying the place as the Dearborn Arms.

"Wait for me," July said to the driver, handing him a few coins.

Maggie began to climb out of the taxi. "I'll go with you."

"No, Maggie. Stay here. I won't be long. I promise."

"July—"

"Stay here, Maggie…please."

July kissed her, then bounded up the steps of the Dearborn Arms. There was no doorman and he slipped a key into the lock of the front door, murmuring thanks to Fat Ernie, the lazy superintendent who dependably pocketed money the building's owner provided to change the lock between tenants. He then climbed four flights of steps to the top floor and quietly made his way down the corridor, expertly avoiding spots on the carpet runner that he knew would elicit a creak from the floor beneath it. The halls were deserted, the building's residents inside their apartments, the sounds of day's end easily heard through the thin walls: radios blaring, children shouting, lids banging onto pots. And conversations…loud conversations.

"And so I said to Mr. Nicodemus, 'Those figures are correct. You can check them your own darn self if you want.' And he looks at me like—"

"It was on sale! Can you believe it? They were practically giving them away."

"Just you wait until your father gets home. Just you wait."

"This is what we're having. If you want steak and caviar I guess you'll have to head down to the Drake Brothers, and along the way, you might think about where you're gonna find twenty dollars, 'cuz you sure ain't got it unless your name changed to Marshall Field since this morning."

"A guy busts his butt all day long and oughta come home to a respectable dinner. Whaddaya call this slop? I call it garbage, that's what I call it. Never marry a bar slut, I tell ya. I shoulda known better…I shoulda."

Outside one of the numbered entries along the hallway, July stopped and then dropped to his belly to peer through the crack beneath the door. It was dark inside. He stood and put a key into the lock. The bolt slid back with a reassuring click and he slipped inside, then softly closed the door behind him. Slowly, shapes emerged from the darkness: a round, drop-leaf table with three chairs, a free-standing shelf, an armoire, a small sofa, a double bed on a circular area rug, a crib shoved against one wall. Except for the crib and the competing smells of perfume and baby powder, the small, furnished flat seemed little changed since he'd left almost a year ago.

July crossed the room and raised a shade to allow light from the street to partially illuminate the apartment, then moved to the bed and pulled it away from the wall. Kneeling in the space behind it, he slid a hand across the smooth floorboards until his fingers brushed over a joint not more than a hair wider than the others. Using his apartment key he jimmied the floorboard, then lifted it out just as a loud knock reverberated throughout the shadowy apartment. He momentarily held his breath, his fingers closing over the grip of the .22 he'd tucked into his belt before leaving the hotel. A second knock sounded followed by the familiar hiss of the apartment's temperamental radiator. July relaxed. Fat Ernie was supposed to bleed air from the pipes to prevent knocking. He never did.

In the apartment next door an argument continued, the angry voices penetrating the wall as July shoved his hand between the joists below the floorboards. The husband was mad because his dinner wasn't on the table. The wife was mad because he didn't make enough money and had called her a bar slut. With the voices growing louder July swept his arm back and forth. When a plate crashed against the wall next door he hesitated, reaching for his pistol, then resumed his search. Less than a minute later, he slumped against the wall, his face in his hands. The money he'd taken from Bugs Moran's safe was gone—the entire ten thousand dollars.

"It was a harsh comeuppance," Grammie Willa told me. "At long last, July understood how one of his marks must have felt at the exact moment the fantasy of easy riches was replaced by the reality of the sting."

The voices of the arguing couple pierced the wall, their

words increasingly more vile. *You lucky bastards*, July reflected. *You can have an argument and not care who hears it. There aren't any cops outside your door, no snitches or mob bosses.*

"You lucky, lucky bastards," he whispered aloud.

He slowly got to his feet and went to the window. In the street below, the taxi still waited. Maggie waited, too, and he sighed, the sound rushing into the room so forcefully he didn't hear the lock turn or the door to the apartment open. He was still looking out the window when a voice made him feel like a tightrope walker about to fall.

"Hello, brother," Ransom Thornton said.

Grammie Willa always claimed that the story of July and Maggie would have been different if July had been able to wrestle the .22 free of his belt at that moment. Instead, the hammer got caught on a belt loop, allowing a second or two for him to recognize his brother, even though the younger Thornton was a mess—eyes blackened, his lip swollen, a tooth missing. Although he'd nearly levitated at the sound of his brother's voice, July quickly recovered, appraising Ransom as if no more than a day, rather than a year, had elapsed since their last encounter in the Miagrammesto jail.

"What happened to you?" he asked.

"One of Capone's boys," Ransom answered. "Don't worry about it. I'm okay." He moved to the space behind the bed and peered into the opening in the floor as if looking into a freshly dug grave. "So it *was* there," he said.

July responded with a blank face.

"Oh, c'mon," Ransom scoffed. "Bugs's wad. The money you lifted from his safe."

"How did you know about that?"

"Hell, July, everybody in Chicago knew about it," Ransom replied. He sat on the bed, and after a moment, July joined him as someone in the apartment below began to play a violin. July recognized the piece as something from Mendelssohn. The violinist was skilled, the notes assured and nuanced.

"How did you get a key to this place?" July asked.

Ransom grinned, revealing a gap where an incisor had resided before Capone's unexpected visit a few days earlier. "This is my apartment now," he said. "I figured you hid the money here even though Moran's boys tore the place apart after you left. Some actress rented it before I could, but I got her tossed... bribed your super to evict her. The big idiot did it for ten bucks. I would have paid a hundred."

"Fat Ernie," July muttered. "Never met a nickel he wouldn't steal."

"I found the hiding place under the floor right away," Ransom went on. "It was empty." He gently ran his tongue across the space in his teeth, wincing. "The actress must have taken it," he said. "Thieving bitch." The brothers sat in silence for a few moments, their shoulders rounded, thoughts of lost treasure competing with the violinist. Suddenly, Ransom tipped his head thoughtfully, fashioning a puzzled expression. "Wait a minute, July," he said. "Who the hell is Fat Ernie?"

Grammie Willa always loved telling the next part of the story. "Those Thornton boys must have looked at each other like a pair of cowboys staring at an empty corral and an open gate," she recounted, describing a moment or two of the sort of silence that occurs when inescapable truth and indisputable comprehension join hands. Then, the brothers began to howl with laughter, the years peeling away as if they were back on Wall Street in their short pants and misshapen hats, blue eyes clear and hopeful, voices pure and resounding—just a pair of Irish lads dancing and singing for pennies.

"The super's a Polish fella. His name is Pavel," Ransom sputtered. "The old super...your Fat Ernie...he moved to Miami. Pavel said he got an inheritance from his uncle."

"Uncle Bugs," July countered, which caused the brothers to hoot like schoolboys until the music of the violin stopped and a muted, thickly accented protest penetrated the floor. They quieted and the violinist resumed playing, his new melody wistful. They listened for a few measures.

"Tchaikovsky," July murmured. "Souvenir d'un lieu cher."

"Tchai-whosky?"

"Tchaikovsky," July corrected his brother. "It's *Memory of a Dear Place*. Tchaikovsky wrote the music right after he left his wife. They had only been married a few weeks." He lifted his chin toward the crib against the wall. "What do I have," he asked. "Niece or nephew?"

"Nephew," Ransom said. "We named him Declan. Bridget's family is old country."

"Declan," July repeated.

"Uncle July," Ransom replied softly.

July studied his brother. This Ransom seemed settled, even stalwart, unlike the reckless little brother who'd given the nuns fits at the parish school. "How did you know I was here?" he asked.

"Capone paid me a visit last week," Ransom told him. "I figured he must have heard something…that you were on the move again. Bridget and the boy and I have been staying with her folks since then. Her dad's a cop…Finnigan…You remember him, don't you?"

July did. Tommy Finnigan was a ward captain and crooked as a cobbler's back.

"I've had the fellow in the tobacco shop on the corner watching for you," Ransom went on. "He called me."

The sound of footsteps in the outer corridor caused both brothers to stiffen. July pulled the .22 from his waistband, quietly padded over to the door, and kept an ear against it until the footsteps receded. When he turned back, the face across the room was that of the Ransom he remembered—the one caught lifting an orange from the bin at Goldman's Market or pinching a nickel from the Salvation Army bucket. The one now looking to his big brother for help.

"I have to tell you something," Ransom began.

"I know," July interrupted. "You made a deal with Capone. It's okay. I understand."

Ransom frowned. "July! Would you shut up and listen? I didn't make a deal. I didn't come here to turn you in, okay?"

He went to the window and peeked out. "We've got to get out of Chicago," he said, "and just the two of us." He faced July. "You can't bring the girl in the car. Who is that anyway? I could have sworn it was Maggie Westinghouse."

"It is," July admitted. "She's my wife… We're married, Maggie and I."

Ransom's lips parted in disbelief. Then, he nodded thoughtfully. "Of course," he said. "You and Maggie. That makes sense. She was always too much for that little town. Lots of fellows took a run at her when I lived there, but it always seemed that she was waiting for someone."

He chuckled.

"So it turned out to be you. I'm not surprised."

Ransom pulled out his wallet and extracted a picture of his wife and son. July took it. Bridget Thornton looked beleaguered and thin, Declan sturdy with a sheaf of curly hair like his father.

"Nice family," July said.

"Maggie can stay with Bridget's family tonight," Ransom said, putting the photo back in his wallet. "Tomorrow they'll help her catch a train home. We'll try to find a safe place and then maybe we can send for all of them…Bridget, Declan, Maggie."

"Safe place?" July repeated. "And where would that be?"

Ransom shrugged. "I don't know. Maybe California or Mexico… I hear Australia is nice. Maybe we could go to Australia and start over. I could be a coach or something. And you…why, you can be anything you want, July. You always could. I'll bet you could become the king of Australia."

"Australia doesn't have a king."

"President then…president of Australia."

"Maggie's pregnant," July said.

As if he'd heard the announcement, the violinist in the apartment below switched to a rhapsody by Bartók.

"Jesus Christ," Ransom whispered, his face sagging as the possibilities afforded the king of Australia and his little brother were abruptly erased.

July didn't respond, listening to the violin. Despite its dis-chords, he found the piece oddly comforting. It was a sense of calm amidst crisis that resurrected memories of those few moments of sublime relief he'd always felt just before lead-ing his men on a charge during The War To End All Wars. He'd learned early in his deployment that identical gravestones awaited the man blasted into hamburger while quivering in a trench and the one ripped to shreds as he charged the enemy. It took the teeth out of death for him, and July had subse-quently prepared for battle figuring he'd either be overlooked by demon Fate or permanently released from the mud and cold and dread. Neither outcome was his to choose. He could only choose whether or not to give a damn.

"Go to your friend in the tobacco shop," he told his brother. "Use his phone and call Capone. Tell him I'm here, waiting. Then go to your wife's family. Don't come back until Capone comes to you with the okay."

"July—"

"Don't be stupid, Ransom. There's no *we* in this. You have a wife and a son. Besides, your father-in-law is on Capone's pay-roll. Capone needs him. He won't kill anyone in his family. He'll want to, but Ricca will stop him. Ricca's an animal, too, but he never foams at the mouth. He'll convince Capone to keep you close enough to stay quiet. Hell, Al will probably hire you back. He'll enjoy having you around. You'll be a pleasant reminder of how he got his revenge… Like a trophy."

He handed the .22 to his brother. "Put this in a locker at Union Station. Leave the key with the desk clerk at the Clark Hotel. His name is Quill. Give him two dollars and he'll keep his mouth shut .for a while, anyway."

He handed his brother some money. Ransom took it, staring at the wad of bills.

"There must be a hundred dollars here, July," he sputtered.

"Pay Quill and keep the rest," July said. "Buy something for your wife…a belated wedding gift." He took his brother's hand and shook it. "Ransom, you have to make the call," he said.

"Don't worry about me. I'll be okay. I promise. Just make the call."

"July—"

"It's good to see you again, little brother," July cut him off. "I've missed you. Now make the call."

Maggie was relieved when July emerged from the Dearborn Arms with his chin up. "Slight change of plans, Mrs. Fitzwalter," he said as he slid back into the cab, leaving the door open. He gave her the rest of his money. "Go to the train station and buy two tickets for New York," he went on. "Get aboard, even if I'm not there. I may be late." He squeezed her hand and winked. "Get a Pullman cabin, doll. It'll cost five bucks more, but I'll make it worth your while."

Maggie clutched the money her new husband had given her, a distant roar in her ears. "Take me with you," she pleaded.

"You can't go with me," July answered.

"July, please—"

He put a finger to her lips and then replaced it with a kiss. "You remember the name and address I gave you?" Maggie stared at her hands. They lay in her lap, as limp and forlorn as dead birds, the gold band still on her ring finger.

"Maggie?" July pressed. "The name, the address... You remember them?" She nodded. "Don't write them down...ever." He kissed her a last time, then slipped out of the taxi and closed the door, flashing the same grin Maggie had first seen from the doorway of a railroad switch-house.

"July—" she whispered through the open window.

"Don't worry, doll," he said. "'Journey's end in lovers meeting.'"

He stepped back and the car sped off. July watched until it reached the end of the street and turned onto Grand Avenue. Then, he crossed to the stoop of his old apartment building and sat. Less than an hour later, a black limo eased to the curb in front of the Dearborn Arms and a husky man emerged from the front passenger seat. He lumbered over, one disobedient eye angled sideways no matter the aim of the fellow's gaze.

Aldo "Lop-Eye" Tonelli reached July and sat next to him on the stoop, one hand disappearing inside his coat. A moment later July felt the barrel of a gun in his ribs.

"Somebody wanna see you," Lop-Eye muttered. "I ain't sayin' who so don' ax." He poked his gun deeper into July's side. "Move," he said, gripping July's arm. They went to the car and climbed in. Two plush, opposing bench seats were in the passenger compartment of the limo, a small, dapper fellow occupying the one facing the front. Lop-Eye shoved July in next to him and then joined Frank Nitti—Capone's chief enforcer—in the seat facing the rear.

"Docks," the dapper little man said using a soft voice with an obvious Italian flavor. He wore a caramel-colored topcoat and a stiff-brimmed Homburg that struggled to stay atop his huge head. July knew him. Paulie "The Waiter" Ricca was the underboss of the Capone mob, a fellow whose murderous reputation rivaled his boss's. "Capone is a caveman," Bugs had once told July. "He'll beat you to death with a pipe wrench and then eat your liver raw. Paulie the Waiter is more civilized, but he's still a killer. He'll put one in your ear and then take his priest out for oysters. Murder don't make him no never mind."

"I heard'a you sing once," Ricca said to July as the car pulled away from the curb. "It was at'a McGovern's. You gotta good voice. You shoulda been a singer…not a soldier. Singers live'a longer."

"So I'm told," July replied. "How's *your* voice?"

Paulie the Waiter laughed. "You gotta sense o' humor. That's'a good. You're gonna need one."

"Anybody else would have soiled themselves about then, but July was a cool customer," Grammie Willa recalled when she spoke of his encounter with Paulie the Waiter. "Even with Lake Michigan and a bag of cement in his immediate future," she claimed, "he was thinking three steps ahead."

"I've a proposition if you're interested," July said to Ricca as the car headed east toward the Chicago docks.

A slow smile spread across the little gangster's face. "You

ain't exactly gotta good bargainin' position," he said. This was a remark Nitti and Lop-Eye found hilarious and they nearly choked with laughter, snorting and spraying spit, as Paulie the Waiter eyed July with the same blend of menace and approval a Shakespearean king might bestow upon his Fool.

"Ah, Mr. Ricca," July replied, producing a cigarette as if from thin air, "things are not always as they seem." It was a tidy bit of sleight-of-hand, but the wily mob boss had shark's eyes, constantly moving as if searching for errant movement, for something amiss. He took the cigarette from July and slowly ground it between his fingers, allowing the tobacco to drift to the floor.

"Sometimes t'ings exactly whatta dey seem," he said.

"Brother Billy had taught July to exploit the ego of a boaster, the faith of the devout, and the greed of the opportunist," Grammie Willa remembered. Ricca was the fourth type, a savvy fellow more likely tempted by a closed mouth than an open one, and the former Knight of Zeus kept his shut as the car turned onto a lakeside service road lined with an uneven row of graying, weather-beaten warehouses. The limo negotiated a sharp turn and then another and another, eventually curving into a reveal of the lake. A dock was there, a huge cabin cruiser moored alongside it. Ricca had spent the last part of their trip dissecting July with his eyes, and as the car eased to a stop, it seemed that silence had, indeed, proven provocative.

"Okay, singer, let's'a hear it," Ricca said as his driver cut the engine. "I know you gotta pitch'a to make, so go ahead. I needa good laugh."

"Are you sure? Maybe you've got enough money already."

"So it's about money?"

"Isn't everything?"

"Don't be a fuckin' sapientone, unless'a you wan' I have Lop-Eye kill'a you right now."

"Mi dispiace," July apologized.

Ricca was surprised. "Tu parli Italiano?" he observed.

"Un po," July replied.

Ricca nodded approvingly and July went on, this time in English. "You may have heard that I was once a magician," he began. "However, I am truly less a magician than an alchemist."

Ricca's face darkened again. "You a fuckin' Communista?" he scowled. The little underboss hated Communists, preferring the democratic principles of America, a place where a man could live like a king if he was willing to work hard at stealing everything he could get his hands on.

"Not a Communist…an alchemist," July said. He leaned closer and began to whisper so that only Ricca could hear. When he was finished the mobster laughed, the sound not unlike a wolf ripping meat from bone.

"Dis mope claim he canna turn metal into gold," he said to Nitti. He faced July again. "You canna turn a doorknob into gold? You canna turn a hubcap into gold? Dat's whatta you claim?"

July nodded solemnly. "Give me a nickel and I'll show you."

Ricca settled back into his seat, forming an expression that made it seem as if he were dangling a strand of yarn just beyond a cat's reach. "You even more full o' shit den I t'ought," he said. His lips parted as if he were whetting his appetite, and for a moment, it seemed he might order Lop-Eye to garrote July on the spot, afterward tossing his body from the vehicle as if disposing of an empty candy wrapper. Instead, the little underboss began to tap his chin with one finger, lips pursed thoughtfully.

"Okay," he said at last. "You gotta balls. I give'a you dat. Gimme a nickel, Lop-Eye."

He held out a hand while Lop-Eye dug through his pocket, the ex-prizefighter coming up with a handful of change that he dropped into his boss's open palm along with two loose keys, a book of matches, and some pocket lint. Ricca picked through the grimy coins, plucked out a nickel, and then tossed the rest at Lop-Eye. "Fuckin' cretino," he muttered. He handed the nickel to July who expertly rolled it along his knuckles, finger-to-pinkie and back.

"So here's my proposition," July said. "I turn this nickel into gold and you square things with Capone. Afterward, I can be your alchemist. I'll work for you."

Nitti suddenly spoke up. "I don't care if he can turn a dog turd into gold, Paulie," he said. "Al wants him gone. You know that."

"He can't make nuttin' into gold if he's dead, Frank," Ricca barked.

"But—"

"But nuttin'...shuddup!" Paulie the Waiter glared at Nitti long enough for the enforcer to consider putting his personal affairs in order, then looked at July. "Okay, singer," he said, "you gotta deal. You make'a dat nickel into gold, I fix'a t'ings wit' Al." He rested his hand on July's wrist, a thick-browed snarl of a man about to become the most important audience of July's life. "But dis better be legit," he said. "You do not wanna fuck wit' me, singer. You do not want'a dat."

"Any normal fellow sitting in the back seat with Paulie Ricca would have been petrified," Grammie Willa always thought, "but not July." His breathing was even and his gaze steady as he closed his fingers over the nickel and began to chant in a singsong voice.

"Betta dar es laam en thur," he intoned, "betta dar es laam en thur." He slipped off the seat and onto his knees, facing Ricca, his voice rising.

"BETTA DAR ES LAAM EN THUR...BETTA DAR ES LAAM EN THUR!"

July leaned into the mob underboss, grasping the lapels of the gangster's cashmere coat.

"BETTA DAR ES LAAM EN THUR."

July's fingers slipped off the coat and nearer Ricca's neck, prompting Lop-Eye to make a fist with one hand and pull July off his boss with the other. He was about to reposition the erstwhile alchemist's nose and cheekbones when his eyes grew suddenly as large and round as quarters.

"Jesus," he whispered, staring at July's open palm.

For a few moments, only the coarse rushes of the ex-boxer's

nasal breathing disputed the silence, as July slowly scrolled his hand in front of the three men, allowing each a closer look. The oily nickel Lop-Eye had dug from his pocket was gone. In its place, lying in the palm of July's hand, was a gold ring.

"Jesus," Lop-Eye repeated

"I'll be a sonuvabitch," Nitti muttered.

Paulie the Waiter plucked the ring from July's hand and peered through it as if the wedding band were a monocle. Then, he pocketed it.

"Back inna Napoli, gypsies useta try da shell game on me," he cooed. "Dey t'ink dey smarter den Paolo Ricca, but dey just fuckin' gypsies." He leaned forward, close enough for July to see his dappled acne scars and a spray of stubble in the cleft of his chin. He was small with a dangerous slice of a smile, tailored clothes, and breath that smelled of garlic; indeed, he might have been mistaken for the owner of a trattoria or haberdashery in Chicago's Little Italy if not for the reptilian eyes.

"Nobody fools Paulie da Waiter," the little underboss went on. He grabbed July's other arm in a vice-like grip and then pried open his hand to reveal the missing nickel. "I always spotta da pea, singer. Dat's'a my talent. No matter how fast you move'a da shells, I always spotta da pea."

He eyed Lop-Eye. "Make'a 'im go away," he said.

Lop-Eye dragged July from the car and dumped him onto the aft deck of the cabin cruiser where another army tank in an ill-fitting suit waited. Like Lop-Eye, this one had the dull eyes, lumpy nose and cauliflower ears of a former professional fighter. A heavy lug chain lay at his feet, its links clinking softly as the boat gently swayed and bobbed in the water. Next to it were a folding chair, an empty wooden tub, and a sack of cement. Lop-Eye cuffed July's hands behind his back, then shoved him onto the chair and wrapped the chain around his chest several times before securing it with a large padlock. Grinning with teeth as wide-spaced as an ogre, he held up the key for July to see, then tossed it into the frigid water lapping against the side of the boat.

Nitti and Ricca had exited the limo to watch from the dock above, and as the two army tanks moved to the helm, Paulie the Waiter touched the brim of his hat. "Bye-bye, singer," he said. He and Nitti then returned to the long car and climbed in as one of the ex-fighters revved up the throaty engine of the cabin cruiser and the other thug released the dock-ropes. By the time Ricca's car had curled through a smooth U-turn on its way back to the city, the boat had edged from its mooring, its prow pointed into the darkness as the cruiser headed for the black, open water of Lake Michigan.

෨

The cabin cruiser bobbed and lurched, anchorless in the choppy lake, with July's feet in the wooden tub on the aft deck, a slurry of unhardened cement up to his ankles.

"Too much water. We need more cement," Lop-Eye observed.

"It's freezin' out here. Let's just toss 'im in," Tony the Camel suggested. A former professional wrestler with joints that crackled from his days in the ring, Tony had piloted the boat to a spot two miles offshore before cutting the engine. "The chain's heavy enough," he added. "It'll take 'im down."

Lop-Eye scowled. "Of all the fuckin' idiots...you wanna 'splain to Mister Ricca when this mope come floatin' up in Evanston or Highlan' Park? You wanna 'splain it to Mister Capone? I don' t'ink you do. Now get me some water. I'm goin' below for more cement."

Tony the Camel exhaled noisily, his jaw thrust forward. "Let me go below. It's your turn to stay up here in the fuckin' cold."

"Paulie put me in charge," Lop-Eye growled. "I'm da boss. I'm goin' below."

Tony the Camel picked up the bucket. "Better we shoot you," he said to July.

"Quicker anyway," July replied. The erstwhile Knight of Zeus watched Tony stumble toward the rail to retrieve more water, while Lop-Eye went below.

"Even though he was in a pickle, July wasn't all that worried, because he had actually been a magician and escape artist at one time," Grammie Willa always claimed. "He wouldn't have been able to argue with a bullet to the head, but the chain and tub of cement were just another pair of stage props, Lop-Eye and Tony the Camel no more frightening than a pair of volunteers from the audience. He just needed to seed their clouds." Tonelli was the tougher nut of the two. Thus far he'd treated July like a squirrel trapped under a dog's paw, but Tony the Camel was beginning to soften. He was a big White Sox fan, and when Lop-Eye reappeared on deck from below, the Camel and July were talking baseball.

"I agree with you one hundred percent, Tony," July held forth. "Shoeless Joe Jackson could hit anybody. Why I saw Christy Mathewson, himself, try to walk him one time. Shoeless Joe simply leaned over the plate and hit a triple."

"Best goddamned player ever," Tony concurred.

"Of all time," July added.

"Quit jawin' wit' him, moron," Lop-Eye snarled, his good eye on the Camel while his other eye wandered about, quivering like an egg in a pot of boiling water.

"Aw, c'mon, Lop-Eye—"

"And don't call me Lop-Eye. I don' like bein' called Lop-Eye. Now shut da hell up!"

"You shut up!"

The pair suddenly seemed to forget July, glaring at each other as if they were back in the ring, their breath steaming the air around their heads. Suddenly, Lop-Eye threw a punch that Tony neatly ducked before throwing himself at Tonelli's knees. They went down, the pitch and sway of the boat dangerously increasing as they wrestled about for two or three minutes. Eventually, the ex-wrestler put Lop-Eye in a stranglehold that exhausted both of them, the two goons left sprawled on the deck, panting and sweaty. Tony sat up first, reaching inside his coat for a cigarette. Lop-Eye bummed one and the two men sat, smoking ironically as they tried to catch their breath.

"July knew that the secret to a successful con came from

understanding when to open the spout and let the bull-twaddle
run out," Grammie Willa asserted. "The weather and an uncooperative tub of cement had primed the pump for him. He had
only to turn on the spigot."

"Listen," July interjected, as Lop-Eye and the Camel smoked
and wheezed, "you boys deserve a warm fire, a stiff drink, and
a hot water bottle."

"No shit," Tony agreed.

"But you aren't going to get them if you don't change the
way you're mixing this cement."

"Whaddayou mean?" Lop-Eye growled.

"The cement," July answered, nodding at the slurry inside
the wooden tub. "It's too cold. It won't set at this temperature."

"Yeah? Howdayou know?"

"You've heard of the Parthenon, right?" July continued.
"Well, I helped build the Parthenon and I can tell you that
freezing weather and too much water in the cement put us
more than a year behind schedule. That's why it wasn't finished
until just before the war. You fellows knew that, right?"

The two thugs exchanged glances.

"Yeah, I t'ink I heard dat," Lop-Eye said.

"I heard dat too," the Camel lied.

"My fate is inevitable," July went on. "I've made my peace
and I'm cold. I don't want to sit here and freeze nor float around
any longer than necessary so I submit to you the well-known
scientific discovery by the esteemed Thomas Edison—to wit,
the addition of granular sodium chloride to a mixture of cement will accelerate chemical bonding when water is added,
resulting in instantaneous solidification."

Lop-Eye and Tony the Camel looked at each other with the
same expression one end of a brick wall offers to the other.

"Add salt to the cement and throw me overboard," July sum-
marized. "When the mixture hits the water it will immediately
set and take me down."

"Salt?"

"Morton's best."

Lop-Eye squinted with suspicion, then looked at Tony. "Whaddayou t'ink?" he asked.

"It's damned cold," the Camel replied. "And he says it's good enough for Thomas Edison. I guess dat's good enough for me."

"Most people aren't stupid and nearly all aren't as stupid as they look," Grammie Willa always taught me. "But there are exceptions to every rule. Lop-Eye and Tony the Camel looked as dumb as a pair of church bells without clappers and they were."

The two thugs gingerly regained their feet. Then, Lop-Eye dumped the unset slurry overboard, afterward pouring more dry cement into the tub while the Camel rummaged through the cruiser's cramped galley. He returned with a glass shaker and began to cautiously sprinkle salt into the tub. Lop-Eye grabbed the shaker.

"Idiot," he grumbled. "Dere's still a little water in da tub. You want dis should set up too soon? What da hell's wrong wit' you?" Lop-Eye then dragged the tub to the swim deck behind the stern while Tony the Camel picked up July, the chain, and the chair as if the bundle weighed no more than a doll. They set the tub and July on the swim deck behind the stern, put his feet in the powdered cement, dumped in the salt, and then shoved him into the lake.

"July figured the chair and chain would be heavy enough to take him down a few feet before the wooden tub achieved buoyancy," Grammie divulged, "which is exactly what happened." Once out of sight from Ricca's goons, he picked the lock of the handcuffs with the collar pin he'd lifted from the little underboss while chanting in the back seat of the limo, wriggled free of the chain, and then waited for the faces overhead to disappear before re-surfacing. Less than a minute after he'd gone into the water, he was back on the swim-deck of the boat, his body flattened against the rear side of the stern, safely out of sight as Lop-Eye and Tony the Camel re-manned the helm. He felt the cruiser tremble as the engine was powered up. Then, the boat lurched, leaning into a narrow arc as it turned

and headed for a marina south of the dockside warehouses
where they'd put in. Five minutes later, with the cruiser about
thirty yards from shore, July slipped back into the lake, afterward clinging to a buoy as the boat eased into its slip. Once the
cruiser's engine was silenced, he heard Lop-Eye and Tony. They
were in the middle of a new argument, this one about boxing
versus wrestling.

"You wouldn'ta lasted two minutes in da ring wit' me," Lop-
Eye boasted. "I woulda punched yer stupid face out da back o'
yer head!"

"You didn't last two minutes on da boat wit' me!" the Camel
rebutted. "I coulda strangled your fat ass if I wanted!"

The water was bitterly cold and July's muscles began to ache
as the two men secured the boat, briefly going jaw-to-jaw before
lumbering up a wooden staircase to a Cadillac roadster parked
on the access road above, their descriptions of what they might
have done to each other in their respective hey-days growing
more creative and profane with each step.

"Get going," July pleaded under his breath, and as if they'd
heard him, Lop-Eye and Tony the Camel suddenly stopped
bickering. They climbed into the car and July next heard the
throaty rumble of the Caddy's engine, followed by the hum of
the tires as the roadster pulled away. Once the car's tail-lights
had faded, July Thornton Pennybaker swam ashore and van-
ished into the night. A day later, Maggie Westinghouse Pennybaker's train wheezed into Grand Central Station in New York
City.

"When Maggie went to the Fifth Avenue address July had giv-
en her, the snooty butler took one look at her thin cloth coat
and sent her packing," Grammie Willa told me. Afterward, she
walked aimlessly around Manhattan until the baby forming in
her belly protested, provoking cramps and then blood. She collapsed in front of the Flatiron Building near Madison Square
and woke up hours later in the hospital. She was no longer
pregnant. Sitting beside the bed was a steaming Mrs. Edith Van

Buren Pennybaker, wife of July's old college roommate: C.F. "Junior" Pennybaker.

"You kept repeating my husband's name. Was C.F. the father?" Edie asked, her voice etched in acid. Formerly Rubenesque, marriage to Junior had given Edie a nervous condition that left her unfashionably thin and ghostly pale. Her husband had preferred the buxom young Edie and his dissipated interest in his wife had produced premature wrinkles in her forehead and tiny lines around her mouth, the unfortunate consequences of too many cigarettes and not enough kisses.

After Maggie explained her situation, the Manhattan socialite was positively giddy. Junior's wife well knew the story of her husband's misguided fraternity brother, a poor Irish boy from the Lower East Side who'd been unable to outrun his working-class pedigree. She gleefully enlightened Maggie.

"Thornton?" Maggie repeated when Edie mentioned July's real name. "So our husbands aren't related?"

"Oh, goodness no," Edie bubbled. "Your husband was from Five Points. An awful part of the city, that place."

"Did he have a brother?"

"I believe he did," Edie replied.

That evening, Edie told her husband about the beautiful girl, the miscarriage, and the girl's husband.

"Junior was the head of his father's company by then and had made a bundle during the war, outfitting their factories to produce military equipment," Grammie revealed. Frequently among the speechifiers who regularly greeted returning troops at New York Harbor after the Armistice, he was there on the day July's troop ship docked. "Junior spotted him walking down the gangplank with a chest-full of medals," Grammie claimed. "He was terrified that one of the reporters in attendance might dig up the story of a prominent New Yorker who had violated the Mann Act and then pinned the crime on a newly minted war hero. It encouraged him to pay July to go away and he did."

"If you ever need help, do not hesitate to ask," he lied to his

former roommate as he saw him onto a freighter at the Port
Authority a few weeks later.

"If I ever ask for help, do not hesitate to give it," July warned
him in reply.

Junior promptly buried his vow next to a proverbial mau-
soleum of unkept promises and he was substantially rattled by
the sudden appearance of July's wife seven years after he'd bade
his ex-roommate farewell. It triggered his instinct to lie about
such things. "I've never heard of him," he told Edie. "I don't
know any Thorntons and he's certainly no Pennybaker." Junior
then escaped to his club followed by a night with his mistress.
He returned home the next morning with the apocryphal tale
of a promise to an old friend and war hero. "I was embarrassed
to admit that we knew each other, Edie," Junior told his wife,
"but the truth is that we were both Zetas at Yale…brothers for
life and all that…through thick or thin, good times and bad.
We took an oath to stand by each other. And besides, July was
a war hero. The nation owed him a debt that I felt duty-bound
to pay off."

He manufactured a few tears and then went on. "After I
saw him get off the boat, I offered right away to help, but he
turned me down. July is prideful that way…so I said, 'July, I
know you've made mistakes in life, but every man deserves a
second chance.' Those were my exact words, Edie, and July
says, 'I don't need no help,' his grammar not being the best as
you can tell, but I didn't back off. 'All the same, July,' I said to
him, 'I want you to know that C.F. Pennybaker, Jr., is a man
who believes in redemption. So I'll be here to redeem you if
the need arises.' And then I gave him our address and we parted
company. That was seven years ago and I've not heard from
him since. That's the truth…the gospel truth. I know it was
impulsive, Edie, but I felt it was my Christian duty… 'But for
the grace of God, there go I,' and all."

Edie knew that her husband and the truth generally slept
in separate beds, but marriage to a liar had forced her to turn
denial into art. So, she convinced herself that Junior's promise

to July extended to the brother Zeta's wife, subsequently inviting Maggie to recuperate with them. With nowhere else to go, Maggie accepted, spending the next year in a beautiful guest room overlooking Central Park.

"Edie grew fond of Maggie," Grammie Willa told me. Junior was gone much of the time, philandering with showgirls and secretaries, and another voice was a welcome change to the ponderous silence that typically filled the spacious, high-ceilinged Pennybaker townhome. Edie bought Maggie a new wardrobe, shared her hair stylist, and dragged her new friend to high society parties and events where people were fascinated by the imperturbable young beauty with the mysterious, missing husband. When several potential suitors made their intentions clear, Edie determined to have July declared dead, engaging a private detective to prove it. Maggie agreed to meet with the gumshoe despite her skepticism. "It's no use," she told the flinty-eyed ex-cop when he probed her for clues. "If July wants to be lost, you won't find him."

A few months later, as 1926 was coming to a close, the detective was shown into the drawing room of the luxurious Pennybaker townhome. His hair was combed, his face solemn.

"I'm afraid I have bad news, ma'am," he said. He produced a weeks old clipping from the *Chicago Tribune*. A gory picture of Hymie Weiss riddled with bullets was posted above an account of the thug's murder. The article claimed that another suspect in the attempted assassination of Papa Johnny Torrio had allegedly met his end in the waters of Lake Michigan. "Your husband, I'm afraid, ma'am," the detective mumbled, his eyes downcast. "I'm sorry." Maggie thanked him for his trouble and packed a bag.

"I'll so miss you," Edie wept, before Maggie boarded the train at Grand Central Station.

"Leave your husband," Maggie replied.

"What?"

"Leave the bastard," Maggie repeated.

"Leave my husband?" Edie gasped. "I can't leave my

husband. What would I do? Who would take care of me?"
Maggie frowned. Despite her advantages, Edie Van Buren Pennybaker was as small and defenseless as a bird under a cat's paw,
her words issued in a ninny's voice that reminded Maggie of her
own mother—a fading southern belle still yearning for a life of
needlepoint and card parties.

"Do what you want. Take care of yourself," Maggie replied.

The notion of a life unbuttressed by matrimony nearly sent
Edie into a swoon, her face turning ashen, her balance uneven.
The headier notion of her husband's net worth helped her recover. "Oh, that's just your loneliness speaking," she argued.
"It's terrible to be alone. I could never do it, but I understand
why you might think it better. Dear, sweet Maggie, sometimes
people must convince themselves that it's best to be alone or
they couldn't carry on. But you don't have to be alone. You're
so beautiful. You can have any man you want."

Edie's face darkened.

"It wouldn't be so easy for me," she added.

For a moment it seemed the New York matron might cry.
Her eyes welled with tears, her lower lip quivering. Then she
smiled, a gaping, toothy thing that made her seem frantic. "I
just know you'll find someone," she said. "Someone who will
take care of you too."

"I can take care of myself," Maggie said.

And she did. Maggie returned to Delphic Oracle, and within
weeks, had married Obie Penrod, the rapid courtship and improbable wedding flushing out the usual covey of busybodies,
led by Violet Roberts. "I was at Christmas Tree Lane a year
later in 1927 when Violet tried to take a bite out of Maggie,"
Grammie Willa once told me. "Violet's dirtiest mudballs were
typically thrown at someone's back, but she'd come over to the
church that day after hitting the eggnog pretty hard and was
ready to go toe to toe for once."

"Whatever happened to that Pennybaker fellow?" Violet
asked Maggie, smirking for the benefit of the gaggle of hens
who had gathered to watch her take down a woman who made

them all feel plain. Maggie was unperturbed. She looked her father's wife up and down.

"That's an interesting dress, Mrs. Roberts," she said. "I once saw some curtains in New York City with the same pattern. That was last year, of course."

"Then Maggie threw up," Grammie Willa reported. "That's how I knew she was pregnant."

Grammie Willa bundled Maggie off to Doc Penrod's clinic where the impending birth was confirmed and in July of 1928—seven months later—little Felicity Penrod came into the world with a full head of hair and more than a few opinions.

Maggie was inexplicably gripped by melancholy after the baby was born. She handed her infant daughter to a wet-nurse and saw her only sporadically for the next three months. "I'm worried she might do something to herself," Obie told Grammie Willa. My great-grandmother reassured him that Maggie's affliction would pass. "Lots of women get the blues after a baby," Grammie Willa told him. "They need a few weeks to tame their hormones again."

Obie hired a private duty nurse to take care of Felicity and watch over Maggie during the day. Nights, he slept in a chair outside his wife's bedroom. One morning, Maggie awoke, fixed her hair, applied makeup, and then called out to her husband. When Obie entered the room he found Maggie cradling Felicity in her arms, vowing to imbue the young lady with independence and more than a dollop of suspicion, lest a fast-talker with a handsome face wander into town from the railroad tracks, spewing a line of bull while putting his hand up her dress.

"The remainder of that summer passed uneventfully," Grammie Willa recalled, and as 1928 eased toward the new year, farm prices went down a little while stock values went up by slightly more than a bit. September enjoyed balmy weather and October hosted the event of the season when Johann Van Cleave married Leticia Irby. By Thanksgiving, July Pennybaker had been missing for more than three years, the townsfolks' memories of him replaced by conversations about the weather or the latest picture at the Rialto. Maggie seemed to be all right, quieting Violet Roberts and the rest of the tonguewaggers. Months would elapse before people in town once again had something truly interesting to talk about.

ૐ

In late June of 1929, July was picked up by a trucker just outside St. Joseph, Missouri. The teamster's name was Lou and he was a curious fellow. Hoping for a good story, he immediately learned that both he and his hitchhiker had served in The War To End All Wars with the Big Red One—July with the legendary 16th Infantry, the driver a member of the 1st Engineers. Otherwise, Lou discovered that his passenger was as tough to open up as a Chinese cricket box, and despite bombarding July with questions, the big truck driver hadn't made much progress as they neared Omaha with dawn a couple of hours off.

"You from Omaha?" Lou asked. "You still ain't told me much about yourself."

"Not much to tell," July replied, even though there was. After slipping out of Chicago he'd given up grifting, instead wandering the country, mostly in the Great Southwest. "He liked New Mexico in particular," Grammie Willa disclosed. "It was a place close enough to its outlaw days not to question rough-looking types with hazy backstories, particularly if they were willing to take on any work for a meal and four bits."

"Not much to tell?" Lou echoed, chuckling. "C'mon, everybody's got a story to tell."

July now had a long beard. It was dense and scraggly, and with his shoulder-length, prematurely graying hair, callus-thickened hands, and affected stoop, he was unrecognizable as the glib fellow who had convinced the citizens of Miagrammesto Station, Nebraska, that an authentic oracle lived among them. He pulled at his beard, wondering if he would ever again appear barefaced in public, wearing a good suit with a flower in the lapel. Even though four years had passed since his disappearance, he still feared the long arms of Al Capone, Paulie Ricca, and Bugs Moran, knowing that Maggie and their child, Ransom and his family, and Brother Billy were safe only as long as the Chicago mobsters believed July Thornton Pennybaker sat in a chair on the muddy bottom of Lake Michigan.

"What happened to you, anyway?" Lou asked. "Seems like you been knocked around a bit."

"'True is it that I have seen better days,'" July recited, "'and have with holy bell been knoll'd to church and sat at good men's feasts.'"

"What?"

"Just something I remember from college."

"College boy, huh?" Lou replied, chuckling. "I didn't get past eighth grade. Tell ya the truth, I didn't see much use to school after that. Figured a fella who plans to be a workin' man oughta get workin' as soon as possible. I ain't got no regrets. I can add and subtract and read the box scores in the paper. I got enough schoolin' for that. You were a college boy, huh?"

"For a time."

"Where at? You go to the university in Lincoln?"

"No."

"I knew some guys went there. One of 'em is a banker or insurance guy or somethin'. The others dropped out. You finish?"

"In a manner of speaking."

"Yeah, the banker fella, he finished. The rest, like I said, they dropped out. Where'd you say you went?"

"Yale."

"That a good college, that Yale?"

"It's pretty good."

The distinct aroma of manure wafted into the truck as a few buildings emerged in silhouette from the shadows alongside the highway. There was another smell too: blood. They were on the edge of Omaha, downwind from the stockyards and close to the packing plants and slaughterhouses on the city's bustling south side. Soon, buildings began to appear with greater frequency, the city concentrating and forming as they drove along, the unpleasant fragrance of the stockyards growing more pungent.

"Smells like money, don't it?" Lou quipped as he negotiated his big Atterbury through a slight bend in the road. Once they had cleared the curve, a solitary streetlamp appeared in the distance. Just beyond it was a railroad crossing.

"Up there," July said. "That'll be good."

The big trucker didn't answer, his face suddenly so grim July caught his breath. Lou didn't look like one of the apes Scarface and Bugs preferred for their entourages, but he was a large, stout fellow who could probably do a lot of damage to a half-starved grifter more than ten years removed from his soldiering days. July eased one hand onto the door handle, then relaxed when light from the streetlamp flooded the cab. Lou's face was rumpled and in need of a shave, his hands nicked by a thousand crates, his clothes those of the working man he claimed to be.

The genial trucker braked his rig to a stop on the side of the road and July climbed out.

"Hey," the big man said before July closed the door. "No mission too difficult."

July leaned into the cab to shake Lou's hand. "No sacrifice too great," he responded.

"Duty first," the men said together, invoking the motto of the Big Red One.

With July on the road's shoulder, Lou steered his Atterbury back onto the highway, offering a final wave as he drove away. July watched until he could no longer see tail-lights, then hiked to the railbed and stepped between the tracks, heading west. He walked until long past sunrise, eventually finding himself surrounded by cornfields. It was nine a.m. by then, the cool of the night worn off, and he sat on one of the tracks to eat a sandwich Lou had given him before they parted. He was about to resume his hike when a distant whistle sounded. Still seated on the track-rail, he rolled onto his belly and put his ear against it. The buzz on his cheek suggested a lengthy train.

July sprang to his feet and ventured into a nearby field where he uprooted a dozen cornstalks and piled them onto the tracks. The whistle sounded again, closer, and he slipped back into the cornfield to hide among the tasseled stalks. A minute or so later the flat face of the lead locomotive emerged from the eastern horizon, a plume of oily smoke billowing from its stack. The big engine spanned the remaining distance quickly and when the engineer saw the pile of cornstalks he sounded his whistle, slowing the train for a few seconds, before plowing through the obstruction. It was merely a hiccup on his day's journey, but enough delay for July to dart from the cornfield, wrap his fingers around the ladder of a car near the end of the train, and then hoist himself aboard.

It was a passenger train, and as he climbed onto the roof of the carriage, July knew he'd have to ride atop it, balancing precariously while choking on exhaust from the diesel engine. But he didn't mind. This train—a spur of the Union Pacific line—was the one he'd wanted. It would take him all the way to Delphic Oracle.

Eighty-five years, nearly to the day, that my little brother, Teddy, ran away from home for the last time, Ulysses Wounded Arrow was headed for his outhouse when he saw a stranger trudging down the railbed that ran behind his home. "He's five feet-four inches tall and a hunchback," Ulysses told his wife, who then reported to a neighbor that the man was rotund with one hand replaced by a hook. Still others described the mysterious hobo as a giant who was seven feet tall, weighed at least 300 pounds, and had sharp, blood-stained teeth. All agreed that the man was heavily bearded with hair cascading to his shoulders in waves. After Lettie Penrod—Doc's wife—caught the fellow pawing through their trash, she gave the scrounger a hard-boiled egg and a tumbler of lemonade. "I suspect he's more than six feet tall," Mrs. Penrod told Sheriff T.J. Goodfellow, "but he's kind of stooped over. It makes him look shorter. Also, I think he might be deaf and dumb." After a brief search, the sheriff discovered the fellow asleep in the railroad switch-house near the fairgrounds.

"Hey there, wake up," T.J. called out from the doorway.
July didn't move.

"You there…rail-hopper! Get up! C'mon now, move it!"

In the past year the sheriff had increasingly found the switch-house occupied. One of the squatters had recently lunged at him with a dull knife, prompting T.J. to keep a hand on the leather sap that hung from his service belt as he cautiously pushed on July's shoulder with his toe. The former Knight of Zeus sat up, hands shielding his face.

"All right now, get up!" the sheriff demanded.

T.J. Goodfellow was little changed, July thought—perhaps a little thicker in the waist but with the same iron jaw and hunter's eyes. *A bloodhound*, July mused, hoping his gray-streaked hair, long beard, and angular, weathered aspect would be enough to defer suspicion. He put his hands over his mouth and then his ears.

"I understand," T.J. said, recalling Lettie Penrod's hunch that the raggedy fellow couldn't hear or speak, "but you still can't bunk in here. Get up now."

With a finger, July began to draw in the thick dust of the switch-house floor.

"C'mon now, son," T.J. said. "You really can't stay here. I mean it. Let's go."

July continued to draw, forming letters. He finished and looked at the sheriff, head atilt like a dog awaiting a treat

"Charlie?" the sheriff said, reading the name July had scrawled in the dirt. "That's your name…Charlie?"

July squinted as if reading lips, then nodded.

Goodfellow pulled off his hat and used a handkerchief to wipe sweat from the band. "What am I gonna do with you now?" he muttered.

"The best T.J. could offer was a cell in the Delphic Oracle jail," Grammie Willa told me. Of course, my tender-hearted great-grandfather first took the wild-haired stranger home where July sat at the big table in the Goodfellow dining room and feasted on chicken-fried steak, mashed potatoes and gravy,

and garden-fresh string beans. Before dinner little Grey—now
almost seven years old—dragged July into his parents' bedroom and made him stand next to the painting of Jesus that
hung over the bed, giggling at the resemblance. After the meal,
Sheriff Goodfellow delivered his guest to the jail. "It's for your
own good, Charlie," he told him. "Just until I can figure out
where your people are." July waited until Goodfellow was gone
and the night deputy out on rounds, then picked the cell door
lock with his pocketknife and explored the outer office. Inside
the sheriff's desk he found a stack of WANTED circulars, his own
picture on one of them. He tore it into pieces and flushed it
down the toilet in his cell, afterward collapsing onto his bunk.

For a few hours, July tossed and turned on the thin mattress,
haunted by a persistent dream. In it, Maggie was framed in the
doorway of a railway switch-house. Each time she reached out
to take his hand, he was suddenly transported back to Lake
Michigan—struggling to escape chains that squeezed tighter and tighter as he plunged through the icy depths. Around
four in the morning, he gave up on sleep and rose to look out
the cell's only window, his fingers curled around the bars. The
Penrod Hotel stood across the street, its lobby lights lending a
warm glow to the night.

Sheriff Goodfellow delivered breakfast around eight a.m.,
studying his prisoner as the strange vagrant ate. Afterward, the
big lawman sat at his desk for nearly an hour, perusing the same
circulars July had reviewed the night before. When it was time
to make his rounds the sheriff approached the cell and looked
through the bars. "Who are you, Charlie?" he asked.

After T.J. left, July once again went to the window, painfully
aware that an egg he'd hatched in New Mexico now found itself in Delphic Oracle without a chicken. He looked out. The
day was overcast and cool—more like one in late October than
mid-summer. Low clouds hung in the sky, although the threat
of rain had not discouraged Angus Penrod. The old man sat
alone on a bench in front of the hotel across the street, intently
surveilling every passing car, every bird and squirrel in the trees

surrounding the courthouse across the street, every pedestrian passing by on the sidewalk. After nearly thirty minutes, Obie Penrod emerged from the hotel. He helped his grandfather stand and then took him inside. A minute later, the gangly hotelier re-appeared. He walked to the edge of the street, checked his pocket watch, and then went back to the bench and sat, hands on his bony knees. A few minutes later a late-model automobile slanted into a parking space in front of the hotel. The driver of the car stepped out and July caught his breath.

Maggie.

The former Oracle of Delphi had changed. No longer girlish, she was fully a woman and more beautiful than ever. The thin cotton frock worn by the girl in the switch-house doorway four years earlier had been replaced by a fashionable dropped-waist dress with a pleated skirt. Her once long hair was now jazzily cropped and peeked out from beneath a felt cloche hat. Maggie leaned back into the car, and when she re-emerged, July's heart nearly stopped beating. She held an infant in her arms.

Ours? No...our child would be more than three years old now.

Maggie handed the infant to Obie and they moved toward the hotel. Just before entering she turned, her eyes settling on the face in the window of the Miagrammesto County jail across the street. A moment later she was nearly knocked down by a large man on his way out of the hotel. The fellow was broad-shouldered, his nose lumpy and crooked, his charcoal fedora sporting a wide, white ribbon. One eye wandered about, independent of the other. July quickly dropped below the window sill and slumped onto his bunk, the blood draining from his face, his entire body turning hollow and desperate.

"Lop-Eye," he murmured. "Fucking Lop-Eye."

The former con man had once considered himself lucky, but after four years of hard times on the road, had learned that his life before Maggie had merely been filled with coincidence disguised as good fortune. And coincidence, he knew, was inescapably statistical. The fellow who won on a long shot lost it all on the next race, the investor profiting from a short sale was hornswoggled on the bad end of a land deal, a man who wriggled free of the chain dragging him to the bottom of an icy lake suddenly found himself staring into the cold, dull eyes of Aldo "Lop-Eye" Tonelli.

July looked between the bars of the cell door. On the sheriff's desk, stacks of paper competed for space with a coffee mug, baskets overflowing with correspondence, a jar of pencils, a baseball, and the tray with his breakfast dishes. The items were as jumbled and disorganized as his thoughts.

Calm down, he told himself. *Think. You need to think.*

But he couldn't.

"July was as close to stumped as he would ever be," Grammie opined. "He'd spent four years underground only to resurface with the hound still baying at the fox's den. It temporarily deprived him of ideas, an unusual state of affairs for a conniver of July's proficiency."

I could confess, he thought. *T.J. helped me once before. He might do it again.*

He reached under the bunk for his rucksack and then slipped a hand inside, curling his fingers around the handle of the .22 caliber six-gun Ransom had left in the Union Station locker. The feel of the grip was comforting. It provided enough courage to send July back to the window. Tonelli stood on the curb, his dim-witted expression making it seem as if he didn't know how to step off it. July rested the barrel of the gun on the window sill and sighted down it with one eye. *A bullet would solve at least one of my problems,* he thought. Tonelli was huge, hard to miss. The .22 was not a certain killer, a slug to the body shrugged off, but one in the skull? It would be enough.

And then?

July moved away from the window and again sat on the narrow bunk, shoulders rounded, face sagging.

Maggie has a different husband…a different child.

He stared at the gun in his hand, then slowly pressed the barrel against his temple, his finger gently squeezing the trigger.

And what about our child? What's become of our child?

He did not move for a very long time, the gun poised against his skull. And then, as if Brother Billy were there, July recalled the campfire at the fairgrounds, the sharp pain when the back of the Brother's hand hit his face, the big preacher's words as he stood over him.

Crissakes... for crissakes!

July lowered the gun to his lap.

Everybody's milk spoils eventually. No need to make yours turn sour any sooner than it will on its own.

July stared at the revolver, Brother Billy's words still resonating.

Crissakes, young July... for crissakes!

July suddenly laughed, the sound echoing throughout the cell block.

"For Christ's sake, indeed," he snorted, shoving the gun back into his rucksack.

When Sheriff Goodfellow returned, the cell was empty and the big lawman moved on to a new concern: the brutish fellow with the flashy hat who had arrived on the 8:50 from Omaha and then checked into the Penrod Hotel. Four years had turned up nary a trace of July Pennybaker, but T.J. had never forgotten the Knight of Zeus's ominous claim of dangerous men willing to hurt Maggie if it would put July in their sights. He sat at his desk and reviewed WANTED circulars, carefully examining each face. It was slow going, the images revealing a collection of sneering thugs with lifeless eyes. After an hour or so he set the flyers aside and escaped to the coffee shop of the Penrod Hotel for a slab of peach pie and a glass of milk. When he returned to his office, the cell that had held the deaf-mute, Charlie, was still empty.

For years, Waring Dolny had hosted a Friday night poker game in the basement of the Cozy Lunch and July sighed with relief from his hiding place in the bushes across the street when players began to arrive shortly after a single chime from St. Mary's proclaimed the half hour. It was 10:30 p.m.

One by one, they came: Doc Penrod, Myron Van Cleave, General Bill Dogberry, and lawyer Carl Irby. Ulysses Wounded Arrow was last, driving a new Chevy pickup—the very same pickup that Francis Wounded Arrow still drives. The station agent parked his truck on the street and went inside. A few seconds later, the establishment went dark, save the light from a single basement window.

July slipped from the bushes and ran to the pickup. As expected, Ulysses had left the keys dangling in the ignition and July fired up the engine, drove to the alley behind the three-story Penrod Hotel, and then quietly eased out of the cab. A rusty wrought-iron fire escape clung to the hotel's rear elevation like the cast-off shell of a giant cicada. A ladder from the lowest platform dropped to the alley below and July was about to climb it when a window on the second floor opened. He instantly flattened himself against the building, listening as a man coughed in great whoops for a few seconds and then spat a wad of phlegm the size of a small mouse. It splattered onto the bricks of the alleyway and was followed by a second round of whooping and spitting. Once the eruption had subsided July scrambled up the fire escape, jimmied a window lock, and slipped into the third floor corridor. His footsteps muted by the thick carpet runner, he then glided down the hallway to a door at the end.

"He'd figured that an experienced murderer like Lop-Eye would make it harder to be murdered, himself, opting for a top-floor room as far from the fire escape as possible," Grammie Willa revealed, "and he was right."

"Yeah...who is it?" Lop-Eye called out from inside the room after July knocked on the door.

"Western Union, sir."

"Who?"

"Western Union. Telegram from a Mister Alphonse Capone."

"Jes' a minute."

July heard the bedsprings creak. A few seconds later Lop-Eye's good eye appeared in a slivered opening and July put his weight against the door, twice slamming it into the big ape's forehead. Lop-Eye went down and July was quickly inside and upon him, the barrel of his .22 nearly filling one of the ex-prizefighter's nostrils.

"Not a sound," he whispered.

"Who da fuck are—?"

July shoved the gun farther up Lop-Eye's nose. "Not a sound," he repeated. "Got it?" He climbed off Lop-Eye and went to a dresser shoved against the wall. Inside the top drawer were a train ticket and a .45. July took the mobster's gun and tucked it into his belt.

"Pack and let's go," he ordered.

Lop-Eye had spent much of his boxing career studying his opponents from the canvas and seemed neither surprised nor uncomfortable to be on the floor, looking up. "Where am I goin'?" he demanded. July answered by cocking the hammer of the revolver and the ex-boxer got to his feet. "Who da hell are you?" the big man asked.

"Pack your things," July repeated.

Lop-Eye stuffed his few belongings into a valise. Afterward, they took the service elevator to the first floor, snuck through the darkened kitchen, and exited into the alley. July climbed into the passenger side of the pickup with Lop-Eye taking the wheel.

"Where to?" the mobster asked.

"Train," July answered.

Lop-Eye laughed. "Dere ain't no train tonight, genius. Besides, how you gonna make me get on it? You gonna wait in da station wi' dat gun on me?"

"Drive," July replied.

"Didja hear me? Dere ain't no passenger trains tonight."

"Drive."

With July pointing out directions Lop-Eye drove to a lonely section of track at the edge of town. From there, they pulled off the road and bounced alongside the railbed for another half mile.

"You gonna kill me?" Lop-Eye asked, peering at July with his good eye as he wrestled the truck over the bumpy trackside. He seemed oddly disinterested, as if the idea of losing his life was merely another blemish on his boxing record.

"Stop here," July responded. Lop-Eye braked the pickup to a halt. They climbed out and began to walk down the railbed, Lop-Eye in front, carrying his valise. Suddenly, Lop-Eye dropped the small suitcase and turned to face July. He twisted his head from side-to-side, the motion popping the bones in his neck.

"I ain't goin' no fur'der till I know da name o' da guy dat's doin' me in," he said.

"Nobody's doing you in," July replied. "There's a train coming through. We're catching it."

Lop-Eye laughed, the sound like a dog regurgitating a dead bird. "What kinda train? I ain't ridin' in no cattle train."

"It doesn't matter what kind. We're jumping it."

Lop-Eye squinted suspiciously.

"Relax," July reassured him. "As much as I'd like to shoot you, I won't if you behave yourself."

"Where we goin'?"

"Don't worry about that. You'll be rid of me soon enough."

Lop-Eye appraised July with his good eye. "Who da hell are you?" he asked.

"You know who I am."

"Fuck I do," Lop-Eye replied. He squinted, mouth pulled to one side, his entire face pinched in concentration.

"Once I let you go," July went on, "you'll have no reason to come back here. I'll be somewhere else...for good. You can tell that to Capone. I won't come back here...ever."

"Once I tell Capone? What da fuck am I tellin'...?"

Lop-Eyes eyes abruptly widened, his lips curling into a wolfish grin. Then, he pointed with one hand, his other forming a fist.

"SINGER!" he shouted as his shoulders dropped and he hurled himself at July, a gunshot simultaneously ringing out.

They both went down, the impact slamming July's head onto one of the crossties, the .22 knocked out of his hand. For an instant he saw sparklers, then fluttering darkness. Seconds passed and the sparklers dissipated. Seconds more and his head began to clear. Lop-Eye was still atop him and July groped about for his gun, the big man's weight pinning him to the sharp cinders of the railbed, the knuckle-swollen fingers of the ex-boxer's hand curled around his throat. A moment later, July relaxed. The goon's fingers were limp and lifeless and he next squeezed out from under the bulky mobster and sat up, tentatively fingering a fresh lump on the back of his head. Beside him, Lop-Eye was sprawled on his face, legs oddly splayed, a pool of blood around his head. July touched the gangster's neck, searching for a pulse. There was none.

The night was eerily quiet and July abruptly stiffened when a dog barked in the distance. He held his breath, waiting for shouts or the sound of a siren. A few yelps and single howl later, the barking subsided and the former Interpreter for the Oracle of Delphi got to his feet. He dragged Lop-Eye's body into the weeds a few yards off the tracks, then hiked back to the truck and drove across town to the service road along the rear of the Penrod estate. Back in his Knight of Zeus days, July had been given a tour of the Penrod grounds, including Obie's pride and joy: a fastidiously organized garden house. Now, he slipped into the shed where he found a shovel, a stack of empty gunnysacks, and a half-full bag of granulated limestone. A few minutes later he was back at the remote railbed where he covered the floor of the truck bed with the gunnysacks before dragging the mobster's dead body to the pickup. He hoisted Lop-Eye into the rear and then climbed back into the truck cab, wrestled the pickup into gear, and began to slowly drive along the uneven slope next to the tracks, searching the moonlit landscape for a grove of trees or a hedgerow. Eventually he came upon an unplanted field filled with knee-high grasses.

"It'll have to do," he muttered, praying that the first pink shades of dawn in the eastern sky were imaginary and that

Ulysses Wounded Arrow's luck had been good enough to keep him in the poker game at the Cozy Lunch.

He braked to a stop, then retrieved the shovel, hiked about twenty yards into the tall grass, and dug a hole. Afterward, he hauled Lop-Eye off the truck and dumped him into the grave along with the gunny sacks, the valise and the mobster's .45. He covered the body with limestone granules and was about to spade dirt back into the grave when he hesitated. July had not killed a man since The War To End All Wars—indeed had killed mostly from a distance in that conflict, save one fellow dispatched with a field knife. It had happened near the end, the outcome between countries already decided. Both soldiers knew it and yet struggled mightily, the tip of the knife moving back and forth between them like a metronome. July had been young, the German younger, and when the enemy soldier died—the knife plunged into his throat—July was filled with both relief and sorrow.

He looked into the shallow grave. The big mobster was dead, a bullet hole in the center of his forehead. July had seen other dead men with bullet holes. In war, they had been linked to righteousness and glory, to medals and cheering. But this time, there were no medals to be won, no cheers from a grateful nation. July had not dispatched an enemy to save a fellow soldier or for love of country. He had committed murder. The thug may have deserved it, but it was still murder.

July dropped the shovel and slumped to the ground next to the grave. White limestone covered Lop-Eye's face, making him resemble one of the street mimes the former doughboy had seen while on leave in Paris after the war. *That was a time*, he remembered. The powdered face made Lop-Eye seem curious and July was inexplicably reminded of his brother. After they'd parted, Ransom had made the newspapers, too, but not as an unnamed assailant or a bullet-riddled corpse. Indeed, just as July predicted on that fateful night in his old Dearborn Arms apartment, Capone had been reluctant to rub out a police captain's son-in-law. He'd actually rehired Ransom, installing the younger Thornton first as a ward captain and then a Cicero councilman. His little brother was in politics, the career many had supposed July might pursue. He probably lived with Bridget and Declan in a big house, July mused, maybe with a whole brood of little Thorntons. He wondered if Ransom knew that his big brother was alive. Did he think July's eyes as dark and lifeless as Lop-Eye's? Did he imagine him rotting at the bottom of Lake Michigan—food for the fishes, his bones pale and fenestrated?

July began to cry, whimpers at first, then great wracking sobs that shook him, his face awash in tears. He cried with anguish and frustration, with anger and despair. With regret. He cried until distant barking once again sounded. Then, he rose, swiped at his tears with a shirt sleeve, and erased Lop-Eye Tonelli's fixed expression with a shovelful of dirt. Within minutes, the dead mobster was buried and July hiked back to the truck. He returned the shovel and bag of limestone to the garden house on the Penrod estate and then headed for the Cozy Lunch. The basement window was still illuminated and he parked the Chevy where he'd found it, afterward returning to the darkened Miagrammesto County jail. When the night deputy returned from his patrol at 5:30 a.m. he found the deaf-mute named Charlie asleep in an unlocked cell.

Grammie Willa always claimed to have immediately recognized July when he turned up for dinner on his first night in town. "I think T.J. knew too," she suspected. "We avoided talking about it. I know T.J. wouldn't have wanted to arrest him and I'm not naturally chatty." Of course, Grammie Willa was tremendously chatty, having never met an ear she couldn't fill with a story. But she also knew that July had returned to redeem himself and she was a sucker for redemption. "Sure, Lop-Eye had been murdered, but we didn't know that," she justified. "Lop-Eye was just missing and as far as T.J. was concerned it was simply a matter of a big-city crook skipping out on his hotel bill."

After Charlie woke up, the sheriff took him to a diner for breakfast and then to Doc Penrod's clinic. "I was working that day," Grammie remembered. "Doc looked our Charlie over pretty carefully…listened to his heart and lungs, percussed his abdomen, shone a light into his eyes. Eventually, he banged a tuning fork and set it to vibrating all over July's skull."

"I suspect he lost his hearing after childhood measles," Doc decided. "I can't find anything else to explain it." Afterward, Sheriff Goodfellow gave Charlie to the Unitarians. "He figured they were indecisive enough not to argue about taking him in," Grammie always chuckled and soon, the odd deaf-mute was comfortably ensconced in a spare room of the Unitarian rectory. In return, he mowed the lawn and trimmed the shrubbery that footed the church, adding handyman chores as summer meandered into autumn. Eventually, Charlie branched out, taking jobs with parishioners, then all-comers. His stamina and cheap rates earned respect. His odd gait—twenty-four shuffling steps followed by a pause to survey his surroundings—gave him the nickname "Twenty-Four Step Charlie," a fellow who assiduously kept to himself, his idiosyncrasies viewed with equal measures of amusement and pity.

There was a good deal of smirking and finger-pointing when Charlie began to scrounge old materials and haul them to a vacant patch of land. He accumulated shredded tires, discarded scraps of plywood, irregular pieces of corrugated roofing, a copper vat once used to brew beer, pipes and valves, cast-off two-by-fours. Soon after, he was hard at work, constructing a home to replace his housing at the rectory. When it was completed, townsfolk christened it "Charlie's Last Resort," even though it was merely a one-room shack with a single door, screened windows on each wall, and a hatch that opened to the flat roof. Inside were items donated by the Unitarians: a bed and a rocking chair, shelves with books and magazines, and a wood stove. A curious fountain occupied the center of the shack's only room. It was a clever bit of engineering with rain and snow collected in a copper cistern atop the roof and then directed through a cheesecloth-and-sand filter to the fountain below, water pressure provided by gravity. "Heck of a contraption, Charlie," visitors told him, never suspecting their host to be the former Knight of Zeus, July Pennybaker, the fountain quenching their thirsts directly atop a shallow grave hiding the body of ex-prizefighter and Chicago mobster Aldo "Lop-Eye" Tonelli.

Three years later, in August of 1932, a stranger stepped off the noon train. He was large with a flat nose, huge misshapen ears, and a barrel chest that threatened to burst the seams of his suit. As usual, Charlie was on the platform. He met every passenger train that passed through. "He's harmless," natives reassured out-of-towners taken aback by the long-haired, bearded oddball. "Charlie just loves them trains."

Twenty-four Step Charlie—July Thornton—followed the stranger from the train station, pushing along a wheel barrow with his tools. The fellow went into the Cozy Lunch and July then worked at trimming the shrubs in front of the mortuary across the street, keeping watch on the bar and grill. About twenty minutes later, the man re-emerged and angrily shouted something unintelligible at Waring Dolny from the doorway. Afterward, he headed across the town square to a building where lawyer Carl Irby kept his ground floor office. July trailed him, and after the man entered, he moved to the alley side of the edifice.

There were two upstairs apartments in the building, one doubling as a hair salon, the other home to hostess-for-hire Mona McQueen. It was a warm day and windows were open, the pungent smell of tar and ammonia emanating from the salon, music from a phonograph record streaming from Mona McQueen's flat.

"After you've gone," a honey-smooth baritone crooned, "... and left me crying."

July crouched below the window of Irby's office and eavesdropped on the lawyer and his client. "You really have only one option," Irby said after listening to the fellow's complaint. "You can put a lien on the Cozy Lunch, but you'll have to provide evidence of indebtedness…a contract or a signed IOU."

The stranger protested with a flurry of profanity aimed, specifically, at Waring Dolny, and generally, at the entire town of Delphic Oracle.

"Now see here, sir," the lawyer interrupted him. "There's no call for such language."

The gravel-voiced fellow wasn't discouraged and promptly fired off another barrage of expletives. Irby cut him off.

"Good day, sir," he said, afterward calling out to his wife-secretary. "Mrs. Irby! Would you be so good as to call Sheriff Goodfellow?"

July hurried back to the front entrance in time to see the burly visitor exit the building and then walk up the street toward the train station. The out-of-towner only made it as far as the Rialto Theater—about a block—before Sheriff Goodfellow accosted him, his patrol car screeching to a stop with its front wheels over the curb.

"T.J. wasn't even out of the car before that big fellow launched into a fit of yelling and arm flinging," Grammie Willa told me. "He was madder than a shaved cat in a wet bag," The stranger was beefy and at least ten years younger than the sheriff. Nevertheless, my great-grandfather made short work of the confrontation, leaning forward and speaking softly until the man's arms fell to his sides. July was nearly upon them by then, and when the raspy-voiced fellow became aware that the spitting image of Jesus Christ was at his elbow, he was understandably startled, forming the expression of a man who has just discovered a severed head in the icebox.

"Holy crap, where the hell did you come from?"

July put hands over both ears, then his mouth.

"What the fuck is that supposed to mean?"

"Mind your manners," Sheriff Goodfellow cautioned him. "This is Charlie. He's deaf and dumb."

The stranger took a deep breath and released it, carefully

appraising July. "Sorry," he apologized, "but you oughta wear a cowbell. You scared the shit outta me."

He took a few steps up the street, then turned.

"Buddy," he said, tipping his head toward the Cozy Lunch, "don't ever loan money to a relative."

The man headed for the train depot. July followed and waited on the platform until the husky stranger boarded a train bound for Denver by way of Grand Island and North Platte. Once the caboose had slipped over the horizon, he trudged the mile to the Penrod estate, a canvas rucksack slung over his shoulder. He retrieved a lawnmower from the garden house and cut the grass, afterward taking a long time to clean the machine and sharpen its blade, wary of each car or wagon that made its way past the mansion. When Obie arrived home from work, little four-year-old Felicity dashed out the front door and into her father's arms. Maggie waited on the porch, and once Obie had climbed the steps to join her, she offered a cheek for her husband to kiss. That's when she noticed Charlie, watching them from across the lawn. She lifted her hand in a wave. He waved back.

And you'll call me Miss Westinghouse or nothing at all.

Ah…that I will.

July returned the lawnmower to the Penrod's garden house, gathered his rucksack, and made his way to a huge oak at the rear of the estate. It was a very old tree, thick with broad leaves, its branches sagging with the weight of age. He scrambled up the oak until level with the second story of the home, then nestled into a crook and opened his rucksack, pulling out a canteen and a ribbon of beef jerky. He ate slowly and waited. After dinner Felicity and her father played in the backyard, the little girl shouting with delight as Obie chased her about like a besotted crane, whooping in a bird-like way, his long arms and legs akimbo. July watched, imagining the little girl to be his, even though he had learned shortly after returning to Delphic Oracle that their child—his and Maggie's—had been lost on the cold streets of New York City. When the tail-lamps of fireflies began to blink Maggie called Felicity inside, leaving Obie to gather up the little girl's toys.

It had been a bad day, the appearance of the stranger reminding July that Maggie would never be safe as long as Al Capone was alive. The mob boss was in jail—sent up for income tax evasion—a sentence that seemed akin to rapping a rabid dog on the nose with a rolled-up newspaper. Still, he worried that prison had not loosened Capone's grip on his band of thugs, and even if it had, Bugs Moran was still alive and on the loose.

By ten o'clock the windows in the Penrod home were dark, a single porch light casting a timid arc onto the back yard. July remained in the huge old oak, listening to the rustle of his only neighbors: robins settling in for the night. Eventually, he dozed, tucked into a curl of the broad trunk. A few hours later the clatter of a trashcan caused him to jerk awake and reach for the .22 in his rucksack. Below, a pair of shadowy figures scurried across the lawn, passing directly beneath him as they headed for the stream bordering the rear of the property. July smiled in the darkness.

Raccoons.

Once the ring-tailed scavengers were gone he remained awake, watching the house. Its windows were dark, but a bright three-quarters moon fully illuminated the second story. Suddenly, Maggie appeared in one of the windows and he drew back until awash in shadows. Framed in the window with her hair once again long and loose around her shoulders, she searched the moon-drenched landscape like a sailor seeking shore from the crow's nest of a sailing vessel.

"Maggie," July whispered as she lowered the shade. "Maggie."

July kept watch on the window for the rest of the night. It remained quiet, the birds asleep, the raccoons rummaging through someone else's trash. No cars passed by the house and the neighboring homes remained dark and peaceful. As first light approached he heard the low whistle of a train. The whistle grew louder and July suddenly wanted to scramble from the tree and make for the railbed near the fairgrounds. He cocked his head to listen, recalling the thrill of anticipation, the mad dash alongside the tracks, the triumph once his fingers had a firm grip on the ladder of a railcar, the sensation of flight as he pulled himself aboard. The whistle sounded a third time, a distant melancholy thing that inexplicably recalled the dingy walk-down in Five Points, his cell at Rahway, and the trenches in France. He looked at the window on the second floor. Maggie was behind its shade, asleep, and July knew that she would sleep for the rest of that night, and the next one, and the one after, never knowing that less than a mile away Lop-Eye Tonelli lay in a shallow grave, the worm-ridden earthly remains of a man who would have killed them all without reluctance or regret.

July leaned into the massive tree trunk, using his rucksack as a pillow. With dawn approaching he remained awake high in the protective branches of the oak, watching the house, listening for sounds that didn't belong. He was gone before the Penrods arose for breakfast, but returned on the following night and once again climbed the oak at the rear of the estate. During the evening he heard music coming from inside the house, but the windows were dark by ten o'clock, leaving him alone to wait for the raccoons and the train. Once again he watched the house with the wide veranda and the shaded window where Maggie had appeared the night before. He remained there for a long time, until well after the robins had settled in and the raccoons had finished their nightly repast. He was there when the moon rose and when it descended, when the whistle heralded the train's approach and bade its farewell. The hours passed slowly, but July remained at his post, watching, listening. He was there for the rest of the night, and was still there when morning light slanted softly through the shaded window and Maggie awoke.

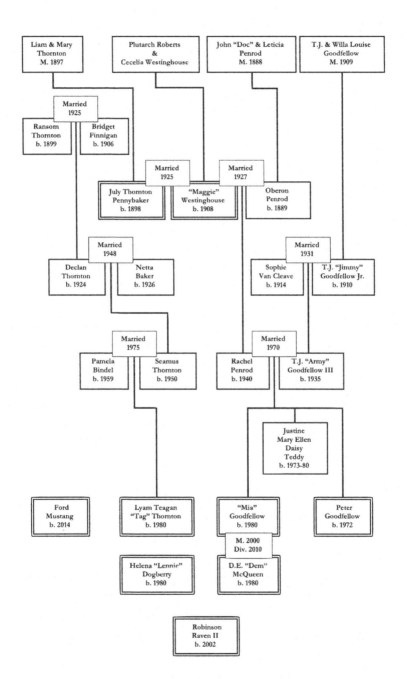

12

MIA AND TAG

On the outskirts of Delphic Oracle, nestled between a cornfield and the rolling hills of the municipal golf course, is the place I would continue to call home for the next few months—at night, anyway. The Luther Burbank Correctional Facility was once a college that nurtured undergraduates largely committed to a future in agriculture, its curriculum varied enough to produce a governor, three state senators, a best-selling author of gardening books, a Navy Cross winner, and an Olympic archery champion. In its heyday, the Luthers were a respectable NAIA football team, the college's debaters more than formidable, and the agronomy program unrivaled, turning out some of the finest farmers and county extension agents in the entire Midwest. However, by 1965, veterans of the wars in Europe and the Pacific had spawned a sulky generation that unfavorably compared the sweat and narrow profit margins of farming to the padded bank accounts and weekend golf that accompanied degrees in business, medicine, and law—courses of study better pursued at the state university in Lincoln.

Luther Burbank College made a valiant effort to change with the times, revamping its curriculum to reflect the turbulent 1960s with courses like *Revolutionary Botanical Thought and Criticism* and *Plant Genetics and Hallucinogens: A Philosophic Conundrum*. But it was no use. They went belly up just as Neil Armstrong took his first steps on the moon. For twenty years the college lay fallow and was about to become a driving range for the golf course when Mayor Ed Dogberry came up with a way to put the old campus to use. "Correctional facilities are the future," Ed opined to the boys hanging out at the Y-Knot Drive-In. "Why, I'd be willing to bet there's more young people going to prison than college right now." Ed was in his second term as mayor of Delphic Oracle with a short but effective history of delivering most of the county's votes to the right folks at the statehouse. And so, not long after he proposed converting the defunct college into a prison, the great state of Nebraska resurrected it as The Luther, a turn of events that brought July Thornton's great-nephew to Delphic Oracle.

The same day Teddy ran away from home for the last time, Lyam Teagan "Tag" Thornton became my new cellmate at The Luther. Processed by grandmotherly Jewel Tomek, Tag was escorted to his cell by my ninety-three-year-old great uncle, Grey Goodfellow, a talkative fellow who ran the family's insurance business until my sister, Mary Ellen, took over about fifteen years ago. Retired now, Uncle Grey works a few hours each week at The Luther as a guard, the rest of his time spent at the pinochle table with his buddies at the Saint Aquinas Retirement Village.

"This is my nephew, Father Peter," Uncle Grey told Tag as he showed him into our cell. "'He's a good bunkmate. He knows everything about this place." Tag ignored me, instead studying our room. We each had a trundle bed with a cushiony mattress and large drawers for storage beneath the sleeping platforms. A small desk was tucked against the wall above the head of each bed and sunlight streamed through a cheerfully curtained tri-paned window with two operating casements. Neither bars nor wire mesh impeded the sunbeams. Likewise, there was no door to keep us in. We were free to come and go as we pleased.

My new roomie threw his gear onto the open bunk and then went to the window. It overlooked an immaculately mown and edged Common bordered by beds of vibrantly colored flowers. A small, semi-circular bandshell occupied the center with criss-crossed sidewalks fanning out like four spokes of a wheel. Towering trees provided shade and a few picnic tables and benches were scattered about. Two men at least as ancient as my uncle Grey stood in one of the flower beds, leaning on their rakes as they chatted, wide-brimmed straw hats shading their faces, the badges on their coveralls reflecting sunlight.

"Home sweet home," Tag muttered.

Tag Thornton was sort of famous. Grandson of legendary Cornhusker pigskin star and former Nebraska governor Declan Thornton, he was thirty-four years old with rangy shoulders, an undisciplined tousle of blondish hair, and startlingly blue eyes. Fully two inches over six feet with a trim waistline and narrow hips, Tag still looked very much the player the U had recruited to dazzle their fans on the football field. The dazzle had been short-lived. Bounced from the team after accepting money and a car from a well-heeled booster, he had a cup of coffee in the NFL with night-life and disinterest ending his career after two seasons. "If the Super Bowl is the ultimate game," he once scoffed to an ESPN interviewer, "why do they play it every year?" Tag had previously served three years for burglary at Niobrara, a real prison up north. Forgery—a white-collar crime—had landed him in The Luther.

I pulled out my harmonica, tootling a few notes as a conversation starter. Tag continued to ignore me. I didn't take it personally. I'm slender and graying—not the forklift with tattoos one sees in prison movies—but Tag's stretch at Niobrara had taught him to keep his head down until he knew the gangs and the gang leaders. The Luther is different. We don't have gangs. We have Trivial Pursuit night and a chess club. By the way, I'm a three-to-five for assault with a deadly weapon after shooting my sister Mia's ex-husband, Dem McQueen, through the ear lobe with a BB gun. I would have gotten probation and community service, but expressed no remorse and Judge Hardy Irby is a Calvinist who believes all Catholic priests are tax-evaders who belong in jail.

"Let's go eat," I said.

Tag carefully appraised me for a few moments and when he finally answered, his voice was as flat and noncommittal as the prairie landscape outside our cell.

"Tag Thornton," he said.

"Peter Goodfellow," I answered.

After a gourmet lunch overseen by prison chef Marcel Du-mont, Uncle Grey and I gave Tag a tour of campus, probably talking more than we should. As I said, Tag was sort of famous and I guess we were a bit star-struck.

"The landscaping did them in," I told him to explain our relaxed prison security. "Mayor Dogberry thought beautifica-tion would put Delphic Oracle on the national correctional facilities map and he blew the start-up money from the state on flowers and shrubs. But Ed miscalculated, and by the time they completed the grounds, there was no money left for bars and locks. Ed had connections at the statehouse and figured he could wangle a little extra time and money. But the penitentiary at Niobrara was overflowing and its warden was the governor's brother back then. So they had to start taking prisoners here. That was about twenty-five years ago."

"So, what keeps inmates from running?" Tag asked.

Uncle Grey and I exchanged smiles. "We're hospitable," my uncle revealed. "We make it more pleasant to stay than to es-cape."

Tag shook his head. "And that works? You've been getting away with this for twenty-five years? I find that hard to believe. Aren't there inspections? Visitors? People from the govern-ment?"

"It sounds crazy, I know," I responded, "but here's the thing. We are the only prison in the United States that has never had an attempt at escape. I'm not talking about actual escapes. I'm talking about *attempts*."

"Attempts!" Uncle Grey echoed. "We've never even had an *attempt*. Do you know what the statistical probability of no es-cape attempts is?"

"It's like healthcare," I added. "To politicians, no malpractice lawsuits means good medical care even if all the patients are dead. In the prison business, it's no escapes and a low person-nel budget. As far as that goes, we spend virtually nothing on security. Other than the warden we don't have many employees. The guards are volunteers from Saint Aquinas and prisoners run the rest of the place, so we're incredibly cheap from the taxpayer's standpoint. We cost the state far less per prisoner than any other facility they manage. The boys at the statehouse in Lincoln love us, and believe me, they don't want to know *how* we do it. They just want us to *keep* doing it."

We stopped in front of Penrod Hall, a brick-walled edifice with an archway over the entrance evocative of French gothic cathedrals. Unlike The Luther's other buildings, iron bars entwined with green ivy filled the ground floor windows.

"This is the administration building," Uncle Grey proudly revealed. "It's the only building on campus with bars. About once a year a few muckity-mucks from Lincoln or Washington DC show up to inspect us. We dress up some folks in prison stripes, then trot them over here. I always get to play a convict. I sit in one of the cells with the *700 Club* on TV, reading the Bible and looking contrite. Politicians love that stuff. They're crazy for the Bible. It's like heroin for them. I quote a little scripture, they get teary, and we get funded for another year."

Uncle Grey grinned. "Of course, that's not our only source of income. Most of the inmates have jobs in town so they can pay a little rent. And then there's Marcel."

Over a lunch of grilled salmon with rosemary mashed potatoes and tender asparagus shoots, I had explained how the cafeteria doubled as a cooking school headed by Marcel Dumont, a razor-thin man with a bristle of hair only slighter darker than his hawkish eyes. "He's not really French," I told Tag, revealing that our prison chef had morphed from Gerald Matulka to Marcel Dumont somewhere between the Culinary Institute of Cheyanne, Wyoming and his trial in Scottsbluff, Nebraska after embezzling from a local Olive Garden. "He's worth every penny, don't you think?" I opined. "I mean, you ate that lunch, right?"

Tag didn't respond, his eyes on a figure fast approaching—a tall, beautiful woman with a tousle of honeyed hair under a wide-brimmed, floppy hat. She wore a sundress with a flowing skirt that ruffled about her legs as she walked down the center of the wide sidewalk, taking long, coltish strides. The woman reached us and kissed Uncle Grey on the cheek before greeting me with a hug. Then, she offered Tag an astonishing smile as she extended one hand. He took it and the moment they touched it was obvious to anyone, who believes in romance and fate and magic, that Tag Thornton was dizzily, ridiculously, and irretrievably in love with my little sister, Mia Goodfellow: ex-wife of Dem McQueen and the warden of The Luther Burbank Correctional Facility.

Around the same time Tag was falling for Mia, her ex-husband—Dean Emmet "Dem" McQueen—woke up from another bender, rolled over, and groped at the dirty jeans next to the couch. He needed a smoke.

"Sonuvabitch," he muttered when his search yielded only an empty package. He crumpled it in one hammy fist and then sat up. "What the hell?" he murmured in surprise. A large man with the burgeoning thickness of Elvis-the-later-years, he was dressed in a T-shirt and briefs, somehow removing his pants the night before without taking off his shoes and socks. Moving slowly, he rose, crossed the room, and then threw back the heavy curtain that shaded the front window. A cloud of dust billowed outward, the particles floating in beams of sunlight that slanted into the room.

Another goddamned beautiful day...just like my life used to be.

That was before Mia left, before he chased after her with a baseball bat, stopping when the one-eyed barrel of his service revolver stared him in the face. He had once been a respected and feared cop. Feared, anyway. That was before Mia got mouthy, before she forgot what a wife was supposed to be, back when she put three squares on the table and understood that a fellow had to cat around a bit to keep things fresh. She'd always had spunk, Dem allowed. He'd liked it most of the time.

It was sort of sexy and he could always smack it out of her if she went too far. But that was before she screamed at him, her beautiful face narrow and poisoned with hatred, before she halted him in his tracks with cool deadly eyes, the heavy gun she'd taken from his leather holster held steady and unwavering. It was before the separation and the divorce; before the nights got longer and the missed roll calls at the station; before the beers that went down too easily and the last calls that arrived with dawn at their heels.

Dem went into the kitchen. The table was cluttered: old newspapers, unopened mail, empty pizza boxes. He found a half-smoked cigarette and lit it, then picked up one of the letters and extracted his latest unemployment check, afterward belching and scratching his balls. Other than coaching the Pease-blossom Giants, this was pretty much what Dem McQueen did most days. After Mia walked out he'd been fired from the Delphic Oracle Police Department for drinking on duty, and over the next few years, jobs of descending prestige followed. He'd been fired from the latest about six months earlier and was currently in the business of smoking Camels, drinking beer, ordering pizza, and scratching his balls. Every so often an unemployment check showed up, although an end to his latest incarnation on the government tab was fast approaching and Dem knew it. He idly fingered the hole I'd put in his earlobe.

"Sonuvabitch," he said again.

His doorbell chimed, but Dem ignored it, instead returning to the living room where he collapsed onto the couch and aimed the remote control at the TV. Before the set turned on, the doorbell sounded again. He angrily dug out an empty beer bottle from between the couch cushions and threw it at the door. It missed, crashing through the sidelight window followed by a third ring of the bell.

"Goddamned sonuvabitch!" Dem bellowed. He lurched to his feet and staggered to the entry where he flung the door open, his teeth bared, one fist clenched, a piece of his mind ready to be hurled at whomever was on the other side. Helena

"Lennie" Dogberry—daughter of car dealer and town Mayor Ed Dogberry—stood on the porch, inspecting the broken glass scattered about. She wore little makeup and had pulled her hair into a ponytail, a questionable decision as it made her nose seem too long, her chin too pointed, her algae-green eyes too narrowly spaced. A pair of gaudy, junk earrings dangled below the angles of her jaw. Dem relaxed, unclenching his fist.

"Hey, Lennie," he said.

"Hi," Lennie replied. "Where're your pants?" She bent to retrieve the bottle Dem had thrown through the sidelight window and then brushed past him. "You should recycle," she said, setting the bottle on the entry table.

"Cut me some slack, Lennie. I'm havin' a bad day."

Lennie eyed the jagged glass still clinging to the panel frame. "So I see," she remarked, afterward moving into the living room where she immediately began to straighten up—collecting dirty dishes, emptying ashtrays, gathering up paper plates and plastic dinnerware. Meanwhile, Dem pulled off his shoes and wriggled back into his jeans, then picked up a hand gun from a side table and tucked it into his waistband. Afterward, he flopped back onto the couch. When the phone rang, he let Lennie answer it.

"Dem there?" Estelle Nixon began. Once married to Snug Nixon, Estelle had slummed around with Dem for a few months after leaving her husband. She still called once in a while to see if the embers had any fire left.

"Who is it?" Dem growled.

"Estelle," Lennie answered. Dem pulled the gun from his waistband and pressed the tip of the barrel to his temple.

"What's he doing?" Estelle asked.

"He's about to blow his brains out," Lennie replied.

"Is the gun loaded? Tell him to either put bullets in the damned thing or stop threatening to shoot himself. Are you gonna stay?"

"For a while," Lennie said.

A click sounded, followed by the dial tone, and Lennie hung up the phone.

Across the room, Dem turned on the television. An old movie was showing—one about a handsome, perfect man who writes a letter to his beautiful dead wife, afterward putting it in a bottle that he throws into the ocean. A different beautiful woman finds the bottle with the message and chases after the man.

"I love this movie," Lennie said, plopping down next to him on the couch.

"Yeah, Mia did too," Dem replied, recalling that his ex-wife had turned blubbery and uncharacteristically affectionate when they saw it at the Rialto. "I thought it was boring," he added. "I couldn't stay awake." He pulled off a shoe, smelling the inside before throwing it at the TV. It badly missed, clunking against the wall.

"Sonuvabitch," he muttered.

Dem surfed through a few channels, settling on a baseball game for less than a minute before leaving it to go inspect the broken sidelight window. Lennie trailed and stood behind him, running a finger along his arm. Most of the glass in the frame had fallen out, but a few shards remained. Dem flicked one, smiling grimly when it crashed onto the porch.

"Oh, Dem," Lennie whispered.

I should marry her, the ex-cop mused. *I could work at Ed's dealership... Take over the credit department and wear a tie to work.* A moment later, he dismissed the idea. He liked Lennie, and had to admit that she could be pretty when she let her hair fall around her shoulders. But they were just friends and Dem firmly believed that friendship ruined marriage.

Besides, he thought, *it ain't over for me and Mia.*

He looked at Lennie. "One of these days, Mia's gonna come to her senses. Wait and see. The divorce was just a hiccup."

"No, it wasn't, Dem," Lennie replied.

He studied her face for a few moments and then pressed the gun to his temple and pulled the trigger. A loud click echoed about the room.

"Dem, you're not in love with her," Lennie pleaded. "You never were. You're just obsessed. There's a difference."

"There *is*?" Dem replied. He gave her observation some thought and then pulled the trigger of the gun a second time.

"Dem," Lennie said softly, "give me the gun. It's not even loaded." She touched his arm, but he pulled the trigger a third time, adding a hollow click to a commercial jingle playing on the television.

"Dem…" she whispered.

The former cop looked at her, then handed over his weapon. *Lennie's a true pal*, he thought…*loyal and dependable*. He suddenly brightened.

"I should get a dog," he said.

Lennie led him back to the sofa and they switched the channel back to the old movie. Lennie wept at the end, while Dem perused an old *Sports Illustrated* swimsuit issue. When the movie was over, Lennie rose.

"I've gotta get back to the dealership," she said. "Daddy will wonder where I am."

Dem didn't respond and Lennie crossed to the door.

"I'm leaving," she said.

Dem pointed the remote control at the TV and switched the channel back to the baseball game. "See ya, Lennie" he said without looking at her.

Lennie went out to her car, but didn't leave, instead watching the Reverend Oscar Redwine mow the lawn of the Baptist church across the street. When she began to cry, the reverend noticed and approached.

"What troubles you, child?" he asked. To someone susceptible to the faintest suggestion of sympathy, his voice was like a warm blanket and Lennie promptly came undone. "Oh, my poor girl. You must come inside," the reverend consoled her. He dried her tears with a clean handkerchief and then brought her into the parsonage where his lovely wife brewed a pot of blackberry tea that was aromatic and bracing. Afterward, they listened without interruption as the lovesick car dealer's daughter poured out her heart. She was in love with Dem, Lennie told them, the poor thing discerning something in the ex-cop that was invisible not only to the Reverend Oscar and his wife but to everyone else in Delphic Oracle.

"When he married Mia, it broke my heart," she lamented, revealing that she'd never loved the Honda dealer's son from Zenith that she'd subsequently wed on impulse. It hadn't worked out, and now, both she and Dem were divorced with Lennie determined to wear him down with devotion.

"Dem seems a bit too durable for that," Reverend Oscar suggested, diplomatically substituting "durable" for "thick-headed." He put a huge arm around her, his hug nearly rendering her breathless. "Just remember that God loves you, Lennie," he said.

"If only that were enough," she sobbed.

After she left the Baptist parsonage Lennie drove to Dogberry Motors and went into the shop, a place she much preferred to the showroom. It was cool and filled with the clank and jangle of work, the aromas of oil and rubber and gasoline oddly comforting. "Hey, Lennie," one of the mechanics called out, "there's a clunk in that rig over there. Can you take a look?" Lennie changed into coveralls and was soon up to her elbows in the transmission of a gigantic SUV. She finished the job and moved to a brake pad replacement and then a driveshaft repair followed by investigation of a mysterious engine knock in an old Taurus. The knock proved elusive and she skipped dinner, working on until the dealership was deserted and dark, save her work lamp. She finished with the Taurus around nine p.m. and treated herself to a candy bar and a Coke in the employee lounge. A radio was on the counter and she turned it to an oldies station, then sat at a round table, humming along with the music. A song by the Beach Boys came on followed by one from the Rolling Stones. Halfway through Art Garfunkel's anthem, "Bridge Over Troubled Water," she stood and turned over her chair. Like the table, it was a castoff from the house she still shared with her parents. Words written in crayon were on its underside. Although faint with age, the dedication was still readable:

Lennie + Dem

She traced the letters with her finger, recalling how she'd lain on the floor beneath the chair those many years ago and reached up with her crayon. Dem had kissed her on the playground at school that day. Only six years old, she was already in love with him.

Lennie flipped the chair upright, then went back to the repair shop and started on the next job. She could still hear the radio in the lounge and sang along, her vocals loud and tearful. The night deepened, then turned to morning, but Lennie Dogberry worked on. Spotlighted by the haloed light of her work lamp she snugged a bolt or tightened a screw, thrilling to the purr of her only remaining companion—a classic Galaxie 500 from the 1960s—a pristinely maintained automobile that responded to her every touch, the rumble of its mighty engine obediently rising and falling as her hands moved expertly and with agile tenderness.

The Luther is populated with non-violent criminals—forgers, embezzlers, once-in-a-lifetime criminals like me. Most are first time offenders whose relief is palpable when they find prison to be more like a few years at a Holiday Inn than a stretch at Alcatraz. A handful work on the main campus. The rest are given work in town and Tag took a position in sales at Dogberry Motors after Ed won a coin flip with Big Bob Peaseblossom. His job gave him access to every car on the lot and he well knew that the prison without a single escape attempt would never report his disappearance. Still, after a few weeks, he'd not escaped, and on those increasingly rare occasions when Mia was not in his thoughts, it baffled him. Meanwhile, Ed Dogberry had made it clear that he wanted the ex-football star to marry his daughter, Lennie.

"She doesn't want to marry me Ed," Tag told his boss the morning after Beagle Gibbs attended his first and last Quaker service.

Adept at separating serious customers from window

shoppers who merely needed a whiff of new car smell once in a while, Dogberry knew that Tag wasn't in the market for a wife. But he was also a salesman who could convince a customer to put fog lights and a luggage rack on a riding lawn mower. He wasn't about to give up.

"Not marry you? Of course she does, Tag," he blustered. "All women want to marry you. Women chase after men like you with a marriage license in one hand and their panties in the other. Now, I'll admit that Lennie hasn't shown a lot of interest, but be fair. Have you really tried? Pay a little attention to her and she'll be shopping for a wedding gown before you can say 'sizeable inheritance.'"

He winked slyly, pausing to let his ham-fisted implication take root. "And she may not look like much, but Lennie's a catch," the car dealer went on. "Doesn't show it. Too shy. That's her problem. Hides her light under a basket. Tries to do what people want. But she's a pip. She's a corker, Tag. Lots o' hidden talents. And sweeeet...sweetest girl in the world. Not a malicious bone in her body.

"You've a future here, son," Ed continued, using the voice he believed made a new convertible sound every bit as effective as Viagra. "You're past entry level. No Korean or Jap tin cans for you, Tag, boy. Why, you're a man with Ford Mustang written all over you."

As his boss went on, Tag gazed past the showroom outside Ed's office to the floor-to-ceiling windows that dominated the front of the dealership. Delphic Oracle's main drag—Scout Street—fronted Dogberry Motors. Running north and south, it was interrupted by an east-west railbed just a few yards past the corner edge of the business. Suddenly, a distant whistle sounded and the railway crossing bar immediately began to descend, creating the impression of a showroom on either side of the glass wall as a short line of cars formed on the street. Less than a minute later, a westbound train lumbered down the tracks.

Tag knew that rail-hopping was in his blood, his notorious great-uncle July Thornton allegedly a freight-jumper of considerable proficiency. *Not for me*, he mused as the caboose cleared the crossing and the bar swiveled upward. *When I escape, it won't be in a cattle car.*

"Lennie's not so bad," Ed interrupted his thoughts, gesturing at a photograph of his daughter and her late mother, the pair bearing similarly startled expressions, "once you get to know 'er, anyway." He fashioned a fatherly face, pointing his chin at the auto showroom just outside his door. Lennie was on the sales floor, half-heartedly pointing out the features of a fully loaded SUV to a young man with raging acne and a pair of pants so far off his rump they seemed about to fall off. Ed frowned. He loved his daughter, but she was a terrible salesperson, preferring the repair shop to the showroom. "She can't tell the difference between the sharecroppers and the plantation owners," he had once complained to me during an unauthorized visit to the confessional at St. Mary's. He half rose from his chair, then relaxed when the young man shifted his attention to an affordable compact.

"Now, you and Lennie...you're not in love...yet, anyway," Ed went on, "but, Tag boy, love isn't all it's cracked up to be. There're other things. Like meatloaf and potato pancakes. My old man was married to my mother for almost fifty years and didn't love her for more than three of 'em...four tops. But he loved her meatloaf and her potato pancakes his whole life. That's reliability, son...reliability. After a while the paint fades and the upholstery has a rip or a coffee stain or a cigarette burn. What's under the hood is all that counts then, Tag, and that's gotta be reliable. You don't have to love a car or a woman, but you gotta be able to rely on 'em both."

Tag glanced through the doorway where Lennie was now alone, longingly running her finger along the surface of a red Mustang as if she and the car were lovers. A couple of weeks earlier Ed had orchestrated a date for the couple where she tearfully confessed her love for Dem McQueen. "He's different around me," she told Tag. "He wants to be a good person. He just needs someone to show him how. He needs nurturing."

Tag was skeptical. He'd seen enough of the ex-cop to know that Dem McQueen was the sort of fellow best nurtured with a chair and a whip. Lennie seemed far too good for him, but Tag knew better than to argue with a woman who had made up her mind and he didn't. The date had ended without a kiss, the couple merely friends.

"Give up, Ed," Tag said. "Lennie doesn't love me and I don't love her. She's a nice girl. You're right about that. She's great. But she knows what she wants and it isn't me. Besides, she can do better than me."

"You're talking about Dem McQueen?"

"She can do better than him too."

Ed hesitated, then reached inside the pocket of his sport coat, a green-and-orange thing that made his lime-hued trousers seem demure. Offering an expression to suggest that Tag had so out-bargained him further negotiation would be downright mean-spirited, the car dealer extracted a set of keys and tossed them onto his desk.

"Take that Mustang out there in the showroom, Tag," he said. "Keep it for a few weeks. It'll be your company car."

"Ed—"

"Just listen to me for a second. I understand your hesitation. A fellow can't decide without a test drive. I get that. I wouldn't have much respect for a man who thought otherwise."

Ed rose and took Tag by the arm, guiding him into the showroom where they joined Lennie beside the Mustang. "Here she is," he said with pride. "Five point eight liter V-8, three hundred five horsepower, fully loaded." He grinned, then stood between Tag and Lennie with an arm around each of them. "Beats the heck out of a Jap car, don't she?" he said.

Despite Uncle Grey's claim, The Luther's record was not pristine. A couple of runners had fled in the past. Both voluntarily returned before reaching Three-Mile Corner south of town, shamed by our barless honors system and appreciative of Marcel

Dumont's haute cuisine. However, Tag was a problem not previously encountered—a guest of the state with the potential to
become an actual fugitive. Nevertheless, as we meandered into
August with the Little League championship game and Felicity's
adventure on the Platte River fast approaching, Tag remained
in Delphic Oracle, finding any excuse at all to bump into Mia.
Eventually, people around town felt as if they had no choice
but to gossip, most weighting the scales in favor of an affair. It
made for juicier chinwagging and put aside the genuine worry
that Tag might actually flee the jurisdiction. "They're in love,"
folks opined. "At first sight, I hear tell."

It was true. Tag remained dizzily, ridiculously, and irretrievably in love with Mia, and even though she refused to admit she
might be in love with him, my little sister was certainly leaning
into it. "She's just the warden. I don't think of her as a woman,"
Tag claimed, even though I'd not asked him to state his intentions. It was the attitude a sensible Don Juan evinces to convince himself that he's not ready to stop Don Juan-ing. "He's
just another inmate," Mia insisted from her side of things, the
response a sensible woman volunteers when she's been burned
once and isn't looking for another fire. But that's the problem
with love, isn't it? There isn't anything sensible about it.

A couple of weeks after Felicity rescued Daisy's horses from
the sandbar, I visited Mia in her office. It was lunchtime and
the Common below her window was crowded, the grassy plaza
a popular gathering place since The Luther's days as a college.
Picnickers munched on sandwiches, young mothers gabbed as
their toddlers waddled about chasing birds, senior citizens from
nearby Saint Aquinas dozed on benches, and a couple of boys
sat on the stage of the small Romanesque bandshell strumming
guitars, their cases propped open to invite spare change. Mia
watched it all from her second-floor office in Penrod Hall, as
red-faced Mayor Ed Dogberry paced about behind her, hands
alongside his head as if it might otherwise fly off his neck. I sat
on the sofa, watching.

"I'm tellin' you, Mia, the boy's about to run," Ed moaned. "I tried to buy him off with a car, but that won't be enough, either. It's in his nature. He's like his great-uncle. My grandpa, General Bill, told me all about that fella and I think Tag's cut from the same cloth. I like 'im, mind you, but he's no roostin' pigeon. He's a flyer, and I'm tellin' you, he's gonna run!"

"Calm down, Ed," Mia sighed, but the Delphic Oracle mayor was undeterred.

"We can't have an escape, Mia. It'll bring federal investigators in here. We'll have the Justice Department on our backs. We'll be on *60 Minutes* and not in a good way. Just think about it. Sixty dad-burned Minutes hangin' us up by our privates on national TV…by our dad-burned privates!" The mayor stopped in front of the office's large window just as Tag emerged from the cafeteria building below. "This is your fault, Mia," he exclaimed. He whirled around and pointed at me. "And yours, too, Father. We put 'im in with you. You were supposed to keep a leash on 'im. If he runs, I'll bring you up on charges… Aidin' and abettin' or—"

"Accessory after the fact?" I offered.

"Yeah, thank you…accessory after the fact. I'll have you charged with that."

After the mayor was gone, Mia stood at the window, watching the last of the picnickers reluctantly pack up. It was a beautiful day although the faint grayness of a storm dulled the horizon. The bend of the treetops and a high bank of sooty clouds predicted that it would miss us, swinging to the north, but Mia was uneasy. In a place where plains twisters sometimes flitted from low-hanging clouds or a capricious bolt of lightning sent a cornfield smoking into the summer sky, catastrophe was always a possibility, even on a day ambling along as innocently as this one. For her, Tag Thornton was a low-hanging cloud, an ominous crackle of light in a dark sky.

I rose from the couch and joined her. Below, Tag had stopped in the Common to chat with one of the guards. "I went to the dealership a few days ago," Mia suddenly offered. "Pretended I was interested in a new car."

"I heard."

"He asked me to dinner."

"I heard that too. Not a good idea, Mia. An inmate having burgers with the warden at the Y-Knot will likely make it onto the front page of the *Banner-Press*."

"I know."

"You wanted to say, 'Yes,' didn't you?"

Mia nodded, sighing. "I must be out of my mind," she muttered.

I understood. Tag had a way about him. He was wanderlust, personified, and it had affected me, as well; indeed, I'd recently told the bishop that I wouldn't be opposed to a new assignment…someplace exotic or even dangerous. We watched as Tag headed across the Common alone, a sudden gust of wind lifting his hair and shifting the curve of the treetops. He moved quickly with long strides and I felt Mia shiver, the distant, somber grayness hugging the horizon suddenly closer. A moment later the wind settled and Tag disappeared behind an ivy-covered building at the far edge of the Common.

"This is ridiculous," she said, moving to the chair behind her desk. "I'll meet with him this afternoon. Put an end to this nonsense, once and for all."

"Do you want someone here with you?" I asked. I'd heard confessions from more than a few folks who'd scheduled meetings to put an end to things, only to have their lower ends meet during the "New Items" portion of their agenda.

Mia frowned. "It's a meeting, Peter, not a tryst. I'm a professional. Good God, would you ask that question if I were a man?"

Later that afternoon, Uncle Grey escorted Tag into Mia's office, where she spent nearly an hour trying to convince The Luther's most famous inmate to serve out his time. "This town may not mean anything to you," she told him, "but it's home to a lot of good people who depend on this facility to support their businesses. Besides, we have a system that works. There's no recidivism. Our guys get out and stay out. The state is happy.

Society is happy. Justice is served. In exchange, we get money to support the institution. That money stays in Delphic Oracle. It sustains jobs, builds things. Things that last."

She made her voice earnest, her gestures emphatic, because her job called for her to be earnest and emphatic. Yet, even as she begged him to stay, Mia couldn't help wishing that he might turn out to be exactly the man she thought he was—a fellow who knew it was time to go at exactly the moment a woman was ready for him to leave. Eventually, her frustration with his piercing blue eyes got the best of her.

"I should throw you into solitary," she grumbled.

"Do we have solitary?"

"No, but I can lock you in a room for a few hours with Ed Dogberry. You'll wish you were in solitary after that."

Tag laughed. "Can't you just beat me?" he quipped.

She glared at him, which is what a reasonable woman does when she's made one bad mistake named Dem McQueen only to find herself over the moon for a handsome disaster with good hair. He responded with a quizzical expression that made him even better looking.

That's it! Mia decided. *I'm transferring him to Niobrara.*

"You're dismissed," she said.

I'm done with him.

"Get out of my office."

Done!

And then, she wasn't, because as I've learned after hearing thousands of confessions, you can't run away from love. You can't even hide from it. Love follows you home, lurks under the porch, then jumps out just when you begin to feel safe. Love has no manners nor sense of propriety, and despite the mooning of poets, isn't at all poetic. It's messy and a bit sweaty, and until one gets used to it, altogether terrifying. Or so I'm told.

Tag was halfway to the door, when Mia stopped him.

"Do you still want to have dinner with me?" she asked. It seemed less an invitation than a reproachment.

Tag turned. He was surprised, but only a little. "Sure," he said.

"Stop grinning."

"Okay."

"I mean it. It's makes you look smug. It's unattractive."

"Sorry."

"Don't be sorry. Just stop it."

"Okay."

"Come to my house at seven-thirty. And don't tell anyone you're coming."

"Seven-thirty?"

"Yes."

"It's a date."

"It's not a date. It's just dinner. Now, get out."

Tag arrived at seven-thirty that evening, edging the loaner Mustang to the curb in front of Mia's little Craftsman house. She sat on the top step of her porch, hair pulled back in a ponytail. Her dress was coral—sleeveless with spaghetti straps. Her legs were bare. She wore sandals and a cat was on her lap.

"This is Betty Comden," she said when Tag approached. She moved the cat's paw in a wave. "Betty...meet Scarface Thornton."

"A promotion...thanks," Tag joked. "Ironic choice. My great uncle was supposedly rubbed out by Scarface Al Capone."

"Why am I not surprised?" Mia said.

Tag took the cat from her arms. "Hello, Betty," he said. "Are your manners any better than your mommy's?"

"Oh, she's not mine," Mia told him. "She belongs to our chaperone."

Tag's face fell. Typically, when a woman invited him to her home, the evening was chaperone-deficient and ended up in her bedroom.

"Really?" Mia sniffed. "Did you think I was joking about solitary?"

"Sorry," he said.

"I should think so," Mia answered, although she was smiling.

She eased Betty Comden off her lap, then stood and took Tag's hand, afterward leading him across the street to a tall Dutch Colonial surrounded by disorderly plant beds and trees in need of pruning. Mia rang the bell, and when the door opened, they were greeted by the prison matron who had checked Tag into The Luther.

"Come on in," Jewel Tomek greeted them. She wore a dress that was a bit too short on hemline and more than a bit too long on cleavage for a seventy-one-year-old woman. "My God, you're good-looking," she said, taking Tag's arm and leading him into the parlor. I was there, standing near the fireplace with a dish towel draped over my shoulder. Tag was surprised to see me.

"I'm here to cook," I told him before he asked.

"I can't boil water without burning it," Jewel added.

"Where's Ed?" Mia asked. Jewel had recently agreed to marry the long-time Delphic Oracle mayor after Ed's first wife, Vivian, decided shortly after the Fourth of July that death was preferable to another day with him.

"I didn't invite him," Jewel replied. "We're not a couple. I accepted his proposal to shut him up. With luck, one of us will die before there's a wedding."

I watched until Tag had managed to pry Jewel off his arm and then retired to the kitchen to put the finishing touches on a beet and arugula salad. Meanwhile, Jewel—a singer and dancer on Broadway in the 1960s—sat at her piano and entertained Tag and Mia, providing musical accompaniment to a litany of show business stories that built to a salacious anecdote about her trysts with both the leading man and his understudy in *The Fantasticks*. "After that, I was in *Hello Dolly, How to Succeed, Finian's Rainbow, Bye Bye Birdie*," she added. "*Birdie* ended my career. I was in the national touring company and met Mister Tomek when we made a stop in Omaha. I always told Arthur that he swept me off my feet, but truth be told, he wasn't the feet-sweeping type. I was just tired of the theater. I was only twenty-five, but I'd been at it for ten years and was still in the chorus. I was ready to quit and be a normal person."

By the time I called them to dinner Jewel had abandoned her effort to seduce Tag, and we worked our way through four courses. As we ate, Jewel talked a lot about Jewel, while I didn't talk much at all, keeping to myself the request for transfer I'd made to the bishop. It was Tag and Mia's first genuine date and I figured they might stutter and fidget a bit. However, they seemed to welcome the chance to be with each other absent prying eyes. Over a dessert of vanilla bean gelato with blueberries and caramel syrup, the conversation turned serious. My little sister is passionate and Tag listened as she carried on about things that mattered to her. Occasionally, he challenged her, but she easily debated him into submission.

"How does one win an argument with you?" Tag teased her.

"One stops being wrong," Mia replied. She was joking but only a little.

Eventually, we transitioned back to the parlor where Jewel played the piano and sang show tunes. Jewel is a very good singer. Mia and I are pretty good too. Tag tried. He had a decent voice, but knew none of the lyrics. Around eleven, Jewel abruptly left the piano and went into another room. She returned in pajamas and a bathrobe.

"That's it," she said. "Party's over. Thanks for coming."

We made our way to the front door for our goodbyes, but when Tag and Mia stepped onto the porch, Jewel grabbed my hand.

"I need to confess, Father," she said. She looked at Tag and Mia. "I have to confess," she told them. "You two go on now." She closed the door, afterward pulling me into the darkened dining room. From there, we spied on the couple as they strolled across the street with the moon casting beams of spectral light through the trees.

"Five dollars says he kisses her," Jewel proposed.

"That's a sucker bet," I replied. "Mia's tipping, but she hasn't fallen yet. She might never fall."

Tag and Mia reached her house, arm in arm, but when he leaned in for a kiss at the entry, she put a finger to his lips and then went inside. A few seconds later, the porch light went out and Tag stood alone in the dark.

I smiled triumphantly at Jewel. "Pay up," I said. She went for her purse, while I watched Tag make his way back to the Mustang parked on the street. A hedge of reblooming lilac bushes lined Mia's front walk, and when he climbed into his car, I saw a low-hanging bouquet of leaves and blossoms rustle irregularly. It happened a second time, and then a third as Jewel returned with my money.

"Did you see that?" I asked her.

"See what?"

"The bushes. They moved."

Jewel shrugged. "Probably one of my cats. They love to hide in there."

She was wearing a date dress, Dem McQueen silently fumed from his hiding place within the lilac hedge. *A date dress!* Mia had always loved summer dresses—long, fluttery things that bared her lovely shoulders. "What do you think of this one?" she'd often asked in the first year of their marriage, holding up a catalog filled with glossy photos of women in seasonal fashions. "How long will it take to get it off you?" Dem had predictably responded.

McQueen had gone to Mia's place with a carefully rehearsed speech he was sure would win her back. Instead, he'd arrived just in time to see his ex-wife and Tag Thornton holding hands on their way to the old prison matron's house. Resisting the urge to tackle his rival and rearrange his face, Dem had instead sought cover in the lilac hedge. From there, he'd had an unobstructed view of Jewel's guests through the dining room window. Ominously gripping the handle of the revolver tucked into his belt, Dem sullenly watched the party-goers eat and drink and talk and laugh. Mia and Tag were seated with their backs to him, and as the evening progressed, his ex-wife frequently leaned into The Luther's most famous inmate, putting an occasional hand on his arm that stopped being occasional about an hour into the dinner. Eventually, they'd left the dining room, and minutes later, he'd heard a piano and singing through an open window on the other end of the porch. Around eleven o'clock, Mia and Tag re-emerged and crossed the street, her arm linked in his.

After Mia went inside and Tag drove off, the ex-cop scrambled from his hiding place and then stretched out on a shadowed section of Mia's front lawn to contemplate what a baseball bat might do to Tag Thornton's face. The notorious convict wasn't the first man to pursue Dem's ex-wife since the divorce, but he was the first she'd allowed to catch up with her. It was a snag in their reconciliation that Mia's ex-husband hadn't anticipated.

"Sonuvabitch," he muttered.

The moon was at half-month, and when it cleared the edge of Mia's roof and erased the shadow that hid him, Dem began to punch at the air, hissing curses at the night. Slowly, his anger was consumed by despondence and the long-lapsed Catholic searched the heavens for guidance. "What am I gonna do?" he lamented, drawing lines between the overhead stars as if an answer was hidden within an undiscovered constellation. His plea went unanswered, leaving him to his own devices, an unfortunate turn as Dem's device box was pretty empty. Indeed, original thoughts in his universe were mostly extinct; hence when one unexpectedly worked its way into his thick skull, he sat up, grinning.

Lennie thinks the sonuvabitch might try to escape…and the man who catches him will be a hero… A fellow the town might once again want on its police force…one whose ex-wife might be less happy about the "ex" when I save her goddamned, stupid job!

Dem lay back in the grass, imagining the hoopla if he were to capture Tag Thornton and save the town. His picture would be in the *Banner-Press*, shaking hands with a beaming Mayor Dogberry. There would be a dinner in his honor with Mia seated next to him at the head table. She would wear a new summer dress and no underwear. Dem already knew what he would say to her.

Nice dress, honey.

The sounds of night were interrupted by the distant hum of an approaching automobile. The hum crescendoed as the car neared, then faded after it passed, making room for the ar-rhythmic chirp of a cricket. By then, the fantasy of a hero's fete had been replaced by the memory of Tag and Mia crossing the street, arm in arm. At her door, they had nearly kissed, their fac-es merely a whisper apart. Dem clenched his fists and exhaled hard through his nose, the sound of it muting the half-hour chime from St. Mary's. It was eleven-thirty.

The hum of another approaching car interrupted the quiet as one of Jewel Tomek's cats slinked out from under the bushes and climbed onto his belly. Dem hated cats and might have giv-en her a toss, but instead gently pushed the silky creature away and then slipped back into the lilac bushes as Tag's red Ford Mustang glided to a stop on the other side of the hedge. The purr of the engine was silenced, but the car's radio remained on. A baseball game was in progress, the announcer an old hand who spiced a seemingly limitless supply of anachronistic baseball metaphors with vocal inflections that made him seem perpetually flabbergasted.

"Hard to believe it's top of the eighth. It's been a tough outing for our hometown Haybalers who look ready to call it a night. If you've just tuned in, the Milkmen of Fairbury have jumped to an eight-two lead and their big first baseman, Miguel Castillo, is up again. Seems like he was just at bat. What're you gonna say? Time flies. Here's the pitch. There's another well-hit ball to centerfield! Marcosi gets on his horse… He's headed for the wall! Back…back…back…and…it's outta here! This one's a souvenir, folks. It's a loan to your brother-in-law, a check to the IRS, a letter to Maria! It ain't comin' back! It's a—"

ல

On the other side of the lilac hedge, Tag turned off the radio. The hyperbolic broadcaster recalled for him a time when his own exploits on the football field had generated similar excite-ment. He'd liked the attention, at first, but eventually came to resent it, feeling as if he were more a headline than a person.

Even after football, he'd made headlines, the burglary conviction that sent him to the prison at Niobrara in 2004 a page one item in the *Omaha World Herald*.

"Is this the life Declan Thornton would have wanted for his grandson?" the judge had asked at Tag's sentence hearing, alluding to the former Nebraska governor. "You're a young man. You can still make your grandfather proud."

"I was always told to try my hardest," Tag had smart-assed the judge, "and I've tried hard to be a good outlaw."

Now, as he sat in the Mustang, gathering his nerve, the memory was painful. Mia wouldn't have been impressed. She'd have thought him childish. He studied the face of her house. The windows were dark, the neighborhood quiet, the front door aglow with invitation, stolen from the surrounding darkness by light from a streetlamp. A familiar soft whimper sounded and Jewel Tomek's cat, Betty Comden, emerged from the thick, soft leaves of the lilac hedge. Tag opened the door of the Mustang. She jumped onto his lap, then put her front paws against his chest, her whiskers twitching with expectation.

"What do you think, little girl?" Tag said. "Do you believe love changes a person?" He began to pet her. She lay down and then rolled over to offer her tummy, purring like one of his old girlfriends. "Okay," he said, "but I blame you if this doesn't go well."

Tag climbed out of the Mustang and approached the house with Betty Comden in his arms. When they reached the porch, he put her down and she watched as he rang the bell, her face tipped upward, nose wiggling. From inside came the sound of footsteps, followed by the porch light, and then Mia, wearing a fuzzy blue robe and no makeup. Her hair was tousled, her feet bare. She didn't seem surprised.

"Which one of you rang the bell?" she asked, eyes moving from Tag to the cat. When Tag remained silent, she shrugged. "Well, as long as you're here and I'm up…"

Tag moved to step past her.

"I was talking to the cat," Mia added.

Tag immediately froze, remaining motionless until Mia laughed, the sound soft and musical. "I'm joking," she reassured him. "I suppose you can come in, too, if you promise not to pee on the carpet."

Tag slipped past her and into the foyer, catching the faint scent of her face soap and hand lotion.

"Right," he said. "I get it. That's funny… You're a funny woman…I love you."

Despite the romantic marvels depicted in movies and on television, clocks don't stop ticking at such moments. The earth doesn't stop spinning on its axis nor does the moon cease to orbit our planet. But it sometimes seems as if all of those miraculous things happen; indeed, it seemed exactly like that to Tag as Mia caught her breath, her lips parted. She reached out and flipped a switch. The porch light went out.

"Did you hear me?" Tag repeated. "I love you."

Mia nodded. "Yeah, I know." She closed the door. "I heard you." She left him in her entry and went into the living room. Tag followed.

"Sit," she said, indicating the sofa. She clapped her hands, and across the room, a lamp came to life. "Stay here," she added, afterward disappearing into her kitchen. A minute later, she returned with two tumblers, a narrow rim of bourbon in each. Her hair was brushed, the sleep splashed from her face. She handed one of the glasses to Tag and then joined him on the sofa, the tails of her robe parting to expose her legs to midthigh. Tag stared.

"Jeez, Tag, grow up, would you?" she said, tucking her robe back into place. "Just grow up."

A nearby bay window was open and a single owl hooted as midnight approached. Mia tipped her head to the sound, her eyes somber as if visualizing things both near and far away, things long kept hidden. Suddenly she seemed discomposed, her eyes downcast, one hand patting down a fold in her robe, pushing her hair up, touching the feathery gold chain at her throat. She sipped at her bourbon, then spoke.

"You and I," she whispered. "We don't know each other." With her hair pushed up and off her face, Mia's nose was bigger than Tag remembered. And there was a faint white scar near one ear with lines at the edges of her eyes.

"You're not perfect," he said.

"What?"

"You're imperfect," Tag replied. "Perfectly imperfect."

Mia's forehead momentarily wrinkled, then relaxed.

"That might be the nicest thing anyone has ever said to me," she responded. She set her tumbler on the coffee table, then went to the open window and took a deep breath. "I love the smell of the night in summer," she said. She turned to face Tag. "It's late...or early, I guess. Which one? What time is it?"

Tag peered at his watch. "Still late," he said. "Just barely."

Mia stepped away from the window and clapped her hands. The lamp across the room went dark and soft moonbeams streamed through the window, bathing her in ghostly light. She loosened her belt and let the robe slip from her shoulders. It fell to the floor, leaving her naked. Tag went to her and they kissed.

"I've changed my mind," Mia whispered, her lips touching his ear. "You should probably escape."

Tag let his fingers trail down her back.

"I don't want you," she went on, unbuttoning his shirt. "We don't know each other." Her eyes suddenly flashed with anger and she cupped his face between her hands. "One night," she said. "One night and we're done."

"Mia—" Tag whispered.

"I mean it, Tag," she interrupted. "I can't have you here." She took his hand and led him up the stairs to her bedroom. "I've already escaped from one man. I can't do it again. I have a life."

She helped Tag slip out of his clothes and they fell into her bed.

"I have friends. I have a job. I can't leave. It has to be you. Not me."

She moaned, drawing up her legs as Tag entered her.

"You have to go."

They made love, slept, made love again, slept again. As first light approached scattered sprinkler heads popped up on the neighbor's lawn, evoking an irritable twitter from birds settled in the trees. Not long afterward a car glided past with a small boy running alongside, flinging newspapers at the houses along the street. Tag and Mia rose and went to the kitchen. She put on a pot of coffee and talked, eventually getting around to her ex-husband.

"I should explain Dem...our marriage," she said.

"You don't have to."

"I was too young...just turned twenty. I didn't know how to stand up for myself," Mia persisted. "I didn't want to marry him, but I already had the dress and Mom and Dad had spent so much money on the wedding. I didn't think I had a choice." She continued, telling Tag about the nine years she'd stuck it out with the big ex-cop and the day he taken the last of too many swings at her; how she'd turned up on my doorstep at the rectory with yet another bruise on her face; and how I'd gone after Dem at the Y-Knot Drive-In, shooting the big ape through the ear lobe with the BB gun I kept to scare rabbits away from Sister Josepha's herb garden. She told him about the four years since the divorce with no romance in her life and how she'd become convinced that she liked it that way.

"I'm doing all the talking," she apologized as the sun cleared the horizon and began to burn off the dew beading the grass.

"You're the one with things worth saying," Tag answered.

They returned to the bedroom and made love again. Then Mia walked Tag to his car, lingering for a kiss before turning away. She didn't look back until reaching the lilac hedge along her front walk. There, she paused to take in the scent of its leaves and the wet earth hidden below, a musky aroma still pungent with night as it awaited the ascent of the sun and the dry heat of the day.

ॐ

"Sonuvabitch," Dem McQueen muttered. "Double sonuvabitch."

He was high in the branches of the elm tree in Jewel Tomek's yard, a spot that gave him a better view of the second-floor bedroom window in Mia's house. After relocating from the lilac hedge, he'd kept watch all night—long, seemingly endless hours, his only companion a tortured imagination. Dawn arrived and Tag remained inside Mia's house, Dem alone in the neighborhood save a tawny tomcat with sharp ears that turned up on Jewel Tomek's lawn, yowling incessantly until Jewel opened her front door around eight o'clock. Betty Comden promptly bolted from the house and then streaked across the former showgirl's porch and onto the lawn, where she and the tom began to lasciviously clean each other with pink, ribbon-like tongues. Dem scowled. The cats were an uncomfortable reminder that his ex-wife and Tag Thornton were probably still in bed together behind the curtain of the second-floor window.

Eventually, the two felines wandered off, but Betty Comden eventually returned. She gracefully climbed the huge, gnarly elm and began to test her claws on Dem's thigh, just as a blue-and-yellow helicopter passed overhead. At the same time, Tag Thornton re-emerged from Mia's house and strolled out to the parked Mustang with Dem's ex-wife clinging to his arm. Dem swallowed a curse as Betty Comden continued to sink her claws into him, seething as he watched Mia—*his* woman—kiss the handsome inmate, then saunter back to her house, pausing at the lilac hedge to offer a parting affection, something said with half-lidded eyes and a seductive tilt of her hip.

After Tag was gone and Mia inside her house, Dem remained in the elm, his fingers on the revolver crammed into the beleaguered waistband of his jeans. He could feel the raspy cross-hatching of the tooled handle and smell the freshly-applied oil. *It's all going to shit*, he fumed—his heroic capture of Tag Thornton, Mia's sorrowful contrition, his deliverance from the hell that had become his life. The gun was loaded this time and Dem pulled it from his belt, his finger stroking its curved trigger, a thumb drawing back the hammer as he placed the perfectly bored barrel against his temple.

"Officer McQueen…Officer McQueen! Is that you?"

The ex-cop eased his finger off the trigger.

"Officer McQueen! Can you hear me?"

He looked down. Jewel Tomek stood at the base of the tree.

"I can't believe you arrived so quickly," she called out. "I just got off the phone with the station and you've already rescued her. You've found my Betty Comden."

Dem sighed with relief.

The old battle-ax thinks I'm still a cop.

He carefully reset the hammer on his revolver and then slipped the gun into the waistband of his jeans, pasting on a cracked-egg grin. "Good morning, ma'am," he called out. "Don't you worry. I've got her and I'm on my way down." With the cat held in one arm, McQueen cautiously descended, twice nearly falling. Upon reaching the ground, Jewel looked him up and down.

"Where's your uniform?" she asked.

"I'm…uh, undercover," Dem stammered.

"Haven't seen you around in a while. I'd forgotten what a husky specimen you are," Jewel said, loosening the top button of her pajamas. "Come in for a cinnamon roll."

They went inside where Dem accepted the cinnamon roll, but declined the proposition. Afterward, he walked home, climbed into his pickup, and headed for his cousin's abandoned farmstead near Three-Mile Corner, a place where he often went to shoot at things and think.

As Tag and Mia whiled away the morning with Dem hiding in the branches of the elm tree across the street, it had been a busy day in Delphic Oracle. In an effort to head off *60 Minutes,* Ed Dogberry negotiated a tentative pardon for Tag Thornton in exchange for taking on the governor's no-account nephew as a paid intern in the city clerk's office. "I'll fax you the form, Ed," the governor told our town mayor over the phone about nine-thirty. Ed then asked Regretful to set up the fax machine the city had bought six years earlier. My nephew had the thing

running in minutes, and soon, the official application for a gubernatorial pardon emerged from the magical device. Ed hur-
riedly filled it out and then began an hour-long effort to fax it
back to the governor's office.

Meanwhile, Beagle Gibbs and my sister, Daisy, were to be
married that evening, but despite the impending nuptials, the
bridegroom had gone fishing with Francis Wounded Arrow
the previous night. Six beers in, Beagle asserted that Francis's
adaptive shamanism was not evidence-based—a term he'd
picked up after matriculating at Zenith State to pursue a major
in theology.

"Why don't you go evidence-base yourself," Francis eventually suggested when Beagle wouldn't shut up about it, afterward
submitting to the prospective theologian that people in hell
were likely to get ice-cold Pabst Blue Ribbons before he gave
his fishing buddy another ride to class.

"C'mon, Francis," Beagle pleaded the next morning, around
the same time Ed Dogberry was on the phone with the governor. "I've got an exam in my mythology class."

Francis refused to give in, and while Beagle sniffed around
for alternative transportation, Ed gave up on his fax machine
and murdered it. The uncooperative device had repeatedly spit
out the completed application for pardon until the mayor was
so furious he jammed his letter opener into the document slot.
He called Regretful to administer first aid, but it was too late.

"It's dead," my nephew solemnly pronounced. "You killed
it."

With the fax machine in the morgue, Ed employed his usual
approach to things that perplexed him, rocking back and forth
in the chair behind the big desk in his courthouse office, a low
moan occasionally escaping his lips. It was about ten minutes
before eleven by then. Tag and Mia were about to say their
goodbyes and Beagle had secured a ride in the little blue-and-
yellow chopper used in the horse rescue on the Platte.

"Thanks," Beagle told the pilot as he climbed into the passenger seat. "I really appreciate this."

Moments later they were high above the airport. To the north Beagle could see the streets of the town, cross-hatched in perfectly straight lines while Three-Mile Corner was visible to the south. With Zenith only fifteen minutes away by air they had some time and swung over Francis Wounded Arrow's house, hovering above the roof until Francis dashed out the back door in his pajamas, shaking his fist. They flew low over the town square next. Ed heard the chopper and vaulted from his chair, hurtling out the front door of the courthouse and then chasing after it.

"What's got into him?" Beagle remarked to the chopper pilot as they outdistanced the mayor, next flying over Jewel Tomek's house. A red car was parked on the street in front of Mia's little two-story home.

"Did Mia buy a Mustang?" Beagle shouted at the pilot, his words nearly lost in the whine of the chopper's engine.

"Loaner," the pilot answered, pushing the stick of the aircraft. They immediately veered north, passing over the water tower and the town square, climbing higher as they made for Zenith above lush-green fields of corn—climbing so high Beagle imagined the chopper's blades might melt from the heat of the sun, dashing the cabin's wingless mortals to earth as in the story of Icarus, a tale he later recounted in response to the third question on his mythology exam.

Thirty minutes after the helicopter cleared the town limit, I left St. Mary's and walked ten blocks to The Luther for Marcel's TGIF pasta special. Volunteers were in the Common when I reached the prison campus, hanging lights between the trees in preparation for Daisy and Beagle's wedding that evening. After a delicious lunch of orecchiette pasta with sundried tomatoes and broccoli rabe, I went outside to check on the bandshell where I would perform the nuptials. Across the grassy plaza, Tag was entering our residence hall and I called out. He didn't hear me. It was Friday, August 22, 2014, almost ninety years since July and Maggie were married by a sleazy justice of the peace in Omaha and nearly sixty-five since Maggie and a companion ran away together only to meet their end at a lonely railroad crossing just south of the Platte River. Ironically, another wedding—Daisy and Beagle's—was scheduled for that night. And another runaway was about to make his break.

I followed Tag into our dormitory and found him in our cell, stuffing his belongings into a pillowcase.

"What are you doing?"

Tag looked at me, then shook his head.

"Are you leaving? You can't leave."

He paused, retrieving a book I'd loaned him from the shelf above his desk: *501 Minutes to Christ*. "I'm sure this is good," he said, "but I won't have time to read it." He held it out.

"Keep it," I said.

He stuffed the book into his pillow case, then twisted shut the open end of the makeshift pack and slung it over his shoulder.

"Unless it's reported, the boys in Lincoln will never know I've escaped," he said. "Even if they find out, they won't cut your funding. Niobrara costs them far more per prisoner than this place. They'll keep The Luther open."

He headed for the door. I blocked his way.

"Move, Peter," he said. "I have to go."

"No, you don't, Tag."

"Yeah, Peter...I do. I've no choice."

"God always gives us a choice."

Tag shook his head. "Not this time." He tried to push past me, but I stopped him again, this time with a question.

"What about Mia?" I asked. "What will she think? Did you even say goodbye?"

"This is what she wants."

"No, it isn't,"

"Yes, it is. She wants me to go. She can't have me here... Her words, not mine."

"But she loves you," I argued, "and you love her. Doesn't that matter?"

"Yeah," he said, "but for once in my life, Peter, I'm going to do the right thing. Mia deserves better than me. I think she knows that. And even if she doesn't, I do."

A lot of good Catholics think that priests always know what to say—that we have a deep well filled with fit-the-occasion aphorisms to draw from. Some may, but I don't. The world is too filled with uncertainty and I often find that I merely have questions or a strong desire to smack some sense into a big dope like Tag who would rather be noble than open his heart to love—one of life's few absolutes. Frankly, enough unrequited love has floated through the screen of the confessional over the years to make me realize that there's no place for nobility when true love is in the mix. One shouldn't give up or run away from love. One should take a deep breath—inhale it until your lungs are filled with it. Screw nobility.

I was still in his way and Tag gently shouldered past me. In the doorway, he paused. "You're a good friend, Peter," he said, facing me. "I wish I were like you. You know…dependable."

I knew his remark was meant to be a compliment, but I immediately frowned, still bristling from the phone call I'd received that morning from the bishop. "You don't really want another posting, Peter. You're a good fit in Delphic Oracle," the monsignor had condescended. "Let's face it, you're not the adventurous type." He'd gone on, using the same word Tag invoked—*dependable*—a word that now made me feel like a pitiful gelding in a stable full of proud stallions. I must have looked it, too, and Tag noticed.

"It's not an insult, Peter," he said.

"It's not?" I argued. "What would you call it then? You make *dependable* feel like *pathetic*."

"You know what I mean."

"No, I'm not sure I *do* know, Tag," I sniffed. "Granted, I've never been a big-deal celebrity football player or an outlaw like you, but I've had my moments." I recounted for him the day I'd angrily gone after Dem McQueen at the Y-Knot Drive-In.

"You've never shot anybody," I huffed as I gathered steam,

"but I shot Dem McQueen. Let's check the score on that one, Mister All-American. I think it's me, one, and you, nothing."

"I'm sorry, Peter. I didn't mean to offend you."

"You think I'm noble or something? Is that it? You think I'm Sir Dependable of St. Mary's?"

Tag fought to suppress a smile.

"It's not funny," I snapped. The memory of the crime that had landed me in The Luther was suddenly vivid—the *pfft!* as the pellet was fired, Dem clutching his ear, the look of shock on his face. Of course, I'd run for my life afterward with Dem chasing me like a bull at Pamplona, but still....what a day that had been! Oh, my gosh, what a day!

"Screw nobility, Tag," I blurted.

"What?"

"Screw nobility... I'm going with you."

Tag was momentarily taken aback, head cocked, lips slightly parted. Then, he laughed. "That's crazy, Peter," he said.

"Yes, it is," I replied. "It's about time I did something crazy. To hell with the bishop. Maybe I *am* the adventurous type."

"The bishop? What are you talking about?"

I grabbed my pillowcase and looked around for things to throw in.

"Peter, I don't know what your bishop has to do with this," Tag said, "but I promise that where I'm going and what I'll do is not for you. It's not what you want. Besides, you've only got a few months left on your sentence."

"How do you know what I want?" I retorted. "Maybe I'm stir crazy. Did you ever think of that? You're not the only one sick of prison. Or maybe the life I've got isn't the one I want. Maybe I'm *too* dependable. Maybe I need to shake things up... be more like you."

"Your family is here, Peter...your church."

"Don't get me wrong, Tag," I said, borrowing from Aunt Felicity, "but you need to shut up now."

I flung a few things into the pillowcase—my Bible, a coffee mug proclaiming me to be the "World's Best Father," a baseball signed by Willie Mays, a paperback copy of Vonnegut's *Player Piano.* By then, Tag had given up arguing with me.

"You might want to pack a toothbrush...extra socks," he observed. "You know...fugitive shit."

"Don't make fun of me," I growled.

Minutes later, we were off, the rag-top down on the Mustang convertible as we cruised past Dogberry Motors, the post office, the stately brick courthouse, and the Rialto Theater with its triangular marquee. We took a couple of turns around the town square, saying goodbye to the Cozy Lunch and Peaseblossom Implement & Auto Parts and the Penrod Hotel. I had nearly lost my nerve and was about to ask Tag to pull over and let me out, when I saw Ed Dogberry in my side mirror. Dangerously red-faced and gasping for air, he chased after us, a piece of paper held up like a banner.

"Keep going," I said and Tag did, not stopping until we reached the pedestrian crosswalk by the Y-Knot Drive-In. There, we waited for a pair of toddlers to cross the road, their haggard mother trailing them, pushing a baby stroller with a third child inside. She smiled wearily at us. *Take me with you*, her eyes said. After the mother and kids were safely on the opposite walk, we went on, skirting the lake and the golf course, before crossing the city line. On the highway, the Mustang accelerated, but Tag strictly obeyed the speed limit until he saw the windsock tower at the airport. Surrounded by acres of open land, it stood like a lonely sentinel—unable to stop us, merely waving farewell. Tag drew back his shoulders and tightened his hands on the steering wheel, a grin slashing his face.

"Let's see what this baby can do," he said.

He floored the gas pedal and the Mustang shot down the highway, the fields of cornstalks on either side blurring into an unblemished ocean of green. The surge pushed me deep into the leather seat as I tracked the needle of the speedometer—90, 100, 110—such astonishing speed it seemed certain we would soon take flight, soaring over the patchwork-quilt fields that surrounded us and then flying west to where mountains made the earth rumpled and angular. With the needle on the speed-ometer nearly buried, we overtook the only other vehicle on the road—Dem McQueen's oversized pickup—a beast of a truck that we passed as if it stood still, racing on until it was mere-ly a dot in my side mirror. Wind roared in my ears as Three-Mile Corner began to form in the distance. There, the road dead-ended into a dirt driveway with Highway 30 going east and west to either ocean. *We're free now*, I thought. *We can do as we please, go wherever we want, have an outlaw adventure.*

Suddenly, the needle of the speedometer began to fall. It hit 100, 90, and then 80.

"What's wrong," I shouted.

Tag didn't answer and we continued to decelerate, the needle edging past 50 on its way to 40 and then 30. With the great machine almost fully reined in, Tag tapped on the brake pedal and we came to a complete stop with the Mustang's tires nuz-zling the raggedy grass that kissed the roadside. He shut off the engine, allowing the growl of a different motor to compete with the rustle of cornstalks in the adjacent field. I looked to the sound and spotted our town's familiar blue-and-yellow heli-copter directly overhead. It lazily circled us, then tipped slightly and headed north toward the airport. At the same time, the wind eased, bringing the sway of the cornstalks in the adjacent field to a complete stop. We sat, motionless, allowing the fading whine of the helicopter to command what remained of morn-ing, its buzz waning until replaced not by silence, but quiet. It was a peaceful thing—the quiet that settled around us—one that lent itself well to reflection. And so we did. We both re-flected; indeed, Tag and I reflected the living daylights out of ourselves. And once I had reflected enough to be honest about things, it was apparent that three miles worth of outlaw adven-ture was entirely enough for me. There was simply no future in the reckless abandon trade for someone with a loving family, wonderful friends, and parishioners I felt so fulfilled in serving. Sure, it had been thrilling to shoot Dem McQueen through his ear lobe, but I knew such things would undoubtedly lose their charm if one could shoot a person through the ear lobe whenever you felt like it. That life would be a bad fit for me. The bishop was right. In Delphic Oracle, I was a good fit.

Tag, too, was reflecting. His great-uncle July had once been as wild as the Mustang, as quick to run. But then, he met Maggie Westinghouse. "July wanted a life with Maggie and was willing to risk everything for it," old Gramps Ransom had often told his great-grandson in the days before his mind lapsed. "I did the same for your great-grandma Bridget. That's true love, boy, true love."

Tag looked at me. "I never got it," he said.

At the time, his remark was puzzling to me and my face wrinkled to show it. "Got what?" I asked.

He shrugged, then reached for the ignition key. "Screw nobility," he added.

A moment later, we were both dragged, head-long, back into outlaw adventure as a gun barrel touched the base of Tag's skull. He glanced into his rearview mirror and was met by a pair of slightly bloodshot eyes.

"Where's the fire, assholes?" Dem McQueen sneered.

Lennie Dogberry banked her Robinson Raven II helicopter and it swooped lower in the sky, a maneuver the little chopper had performed under her sure hands many times. It was a beauty, her little blue-and-yellow Robbie, and she never tired of pushing it a bit. After dropping off Beagle in Zenith, she'd headed home and was about to descend when she spotted Dem's pickup heading south. She'd tailed him—saw the Mustang shoot past, then pull over, and Dem's pickup afterward ease off the highway about one hundred yards behind it. From above, Lennie watched Dem park his truck on a dusty tractor path edging the adjacent cornfield, then exit the vehicle and cautiously approach the red Ford convertible from the rear, one of his arms made longer by the obvious shape of a gun barrel.

She reached for the helicopter's radio handset and issued a few chopped, urgent words. Then she gave the stick a light push and the Robbie descended until it had landed on the tractor path next to Dem's pickup. Lennie leapt from the cockpit before the blades stopped turning and dashed to the truck. Inside the cab, she jerked open the glovebox, discovering a rat's nest of old repair invoices, a pack of cigarettes, and a baseball with a cut in the cowhide cover. She grabbed the ball, then scrambled out of the cab and knelt to tighten the laces on her sneakers. The Robbie's blades were nearly motionless now, and by the time they had stopped turning altogether, former track star Lennie Dogberry was already on the highway in a dead-sprint, heading toward Three-Mile Corner just a quarter of a mile away.

The driveway to the farmstead on Three-Mile Corner was deeply rutted, lined on one side with a windbreak of tall poplar trees. It led to a ramshackle, two-story house opposite an open-faced utility shed. Inside the shed was an ancient tractor with two flat tires. A large barn was set off from the house, its loft door dangling from a single hinge. The house was obviously unoccupied—eaves sagging, splintered front door drooping in its frame. Every window was broken, leaving fragments of glass covered with water spots and bird-droppings. A corral separated the house from the barn with a creaky windmill inside a large, circular watering trough. The entire farm reeked of abandonment.

Dem directed Tag to a garden. It was filled with giant dead weeds, although the electric fence surrounding it appeared dangerously alive, its wires taut with efficient-looking porcelain insulators at neatly spaced intervals. A dead crow dangled from the upper wire of the fence, swinging gloomily in the light breeze, its talons crusty and blackened.

Tag shut off the engine. "So what's the plan?" he asked, slipping his fingers over the door handle.

"Both hands on the wheel," Dem snarled. He then began to wield the gun barrel as if it were an artificial limb—pressing on the button that raised and lowered the window, flipping the sun visor up and down, scratching his balls. He pushed the muzzle tip into the foam dashboard and then pulled the gun back, leaving a shallow, perfectly round dent. When a fly settled into the depression he placed the barrel tip over it, trapping the insect.

"Gotcha," he whispered, afterward glancing at Tag. "I got 'im," he added, grinning.

From the back seat, I could see Tag's eyes in the rearview mirror. He nodded, almost imperceptibly, and I responded with a head shake. I wanted no part of an attempt to overpower Dem. The big ape was not in shape, but he was huge. On open ground we might have a chance, but a fight in the front seat of the Mustang?

A fellow in the back seat could get shot!

Dem had managed to pull his revolver off the dashboard with the fly still trapped inside the gunshaft. "Look at this," he exclaimed happily, holding up the pistol for us to see, a finger over the end of the barrel. "Whattayou boys think o' *that*? Pretty quick hands, huh?"

Tag continued to eye me the way one accomplice eyes another just before they attempt a getaway that gets the smaller of the two killed. Tag is bigger than me, so I headed it off.

"You've got us, Dem," I said, looking at our captor. "You can put the gun down. We'll go peaceably. We don't want anybody to get hurt."

Dem stared at me, blank-faced. Then his expression contorted as if he were trying to squeeze a thought from his brain like dirty water from a dishrag.

"Shut up," he growled, releasing the fly. "Get outta the car, Father." He glowered at Tag. "You, too, asshole…and gimme the keys. We're gonna be here a while. They gotta know you two are gone." Tag handed over the keys, frowning at me. Dem pocketed them and then exited the Mustang, motioning with the gun for us to do the same. "I can't believe my frickin' luck," he told us "Two of you! I'm gonna bring back *two* of you fugitive sons o' bitches!" He laughed, something that turned into a bellicose fit of coughing, his face turning red and then purple, a fist held against his chest as he blinked at us with desperate, watery eyes. Once the coughing had subsided, he sank to the ground and took deep, noisy breaths. "Frickin' coffin nails," he said at last. "Gonna quit one o' these days."

After Dem had regained his wind, he slowly got to his feet and then used the heel of his gun hand to brush dirt from the seat of his pants. The trigger caught on his jeans pocket and the gun went off, kicking up a puff of dust behind his boot.

"Whoa," the big man hooted. "Close one there."

He glanced at me, then let his gaze shift to Tag.

"Whaddayou lookin' at?" he snarled.

Tag smiled. "You don't need the gun, Dem. We're not armed," he said.

"You tellin' me what to do?"

"You have the gun. You're the one in charge."

Dem's lips curled into a sneer. "You remember me, doncha?" he said. "Oh yeah, you remember. You took a pitch and juked our safety...left him with his pants around his ankles... but you weren't expectin' me. No, sir, you weren't expectin' big Dem McQueen to drill you."

I looked at Tag. The former football star obviously had no memory of playing in a game against Dem's team.

"You had tears in your eyes after that tackle," Dem continued. "You were actually cryin'...the big All-Stater. I'll bet the scouts from the U didn't know *that*, did they? I'll bet they woulda thought different about recruitin' you if they'd known, huh? Maybe they woulda thought about recruitin' big Dem Mc-Queen instead?"

He fired off a shot at the farmhouse, aiming for one of the second-story windows, instead sending the squeaky wind-vane atop the roof into a dizzying spin.

"Oh yeah...you remember," he blustered. "You still remember, doncha?"

I'm a priest and do not encourage liars, but gunfire has a way of compromising one's principles and I prayed for Tag to either remember the game or pretend that he did. He had told plenty of lies in his life. One more shouldn't have mattered.

"I think I remember that game, don't you, Tag?" I offered, fingers crossed behind my back to let God know that my fib was exigent.

Tag shook his head. "Sorry, Peter," he said. "I don't know what he's talking about."

Dem's face darkened. "The hell you don't," he growled. He leveled his gun on Tag's chest.

"I don't remember playing against you," Tag reiterated. "I'm sure you were very good, but I just don't remember."

Dem cocked the hammer of his revolver, his finger whitening as he began to squeeze the trigger.

"You lousy sonuva—"

Here's where things got interesting. It turned out that, despite each of us vowing to screw nobility, Tag and I were both determined to be noble, simultaneously lunging at Dem. We were both too late. The gun roared before either of us reached him, the bullet putting a hole in the windshield of the Mustang. At the same time, Dem's expression went as dull as a dairy cow and he dropped his weapon, stumbling backward into the electric fence. A shower of sparks filled the air as the big ex-cop shuddered violently, his arms thrashing about like broken wings. A porcelain insulator on the fence popped, followed a moment later by a second one, and for a few moments, Dem remained stuck on the fence, wobbling like an unstrung marionette. Then, he slowly twirled and fell onto his back, making a great whumping sound when he hit the ground, his face dusky, the round bruise at the center of his forehead displaying a perfect imprint of the baseball Lennie Dogberry had thrown at him with deadly accuracy and speed.

"Get the gun!" she cried, her voice trailed by the mournful wail of distant sirens.

Moments later, Lennie was on the ground with Dem's head in her lap, blood trickling down his forehead from a small split where the baseball had hit him.

"Breathe. Just breathe," she sobbed. "You're all right, you big moron. Just breathe. Please breathe."

Dem leered at her, eyeballs quivering, one hand idly stroking her breast. His face, eggplant purple as he'd spasmed on the electric fence, was now merely florid. "Where's Lennie?" he whimpered. "Could you call her, please? You have a nice boob."

The sirens had grown louder and louder, and with red-and-blue lights revolving atop his car, Sheriff Faron Troutfedder's cruiser shot into the farmstead, trailed by the mobile rescue unit and the fire engine, men clinging to the big rig's siderails as they struggled to stay atop the running boards. A bit of Keystone Kops antics ensued, but the sheriff eventually got things under control, and by three o'clock, everything was sorted out. Tag and I were each given a once-over, despite our insistence that neither of us were injured. "It's protocol," volunteer paramedic Francis Wounded Arrow insisted as he took my blood pressure. "Besides, Father," he grinned, "if I don't check you out, your sister will kill me." Dem was treated at the scene with a Band-Aid and an ice-pack and then transported to the Delphic Oracle Hospital. Meanwhile, the fire engine went back to the station house and Sheriff Troutfedder informed Tag that Ed Dogberry had driven to Lincoln to retrieve the governor's signature.

"Ed probably won't be back until close to Beagle and Daisy's wedding," Troutfedder told him, "and you can't leave without the pardon, so you might as well join us tonight. It's gonna be great. My band is playing."

✿

The wedding of Beagle Gibbs and my sister, Daisy, was to be an outdoor affair in the Common of The Luther. Mom and Daisy were supposedly in charge of planning along with Justine, Mary Ellen, Mia, and Teddy's wife, Monica, but they all had the good sense to let Aunt Felicity implement their vision. I was to perform the nuptials and arrived to find the Common transformed into a world of midsummer magic. Tiki torches outlined freshly mown grass and gardens planted with new flowers, their bursts of color mystical in the long shadows of early evening. As promised, the sheriff's country-and-oldies band, Faron Troutfedder and the Faronistas, had been booked for the affair and broke into "Here Comes The Bride" when Daisy entered, riding sidesaddle on her palomino, Prince Valiant. She was dressed in a simple white sheath, a tiara of delicate flowers in her hair. Her feet were bare. Uneven strings of white lights draped like icicles over the aisle, and as Prince Valiant solemnly delivered the bride to her groom, Daisy reached up, her fingers lightly grazing them.

I presided and kept it short, making it through the "I do's" in record time. The bride and groom kissed, everyone cheered, and then Faron and his Faronistas performed a country-and-western version of the "The Wedding March," before launching the reception with "Toma usted esto Trabajo y Empujarle." Aunt Felicity had hired Marcel Dumont and his prison staff to cater the affair, the pride of the Culinary Institute of Cheyanne, Wyoming personally sculpting a wedding cake topped by an exquisite miniature bride and groom on horses. Regretful, Johnny Mark, and a few of their teammates were waiters, the boys cruising among the guests with trays of appetizers and flutes of champagne they surreptitiously sampled when their parents weren't watching. Meanwhile, I played harmonica with the band, sang harmonies, and was the featured singer for "Someone to Watch Over Me."

My siblings were all there, Teddy and Monica drawing applause that justified the money they'd spent on dance lessons in Zenith. Mary Ellen shuffled through the slow numbers with Big Bob, while Snug Nixon—who has always had a thing for my sister Justine, even when he was married to Estelle—got drunk early and kept trying to cut in on Francis. Eventually, my brother-in-law went after him with a plastic spoon, forcing Chief Johnson K. Johnson to break up the fight and then handcuff Snug to his ex-wife, the divorced couple looking as if they'd both rather be hanged.

Dem McQueen was treated and released from the hospital in time to make the reception. He arrived with a bandage on his forehead and spent most of the night kissing Lennie's hand while occasionally trying to breast-feed. "When he hit that fence," Doc Newhouse speculated, "it must have been like electroshock therapy. There's a period of euphoria that follows. That's probably what we're seeing."

"Will it last?" Lennie asked.

"We can only hope," Doc replied.

Tag was a popular dance partner with more than a few women doing their best to convince him to stay. Jewel Tomek encouraged him move in with her as they two-stepped to "You Got Big Red Lips."

"My place is too big for one person," she told him, "and don't worry about Ed. He and I broke up. He's too old for me."

Meanwhile, Ed made one last attempt to play matchmaker for Tag and Lennie, babysitting Dem long enough for the couple to share a dance. Afterward, Lennie put a cork in his meddling. "Stop sticking your nose into someone else's true love, Daddy," she ordered, advice her father eventually accepted about two glasses into a second bottle of champagne. He dragged Tag out to the parking lot where he gave our famous inmate his official pardon. Putting his finger over the hole in the windshield of the Mustang made by Dem's bullet, Ed attempted a whistle that sent spit flying.

"By gosh, keep the car, Tag," he said, a decision he would regret after he sobered up the next day.

The pardon proved nearly as popular as Tag with a number of townspeople interested in running a finger across our popular governor's genuine autograph. Eventually it became dangerously thumb-worn and Mia confiscated the document, afterward pulling Tag onto the dance floor as the Faronistas' song selection became more languorous. It was a rare August night in Nebraska when the day's heat had been driven off by wind that diminished to a breeze at sunset, leaving the evening balmy and dry. As midnight approached, both Faron's voice and mine grew somewhat ragged and the crowd thinned, but we played on, our music slowing to match the rise of the moon. After our last note floated into the night, Mia took Tag's hand and walked with him to the Mustang.

"You'll be needing this," she said, handing over his gubernatorial pardon. He forlornly accepted it as if receiving a notice of execution.

"Mia—"

"I know," she said, her eyes shining as brightly as the starry lights strung between the trees. "Maybe you'll get back this way."

They kissed and Tag climbed into his car, then started the engine of the Mustang and reluctantly drove away, cruising through the deserted downtown streets, past the city park, the golf course, the town water tower, and finally, the Delphic Oracle airport where Lennie Dogberry's little blue-and-yellow helicopter sat on the tarmac. He reached Three-Mile Corner with nowhere to go and no one waiting for him, then headed west, the highway cutting a swath through endless rows of cornstalks on either side, their tassels shining in the moonlight as if drenched in gold.

He drove at exactly the speed limit, so exactly it was hard to understand why the flashing lights atop a patrol car appeared in his rearview mirror as he neared the Miagrammesto County line. Tag eased the Mustang to the soft shoulder of the highway and waited. Two silhouetted figures, one hatless, emerged from the cruiser and made their way forward. The bare-headed officer stayed back while the other approached the driver's side door, a badge visible on the front of a round-brimmed campaign hat. Tag's gubernatorial pardon was curled into the cup-holder on the console and he retrieved it, the document already wrinkled and smudged. He held it to his nose, imagining that it had retained the scent of perfume. "Mia," he whispered, struggling to recall their final kiss, struggling perhaps harder to forget it. She had walked away as the moon drifted through the tattered clouds in the night sky—her hips gently swaying, her hair shining, their parting kiss lingering.

"Where's the fire?"

Tag looked up. Overhead, the sky was huge and darkly lustrous, refulgent moonlight revealing the face beneath the broad brim of the cop's hat.

"Where's the fire?" Mia repeated.

Tag couldn't answer, his throat full, his eyes welling with tears.

"You got your man, Warden?" Sheriff Troutfedder called out from behind the car.

"I've got him, Sheriff," Mia answered. "He's been apprehended."

Troutfedder chuckled. "Then, I guess I'll be on my way. I'll see you two back in town. Don't lose my hat, Mia."

The sheriff returned to his cruiser and drove away, the hum of tires against the cool road gradually fading into the soft rustle of cornstalks in the nearby fields.

Mia pulled open the door and gently took the pardon from Tag's hand. She tore it in half and then sat on his lap.

"Where's the fire?" she repeated, leaning into him until their lips nearly touched. "Don't you realize how fast you were going?"

EPILOGUE

A LIKELY STORY

In 1940, Maggie and Obie Penrod welcomed a surprise addition to their family. Unlike big sister Felicity, Rachel Penrod was the spitting image of her mother—so beautiful no one was surprised when a talent scout signed her to a contract after catching the 1962 Gotham Bowl telecast, where Rachel was prominently featured as a Nebraska Cornhuskers cheerleader. It led to a nearly a decade in Hollywood where she made a living as one of the beauties who displayed products on *The Price is Right,* sporadically appearing in various movies as an ingenue, a farmer's daughter, a beach bunny, or "pretty girl in background." Weary of a dearth of satisfying roles and an excess of handsy producers, she returned to Delphic Oracle in 1970 and married T.J. "Army" Goodfellow IV—ex-Marine captain, owner-editor of the *Delphic Oracle Banner-Press,* and grandson to Sheriff T.J. Goodfellow, Sr.

Given their late entry into parenthood, Rachel and Army quickly spit out four children—me, Justine, Mary Ellen, and Daisy. The twins, Teddy and Mia, were a surprise, arriving in 1980, nine months after Mom and Dad made a second honeymoon trip to Italy. As you know, I entered the priesthood; Justine married Francis Wounded Arrow and stayed in town, occasionally making herself invisible; Mary Ellen took over the Goodfellow Insurance Agency from Uncle Grey and added a decent pitcher, Regretful Peaseblossom, to the town ranks; while Daisy rode the rodeo circuit for fifteen years after throwing up in Beagle Gibbs's car on prom night. Of course, Teddy ran the theater when not running away, and now you know my youngest sister's story—one that began in 1925 when a down-on-his-luck grifter first saw a beautiful girl framed in the doorway of a railroad switch-house. Maggie and July were star-crossed, but Tag and Mia—July's great-nephew and Maggie Westinghouse's granddaughter—rediscovered and claimed their lost destiny.

When Grammie first told me the story of the Oracle of Delphi, I didn't believe that Maggie failed to recognize her first husband in all those years he lived under her nose as a deafmute handyman. I still don't believe it. I think she knew and maintained the ruse not only to fool the town natterers but for the sake of innocents who might be put at risk should Al Capone or Bugs Moran pick up the scent. Eventually, of course, it was no longer necessary and their tale had its denouement.

It happened in October, 1949, two years after Twenty-Four Step Charlie mysteriously disappeared, leaving behind his Last Resort with its curious water fountain. It was Indian summer, the days languid and warm, the evenings brisk enough to encourage sweaters and blankets as Delphic Oracle's citizens sat on their porch swings. An elegant stranger had checked into the Penrod Hotel, and as usual, gossip and false rumors had to work their way around before a consensus could be reached that he was around fifty years old with thick, snowy hair framing a tanned and goateed face. A day later, my grandma Maggie's yellow Cadillac convertible pulled up to the rear of the hotel. Witnesses saw the stranger emerge from a back exit, climb into the passenger seat, and then kiss Maggie Penrod like a soldier just home from the war. Less than two hours later the yellow Cadillac smashed into a southbound train at a lonely section of track surrounded by cornfields and cloud-filled sky. A fragment from a leather valise was discovered nearby, one blackened buckle still attached. Clearly visible were etched initials: JTP.

Curiously, Maggie and July were not killed heading *away* from Delphic Oracle but *back toward* it. Most figured she'd forgotten something—an article of clothing, a memento, a piece of jewelry. I don't agree. I'm quite certain that she was coming back to stay. Her daughter, Rachel—who would grow up to become my mom—was only nine years old at the time. She was a child.

July may have been the love of Maggie's life, but a mother will always choose her child. I suspect July knew that too. I suspect he didn't argue when Maggie wanted to turn around and go home. Years later I found a box of my grandmother's effects in the attic of the family's mansion. Included were two newspaper clippings and a postcard. The first article was from a 1946 edition of the *Cleveland Plain Dealer* and recounted the imprisonment of Bugs Moran in Ohio. The second clipping appeared in the *Chicago Tribune* in 1947—the same year Twenty-Four Step Charlie disappeared from Delphic Oracle. It reported the death of Al Capone. The postcard displayed a picture of the Temple of Apollo in Greece. Dated August 21, 1949 and addressed to "Miss" Margaret Westinghouse, it contained a handwritten message: *Journey's end in lover's meeting.* A line from Shakespeare's *Twelfth Night*, it was apt when written, although now, when I think of the fate that awaited July and Maggie, a different line—this one from Shakespeare's *Merchant of Venice*—comes to mind: *Lovers ever run before the clock.*

It's been a year since Teddy ran away from home for the last time and not much has changed in Delphic Oracle. Tomorrow is the Fourth of July and Francis still hasn't finished detailing his nearly cherry 1929 Chevy pickup. Beagle dropped out of college, but has proven to be a natural-born horse rancher, Felicity is still at the library, and Regretful is having good first year in the Pony League. Dem McQueen was permanently tamed by his tussle with the electric fence. He and Lennie Dogberry were married and opened up a UPS store here in town. It's doing well and Dem was elected sergeant-at-arms for the Rotary Club. Lennie is president.

Of course, the big event of the year was Mia and Tag's wedding. They're expecting now, fully completing July and Maggie's unrealized destiny. And yet I wonder. Is it unrealized? Is it yet over for the Knight of Zeus and his Oracle? Sometimes at night, after a late visit to a hospitalized parishioner, I pass by the building that used to house Dr. Plutarch Roberts's dental practice. The old place has long been abandoned, its siding warped, its porch sagging lifelessly. I am skeptical of ghosts, but occasionally, it seems as if the grandmother I never met is framed in one of the upstairs windows. Still mysterious, she is no longer young, her hair silver and piled atop her head. She gazes into the night, as if the moonlit fields in the distance are part of an ocean—as if a faraway sail has suddenly broken the distant horizon, its flag bearing the crest of a captain beckoned by a voice carried on the wind. I always stop and wait for a while, searching the night along with Maggie, the long-lost Oracle of Delphi. The phantom ship has yet to arrive. But sometimes, when the moon is full, the sky cloudless, and the stars bright enough to guide a mariner home, I can see that faraway sail too.

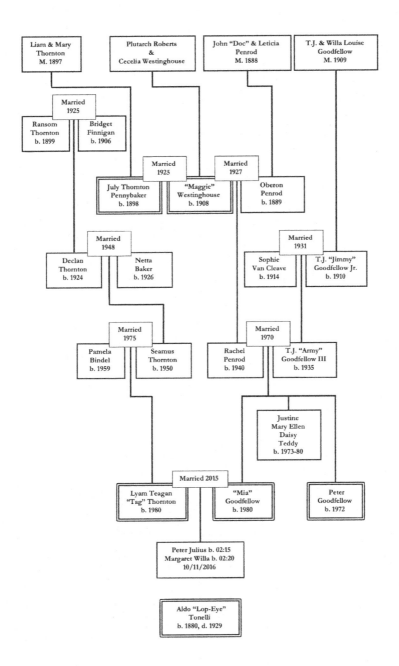

Liam & Mary
Thornton
M. 1897

Plutarch Roberts
&
Cecelia Westinghouse

John "Doc" & Leticia
Penrod
M. 1888

T.J. & Willa Louise
Goodfellow
M. 1909

Married
1925

Ransom
Thornton
b. 1899

Bridget
Finnigan
b. 1906

Married
1925

Married
1927

July Thornton
Pennybaker
b. 1898

"Maggie"
Westinghouse
b. 1908

Oberon
Penrod
b. 1889

Married
1948

Married
1931

Declan
Thornton
b. 1924

Netta
Baker
b. 1926

Sophie
Van Cleave
b. 1914

T.J. "Jimmy"
Goodfellow Jr.
b. 1910

Married
1975

Married
1970

Pamela
Bindel
b. 1959

Seamus
Thornton
b. 1950

Rachel
Penrod
b. 1940

T.J. "Army"
Goodfellow III
b. 1935

Justine
Mary Ellen
Daisy
Teddy
b. 1973-80

Married 2015

Lyam Teagan
"Tag" Thornton
b. 1980

"Mia"
Goodfellow
b. 1980

Peter
Goodfellow
b. 1972

Peter Julius b. 02:15
Margaret Willa b. 02:20
10/11/2016

Aldo "Lop-Eye"
Tonelli
b. 1880, d. 1929

PLUTARCH AKA LUCIUS MESTRIUS PLUTARCHUS

b. AD 40, d. AD 120

Roman citizen of Greek nationality who achieved prominence as a biographer. His most famous work, *Parallel Lives*, is a series of biographies of famous Greeks and Romans arranged, as with chromosomes, in twenty-three pairs. Less concerned with history or myth as with character and motivation, he humanized his subjects, filling his accounts with fascinating anecdotes and trivial incidents. Accordingly, many consider him to be the father of modern literature and he was a powerful influence on writers as varied as Shakespeare, Rousseau, Ralph Waldo Emerson, Montaigne, Alexander Hamilton, Robert Browning, and Louis L'amour.

From AD 90 until his death, Plutarch was a priest of Delphi.

GLOSSARY

Mia grammh mesa (Greek: myâh´ grâh-mē´ may´-suh)…(Def.) A
line in

ACKNOWLEDGMENTS

My thanks to those who read part or all of this book in its various incarnations: Leslie Gunnerson, Chris Dempsey, Mike Christian, Barbara Herrick, Judith McConnell Steele, Shelby Sallee, Jessica Hall, Dana Gonda, Jennifer Bowen and her BookHive readers, and advance reviewers Susan Wingate, Alice Kaltman, and Dan Kopkow. A special thanks to the marvelous author and editor, Mary Rakow, whose "I'm drifting" notes helped reduce the weight of the manuscript until it could be carried without a forklift. My heartfelt and everlasting thanks to Regal House Publishing and its wonderful publisher/editor-in-chief, Jaynie Royal, and senior editor Pam van Dyk. Thanks and love to my beautiful wife, Pam, who pretended to notice the changes between drafts even when confined to the little semicolon that grew into an em dash. And last of all, a posthumous thanks to the late Bernice Slote, long-time *Prairie Schooner* editor and my teacher. A very long time ago, she helped me believe that I could be a writer.